The Perfume Thief

ALSO BY TIMOTHY SCHAFFERT

The Swan Gondola
The Coffins of Little Hope
Devils in the Sugar Shop
The Singing and Dancing Daughters of God
The Phantom Limbs of the Rollow Sisters

THE PERFUME THIEF

Timothy Schaffert

DOUBLEDAY
NEW YORK

This is a work of fiction. Names, characters, places, and incidents either are the product of the author's imagination or are used fictitiously. Any resemblance to actual persons, living or dead, events, or locales is entirely coincidental.

Copyright © 2021 by Timothy Schaffert

All rights reserved. Published in the United States by Doubleday, a division of Penguin Random House LLC, New York, and distributed in Canada by Penguin Random House Canada Limited, Toronto.

www.doubleday.com

DOUBLEDAY and the portrayal of an anchor with a dolphin are registered trademarks of Penguin Random House LLC.

Front-of-jacket photographs: person © Denise Bellon/akg-images;
Paris © Interfoto/akg-images
Jacket design by Emily Mahon
Book design by Pei Loi Koay

LIBRARY OF CONGRESS CATALOGING-IN-PUBLICATION DATA
Names: Schaffert, Timothy, author.
Title: The perfume thief / by Timothy Schaffert.
Description: First Edition. | New York : Doubleday, a division of Penguin Random House LLC, [2021]
Identifiers: LCCN 2020043849 (print) | LCCN 2020043850 (ebook) | ISBN 9780385545747 (hardcover) | ISBN 9780385545754 (ebk)
ISBN: 9780385548151 (open market)
Classification: LCC PS3619.C325 P46 2021 (print) | LCC PS3619.C325 (ebook) | DDC 813/.6—dc23
LC record available at https://lccn.loc.gov/2020043849
LC ebook record available at https://lccn.loc.gov/2020043850

MANUFACTURED IN THE UNITED STATES OF AMERICA

1 3 5 7 9 10 8 6 4 2

First Edition

To Rodney, mon bon ami

Has war affected perfume-making? . . . Ingredients difficult to get now are these: *mousse de Chine,* an oak-moss from Yugoslavia; it gives the green color to some perfumes. Pure jasmine from France or Palestine, used in almost every good perfume. (Last year it cost $275 a pound; this year nearer $1,000.) Oil of bergamot from Italy. And from France—violet, *rose de mai,* mimosa.

—"PERFUME PROPAGANDA," *VOGUE,* 1941

The Perfume Thief

1

South Dublin Libraries
www.southdublinlibraries.ie

If you're picturing me in some ladylike frock printed with posies, lace at the collar, don't. I'm not done up that way. I began wearing trousers long before we ladies were allowed. You'll find me in tweed and neckties, shirtsleeves and cuff links, fedoras and porkpies.

People sometimes say, *She's still somewhat handsome,* and I think they mean it as a compliment.

"Are you whoever you are when you're dressed," a fellow asked me many, many years ago—decades, probably—a bourbon in one hand, his other hand toying with the button of my suspenders, "or are you whoever you are when you're naked?"

I've had aliases. Sometimes I committed my crimes as a man, sometimes as a woman, sometimes as a woman in a man's clothes. I don't think of myself as dishonest, though. Never did. I've told lies, yes, but you can't call me a liar just for being different. I'm an *actor,* if anything. I'm none of those people I pretended to be. Or, better yet, I'm all of them. And I have a good heart, and I'm a damn sight kinder than most of the saps I've snookered. When I was famous for a time, I'd be doing you a favor to filch your fine goods. People practically begged me to fleece them so they could boast of it. They'd pay me double the worth of whatever I took, just for the bragging rights.

I haven't dragged my tuxedo out in years, and though I've never much minded the scent of mothballs, I've doused myself, lapel to sock, in a perfume I've bottled new for the occasion—the pretty, powdery stink of fresh-plucked mimosa smuggled up from the farms south of here, from the unoccupied zones, snuck right past the border by my underground spice merchant. This illegal perfume is my little slap on the nose to any Nazi who comes sniffing around my throat.

Now we've been invited back, we Parisians, to some of the clubs, some of the parties, some of the playgrounds we got kicked out of when our invaders invaded. They need us drunk and happy and batting our lashes at the enemy. They need Paris to be Paris. They need the city they stole to be something worth stealing after all.

It's all pretend, but that's fine, because I was always my most charming when I lied.

···· 2 ····

When the Nazis first hustled their way into Paris, they took all the brothels as their own, setting up camp in the frilly boudoirs with the ruffled pillows and beaded lampshades and roses in the wallpaper. The soldiers soak their long, gangly limbs in the seashell-pink bathtubs of *les montantes* ("the women who go upstairs").

Just inside the front double doors of Madame Boulette's bordello is a cabaret, an entertainment all its own. There's a small stage with space just enough for the singer and a jazz trio, maybe a quartet, a quintet at the most. An upright piano shoved off to one side. A cramped dance floor before the stage, and behind it, a mural of naked women with skin a cotton-candy pink and nipples a candy-apple red, waltzing with lanky men buttoned up undertaker-like in midnight-blue suits. Along one wall is a long mahogany bar sculpted with a frenzy of mermaids. But most of the room is devoted to little tables with linen cloths, and the place is already packed and buzzing, the show still an hour off.

The cocktail waitresses move through the cabaret wearing nothing at all, their naked skin painted with words and numbers, their hands on their hips. One strolls nearby, and I see it's a menu she wears, a list of brands of champagne (Bollinger, Taittinger, Gosset), their prices, and their years, inked across her breasts and her stomach, her back, her ass, and up and down the insides of her thighs.

We're in one of the banquettes at the back of the cabaret. We're tucked into the shadows, and the booth is even draped with chiffon curtains we can draw if we want to turn ourselves into silhouettes.

Our dear friend Day, the cabaret singer who summoned me here, sits with us now, gussying up for her show. She has a secret. A plot. She's up to something, but she hasn't told me what. And though I'd rather Day kept out of trouble herself, I don't mind dusting off my criminal instincts.

She's pinching her fake eyelashes onto her eyelids, leaning in to look in a hand mirror she's propped up against a vase of felt flowers—a raggedy clutch of daffodils. "My first job when I got to Paris was doing exactly what I'm doing right this minute," she says. "Can you believe it? They paid me to sit in an apothecary window, in a flimsy slip, and put the lashes on, take them off, put them on, take them off, on, off, on, off, for hours, all day, showing how easy it was." *On, off, on, off, on, off,* she trills on along, singing it to an invented tune, flapping her lashes frantically, testing them, making sure they're on tight.

Day and I didn't run when we should have, when we Americans would have been wise to leave Paris behind. We've too long considered ourselves exiles. Day came to Paris to become a devoted expatriate when the city's clubs so embraced Black performers and the jazz songs she sang. She even had a popular tune in '21, when *she* was twenty-one, "Where Were You When," her voice mournful and girlish both. Everyone heard in it a sweet grief for all the world's war dead.

Her father had been Nigerian, a sailor on a whaling ship, and her mother an Irish cancan dancer on the San Francisco wharf, and *Oh how they loved each other, and anybody who didn't like it could go straight to hell for all they cared.* Day has told us that story more than once. She says she's been singing since birth, that she left the womb cooing a love song to her mom and pop, then took to the stage when she was only twelve and a half. In America, she could pass for white when she had to, to sing where she wouldn't be allowed otherwise.

With the Nazis banning jazz willy-nilly all through Paris, she's back to passing. And she makes up her own songs; she's heard of people getting arrested just for singing American swing on a street corner.

Day grabs hold of a naked waitress's wrist. She runs her finger along the loops and letters of the cursive across her hip. "Bring a bottle of this," Day says. She winks at the girl, her lopsided lashes slipping from their glue.

But the waitress has her eye on Blue, *my little boy Blue,* who lives in my house and sleeps in my attic. We're both in tuxes tonight, he and I, matching right down to our unknotted bow ties, the ends dangling. We're not exactly twins, of course. I'm old enough to be his grandmother.

The waitress can't resist giving his cheek a playful pinch; he's used to such things. He was orphaned as a boy, and his pretty baby face still begs to be mothered. He's even named for those sweet, melancholy peepers of his, born *Bleu,* with that French pucker-up, *Bluh,* a little lip-flutter and puff of breath, but he Americanized his name for the stage. He's an actor.

Blue the stage actor, Day the cabaret singer, me the whatever-I-am. The perfumer. We're all feint and dodge. We're light and shadow. Art, beauty, champagne bubbles, all the smoke and mirror that gives Paris its character, it's all under siege. We are the alchemists of the city's very soul, the way I see it.

"Oh," I say, remembering, pulling from my trousers pocket the bottle of perfume I made for Day. Since retiring from my life of crime, I'm a halfway respectable businesswoman, with a perfume shop on the Left Bank of Paris, my house above it, all of it easy to miss if you're not out to find it. Day's often in the shop, always wanting my help to stir up her ghosts. Every week, it's a different lover she longs to recall. Last week, it was a boy training to be a priest, a long-ago summer in a rectory garden, with the moonflowers at midnight, their scent like a negligee washed in the sink with soap flakes. I matched some vanilla with some jasmine with the velvet must of a confessional booth.

The week before that, we summoned for her a boyish chap with broken teeth who sucked on candy whistles, always tweeting on the cinnamon sticks, scenting the air with a song that smelled oversweet and red-hot. His kisses tasted that way too.

This bottle I've brought her tonight I've been working on for weeks, with no success. She lifts the glass stopper, holds it to her nostril, inhales, closes her eyes, slowly tilts her head as far back as it goes, like she's been done in by a quaff of morphine. This is encouraging. I've been expecting her to say, once again, *Goddamn, so close, but not yet.* It's her nature to be never-satisfied. I wait for her verdict, tapping my foot, drumming my fingers. "Ah, yes, there he is," she finally says, to my surprise. *"There he is,"* she sings. "We've found him at last." She leans over to give me a smack on the cheek, pressing hard so she'll leave the perfect pucker of her red, red lips.

Day falls *in* love all the time—with men, with women—but she never falls *out* of it. Anyone she's ever loved, she loves still. And madly so.

One of the many things I love about Day is how she always acts as if she's being watched. Or not watched, really, but *seen.* Even now, with just us three in the booth, she lifts her chin and closes her eyes, performing every breath she breathes in, waving the bottle slow beneath her nose.

The lover in this particular bottle was a pyromaniac, so I've singed the perfume with burnt sugar, tobacco, kerosene.

As if inspired by the fragrance that fills our booth, Blue takes out his cigarette case and offers us each a smoke. He's well stocked in cigarettes, beyond just his tobacco ration, his *fumer sa décade,* and liquor too, having quickly mastered that particular edge of the underground. For the most part, though, we avoid the black market. We don't want to reward the *trafiquants,* the marketeers who get fat on our famine. Yes, I've lived the life of a thief, but I've only ever taken from people who didn't need what I took.

Besides, in the black market, you pay too much for too little. The other night, we got our hands on a roasted chicken that was more likely some songbird, a back-alley jackdaw dropped by a slingshot. We cut into his plump breast and found it mostly empty, like he'd died with his lungs puffed up with a half-whistled melody. We ate the little bird like tender wolves, stripping it down to its skeleton, going so far as to break off bones to suck.

Food is scarce in Paris, but the Nazis eat fine.

"I wish you wouldn't," I say to Blue, but I know there's no point. He craves smoke, but cigarettes are bad for his sick heart. *Tobacco heart* was what they used to call a ticker slowed down by nicotine.

Blue lights our cigarettes, three on a match, unlucky. We court superstition these days. Laugh in its face. Believing in luck is a luxury of the past. "My bad heart's good for me," he says softly, giving me a pitying pout with that plump bottom lip after he blows out his smoke. "It keeps me off the front."

It skips too many beats, or maybe it beats too many per minute. Not even he can remember the particulars of the affliction, though it's one he's had since infancy. It somehow hasn't killed him, and now his heart's broken rhythm is likely saving his life. Blessedly so. I can't imagine such a delicate boy surviving a standoff with the enemy.

Nonetheless, we keep to the shadows and silhouettes of the banquette. The Nazi soldiers come to the cabaret in civilian clothes now, so as not to startle. But it's even more startling to see them out of uniform, here among us. Their cheer and charm seem like a trick. A trap.

The waitress brings us the champagne, and a highball of calvados for Day. Day lifts her glass toward Blue and me, like she's toasting us, and says, "What would I do without you?"

"You talking to us or to your glass of hooch?" I say.

She winks with those heavy lashes, then tosses the drink back in a gulp. She likes the burn the brandy gives her vocal cords when she sings, lending her songs an extra shiver of romantic damage.

More and more Germans cram themselves into the club, and they bring along their noise, their bravado and backslapping. To me, even when they're festive, they sound like a pack of snarling, barking dogs straining at their chains. Nonetheless, when I stop listening close, the human racket is a relief. With the Nazis' curfews and ordinances, the nights often sound as if the city is under glass, a giant crystal bell overhead muffling all.

To think, before the war, people mounted campaigns against the noise. They were so churlish as to criticize the laughter and shouts of the puppet shows in the Luxembourg Gardens, and the merchants in the street—*Venez voir mon poulet grillé,* they sang, the peddlers of chicken, eggs, tripe, chocolate. All that food.

"Day," I say, because a woman my age must get on with things, "what sort of trouble you stirring up with these devils?" No need to whisper. We can barely hear each other even with our voices raised.

She takes a deep breath, puts the glass down. But instead of telling me what she's been wanting to, she sighs and asks, "Why'd you bring the boy?" She nods toward Blue without looking his way.

"Aw, come on, tough guy," Blue says to Day. "Don't talk about me like I'm not here."

"You're *not* here," she says. "You're up in your attic, out of the way. Where you should be."

I shouldn't have brought him, but he begged. The show's headliner is Zoé St. Angel. In better days, Blue would see Zoé at the Casino de Paris, a legitimate club, a grand hall, nothing like this little brothel tavern. The Casino de Paris even sold a Zoé St. Angel doll in its souvenir shop, one decked out and painted up to look like the singer, her glass eyes wide and amber-orange, her porcelain lips prettily swollen. The doll wore a wig advertised as featuring one genuine lock plucked from Zoé's own head and woven in among the yak hair. At the Casino de Paris, Blue would cradle that doll in the crook of his arm like a sociopath pansy.

Day knows how Zoé ended up here, but she won't say.

"It's too cold in his attic at night," I say, in defense of bringing Blue along. "We don't have a brick of charcoal. Not a lick of heat. We sneak out to go anywhere there's a pack of warm-blooded strangers we can huddle up next to. Even past curfew. We'll even go to the movies and sit through Nazi propaganda flicks . . . if there's a working furnace and a good plot."

I can tell that Day is reconsidering her invitation to me. Exasperated, she rolls her eyes, and it knocks her fake lashes loose again. This time she just flutters them all the way off, and flicks them onto the tablecloth. She returns her attention to her mirror to repaint her lips, to put back the red she left on my cheek.

"How can you even bear to sing for these sadists, anyway?" I say.

"When I'm on the stage, I'm up in the light, and they're down in the dark," she says. She shrugs. "All I can see are spots in my eyes."

I had wondered why she chose a crowded cabaret, right in the thick of the thieves, to discuss something secret, but I think I know now. Her plot hinges on this bordello.

Old instincts kick in, and I glance across the room, looking for the play of light. Thievery isn't just about being stealthy; it's also about jostling, disrupting, in the gentlest of ways—the touch of an elbow, a half-whispered apology. Throwing a shadow this way, stepping out that way. *Is this yours?* you say, offering the mark something they dropped as you take something else.

I'm nervous about old instincts, though. I never did *retire,* really. I stumbled. More than *stumbled,* I suppose. I failed, to be honest. I broke. I fled. And now I'm thousands of miles from where I was.

As a thief, you balance your confidence with your anxiety. You respect omen and augury. One flinch and you're doomed.

And the fields of war are full of ghosts who wish they could go back to that one split second that separates them from life and death. There've been so many lives undone by a misstep, a wrong turn, a hair trigger.

I pick up one strip of Day's false eyelashes from the tablecloth and try to put it on myself, but my fingertips so close to my eyeball makes me blink too fast. I can't catch my lid. When I get the lashes on, Blue picks up the other strip to stick to his own eyelid, completing our matching costume.

This gets the attention of a photographer who's been popping his flashbulbs all through the cabaret, and he lifts his camera. But Day reaches up to push the drape closed as far as she can reach, shutting us away behind the see-through curtain. She casts a scolding glance at us. *"Shhh,"* she says, but we haven't said anything. It's our eyelashes and tuxedos that are too loud, I suppose. We're too conspicuous.

But I can't help but see the picture that photographer might have taken. And I've heard that the Nazis have all the color film, miles and miles of it, to run photos in the newspapers of the French having fun. Not a care in the world. Not a hair out of place. Paris better than it ever was.

Blue's blue eyes, Day's red lips blowing a kiss. The blush at the tops of Blue's cheeks. Day's saffron-colored freckles. She wears a light-colored wig, a shade of dirty blond she calls "palomino." She used to wear wigs only onstage, but ever since the city was robbed of all its heat, she's had one on always, even when sleeping, to keep her head warm.

My hair's just the dull gunmetal gray of a coffee urn, but Blue cut it close to the quick this afternoon, then slicked it back with vegetable tallow, giving it a hint of shimmer.

Do I even have any photographs of the three of us, color or otherwise? Of course not. I have a bandit's sixth sense for keeping out of sight. The fact is, I don't have any pictures of anybody.

I've led a long life of avoiding friends and lovers, to keep from getting caught in the snare of sentiment. I've not wanted any temptation to linger in a place; but now that I've settled in, so far away from the life I led and the person I was, I've let these two characters into my heart.

I came to this city to hide from my mistakes, to be a little old lady with a shop with no shingle. My perfumery doesn't even have a name, only an address, and not much of an address at that. My building is so narrow, you feel you're always on the stairs, just to get from one place to the next. It's as if the buildings on either side of it have spent a century squeezing mine flat.

When I first moved to Paris from New York, it was still the 1920s, and I had turned sixty. Here, my strangeness was a lure, not a trap, and strange people arrived. They were in costume but without disguise, you might say, entirely and utterly themselves. From this side of the looking glass, I finally recognized myself. *These* people I knew.

Here, a woman could put on a three-piece suit and a gentlemanly monocle without anyone calling the law. And these mischief-makers dared to think this could be the way of things from now on, this manner of living the way they wanted to live, of loving who they loved. Instead of changing themselves to fit in, they decided to change the world. Instead of becoming more like the people they weren't, the people they weren't might feel compelled to become more like them.

"We should have seen it coming, I suppose," I mutter. The shift *away* from such freedom. Even if the Nazis hadn't come along, it was inevitable, wasn't it? Too good to be true?

"Who's *we?*" Day says.

"For a short while there, we could listen to all the clichés," I say, putting my hand on Blue's sleeve, "all the lyrics about kisses and dreams, and it seemed those old songs were finally about us too. How dare we."

"Are you all right, Clementine?" Blue says. He picks up my champagne glass and holds it toward me. He stops just short of putting it to my lips. I take it and take a sip, but I've had too many sips already. I'm becoming maudlin.

Who's we? The queer denizens of Paris, who despite pasts that must pain them, and wounds they're still licking, come to my shop seeking nostalgia. They might ask for the smell of a grandmother's kitchen, of a molasses cake she baked every holiday from a recipe she took to her grave. Or there was the strong coffee and stout brandy in that café that winter, with that girl you loved who never loved you back.

I have a laboratory full of flasks and pots and vials, evaporated smoke, pickled lilac, casks of peach pulp and raspberry mash and candied peel, tincture of basil and ginger, pocketsful of posies, ashes in tins, dusts in apothecary drawers.

Folks also come knocking at my shop for perfume that's distinctly their own, that reminds them of nothing, that's potent and subtle both, a scent they can leave behind everywhere they go. These are often people who have no affection for objects from their past. They've perhaps been tossed from their homes, deprived of their inheritances, punished with loss. They avoid attachment. They come to value the ethereal above all else.

It's not for their *things* that they stayed in Paris with the occupation. As much as they may love their books bought from the stalls along the quai, and the chifforobe they found abandoned on the street, or the silk scarves they bought for cheap at *les puces*, the flea markets, none of that keeps them here. They stayed because to leave would be to admit defeat. They, of all people, believe in the true beating heart of Paris.

We'll get through this, we tell each other. We *all* say it, all of us, always, but how could anyone possibly know what's what? But we try to believe each other, when we can. *Yes*, we say, *yes yes yes*, *it'll end*, *it'll end*, *it'll end*, galloping along like one of Day's impromptu tunes.

···· 3 ····

When Day takes the stage to sing, her voice starts soft, as soft as paper lanterns bobbing in a garden breeze. As soft as a hummingbird flitting from one bell of the honeysuckle to the next.

Her voice purrs along, getting a little louder, then a little louder, then louder still, filling the cabaret, echoing and bouncing off the low rafters, until I feel *her* voice in *my* throat, giving me goose bumps.

And her lyrics are only snippets she lifted from a contraband copy of American *Vogue* backstage: *our fur muffs are from pedigreed foxes . . . don't let your corset pucker . . . as fresh as candy-box doilies . . .*

Most everyone here won't know the difference, because she's singing in English. Everywhere else, English is the outlaw tongue, but here at the cabaret, anything goes. Decadence lives at Madame Boulette's bordello and cabaret. To hear the Nazis tell it, our immorality is what did us in, and yet here they are, sitting in our dark, loving our sin.

Jeder einmal in Paris—this is what the Nazis call their special gift to their soldiers. "Paris for everyone once." Each and every member of the German military is allowed a holiday here, to witness the city's happy captives, to eat the food off our plates and pick the cherries of our maidens.

Madame Boulette used to go through a hundred bottles of champagne a night in the bordello's heyday. When the Nazis limited her to a ration of a hundred a month, she went to them directly. She demanded. She begged. She pleaded with them, too, to lift the ban on her French patrons. *I'll be left to hire girls no one desires,* she said, citing the loss in income. *The girls with rotten teeth and crawling with lice.* The Nazis didn't want undesirable, lice-ridden girls. So days later, a bill of notice posted on her door invited the return of the French bordello dwellers, and business kicked back into a raucous upswing, with as much champagne as they could guzzle.

Day's next number is her popular hit, "Where Were You When," and everyone but us rushes to the floor to waltz slow. The song is twenty years old, but everyone everywhere knows it. The way to dance to "Where Were You When" is to collapse, to hold each other up, like you're completely done in by love and despair. Even the Germans have always adored the song, though it's a tribute to the winners of a war they lost. For a time, you couldn't escape the song; it was on every singer's lips at every club, even in Berlin. And the bars love the money it brings in; it's so melancholy, people sidle up for a stiff drink after they've wept along to it.

"Let's dance too," Blue says, but I say absolutely not. "You're breaking my heart," he says.

"There's no room," I say, and there is and there isn't. There is indeed little room on the floor, but I'm an expert at dancing in small spaces. I spent years sneaking into dark corners, kitchen pantries, wine cellars, maid's closets. Balconies, corridors, box seats at the opera. *May I have this dance?* I'd ask the lady, pulling her closer to me, so I could filch an earbob or a bracelet.

But still Blue holds out his hand to me. I put my hand atop his and bring it down on the tabletop, to hold it there, as if I might somehow keep him in place, keep him from being snatched away.

He upturns my wrist, my unlinked cuff falling open and away. I glance around me, looking for the cuff link. He then smiles at me, a full grin, the sapphire link between his teeth. He winks at me, pleased by his sleight of hand, then plucks it from his mouth. Blue hasn't had much interest in learning the business of perfume, but he has begged me for instruction in some of the niftier tricks of snitching.

Before he returns the link to my cuff, he puts his nose to my wrist and sniffs at my pulse, and he most surely feels my heart in it, the beat of it speeding up. I make a wish. *Never leave me.* He touches his lips to my skin, kissing the fork in my vein.

"What you got on tonight?" he says as he refastens the cuff link. Dressing me.

"You like it or you don't?"

"Of course I like it," he says. "Even if I didn't like it, I'd like it on *you.* You're a genius at wearing perfume."

I taught Blue how to flirt with old women, so it's a tragic irony that I sometimes fall victim to my own art and corruption. I took him in when he was in his teens. Now he's twenty-one, but it seems hardly any time has passed since the first time I saw him.

I met Blue because of my house. I bought the place from the estate of a Monsieur Fleury, who'd finally died at 102. Beneath a thinning toupee the color of a winter fox, he'd managed Monsieur Fleury's Institute for Gentlemen, "a school of every subject." Blue was only sixteen when he arrived, already taller than me. He'd run away from the home of a cruel uncle.

He'd come to Monsieur Fleury's because he'd read about his ramshackle academy in an old book he'd found in a library. *He offered scholarships to young men without means,* he told me. Blue clutched his duffel to his chest as he sat on a stool in my perfume shop, his head lowered, chewing on his lip, shrinking inch by inch before me, more and more boyish by the minute. He was terrified and disappointed. He related to me his entire plan: hitchhike into Paris, put on a necktie stolen from his uncle's closet, and flatter Monsieur Fleury with an extensive knowledge of the man's school and his charitable acts. *I'd be happy to shine all the boys' shoes,* Blue said, looking over at me with those big, baby-doll eyes, as if I could somehow bring back all those boys with their shoes scuffed. *I could sharpen pencils.*

He works at a library now, during the day, in spectacles, bow tie, and baggy corduroy trousers. And at night he pursues his dream of becoming an actor on the stage. Though he's cast every now and again, his voice is too soft to carry beyond the first few rows. But he always has a gig at the theater, as an usher working for tips, helping ladies find their seats, which blossomed into something faintly derelict and fruitful—he's become a gigolo of sorts, a queer lover for those ladies who prefer to remain untouched by their escorts.

All the lonely women who've loved Blue have been warning him lately of the rumors they've heard, of the various armies the Germans are building, troops composed of the lost boys taken off the streets of Paris. It even has an official set of initials, as ominous as the rest of them: STO, Service du travail obligatoire, obligatory service to Germany by young Frenchmen. The old ladies beg Blue to stay with them, locked in their rooms, up in their turrets and towers, shut away from danger. And then there are the other rumors, of the Nazis' moral crusade, of closing the homosexual cafés of Berlin, rounding up the men and putting them in camps.

During the intermission, we drink more. "How can they expect us to just go on?" I ask Blue. I'm a little tipsy, but mostly I'm feeling sentimental. I've been drinking on an empty stomach. I know I'm rambling, but I never quite feel like I'm nearing the end of a sentence. I can't find my way to the commas or the periods. Or the question marks. "And why would we go on, I mean, all my life I've known families that have fought even just among themselves, fighting fighting fighting, part of their daily lives, breakfast, lunch, supper. I grew up among farmers, fathers pitting brother against brother, to test their gumption, thicken their skin, why should they expect all these people to simply give up? Why aren't they frightened by our smiles, and our songs?"

And yet all we can do is apologize. That's all the German we learn.

Ich entschuldige mich vielmals. (I apologize many times.)

Ich bitte recht herzlich um Entschuldigung. (I heartily ask for forgiveness.)

" 'I apologize many times,' " I say. "How clever of the Germans to pack so many apologies into one."

The Germans won Paris in June. It's now the end of January. They want our concert halls to ring with German composers, our theaters to stage German plays, our publishers to print German novels. Meanwhile, they can't stop taking what's ours, dining in our finest restaurants, eating our candy, buying our dresses for their wives. Reeking of our perfume.

They go to my old barber, while the men of France shave their own whiskers or don't shave at all, growing their beards into wild thickets, to face the winter wind that's worse than it's ever been.

I spot a bald German in the crowd of the cabaret, and I point him out to Blue. "Even the bald ones, like that bastard, even they linger at my barber, for a polish with a peppermint tonic, for a hot towel, to lean back in the chair for a few winks of a shallow nap." I breathe in and smell it just now, the barbershop's scents of steam and licorice, an antiseptic sting that bristles in your nose like ice in the air.

But at the nightclubs, at the cabarets—if we manage to squeak in through the front door—the Nazis let us sing along. These popular songs cast a spell over them. I guess all my rambling is provoked by this glimpse of celebration, this reminder of how things were before. Everywhere else we go, however, everywhere in Paris, we hold our breath, to make little noise.

Intermission ends. The lights of the cabaret are lowered, and we're left with the flicker of the candles on the tabletops. The darkness softens our voices, softer, softer, down to a hiss of whispers, then nothing at all.

And up from this nothingness lifts a hum of melody. Even as the stage bulbs brighten, clicking up watt by watt, Zoé St. Angel seems barely there. She's a shadow of smoke.

She sings an old German ballad, a folk song the boys will know from their schoolbooks back home. She's seducing these tyrants with a song their mothers sang them.

We notice that the nicotine-brown fabric of her gown is nearly transparent. Or not. We all get caught up in what you can and can't see.

When she finishes the song, the silence descends again, and then it's gone in a rush and roar of cheers and applause, of shrill, sharp whistles. Her next couple of songs have some swing to them. She steps from the stage and snakes around the tables, her hips sashaying. She sings a verse in French, then one in German, then in French again, then in German again, and every word is about the beauty of youth.

Yes, we're the young ones, she tells the boys, reaching out to tousle some soldier's curls, to pinch an earlobe, to tug on a lower lip. She steals quick kisses and sips of champagne. Age is only for the old, she promises. *We,* we were lucky enough to be born babies. And that luck will keep us young always.

We have what the old can never have, and that makes us the richest of all. *So drink too much and love too hard and study your face in a mirror. Spend every minute, because time's too precious to keep.*

Blue leans over to speak into my ear. "Those Nazis will always be young, all right," he says. "Once they're shot in the head."

I reach up to swivel Blue's chin, so his ear is at my lips. "But at least they won't be cursed with old age," I say.

As if she's in on the morbid joke, Zoé's next song is in English, of all things. It's a soldier's song—a march, really—and she winks, and sings, *Though cuddling in bed is all very well, soon we'll bid you a sailor's farewell.* And though her gown is indeed nothing much more than mesh, none of the men manhandle her. They're especially cautious not even to stumble into the bump of her hips.

Zoé sings of roses blown in by the dozens: *If we can't pluck yours, we'll pluck your cousin's.*

She then takes a rose from a soldier's lady and snaps the bloom from its stem as she walks to our table. I'm terrified that all eyes are on us, but I know that Blue is thrilled to be caught in her sights.

Zoé St. Angel looks at me. She glances down at my tuxedo. Raises an eyebrow. Smiles. I smile back. She presses the rose into the buttonhole of my lapel, her fingers grazing my breast. She gives my cheek a playful slap, and walks away, singing the next dirty verse to someone else.

4

I'm back at Boulette's a few days later, in daylight, up in the parlor where the ladies laze around in silk pajamas, or summery dresses of thin satin, the room so warm, everyone is forever fluttering paper fans at their throats. The Nazis arrange for the house to have the heat that's been withheld from everyone else. So the women sit there and swelter. Such luxury.

These little ladies get the best of everything that's as light as air. Milk to spin into foam for their coffee. Featherlight silk stockings. A dusting of salt for their soft-boiled eggs. A few extra inches of bathwater and a few more suds of soap.

And perfume. Madame Boulette has so admired the fragrances I've bottled for Day, she's paying me a handsome sum to create scents for her and for her every lady-in-waiting. She has more than forty in her employ. I arrive in the morning carrying two cracked-leather satchels—doctor's bags, really—ringing with the rattle of glass bottles and jars.

One girl in the parlor practices dance steps wearing nothing but her underthings, her long legs in long stockings with tiny scarlet bows all up the backs of them. Another girl wears even less—the only thing she's got on is an ice pack on her head, nursing her hangover. And the girl next to her is just as naked as she is, except she's wearing spectacles as she repairs a seam in a dress draped across her knees.

I busy myself at a corner table set up for me, trying not to stare at their nakedness, though I sense they're noticing my quick glances their way. I suspect it feels refreshing to be appreciated from a distance.

"I came to Paris when I was pretty—prettier than them, at least," Madame Boulette tells me, startling me from my covert peeping. She nods toward the naked ones. Her cheeks are plump with broken capillaries freckling her skin, making her look somehow like a little girl and an old lady both.

Boulette is not her real name; *boulette* is a French dumpling. She's as round as one. When she's in the cabaret playing hostess, her heavy breasts are up and out, cinched tight in a frilly bodice of black lace and ivory silk.

She sits at my station and turns up her wrist to me, tugging back a ruffle at her cuff. She's wearing an old-fashioned velvet robe and bedroom slippers. I dab onto her vein a dot of scent—oil of sweet fennel.

Madame Boulette eyes me up and down. She gives me an approving nod, and a wink, but not because of the fennel. She then nods again toward her naked ladies. "Paris," she says, "has always belonged to old women like us. *Us,* not those sweet nothings. Frenchmen are intimidated not only by their mothers but also by all their fathers' many mistresses. If the old women of Paris had been foolish enough to enter government, the city could not have been ripped out from under us so easy."

But where are Madame Boulette's loyalties, really, in serving the Nazis? Those who manage to keep up a good business somehow stay untroubled, even as so many shops have gone dark, one by one. We're all complicit when it comes down to it, just by going on with our lives.

Would Madame Boulette risk housing Jewish girls here? Is she bold enough for that?

She examines the bottles in my satchel, squinting at my handwriting on the labels. When she was a farm girl, she tells me, she read a popular novel about an artist's model. The model wore a military overcoat and carried a tobacco pouch in her pocket. "The book said her voice had notes of peaches, oranges, and lemons," Madame Boulette says. "I've always remembered that. I wanted to get my voice that way, though I had no idea what it meant."

I have a pale blue notebook the size of the palm of my hand. *Peaches, lemons, oranges,* I write in it. She asks what I'm writing, but I don't tell her. I don't say anything in these interviews. I don't want to interrupt, or misdirect. When I let people talk, let them fill the empty air, I can learn the answers to questions I didn't even know I had.

Perfume isn't only about chemistry. It's also about psychology.

I meet with her girls one by one, there in the parlor, to learn more about them, for the perfumes I'll create. One is allergic to perfume—but somehow I can smell on her skin a late afternoon by the sea, the gentle rock of the boat on mostly still waters, the gin and ginger ale.

"I don't know the person I see in the mirror," another girl tells me, in a mouse's tiny tremble of a voice. "I'm . . . *disappointed* . . . when I look at myself."

"I've *never* been disappointed by the mirror," her friend says, with a smile and a wink. "Not once."

For the sad girl, I'll bottle something barely there, a fragrance of white rose and lotus. And for the satisfied one, something *always* there, some common fig, some smelling salts, some camphorwood.

I watch each girl closely, learning her character. Studying her shape. All of the girls' fidgets and shimmies, or their quiet, easy languor, their long limbs and swans' necks, or turnipped hips and squat legs, will inform how the perfume communicates. A perfume can smell different on different wrists, different throats, depending on your habits and tics, and the way you cross a room. I'll tell one girl to wear her perfume behind her ears, another to wear it at the backs of her knees, another along the line of her jaw.

For the perfume to work, they have to believe what I tell them.

I want each woman to breathe in the perfume I conjure for her and to recognize herself in it, to feel she's been properly interpreted. The girls need to feel I've noticed something unnoticed about them.

But it can sometimes be a disguise they're seeking. I can see in some of these girls the desire to disappear, or to become someone else. Sometimes the right scent is the one that seems all wrong. Sometimes a woman goes into a perfume shop seeking adaptation. Or metamorphosis. Or an outright lie.

.... 5 ....

Evening comes, and I'm still at the bordello. These women never leave, but that's not just because the city's shut down. This is where they live. They sleep in the same beds they work in. They call Madame Boulette "Maman," their mommy. Her cook cooks them their dinners, and her laundress launders their laundry. Her doctor gives them their pills and potions.

Everyone is getting ready for the evening, for the cabaret. I find my way to Day's dressing room, which really isn't a room at all. It's nothing much more than a short corridor with a dead end. She sits cramped at her vanity.

When she sees me come around the corner, she gives me a wink with her dangerous eyelashes. She abandoned her fake lashes and their weak glue because an admirer gave her some eyelash dye that's been outlawed and is hard to get, believed to have caused blindness back in the States. "I've never been sick a day in my life," she says when I suggest she not risk it. "Nothing can sink its fangs in me. I sang for the soldiers in the hospitals through both waves of the Spanish flu. Without a sniffle. If a boy looked healthy enough, I even let him kiss my cheek." She looks in the mirror, blinking into a cotton ball to blot some of the ink. The dye's a shiny black, like the silk of a tuxedo's lapel. *I won't give up my upkeep,* she's told me a time or two.

"I did sometimes sing through a mask, though," she says. "It gave my voice a sexy muffle."

"Here you go, Nightingale," I say, holding out today's perfume. Some women choose a scent they wear exclusively, forevermore, but

Day refuses. I'm certain she could make any fragrance distinctly her own no matter how many people put it on, but I do love bringing her a few drops of something new every day or so.

I get to know her a little bit better with each ounce. She tells me of old lovers, of magical nights, of mysteries and fascinations, all of which I try to align with the draughts bottled in my cabinets.

"Is this the bluebell extract?" she says. I say yes, though it's not, really; it's not distilled from the petals. People don't always realize that you can't just bottle the air that rises from a bloom. Squeezing oil from the petals doesn't give off the same stink. To best capture the essence, you fuss and muddle. To me, bluebell smells of fog and, faintly, strings of fresh ginger.

Day stands and takes my wrist but not the vial. She leads me back the way I came. "It's for Zoé," she says. "She wants to meet you."

"Zoé St. Angel?" I say. "Why would she want to meet me?"

"The bluebell oil," she says, as if that should make sense. She's ahead of me, suddenly rushing around sharp corners and up the steps of a maze of corridors and staircases. I practically skip to catch up. The house is enormous, its halls as labyrinthine as a rabbit's warren.

The narrow stairway can barely accommodate the full swing of Day's hips. *It's not an affect, it's a defect,* Day told me years ago, when I first followed her. It's quite a sight, that swing. *My pelvic girdle's been off-kilter since the day I got hatched.*

It's a defect we almost share, though my swing is nothing at all like hers. I've got a crooked skeleton. Years and years ago, I got naked with a surgeon's nurse, and she had me stand in the moonlight at the window. *Your left leg is just a wee bit longer than the right one,* she told me. Or my right was longer than my left. I can never remember, because the difference is so slight. And because it's so slight, I spent days infatuated with the surgeon's nurse for seeing something nearly invisible about me.

When you're someone like me, dressing as I do, you feel like people stare at you in order to make you fade away. The longer and harder they look, the less they want to see you. They stare and squint so you'll dart away and disappear.

"Why the bluebell?" I say, now huffing and puffing to keep up.

"Nightmares," Day says as we turn around one corner, then another quick after that.

"Nightmares?" I say. I squeak it, really. I bump my shoulder into the wall after another sharp turn, jostling a painting of a swarm of cherubs, knocking it off its nail. I stop to set it right.

"They say bluebells chase them off," she calls back to me, then disappears around another corner.

6

Zoé St. Angel has summoned me to her private suite of rooms. *Zoé St. Angel.* I can just hear her name in Blue's voice. A gasp, a swoon.

Zoé is kept in a penthouse that pokes out the roof, a flat with so many windows it is practically all glass, perched above the city like a dovecote or a greenhouse. Some evenings, she leaves the drapes parted, and she blasts the street with all the room's electrical light. Even the Eiffel Tower's gone dark, but never Zoé's *pied-à-terre.* Anyone who looks up of an evening will see her wringing her hands and pacing, singing, rehearsing that night's numbers. Back and forth, back and forth in her glass house, like a doll on a wheel in a music box.

As we head toward Zoé's apartment, Day hears some voices echoing down from up the stairs. She takes hold of my sleeve to pull me back, and around, and through a door. It's a wardrobe closet we've tucked ourselves into, all peignoirs and negligees on padded-silk hangers. I get caught up in one, and the gown is so slight, escaping it is like disentangling myself from a cobweb I've brushed against.

"I haven't the foggiest idea what you're doing," I say.

Day looks up and off, listening, biting her lip. "Might be Lutz," she says. She then leans in, to whisper, to tell me that a Nazi official named Lutz has taken Zoé as his lover. Lutz, it seems, is a handsome thug from Leipzig who studied French novels, who lived in Paris for a time, painting street scenes for tourists—ladies under umbrellas on the Champs-Élysées and other watercolor rot of that sort. That was when he was a college boy, a handful of years ago. His day job now is looting the city's best collections. He shuts down the art galleries of Jewish dealers, robs Jewish homes of their antiques and artifacts, lifts rare books from private libraries. He'll pick the lock of your lovely home, slip his feet into your velour slippers, pour himself a snifter of your best brandy, and shop your valuables.

Already I feel a stab in my gut with worry for Zoé St. Angel. And a little worry for myself, stepping into her constellation.

"Zoé St. Angel was one of the things he wanted most," Day tells me. When he'd lived in the city as a penniless student, Lutz snuck into the Casino de Paris to watch her sing. He'd been caught and hustled out a time or two. So one of the first things he did when he returned to Paris, as an officer of the occupation, was to go to the club and take her right from the stage. He collected other singers too, and he put them to work in the cabaret. The shows he could never afford as a student are now his very own, every night.

"She's his prisoner?" I ask Day as she opens the closet door. We step back into the hallway after she's looked it up and down.

"We certainly hope so, don't we?" she says. She puts her arm in mine, and we walk side by side. "If she's not miserable with him, then she must be a monster." Feeling her against me, I'll let her lead me anywhere. I trust Day in a way that I never used to allow myself to trust anyone. I always feared falling victim to a hustler like myself.

I had my heart broken young. I didn't think I was young at the time, but I certainly was. I wasn't yet thirty years old. He tasted tea for a living, and went by only the letter M. He was strange and remarkable, and the very second I fell in love, I started to fear losing him. And though I'm not inclined toward melodrama, I'm certain I've never quite recovered.

We've reached the staircase that leads to Zoé's apartment. The steps spiral upward to a purple door. "Just knock," Day tells me. "She's waiting for the bluebell." She kisses my cheek and skitters away. "Don't worry," she says as she leaves. "She knows everything about you."

"Don't worry?" I say. "Everything?" But she's already gone.

So I do as Day says, and a chambermaid answers and ushers me in. She tells me where to sit. She brings me a glass of wine I didn't ask for and won't drink. She, too, then leaves me.

All the curtains at all the many windows are drawn. The lamps are turned down, or off. Despite the cool dark of the room, it's even hotter in here than it is in the parlor.

"Day tells me you can keep secrets," Zoé says. She walks in from behind me, passing me, in a silk robe, a silk kerchief tied around her head. She even holds a silk scarf dangling at her side, twisting it a bit as she walks, like it's a streamer. She goes to a phonograph, flicks it on, sets the needle, ups the volume.

"If I couldn't keep secrets, I would've been ruined long ago," I say.

She holds her finger to her lips, as if to shush me. She sits in the fat red chair across from the fat red chair I'm sitting in. She's not looking at me. She toys with the silk scarf, fiddling with it, running it through her fingers, twisting it through her hands, around her wrists. She's nervous.

She looks like she's been carefully dressed to appear disheveled, her robe, her scarf, her kerchief all different patterns, all the patterns competing, a clashing of parrots, cherries, palm fronds. A gazelle stitched in gold thread prances up her sleeve. She wears high-heeled bedroom slippers with tufts of pink feathers at the open toes, and her toenails are painted all different shades of blue and purple.

But it's *my* attire that comes into question. When she finally looks up, she tilts her head. Lifts an eyebrow. "I figured the tuxedo of the other night was . . . a costume," she says.

I start to cross my legs, ladylike, but then I don't. But then I do. I'm wearing a pair of my favorite trousers—a heavy Harris Tweed, checked, emerald green. They're actually meant for hunting, and not to be worn indoors because of their scorched-earth smell—the farm that weaves the tweed also burns peat, to roast barley for whiskey. But the smoky scent is just another reason they're my favorite. And they're my very warmest. Made even warmer by the smell.

"Day told me you know everything about me," I say.

She nods. She then tips her head toward my necktie. "Charvet," she says. Charvet is the *chemisier* in the place Vendôme where I have my shirts made. I buy ties there too. This one is plum-colored with gold thread stitched through for shimmer.

I tug on the end of it. Flutter it. "It's old," I say. We're always apologizing these days for any gesture of ostentation.

Ich entschuldige mich vielmals.

I apologize many times.

Zoé isn't really listening. "How can I know if you will?" she says.

"How can you know if I will?" I say, perplexed.

"How can I know if you'll keep my secrets?"

"I guess you have no way of knowing," I say. But I have no idea what we're talking about. Perfume? I assume this is simply how a woman of mystery speaks: she has to cast all her idle chitchat in riddle and tease. I hold out the vial of bluebell, but she ignores it.

"Tell me about the young man you were with," she says. "At the cabaret." *Young man,* she says, like an old woman. He can't be much younger than she is.

"He lives in my attic." I pick up the glass and take a sip of the wine after all. It's a risk, I suppose, telling this to a Nazi's lover. But I follow those old instincts of mine. She *wants* to trust me. I realize that's why I've let Day lead me into this house and around all its sharp corners, up its twisting staircases, dodging the shadows of Nazis. I'm not here for the naked ladies, as lovely as they are. I'm here in case there's something I can help with. And if there's something I can help with, maybe Zoé can help keep Blue and Day safe. She can help me keep them close.

I say, "How can they bear to send these boys to their deaths?"

Zoé drops her hands into her lap. She nods, her eyes wide, as if she's relieved to hear my concern.

"Men stir up wars because they're too stupid to realize they'll lose them," she says. She looks even younger here, younger than in the cabaret. When she sings, she sounds older. When she speaks now, her voice is almost girlish. "They know they *might* lose, but 'might' seems like something that'll happen to somebody else." She nods toward my open palm, the vial of bluebell. "You know all about perfume," she says.

I hold out the bluebell again. I lift the stopper. She leans forward to put her hand around mine, to pull the perfume closer. "You're the Perfume Thief," she says. "Before, when I said I knew all about you . . . *that's* what I know. I know of your . . ." And here she stops. Looks off in thought. She stands to walk to a credenza along the wall, the top of it lined with liquor bottles, highball glasses, cigar boxes. "Your *peculiar* crimes."

I get a jolt of headache in my temple, the kind of headache that troubles my sight, a play of light and shadow. At the corner of my eye, butterflies flutter and snap their wings, shifting their colors. I close my eyes and they fade away, but when I look around the room, I suddenly notice butterflies I didn't see before. They're in the stained glass of a lampshade. There are a few among the figs in the pattern of Zoé's robe.

Butterflies tend to make me nervous, evoking a touch of phobia. They can be a harbinger.

"I've been rehabilitated," I say.

"Oh yeah, I know all about your sainthood," she says, sharp, like a gun moll in a gangster flick. "Day says you don't use any dead or tortured animals in your perfumes. Your heart breaks for the musk deer. And the civet cats." On the credenza is a novelty box, an alligator made of wood—she pushes down on his tail, his jaw unhinges, and he leans forward to snag a cigarette with his teeth. She takes the cigarette, lights up, then taps the gator's head. "And crocodiles," Zoé says, smoke lifting from her lips.

"Crocodiles?" I say.

"Cleopatra wrote a beauty book," Zoé says. "One of her recipes called for crocodile musk."

"There's no such book," I say. "It's a myth." I shouldn't have said anything so know-it-all, but I've spent years disabusing collectors of the notion they could own Cleopatra's book of perfumes.

I'm one of only a few thieves in all the world who specializes in such artifacts. In my early days, I had to pinch anything within reach worth a nickel, but when I got older, I narrowed my sights. At my peak, I catered to a clientele of perfume fetishists and obsessives. Men who had everything. Ladies who wouldn't take no for an answer. For the rich, the whole world is an open market. What you can't buy, you pay someone to steal. I've peddled hot goods in the backseats of limousines, my face hidden by a veil of lace roses. I've pilfered tulip bulbs and rare orchids, smuggled spices from foreign marketplaces in the drapery of a silk robe. For years, I was the woman you went to when you wanted to spend a fortune on ether and bubbles.

Or the scent of butterflies.

The record has stopped, so Zoé returns to the phonograph. She moves the needle back to the front of the grooves, and the same song plays again. She sits again in the chair across from me. "I need your help," she says.

"If this is about Cleopatra's book," I say, "I *promise* you, it's nowhere. I could have bought and sold it twenty times over by now. I'd have a mansion."

"You *do* have a mansion," she says. "That adorable building on the rue de Vaugirard." She wants me to know, I suppose, that she knows where I live. She takes a deep breath and sighs with boredom. Or frustration. She flicks her ash into the glass of wine the chambermaid left for her. "I'm not looking for Cleopatra's book. I have it already. Or, rather, my family does." I don't even respond to that. But Zoé goes on. "But it's not really a book, so much. A scroll, I guess."

I don't have the heart to tell her she owns a forgery. It doesn't surprise me that someone might deal in such fraud, the demand being what it is. I could have made a mint flooding the market with Cleopatra's beauty secrets. There are plenty of rogue Egyptologists, college professors needing money to fund another plundering of a mummy pit. You pay them to help you fake the thing, then you pay them again to authenticate it. It's all for the underground, so there are no reputations at stake. And, to be honest, if you can convince a client just a little bit, he'll convince himself the rest of the way. He wants so much to believe. *Faith.* It's vital in both thievery and perfume.

But I can't help myself. I'm about to question Zoé about her scroll when she shuts me up by lifting her wrist to my nose for a sniff. And, dear God, there she is. *Cleopatra.* I can't place all the elements of the perfume, but I can practically hear the slither of an asp in it. I still don't believe it, but I respect it as a brilliant sham. I even feel a sting of professional jealousy.

"Cardamom?" I say.

"Cardamom," Zoé confirms. "Sweet rush. Wine. Myrrh. Some other things."

She then invites me to leave. She must get ready for her show, she says, though I know her show is still hours off. "You'll come back tomorrow," she says.

···· 7 ····

Day sleeps late because she works late, so I wait until nearly noon before going to the Café Roche, where she lives upstairs, one floor up. She knows more than she's telling me about Zoé St. Angel. So I'm going to twist her pretty little neck until she sings like a bird.

I call her name up the back stairs. I knock at the wall. I sing the chorus of her own song. *Where were you when,* I sing, off-key. *I looked for you then.* Nothing. I call up to her like I'm calling her to the stage—"*Mesdames et messieurs,* Day Shabillée!," throwing my arms out. But all I get back is my own echo.

She adopted her stage name years ago, inspired by a French word we'd had in America too: *déshabillée,* a state of undress. It tickled her. It seemed like the name of a fan dancer in a burlesque revue.

"I gave her something wicked to knock her out cold," Madame Roche tells me when I take my usual table in the café, right beneath a towering mirror so old, so desilvered and foggy, it barely reflects at all. In that mirror, we're all as faint as ghosts. "Some dust in an envelope to stir into a glass of wine." The old woman produces just such an envelope from her apron pocket. "You'll sleep like I smothered you with a pillow."

"Just the coffee, please," I say. "And milk."

I'm all alone in the café, cold and miserable, still wet from the wind and gusts of snow. Madame Roche brings a cup of coffee that's all chicory and tastes like twigs, with a little pot of hot milk that's mostly steam. Her cupboards are bare, and on the chalkboard, where the menu goes, she's chalked what she *doesn't* have: *900 pigs at market this morning; 600 sent to Germany,* is written in the jumpy scrawl of her angry, arthritic hand. She fills the board with her screed. *I'll go to jail if I cook a rabbit,* she writes. And she lists what the Germans eat at Maxim's, one of the city's finest restaurants, which they've taken for themselves: *langoustes, canard à l'orange, grenouilles sautées provençale.*

Even the menu makes me nervous, though she can easily erase it with a rag. Everywhere you look, there's another ugly truth. Each day that passes, we feel even further from the Paris we knew. We should be more pained by all the injustice, but it still seems impossible. Unbelievable. How could it be as bad as it seems?

The café too is only all echo, but echoes from before the war. I don't even know the place anymore, without Madame Roche shouting orders back to the kitchen, and customers shouting back at her to correct her when they hear her shouting their orders wrong. Whenever she was behind the bar herself, she made every mixed cocktail sound like industry, hammering at ice, clanking a spoon in a glass pitcher. Her espresso machine wheezed and clanked, hissed and whistled.

Now, the place empty, she sits at the bar with a pen and a ledger book, calculating her losses again and again, desperate to find a mistake in her math.

I keep my topcoat on. I pull my wool beret down, tight over the top of my head. I sit near a cylindrical stove of dented metal, a warming oven Madame Roche rolled out. I can barely feel its weak waves of heat, but I set my cup on it to keep my coffee halfway warm.

While I'm twisting Day's neck, I'll twist Blue's too. He's to meet me here. He's been out all night. He rang late in the evening to tell me he was working with his new lover—his new *old* lover—a playwright and director twice Blue's age. This man has cast Blue in a play, and Blue's helping him with research, collecting books from the library, for set and costume details. The Nazis approve only productions of historical plays. They want to prevent commentary and criticism, I suppose, as if history were only ever about the past.

I want Blue to find love, but *true* love, with someone his own age, someone to grow old beside.

Blue finally arrives in a wine-colored coat I've never seen before. And when he leans in to kiss my cheek, I smell a soap I've never smelled on him, a shaving soap, menthol and eucalyptus. His neck and head are wrapped up in three woolen scarves, and before he's even unraveled himself, Madame Roche has brought him his cup of chocolate.

"He didn't feed me," he says, dramatically tossing his scarves across a chair at the next table. "Don't you hate him?" He salts his hot chocolate with extra sugar to tap away at his hangover. His voice is a low, wet rumble from too much liquor guzzled too late.

"I hate *you,*" I say. "I've been waiting all night and all morning to tell you that I met Zoé St. Angel." I hold my finger to my lips. *Shhh.* "It's a secret."

He's so giddy, I forgive him for falling in love with the wrong people. He grabs my hand and kisses my fingers. "Tell me [kiss], tell me [kiss], tell me [kiss]."

"I can't say anything," I say, to tantalize. I don't have much of anything *to* tell, but even a little bit of nothing is still something.

I do, though, tell him about the bluebell perfume, about Zoé and me keeping our voices low beneath the jazz, about the patterns busy in her silk. I tell him she told me to come back tonight.

Day finally arrives, carrying bruised fruit in the sling of an Hermès scarf. And a loaf of papery bread. The cook in the bordello kitchen often sends her home with food that's about to turn. She's in a bathrobe and sunglasses, the lenses literally rose-tinted.

"Find me a husband," Day says.

"What do you want a husband for?" I say.

"I don't *want* a husband," she says. "Nobody ever *wants* a husband. I want someone's money to take."

"Then it's settled," I say. "You'll marry me. And you'll rob me blind."

"I love you too much to marry you," she says. "I'd make the very worst wife."

"At least come live with us," I say. "There's plenty of room." I've extended this invitation many times.

"I love that idea," Blue says, taking a bite of a half-rotten apple.

"But I can't leave my apartment," she says. "All my wigs are here." She's wigless now, a chiffon scarf tied around her head and silver-clipped to a few of her curls.

She's forever getting evicted from one place or another and tumbling back to Madame Roche's rickety upstairs apartment. *Remind me to fire my accountant . . .* That's her standard line whenever she blows back into the café flat broke, laden with all her candy-striped wig boxes, her every fur coat and fox stole draped over her shoulders.

And to be honest, I think she likes living above Madame Roche's. Whenever someone strikes up a tune on the piano, which most often sits silent in the corner, she can't resist. She never learned to play, so whenever anyone does, she's happy to wander down and sing along, no matter the hour. Before the war, when business was brisk, she could pass around the hat for tips, then pay her rent to Madame Roche by simply tipping the hat into her lap.

The bread she brought is so stale, Blue has to gnaw on the crust before he can tear off a chunk with his teeth. Watching him eat makes him seem even thinner. He's wasting away before my eyes with every bite he takes.

"We've gone hungry before," Blue says when he sees me staring. He's struggling to chew the tough bread. But he's talking about history. His *we've* is everyone who's ever lived.

The Germans took siege of Paris in 1870, Blue tells us, during a winter just as brutal as this one. He cites his library books. "The butchers caught rats and cats to cut up," he says. "The better restaurants cooked the zoo animals. Elephant filet. Camel chops."

"We must eat the wolves before the wolves eat us," I say.

Madame Roche brings Day a bottle of Coca-Cola and a glass. During the Great War, or the War Before as we've come to call it, Madame Roche worked in the melt-pot room of a munitions factory, in a lazy haze of dynamite dust that eventually struck her blind in one eye, which she now covers with a patch. I'm thinking again of Day's outlawed eyelash dye, so when Madame Roche leaves us, I whisper to

Day, to nag, "You don't want to end up with an eye patch, do you? From dying your lashes?"

"Nothing's been able to blind me yet," she says, as if this is useful logic. She takes a sip of her Coke, straight from the bottle. She says, "Aren't you going to tell me about it? About Zoé?"

"I was about to ask you the same thing," I say. "Aren't *you* going to tell me about it?"

Day takes off her sunglasses. "It's not my story to tell," she says, but sweetly, her tone apologetic. "She'll tell you what she tells you when she tells you. She's got to go about things her own way." Day means, I presume, Zoé's intention of having me over for a few minutes every night this week. The plan: I'm simply there to bring Zoé bottles of perfume, to establish my visits as an indulgence. A luxury. Her own personal perfumer. I'm to overwhelm her apartment with my fragrances, to stir up a cloud of innocence.

Blue says, "I can tell you anything you want to know about Zoé St. Angel. I've read every word written about her."

There are rumors of a camp in Alsace, I want to tell him once again. I want to worry Blue, just a touch. I want him to be careful. To keep low. What does he really know about the play he's in, and its troupe of actors? This government that's growing is applying new laws to old offenses, scrutinizing records of arrest and arresting again those who served too little time. *Be careful who you mix with.*

I've seen it before. Anything done to free our kind can be undone in an instant. We needn't get too comfortable, whoever we are, thinking the Germans are holding grudges only against the Jews. Just because it's all too grim to imagine doesn't mean we should look on the bright side. *Optimism is just a basket of live bees,* M, that lover of mine of long ago, used to say. And, just like stirring up a nest, he keeps coming to mind now that I've started thinking about him again. I hear his voice, plain as day.

"Zoé was eighteen," Blue says, "when she first sang at the Casino de Paris. She sang sad songs about singing sad songs in dance halls. She sang about running away from home." She sang about dancing the tango-musette on the rue de Lappe, one of those narrow little lanes on its last legs. She sang about derelict lovers with gambling debts. "She insists all the songs are true," he says. "She had a hard life."

"Is that so?" I ask Day.

Day takes a deep breath so she can sigh it back out. "Is there anything that's true anymore?" she says.

I glance up into the old faded mirror, with its speckling of blue and black. "I just don't want to think back to this particular minute, wishing I were sitting here again, so I'd have a chance to do it all over," I say. "Do it all over and do nothing this time. I don't want to regret fussing with something I'm much too old to fuss with." But even as I say those words, I know they're wrong. I *must* fuss with something.

"You're just bringing her perfume, Clementine. That's all," Day says. She takes my hand in both of hers. "I love you with all my heart. And I would never lead you into a problem that I didn't think you could fix." She pats my hand. "You're not nearly as old as you think you are."

"I'm every minute as old as I am," I say. But I'm encouraged by her sense of my age.

"What about *my* perfume?" Day says. "Didn't you bring me a bottle of something today?"

I did. Today's fragrance is another old lover she told me about, a croupier in a club, a dealer at a table of chemin de fer. The perfume: the crisp juniper of gin, the faint vanilla of old playing cards. Day breathes it in, she leans back, and she crosses her legs, her bathrobe falling open enough to show off some thigh. I can too easily picture her as a spy at a baccarat table, interpreting the spots on the cards for their instructions of war.

···· 8 ····

I meet with Zoé every night for a week, for only minutes, and we only talk perfume. She's always in a different robe, different scarf, different pattern: bouquets of flowers, dandelions and their puffs, girls on swings. Bees and ladybugs. Lovers in a rowboat. One of her robes is patterned with a map of Paris.

Maybe all she wants from me is perfume. I should be relieved, but I'm not. Has she determined I'm not up to the task, whatever it is? This evening, she hasn't even bothered to turn on the music.

I've been dressing my most dapper. Waistcoats, watch chains, tie clips. Pinkie ring, polished shoes.

"They tell me now I have a little girl's voice," she says. "But when I was a little girl, they told me I sounded too grown-up." She pets her own throat, which I've just perfumed with winter daphne and coumarin. "My father didn't like to hear me sing. So I didn't sing."

This revelation is just another tease. She dismisses me for the evening. But I don't go. I stand from the fat red chair and walk to the phonograph myself. I thumb through her jazz collection and look for something with a touch of rainy-day. I decide on "Cheek to Cheek," which isn't all that cheek-to-cheek, really—it has a pinch too much get-up-and-go for close dancing—but it does allow for some sway here and there. I nudge the volume up a few notches.

I hold out my hand. "At least let me say I danced with Zoé St. Angel once."

She hesitates; she seems about to refuse. She absentmindedly picks at the bracelet she always wears, that she's always fiddling with, a silver chain laden with charms. I've dabbed enough perfume on her wrist to know the charms well—there's a seahorse, a sailboat, a toy soldier. A woman's shoe, a telephone. At least one charm on every link. There's a story behind each one, she says, but she's told me none of them.

Finally, she smiles politely and puts her hand in mine.

"You grew up on the streets," I say, my voice beneath the tune, my lips close to her ear as we dance.

"No," she says.

"That's what you sing in your songs."

She pauses, then says, "The songs are wrong."

"Zoé," I say, my breath on her neck. "Do you want my help or don't you?"

I feel her body relax just a touch. She leans into me.

And that's when she tells me about her father. We dance slower than the music goes. She tells me her *true* story: of a childhood without songs, perhaps, but bereft of little else. It was a life of riches. Her family owned the Parfumerie Chamberry, one of the most famous of the city's perfume factories.

"Monsieur Pascal?" I say. "Your father is . . . well, he isn't Monsieur Pascal, of course. Is he?"

"Do you know him?" she says.

"Our paths crossed once."

"You robbed him of something, I suppose," she says.

"I've often fancied that *he* stole from *me*," I say. I sweep her around. Forward. Back. And I tell her about meeting her father in Marrakech, when I sought to leave thievery. I was already an old woman, but this was my new beginning. I'd come to the markets to buy spices and oils, to use in opening my own shop. Over a bottle of fig brandy, on a hotel veranda, I told him too much about the intricacies of a perfume I intended to design. I'd simply wanted to impress him. He was one of the world's most famous perfumers, even then. Many months later, I detected in a new fragrance of his a whiff of what I'd described. He'd even titled the perfume Escroquerie, French for "swindle."

"No," Zoé says, and though she's quite light on her feet, she steals the lead from me and picks up the pace of our steps a half beat or two. Her fingers tighten on my hand. "*You* stole from *him*. Your only instinct is theft. You wanted to smell your perfume in his, so you did. Many people have wanted to take credit for his genius. You have no idea. You're just one in a whole den of thieves."

I've upset her. I nod. "I suppose that's true," I say. Her vexation puts an extra kick in her step, and we're suddenly at cross-purposes, both of us leading. She knocks her hip into the phonograph, sending the stylus skipping against the groove, stopping the music, thumping the needle against the record's label. Zoé steps away and turns off the player. When I start to speak, she holds up her finger, stopping me. I wait for her to put on different music.

This time, it's something brassy. We remain standing there, but we don't dance. Zoé fidgets again with her charm bracelet. "My father," she says, "sees perfume as a puzzle to solve. He's a scientist, yes, but he knows that perfume is about passion. Emotions. He sees all the collision of the chemicals"—and here she lifts her hand to flutter her fingers around, the chemicals colliding—"as being part of it. As important as the flowers and the spices. There is all that's at the surface, of course, all that's recognizable, and then there's all that's tipping our brain this way or that."

I know a thing or two about Pascal. Everybody does. The family got rich off scents women could afford, but just barely. Pascal's perfume was just expensive enough to seem exclusive. Every man's first love, every woman he's ever gone to bed with, every girl every boy's ever married. Every mistress he's had. All those women wore one perfume or another from Pascal's factory. Every man in Paris, every woman in Paris—all their ideas of love, of sex, are caught in those bottles.

I'm about to ask after her father, and the perfume factory, and how he's managing in the face of all this. And that's when I begin to put it all together.

If Pascal is her father, then Zoé St. Angel is Jewish. And I instantly sense the danger in the room. The threat she's living under.

Before I can ask anything else, a clock begins to chime. Zoé says, "You have to go."

"No no no," I say.

"Yes yes yes," she says, and she sweeps me along, waving her hands at me. I pick up my satchel, and I begin to collect my perfume bottles. "Come back tomorrow," she says.

"I won't," I say.

"You will," she says, and she's right. She claps her hands, hurrying me. She picks up one of the bottles herself, and she follows me to the door, pinching the atomizer's bulb all along the way, spritzing the air in my wake, scenting my absence.

.... 9 ....

I scoot straight off to a covert jazz club in the Latin Quarter where Day sometimes sings in the late afternoons. I walk because there are no cars to call, no taxis, no gasoline. I'm walking fast enough to keep just an inch ahead of freezing to death, I suspect. I don't have far to go, but it's almost dark before I get there.

So here's how you get into the deepest part of the basement, where the jazz is muffled in a tunnel: At the end of the block, a *marchande de fleurs,* wrapped up in coats and quilts, parks her cart. You say, "Something for my buttonhole," and you pay too much for a few sprigs of some hothouse flower on its last legs. You flash your lapel, with this boutonniere of the day, to the clerk at the back of a secondhand kitchen shop where they sell rusty skillets and chipped crocks. The clerk opens a door to the stairs.

I suspect the flower vendor keeps quiet about the basement operation so long as she can pass off her half-dead posies to the club's clientele needing a passkey. It was only a year or so ago that the nightclub thrived aboveground—you could dance until sunup, then stay for the club's breakfast of chicken fricassee. But these days, you can get arrested for playing jazz, and clubs are raided for featuring musicians who are Black, who are Jewish. Such music, so unrestrained, rots your soul, or so the Nazis say.

Our poor, sickly souls. Even the French who live in the unoccupied zones would have us believe it—our moral failures put us in this fix. We have only ourselves to blame.

I try to sneak into the club and keep to the shadows, but all eyes are on me in a heartbeat. I'm quite a sight, I suppose, in my long coat, and my Tyrolean hat of heavy green felt, a doctor's bag in each hand. Day sits at the bar, and she spots me before I spot her. She gives me a hesitant wave. By the time I get to her, she's had the bartender pour me some pastis. "A little nip of licorice will warm you up," she says, handing me the glass.

I pluck the ratty gardenia from my lapel and hand it to her. "Don't sniff too close," I say, "or you'll get paint on your nose from where she's touched up the dead spots." I take off my gloves and pinch at the fabric of her sleeve. It's a new dress, rooster red. "What is this?" I say.

"Silk crepe," she says. "I took it in and got it blistered." I don't know what that means, but I assume it's what makes the dress wrinkled. Another reason Day's always broke: she doesn't just enlist a seamstress; she'll walk right into the atelier of the world's top silk manufacturer and say, *Can you wrinkle this?*

Before I've even taken a sip, or a seat, Day says, "You need to leave."

"I've been hearing a lot of that today," I say.

"I'm about to sing a song that could get my tongue cut out of my head," she says. She snaps her fingers to the tune, smiles at me, winks, and sings the title: *They Can't Take That Away from Me . . .*

I look around the room, and it's so sparsely populated, it hardly seems worth the risk of arrest. Before the war, when the club was at street level, the place was packed with an international crowd, even Germans, and it became a hot spot for spies, to eavesdrop. "Can't we get you back to America somehow?" I say. "There you can sing whatever songs you want."

"A girl I used to sing with went back to Harlem, before things got ugly here," she says. "Hasn't had a single gig. She spends her days scrubbing hotel rooms, then spends her nights sleeping in a dirty flophouse."

"At least she's alive."

"Oh, is she?" Days says. She fishes the cocktail onion from her gimlet. Pops it into her mouth. She says, "Music will be what saves us, Clem. You wait and see. We'll be singing at the tops of our lungs as we drive the sons of bitches out of town. One of these days, I'm going to sit in a Nazi's lap at the cabaret, and I'm going to sing 'My Funny Valentine' right in his ear, and then I'm going to stab him in the heart."

"Speaking of the cabaret," I say, to shift the conversation away from her rebellion. I take a seat on the barstool. "What's your favorite Chamberry perfume?"

I keep my eyes on my pastis for a moment, then look up at Day slylike, and she's already looking sly in return. She smiles. "The most expensive one," she says. "Galerie des Glaces. They claim the geranium oil is passed through the rose leaves of Versailles." Then she says, "Zoé told you a thing or two?"

"Yes. A thing or two."

"And now you know why I've kept mum," she says. "Lutz, of course, doesn't know. All he knows is the fiction in the songs she sings. He fell in love with the whole idea of her—the beauty who worked her way up from a run-down musette."

He might never learn she's Jewish, or it might just be a matter of time.

"She doesn't know where her father is?" I say.

"All she knows is that the Nazis have taken the house. They've taken the factories. They have it all. And he's nowhere."

"What do they want with it all?"

"I don't know," she says. "Maybe nothing. They've been taking all the Jewish businesses in Germany. So why wouldn't they do it here? They force you to sell for next to nothing. If you make it illegal for somebody to own something, then whatever they own becomes stolen goods." She shrugs, as if it should all already be so obvious, these new extremities.

And it is already happening here. The Jewish shops have to register and post signs. Flyers flutter down the windy streets warning of doing business with Jews. Do I shutter my perfume shop, in solidarity? Should Day stop singing in bars and cabarets? Is that defiance or defeat? Is someone like Madame Boulette serving France or serving Germany by keeping the brothel giddy with delight? Or just serving herself? Those of us wanting to save Paris don't look that much different than those wanting to see it fall, wanting to fall in line with a fascist Europe.

The bartender plunks a few more onions in Day's gin with a tiny pair of tongs. "Tell Clem the trouble we're in," she says to him.

He says to me, "A piano player was dragged off to a camp after playing 'Pennies from Heaven' in a bar in Montmartre."

"So you might best keep your mouth shut," I tell Day.

"I have to sing, darling," she says. "And these are the only songs I know."

She's called to the stage, and she shoots back the gin, then lets the onions roll from the glass onto her tongue. Before she walks away, I grab her elbow. I say, "So what's the twist? In the story with Zoé. Where do *I* come in?"

"This is the part where you save her life," Day says, crunching the onions. She winks at me. "I'd kiss your cheek, but I've had about ten cocktail onions for my dinner." She walks to the stage to a smattering of applause.

···· 10 ····

Zoé holds out her wrist, and I tap some perfume along her vein. I fumble with the charms on her bracelet. A top hat. A martini glass. The letter *Z*. A butterfly.

That butterfly. I pinch at its silver wings. I say to her, "I'm going to ask questions, and you're going to answer them. Or I'm leaving."

She withdraws her hand and leans back in the fat red chair. Fiddles with her charm bracelet. After a moment, she says, "Why are you still here?"

I don't have the patience for this. And if I'm tinkering with something lethal, I need to know. How did I never see that butterfly on her bracelet before? I guess I am still superstitious after all, here in the worst of times. Following butterflies has always led me in the wrong direction, without fail. Butterflies carried me away from M, to be honest. I stand, gather my perfume bottles, get ready to leave.

"No no no," she says. She leans forward to put her hand on my arm. "Don't be silly, Clementine. Sit down. I meant to say, why are you still here, *in Paris*? Why didn't you go home? Back to America?"

I do sit down, but only on the edge of the chair's cushion. "I've never had a home," I say. "No place is mine."

She nods, her eyes in a squint of contemplation. Like she's figuring something out about me. "And that's why you're a thief," she says. "Since you never had a home, you got greedy."

"If you say so," I say.

"When I realized people liked to look at me," she says, "then it wasn't enough that they looked. I wanted them to fall in love too.

And it wasn't enough that *some* men fell in love with me. I needed *all* of them to. How greedy is that?"

"They probably all *do* fall in love with you," I say.

"No," she says. "Maybe *none* of them fall in love. There are those men who say they're in love but they don't know the first thing about it. Have you ever thought that maybe men can't fall in love at all? That they don't feel what we feel? And they don't *know* that they can't fall in love, so they *think* that they do. So they say, 'I love you,' and we have to believe it's the same thing."

"I never think about how men feel," I say.

Her eyes linger on mine. After a moment, she smiles. "You. You know about love; I know you do. You seem sad to me. You have sad eyes."

She can't see anything in my eyes that I don't want her to see. But I shudder with a chill—"someone walked over your grave," they used to say when a shiver worked through you, like we're all ghosts, living and dying in the same breath.

What if I'd stayed put and never pursued my crimes, all those years ago, when I was so in love with M? Decades ago, lifetimes, so much of it nothing more than mist now. I thought I would fall in love again. I was young; how could I not? I still feel the toe-tap in my boot, my quickened heart, the hesitance, as I lingered in the doorway of the train car on the day I left M. One step forward and I would be gone; one step back and I'd have never left at all. But in the station, in that crowd, with all its elbows and whistles and slaps of rushing skirts, there wasn't a single soul watching me. There was no one to see me leave. Or see me stay. I wanted to go because I wanted people to know I was gone. But how do you disappear if you're already invisible?

How different everything, *everything*, would have been if I'd stayed. When I cling to my regret, I keep everyone close.

"Are you in love with Lutz?" I say, to startle Zoé away from studying my mistakes.

I can see the flinch in her jaw, like she just took a sucker punch. She starts to say something but stops. She says, "I'm not answering any more of your questions."

"I've only asked one. You're the one doing all the asking."

"What made you think my father stole your idea?" she says. "When you met him in Marrakech?"

"He didn't know about vendor number 37," I say. "In the spice market. I'm the one who told him about his booth." In no. 37, one of the world's most brilliant perfumers, and one of the oldest, lay slung in a hammock, overcome by his hay fever. He looked like the silkworm cocoons sold in wicker baskets nearby, their pods like spools of cotton. He credited his insights into scent to the narrow nasal passages that were daily strangling him; the nerves of his nostrils were in constant alarm, always sniffing at the air for salvation. As he passed along wisdom, I fanned at him with a banana leaf to help him breathe, so he could suck in some air, and let out some words.

"There's a flower in Cuba," I tell Zoé, "that smells sweet at night, sickly in the daytime. Dama de noche. I wanted to bottle its prettier hours. But I could never quite conjure a match for it. I thought maybe I'd found my way to it with a little pot of ointment I bought from number 37, for scorpion stings, using the Malaki flower of India."

"So *you* took from number 37," she says. "And my father just took what you'd already taken."

"Where is your father, Zoé?" I say. "Why can't you just ask him?"

She pauses. She nods and returns her attention to her charm bracelet. But this time she unclasps the bracelet and takes it off her wrist. She walks to a grandfather clock on the other side of the room. Among the charms is a tiny key, and she unlocks the clock's glass with it. She then puts the key to the center of the clock's face, and with her pinkie, she turns the long hand around and around and around.

Was the clock wrong? What time is it? Paris, our village, has fallen victim to a fairy-tale curse. The sun rises; the moon drops. The cogs of the clockworks tick-tock north-south, or east-west, in whatever direction they've always turned, but time itself has turned to fog. The days: they don't seem short. They don't seem long. What day even is it? To make things worse, the Germans are always jumbling the hours of the curfew. You have to believe them if they stop you in the street to tell you it's night at high noon. *You're out too late,* a soldier might say, so you check your watch, and it tells you nothing.

Finally, with one more twist of the hands, the clock's face pops open. Zoé pulls it open all the way on its hinge, to put that key one more time to the lock of a drawer beneath the workings. She opens the drawer, and takes from it an envelope. On her way to the credenza, she looks at me and nods toward the phonograph. I select a record, and start the music.

At the credenza, I stand right next to her—we're shoulder to shoulder—as she takes a cigarette from her little novelty box, plucking it from the teeth of the wooden alligator. But she doesn't light it. There's an envelope on the credenza; with her fingertip, she slides it toward me.

When I remove the card from the envelope, the paper's scent lifts, blooms, but just faintly. It's fading. I wave the card beneath my nose—I recognize the perfume as one from her father's collection. Ophelia. The scent has something soft and girlish about it, with a hint of cape jessamine.

Now that I've smelled the perfume, she lights her cigarette.

There's nothing written on the envelope but her first name, and the card is unsigned. All it says: *I write about you in my diary. Here's the key to it.* And beneath the writing is an insignia, a little twist and coil of design—part fleur-de-lis, part arabesque, part something else altogether. You could almost see a swastika in it, but these days, with swastikas everywhere, any shape with crossing lines seems suspicious.

"This note was left for me some weeks ago, here at the cabaret," she says. "Or was it months ago? I never know when anything is anymore."

I study the note. *I write about you in my diary. Here's the key to it.* "Where's the key? Is that on your bracelet too?"

"There was no key in the envelope," she says.

I put the card back on the credenza. We both stare down at it. "What does it mean?" I say. "How do you know your father sent it?"

"It's his handwriting," Zoé says. And the handwriting *is* very distinctive. Though the card is unsigned, I can see Pascal's signature in the shapes of the letters and the lines and the slant of the cursive. In recent years, his signature has appeared on all the new boxes of perfume from Parfumerie Chamberry.

Zoé says, "And it's his perfume. Or *my* perfume. He designed it for me."

"Ophelia?" I say. I hold it again to my nose.

"You know it," she says. She seems pleased. Maybe relieved.

"Is Ophelia your real name?"

"It's what he called me," she says. She hands me the cigarette, and though I don't smoke as a rule, I do take a puff, then hand it back. She says, "I did the mad scene from *Hamlet* when I was a little girl. Interrupted him in his studio at the house. I was desperate for his attention. I was always competing with his perfumes." She breathes in the smoke. Breathes it out. She talks fast, rattling off the details. "I made a big production out of it, on a Sunday afternoon. I made a costume out of his smoking coat. I wound a winter scarf around my head. I even staged my drowning, by making a little river out of a blue silk sheet. It was silly—I didn't even know the lines—but it sent my father over the moon. He was full of love for me those days, but he didn't know what to do with me. My mother had just died. He called me Ophelia for all the years after." She doesn't seem emotional, but she pulls a handkerchief from her pocket to dab at her eyes. At her cheek. "But nobody can know," she says.

"Then maybe you shouldn't be telling people about it," I say.

"Don't you get it?" she says. She taps her finger on the card. "It says right here. There's a diary. And I'm in it."

"What can I do?" I say, but I'm not asking Zoé how I can help. I mean to sound defeated. *What could I possibly do?*

"You'll get the diary back," she says. "There's something about that insignia. That's the key he's talking about." And, indeed, the design does look deliberate. Intentional. He drew it once, then drew over it, and over it, inking it blacker and blacker.

"If you're right about all this," I say, "then why didn't he just tell you where the diary is?"

She's disappointed in me yet again. "He was afraid for me," she says, her voice falling soft. "He knew about me. He knew about Lutz keeping me here. He must have. He was afraid people were rifling through my mail. And he was right. He wanted to send a message that might look like any other note I might get. A perfumed note, from an admirer. I get letters all the time. Love letters from strangers. Flowers. Candy." She breathes in the smoke deep. "And, like I told you, he thinks in puzzles. He knew I'd recognize the note as his."

"When did you last see your father?" I say.

"I left home when I was seventeen," she tells me, "to live with a man who said he was going to be my manager. My father was furious, of course. He told me to never come back, no matter what kind of mess I made of my life. 'No matter how miserable you make yourself, you're not welcome home,' is the last thing he told me. 'I promise I'll stay away,' is the last thing *I* told *him*. And I did stay away. I changed my name. I changed my story. And I never heard from him, until he made this perfume for me." She picks up the card, holds it to her nose. "He had the very first bottle of it sent to me at the Casino, a few years ago. He sent a note along then too. He asked for my forgiveness."

"And did you forgive him?" I say.

"I did," she says. "I did. But I didn't tell him. I didn't even thank him for the perfume. Never sent a note back. But I knew I'd go to him someday. When the time was right."

"Do you really have much to worry about, Zoé? Yes, the diary is still in the house, and they have the house. But are they going to sit down and read the thing? When the world is at war?"

She turns a bit so she can speak closer to me, softer. "His diary is more than just a diary," she says. "It's like a cookbook. But it's more than that too."

Inside were not just formulas, not just listings of ingredients like in Cleopatra's beauty book, but key insights into his methods and experiments. And not only that, but personal details, reflections on his influences and inspirations. For Zoé's father, a perfume was not just a combination of oils and extracts, not just a collision of chemicals. It was a peek at his soul. A thump of his heart. His every fragrance told something of his own story.

She says, "I've heard Lutz talk about it. Every night, after the cabaret, the Germans smoke in a gentleman's lounge downstairs. They have grandiose schemes about what the war will win them. They want to keep the perfume in production. They want the fashion, the food, the chocolate, the wine. They see Paris as a parade, a carnival. A holiday resort. They want to keep it all alive, for the New Europe."

"Then why . . ." But how could I possibly finish that sentence? Why *everything*? Why hold us captive? Why punish us? How do you sustain beauty with such torment and quarantine? If they don't kill Paris outright, they'll render the city a relic, a quaint excursion at best.

Zoé puts her cigarette to my lips and leans even closer, lowers her voice even more, so that I have to turn my ear to hear her. As I smoke, she tells me what she knows about me, from Day. She knows about thefts from years ago, from early on, when I mostly worked for widows: young women who'd married old men. They had inheritances to burn through. These women wanted me to bring them something so exceptional it'd stop their hearts. They wanted perfume in their veins. They wanted exotic liquors shot into their tongues with a needle.

I'm flattered, to be honest, that Zoé knows so much. My darling Day. She does pay close attention to me.

"This will take more than just slipping in through a window," Zoé says. "This is going to require some very sophisticated weaseling."

"Sneak out with me," I say, slipping the cigarette back to her, tucking it into her fingers. I keep my hand against hers. "Let's go now. I can hide you in my house. We can walk there." I have Blue in mind too, I confess. Not only do I want to be the one to rescue Zoé St. Angel, but I can't help but think about how happy Blue will be. My building has become a factory, a distillery, cellar to attic, a gasworks of copper pipes corkscrewing through the parlor's ceiling and up through the kitchen floor, winding around the bedposts, whistling like snakes with a lisp. The building's strange acoustics, and all the perfumery's pipes and vents, warp and bend our voices. Sometimes you can whisper in someone's ear from another room. I'm imagining our house filled with Zoé's every whistle and hum, her every private, stifled trill of melody.

"No one's going to let me out of this house," she says. "I can't go anywhere without Lutz. Do you think any of the women in this building can go anywhere on their own?"

I'm naive, I guess. It hadn't occurred to me that the women of Boulette's might be captives. On a short leash, yes, but imprisoned?

"And if I did get away," she says, "Lutz would look for me. And he'd find me. I've been dripping with your perfumes for days. Your potions have been spiking his allergies. You make his eyes water. His nose run. He knows all about you. Your shop is the first place he'd look."

I've had a long career of taking things from people, but rarely things I'd keep for myself. My clients would covet something priceless, and they'd hire me, the international expert at lifting perfume from the skin. But it's always been fairly ignoble. A pursuit of indulgence. The rich at play. And by blaming the greed of others, I've absolved myself of my crimes. Maybe that's how we're all allowing ourselves to just go on along with our daily lives while people are arrested all around us, their homes and businesses taken away. We blame the greed of others.

If I can help Zoé, I might be saving her from arrest, or from something worse.

I do have to be careful myself. I've relied for years on France's lax extradition policies. If the Nazis send me back to America, I'll lose my house, my bank accounts. I'll be arrested for old crimes. Even a short jail sentence might kill someone as old as me.

Zoé picks up the card and puts it in the envelope. She opens my jacket. She keeps her eyes on mine as she tucks the card into my inside pocket. "And wouldn't you like to take a look at the book yourself?" she says. "Maybe you're in it. Don't you want to see what he wrote about Escroquerie? Does he cite you as an inspiration? Does he mention meeting you in Marrakech? You'll finally know if you were robbed by the greatest perfumer in the history of Paris."

She's playing to my vanity, though even my vanity isn't enough to make me take such a risk. Nonetheless, such a prize would be my greatest theft. It's tantalizing, the notion of stealing the scents of Paris back from the Nazis. Paris certainly rescued *me*. But how would I even get my foot in the door of Pascal's house?

Before I can ask, Zoé says, "There are some men I want you to meet."

···· 11 ····

After the cabaret has closed for the night, I make my way back to the gentleman's lounge. The only ladies among the men are Zoé and Day. Day stands amid a few admirers near the fireplace with a brandy; she is still wearing the dress she wore onstage, the sequins half a million itty-bitty hearts, shimmering in the firelight, pulsing with the beat of Day's own heart.

Zoé, meanwhile, has changed out of her see-through gown into a see-through robe, some of her nakedness hidden by the robe's willowy ostrich-feather trim. She's on a sofa surrounded by doting German soldiers, some even in uniform.

Zoé leans toward the cocktail table in front of her, telling the men's fortunes with a handful of hard candy. She shakes the candy in her loose fist, like she's about to toss some dice. She's casting runes. She rolls the pyramid-shaped candies across the tabletop. One tumbles off the edge, and Lutz, who sits on the sofa next to her, snatches it up and pops the confection into his mouth. Zoé taps her pinkie on each remaining candy, contemplating their order.

She predicts rotting teeth and ugly wives, and the men laugh.

Zoé looks up at me. "Should I look into your future?" she says.

As I open my mouth to decline, Lutz interrupts. "I'm going to buy that necktie from around your throat," he says, standing up. "Those silver threads caught the candlelight even out there in the cabaret." He tugs at the end of my tie. "How much for this?" And he gives it another couple of tugs. He's so handsome, it's almost absurd. I wonder if it's embarrassing, how he probably can't go anywhere without getting people flustered.

I speak French when I tell him he can simply have it, but he says, "You're American," in English.

"I am American," I say, in French, unknotting the necktie.

Lutz pulls at the tie before I've quite undone it, so it catches and chokes me. He pauses to allow me to free myself. As I gasp a little, I ask him if he's ever heard of a garrote.

"It's the scarf you'd use to strangle someone," Lutz says. He gives the tie another yank, and it's off my neck with a snap. I can feel the burn of it at the back of my neck. He leans over a cocktail trolley to watch his reflection in a silver martini shaker, knotting the tie around his own neck. He says, "You should scurry on home, Uncle Sam."

Zoé reaches over to pull on the tail of his jacket. He drops back down on the sofa next to her, fluttering his new tie. "Let her stay a minute," she says.

"*Her?*" he says. He looks at me, suspicious, raising an eyebrow. "He's a *her,* is he?"

"She's the perfumer who's been to see me," she says.

"Oh," he says. *"Her.* All that wispy stink makes my eyes water." But he leans in toward Zoé's neck, to inhale the perfume that's there.

Zoé casts a glance at me. She's concerned. *Do your thing,* she seems to want to say. *Worm your way in.*

Whenever I meet a handsome man, I study him quick for flaws. Handsome men know all too well what makes them less than perfect. If they see you seeing the thing they like the least about themselves, you've tapped in. You've rattled their perch. With Lutz it's the flush of his cheeks, round, rosy, and cherubic, as if he's smeared them with rouge. They're like Blue's in that way. Those cheeks were probably often pinched and admired when he was in his baby carriage. They're much too pretty. He's otherwise as square-jawed and steely-eyed as a matinee cowboy. In those plump, pink cheeks is his destiny; their unbearable sweetness has marched him into fight after fight, I bet.

"You're smoking a Punch," I say, speaking American, falling back into my cowpoke's brogue, and though Lutz is first inclined to ignore me, I've made him curious. He picks up his cigar from the crystal dish and puts it to his lips.

"The lady knows cigars," he says.

"I have a good memory for scent," I say. I put my hands in my pockets. "I know that cigar's smoke. And it is *serious* smoke. For serious smokers. It packs a wallop."

"I guess that's why they call it a Punch," he says. "Isn't that the word in English for it? A slug. A punch to the lungs." I don't correct him. It's named after the puppet, a character named Punch, a little boy's toy.

A pop of a champagne cork and Lutz is distracted again. The champagne has sprayed like a fountain among a circle of men near Day; Day laughs and tries to catch what she can in her champagne coupe. Lutz stands up to ridicule the men, but he continues to speak in English, as if he's performing for me. "You have one night in Paris, and you spill your one shot at French champagne?" he says, walking toward them. "Suck it up out of the rug before it dries!"

Earlier, Day told me that she plays along to play against. *I sing them their songs and I sit in their laps and I pour them their drinks. And someday soon, I'll slip under their skin.* They confide in her. She teases out their anxieties. *They're terrified of getting shipped off to some grisly battle,* Day told me. They're all scrambling to build empires in Paris, to dig in their heels, to be indispensable.

Zoé, frustrated, rolls her eyes. She fans at the cigar smoke as the men around her bellow and bark. She picks up the Punch and snuffs it out in the mostly empty candy dish. Suddenly, at her shoulder is a soldier holding open his silver cigarette case. She seems startled, worried that he has noticed her annoyance with Lutz. But she smiles at him, and she takes a cigarette from his case, and she accepts his light.

Madame Boulette brings me my coat, which I'd tossed in a corner chair. She's holding it up for me, wanting me to leave. She says, "No women who don't work here are let in past the cabaret at night," she says.

It's my coat that brings Lutz back to us.

"What kind of beast is that?" he says, giving me a manly slap on the back.

"It would be a gazelle," I say, "if it were real. But it's not. It's synthetic gazelle."

"Synthetic?"

Zoé tells me, "Lutz hates perfume but loves to smother me in fur." She leans back into the sofa cushions, crosses her legs. She sticks the cigarette in the corner of her mouth, to free her hands, so she can count off her list of coats and capes, muttering through pursed lips like a cinema gangster. "Patagonian skunk. A squirrel choker. Cross fox. Marmot. Muskrat. Black rat. Polecat. My bedroom is positively *crawwwwwwling* with vermin."

Lutz chuckles at her, then notices that his cigar's been extinguished. He looks back and forth from Zoé to the dead cigar, his brow furrowed; he playfully thieves Zoé's cigarette, taking it from her lips, then spinning it along his fingers, rolling it over his knuckles in a clumsy, college-boy sleight of hand. But he manages to keep from burning himself, and the cigarette ends up right-side-in at his lips. Even he seems surprised to still have the knack. "Where'd you get this from?" he says, pointing his thumb at the cigarette in his mouth. But the soldier with the silver case is long gone, and Zoé just waves her hand around, in the general direction of all the men in the room, as if to say, *I can't tell them apart.*

They seem used to performing their intimacy for an audience. Though their flirtation appears genuine, it's partly for my benefit. They act like lovers who are most in love when others are watching.

Lutz looks at me, sizing me up. The part in his hair is a work of art, and every blond wave is locked into place with pomade. The pomade will keep his hair from getting ruined when he puts his hat on but will ruin his hat sooner than later with all its oil and slick. "So why's the fur fake?" he says. "France has some of the finest peltmongers in all the world."

"It makes me uneasy," I say. "Fur does."

"Ah," he says; he nods, but not because he's agreeing with anything. He's condescending to me. "What about leather?"

Zoé gives me that look of concern again.

"I don't wear leather," I say.

"And you never eat a steak?"

"Not so much these days," I say. "There's a famine going around, if you haven't heard." He keeps his eyes on mine. "But I do eat meat when I can, to keep alive, mostly."

"But, now, these perfumes of yours," he says. "Nothing dead in any of your scents? No remnant of a carcass? Suet? Musk?"

"No," I say. "None of the fixatives I use come from animals. Except sometimes a bit of ambergris so long as I know it wasn't scraped out of a whale's gut."

"So you know your way around a bottle of perfume," Lutz says.

Zoé says, "That's what I've been telling you."

"That stench you've been leaving behind on Zoé," he says to me. "Those are your own designs?"

"Tell him about Escroquerie," Zoé says, but I'm not sure what she has in mind. In my hesitation, she says, "Clementine worked on that scent. For the Parfumerie Chamberry."

"You worked with Pascal?" Lutz says.

"I . . . I contributed," I say.

"On just the one perfume?"

I try to look Zoé's way without letting Lutz see my eyes shift. Where, exactly, does she mean to lead me with this? "On others too," I lie.

"You don't have to keep any company secrets," he says. "Not anymore."

I'm able to catch a glance at Zoé, who nods me on. "I did consult with Pascal," I say. "We worked together . . . on various scents."

"Don't you think she should meet Oskar?" Zoé asks Lutz, stepping in a bit too soon, I fear.

He pauses. He keeps his eyes on mine, even as he speaks to Zoé. "I think you're right," he tells her. "She *should* meet Voss." He looks over at Zoé, then back to me. "Oskar Voss is an associate of mine. He has a particular interest in the perfumes of Paris. Leave your card with Madame Boulette on the way out. I'll make some arrangements."

He takes the cigarette from his lips, and he makes to return it to Zoé with the same flourish he'd brought to its theft, spinning it along, but this time faster, more deftly. But it reaches her face hot end out, and she flinches, from the coal dangerously near her cheek. Even I start at the sight of it; my hand jerks forward, as if I might need to slap the cigarette from him, to keep it from burning her face. "Pardon me," he says, righting the cigarette, his voice icy, no longer playful. "Who did you say gave this to you?"

"I didn't say," Zoé says. "I didn't know." She hesitantly reaches up for the cigarette to take it from him, but he won't relinquish it. He brings his hand, and the cigarette, to his chest.

"Point him out," he says, pointing the cigarette toward the roomful of men.

"I don't see him," she says without looking around, her eyes not leaving his.

"What'd he look like?"

She pauses. "A Nazi," she says. She leans forward to pluck the cigarette from his fingers. As she brings it to her lips, Lutz snatches it from her, making her flinch again. He grinds it out in the glass dish with a sharp twist of his wrist. I pull my coat on over my shoulders, and I nod toward Lutz and Zoé. "Good night," I say, but they're still eyeing each other, viper-like.

···· 12 ····

I'm chauffeured back to my shop in the backseat of a black car, my driver tight-lipped. Somehow Lutz had arranged for the car and driver without even leaving Zoé's side in the gentleman's lounge.

I've never seen Paris so still and so dark.

It begins to snow.

We stop in front of my building, and the driver, still without speaking, holds up with two fingers an envelope I'm to take. I put it in the pocket of my synthetic gazelle.

Though I've been escorted home in a Nazi car, I'm still skittish about turning on a lamp at this hour, for fear of some night patrolman appearing out of nowhere to knock on my door and slap me with a fine. To needle me with questions. I light a candle. My hands are still shaking from the bitter cold of the night air.

I start toward the stairs but stop when I hear snoring behind me. Blue fell asleep in the shop? I walk across the room and aim my candlelight toward the sound of the snuffling. The flicker of the flame shimmers on some of my perfume bottles strung across the top of the low table. They've been left open. I smell eucalyptus and plum. Juniper. Clove.

Blue is asleep on the settee where my customers sit to contemplate the fragrances I bring them on silver trays. His snores sound muffled, and I suspect he's on his stomach. I lean forward, holding out the candle. I see his naked feet, then his naked legs. It's almost as cold inside as it is out—I read that eleven people have died in Paris this winter, some of them frozen stiff in their own beds. I take a few steps closer, and run the light up his leg, along his thigh, his naked hip. He's a man in a painting I'm certain I've seen somewhere, some skinny-dipping farm boy, sunning himself by a river.

When I reach out to shake him awake, I become distracted by what appears to be a crisscrossing of scars on his shoulder. I assume it's just how the light's falling—I don't know of any such wounds on the boy's skin. I lean in closer. Oh yes, those are scars, and they're deliberate, like from a knife fight. As I lean in yet more, I bump my ankle against another ankle, and there's a rustling. My light falls on Blue's face, his mess of curls, his naked chest. He's been asleep too, on the floor, and he sits bolt upright.

Two Blues, both stark naked. The man I've been eyeing on the sofa, Mr. Knife-fight, isn't Blue at all. He's blond and bearded, and he's been startled awake too. He lifts himself up and looks back at me.

"Oh," I say, stepping away. I blow out the candle, and we're back in the dark. "I'm sorry," I say. "I'm so sorry. Go back to sleep." Blue says my name, but I don't stop until I get to the staircase. I say, "Well, no, actually, don't stay down here. Go to bed, where you can get under the covers. Or you'll catch your death."

"All I wanted to catch was a catnap," says Knife-fight, and I hear them both shuffling themselves into their trousers, the clank of their belt buckles.

I worry I shouldn't have said anything at all. Blue has never brought a man home, that I know of. Did I make things awkward for them? Is it one thing to be naked on a sofa, and another thing entirely to invite a man to your bed? I've complicated the already complicated bob-and-weave of romance.

Blue turns on a table lamp, then closes the heavy chintz drapes to keep the light inside.

"Where do you live?" I ask the bearded man as he ties the laces of his boots.

"Montmartre, madame," he says.

"Well, you . . . you can't go all the way to . . . not at this hour . . ."

He pulls on his raggedy coat as he walks up to me. He smiles. Takes my hand. Leans in to kiss my cheek. "I'll be fine," he says. "I'm very fleet-footed. Now you see me, now you don't." He smells of a spike lavender after-slap I sell in the shop as part of a shaving kit. It suits him. He goes to Blue, tousles his hair, whispers something in his ear, and he's gone.

After closing the door, Blue, distracted, runs his hand through his hair himself. He gathers up his wild locks in his fist, pushes them up off his forehead. From the little telephone table he takes a binder clip from a stack of papers and somehow manages to clip his hair in place. I've often marveled at the architecture of his curls. The very drama of a simple clip.

His shirt is buttoned unevenly. He's barefoot. He seems to look at me for a while before he actually sees me. "You've lost your little noose," he says, his voice scratched with sleep.

"Hm?" I say.

He drums his fingers at his throat. "Your necktie."

"Oh," I say, bringing my own fingers to my own throat. I then bundle up tighter in my coat. "Aren't you cold?" I say.

Blue sort of saunters, sort of half waltzes, into the shop, to where the rest of his costume, from his role in the play, is piled on the floor. "I'm not cold," he says, though he plucks up the military jacket with a flourish, drapes it over his shoulders. "We had much, much, much too much to drink," he says. He takes a bottle of whiskey from the cabinet where I keep liquor, and two glasses. Sometimes the people who visit my shop want colognes that suggest gin, red wine, absinthe. "But just one more sip," he says, pouring us each far more than that.

I pick up his mask from the floor. The mask, made of copper and clay, covers one cheek, and part of his jaw, and his brow, with a half-moon for his left eye to see through. In the play, he's a voiceless veteran of the War Before, one of those men, *les mutilés de guerre,* whose faces were wrecked by shrapnel, and who masked the damage with smooth and pristine cheek-and-jowls of plaster.

I hold it out to him after he hands me my drink, and he puts it to his face.

"Heartbreaking," I say, tapping my finger on his glass jaw. "I can't bear the idea of it." He takes a sip. *Clink,* his glass against the plaster.

"Félix," he says, "—that gentleman who just ran away is Félix—Félix told me he wouldn't have looked at me twice if he hadn't first seen me onstage in the mask." He puts the mask aside. "He says I'm too pretty for his taste."

"All of you boys want to fall in love with a thug," I say. Men who love men seem so often to be seeking the affection of the boys who bullied them.

After the curtain drops for the night, the stage of Blue's theater becomes a makeshift canteen for the lavender crowd. They prop open the alley door with a pink-beaded bedroom slipper from the wardrobe closet, and the ladies and men slink in with their own booze. They sit in the dim lick of candlelight, everyone barely there until you lean in close.

We need a place to lurk. The saloons for us, what few there were, have shut up tight, the Nazis having dragged along with them their laws against queer romance. Even Berlin, which had once upon a time known next to no restraint, has become a ghost of its former self, or so we hear.

"I thought the theater director was your . . . well, I thought the two of you . . . ," I say, then stop. "He wrote you into his play." We sit side by side on the settee, in our coats, warming our bones with the whiskey.

"He is not mine, and I am not his," he says, and I'm pleased to hear it. Félix looks to be Blue's age, at least, unlike the director. But then Blue says, "I'm not with Félix either. They're all just . . . erotic friendships."

Erotic friendships. It sounds to my ear like something he's heard from one of his corrupt, bewigged old widows who pay him to take them to the opera. Those biddies'll give him jewelry to pawn in exchange for a peck on the cheek. But I like that he's not in love. I'll lose him soon enough. If there's one thing I've learned from living forever, it's that nothing lasts.

"How did you lose your tie?" he says.

"Zoé St. Angel's Nazi," I say. "He stripped me of it." And that reminds me of the envelope the driver gave me, and I take it from my pocket. It's an invitation to a fashion show at the Ritz, of a couturier I've never heard of. Stamped all along the border of the card are swastikas in gold foil. And someone has written across the back, *We will see you there*. Tomorrow night.

Blue looks over my shoulder at the card. "I don't think I like the company you're keeping."

"Are you telling me to stop?" I say. "Am I getting myself into something I should be getting myself out of? I won't go if you don't want me to." I'm not sure I even know what I want him to say. And I'm not sure I'd even do what he told me. But I like asking his permission. I've never asked anyone for their approval before I've stirred up trouble.

He seems surprised by the question too. He brings his whiskey to his lips and pauses, thinking. He leans forward to put the glass on the table, and to pick up a few of the perfume bottles scattered there. He untwists a stopper, holds the fragrance to his nose.

"Félix is a professional blood donor," he says. "If his blood's too thin, people in the hospitals in Paris can't be saved. And more and more people are getting sick from the cold. Nearly freezing in the streets. All the donors are going on strike for more rations. They need more sugar, more fat, if they're going to bleed for the whole city." He puts down the perfume and takes another drink. "The poor bastard's opening up his veins. What are *we* doing?"

Before I can think of a good reason we're not bleeding ourselves dry, Blue slaps his hand onto my knee and squeezes tight. He's got a bolt of energy. "You have to let me help you," he says. And before I can insist that he can only help by not helping at all, he takes from his pocket a tiny pistol. He pulls the trigger, and a flame sparks up. "I lifted this from Félix's pocket," he says. "He'll want it. So he'll come back. And I'll get to see him again." This seems to be Blue's evidence that he's capable of my crimes.

I run my thumb over my ring finger, an old, old habit, from when

I wore the ring M gave me many, many years ago. "You're definitely up to my old tricks," I say.

"The Nazis think we're an infection," Blue says, "so let's infect. Let's become an epidemic."

Blue tells me more about Félix, how he's an actor too but has only a bit part in the play Blue's in. Félix does most of his acting in the streets, playing a scoundrel. Americans like to lick at the underbelly. So the tourist guides, back when we had tourists, would pay him to stumble around and look at them crooked. Or he'd try to sell the tourists cocaine, but it was only ever sugar.

Blue seems to slip deeper and deeper in love with every derelict story.

"It's my fault you're so susceptible to slick hooligans," I say. "You came to Paris seeking a scholarship at a gentleman's college, and I poisoned your brain with my moral decay."

He nods, smiles, tilts his head with affection. He puts his glass to mine, and we clink them together in agreement.

···· 13 ····

At Zoé's the next afternoon, all the drapes have been drawn, and the lamps are dim. I walk past vases and baskets, roses of all colors, lilies, irises, and tulips, whole hothouses plundered. I glance at a card on a stick poking up from amaryllis—apologies in both French and German: *Je suis désolé. Ich entschuldige mich vielmals.*

There are dresses too, draped over chair backs. There are fat boxes of new hats and thin boxes of new gloves. Tins of chocolate. The room is cluttered with apology. *I apologize many times.*

I sit on an ottoman that's been pushed up next to the sofa where Zoé lies back, her face draped with a light chiffon scarf. Veiled, like a woman in mourning. She hands me the pamphlet she's holding. *Perfume therapy,* it says in English, *for nightmare victims.* I tip the page toward a thin ray of lamplight, to read. The treatment aims to banish not only nightmares but also something called *depression insomnia.*

I study the pamphlet's instructions. It calls for an eyedropper and calming fragrances. Eucalyptus, rosemary, worn leather. I have all of these. As I sort through my satchel, I ask her about the fashion show I've been invited to. It begins in a few hours.

"I have questions," I say.

She says nothing.

I say, "I just don't know . . . well . . . tell me . . . who am I?"

"Who are you?" she says.

"Who am I pretending to be?" I say. "They think I'm an associate of Monsieur Pascal's. How much do I know about his business?"

She sighs, her breath billowing the scarf. "You best not know too much, I suppose." Her voice is throaty, scratched up, like she has a cold or she's been crying.

"Why not?"

"Well," she says, "you don't want them putting screws to your thumbs. For information. That you don't even have. Do you?"

Why is she acting as if I'm alone in this, embroiled in my own personal turmoil? "Do you know something I don't?" I say.

"I know nothing," she says. "Less than nothing." She says this softly, and gently, and I believe her. Then she says, "What am I paying you?"

"*Are* you paying me?"

"You're a crook for hire," she says. "You'll need to be paid. I need you committed to me."

How is it that I'm insulted by this?

I can't see her eyes through the scarf. They might not even be open.

I begin with the therapy, squeezing the bulb of the eyedropper, dipping it into the perfume bottle. "I gave up crime years ago," I say.

"Why?" she says.

"I got clumsy," I say, to make her nervous, to punish her for insulting me. It is true, though. I got clumsy. "Now *shhh,*" I say, holding the dropper over her scarf.

According to the pamphlet, this is the first step of her therapy—daydreaming out loud. Strolling through pleasant memories. As she talks, I pinch a droplet of perfume on the scarf, between her nose and her mouth. The scarf puffs up with her story, pulses with her breath. Music plays on the phonograph, an aria of some kind, though I don't know much about opera. The idea is that she'll describe the good things, while breathing in scent, while listening to music, and eventually she'll describe the bad things. The nightmares. All the sentiments will get stirred around, and the nightmares will end up defanged. Or so the pamphlet says. The next time she has bad dreams, she'll put on the record and hold the perfumed scarf to her nose.

"I'm with my father," Zoé says. "He's leading me through a field of roses on the Riviera. I'm not even a teenager yet, or maybe I am.

He loved when I'd go to the farms with him." Her blinking shivers the scarf. "Perfume is passed along from father to son. The business, I mean. The oldest perfumeries have been handed off, down, down, down, all along the line for generations. All in a whisper, practically, to keep it all close. My father had no sons. But he didn't care, he said. I had to learn it all. I absolutely had to. But, the thing is, I wouldn't. And I didn't."

And now it's been taken away.

I drip more perfume on the scarf. She breathes in deep, sucking in the silk. "They can't take your father's perfumes," I say. These industries of fashion the Germans want aren't industries at all. Every dress, every shoe, every handbag calls for buttons and embroidery and buckles, and they're all made by different shops, different guilds. And it's not enough to know who to go to for the buttons and buckles; you have to know how to get them to give them to you. You must romance these artisans and convince them that your dress deserves their buttons of pearl.

You would never throw away a dress whole, even if it's worn out or ruined. You'd go at it like a buzzard, picking off all the pieces of it. Collecting ingredients is part of the art of perfumery too. All twisted in among scents and spices, among smoke and color, is religion and medicine and money. Longevity. Eternal life. The search for spice launched ships even when the explorers thought they might sail off the flat edge of the ocean.

Zoé's breath slows, the silk growing still. She pinches at the scarf to lift it away from her mouth, to speak. Her voice is growing faint. She's losing it a little more with every word. "All I know is that Oskar Voss is in my house. And if he finds the diary, and he reads it . . . then he'll be able to put together who *I* am. He'll know I'm Pascal's daughter. And he'll use that against Lutz. That I'm Jewish. I might be a captive here, but in my little glass house, there's an ounce of hope. As long as Lutz thinks I love him, all I have to do is . . ." Her voice catches. "Warble in my cage."

We return to our therapy. I put on a different record, and choose a different perfume. "He promised me butterflies," she says, "my father did, to get me to go with him, because I always get bored on the farms. And I always complained about getting bit raw by bugs. So I bring a little net with me. And I have a book on the butterflies of the Riviera. I've circled the ones with my favorite names. *Camilla. Cleodoxa. Medusa.*"

I don't stop her from talking about the butterflies, and I decide to be relieved. They're not just fluttering in from my deep past, to taunt and terrify. She has butterflies of her own. From her days on the farms.

I listen as she lists them in a sleepy voice: *Icarus, Clytie, Simplonia, Dorilis.*

···· 14 ····

At the Ritz Hotel in the early evening, I'm led to a private salon, where maids have set up a semicircle of chairs. The men move about with leisure, drinking champagne, but no one's going anywhere near the long banquet table littered with all the critters of the forest—woodcock and pheasant, partridge and thrush, goose and snipe and wild boar, nearly every carcass dressed in ribbons of bacon or dripping with truffle sauce. There are baby octopi tentacles, suckers and all, in a glass bowl. The Nazis even have access to everything out of season: the strawberries of Plougastel, blue figs, red grapes on green stems. White asparagus, always the first glimpse of spring in France, sits here somehow on a plate in the dead of winter.

"Try not to look so hungry," Day whispers in my ear, sidling up close. "The food's only here to be ignored."

"Disgusting," I say. I look around. "I wonder if I can fit a few of these lobster claws up my sleeves, to take home to Blue."

Day's wearing a flapper's jet-black bob, shiny, like the wig's been waxed with brilliantine. And she's wrapped up in a fur jacket.

"Whose hide is that?" I ask.

"Kangaroo," Day says. "It was a gift."

"You should give it back," I say.

"To the kangaroo?" she says.

Day plucks a strawberry from a basket, then holds it to my lips. I bite it from the stem. I say, "I didn't expect to see you here." I lower my voice to a whisper. "You're everywhere the enemy is anymore. It's enough to make a person suspicious."

"Shhh," Day says, a shush she then muffles with a sip of her champagne. I turn to see Lutz approaching.

Lutz takes Day's champagne away from her and hands her a different glass. "Don't drink that," he says. "This is better. Pol Roger, 1928." He has a glass for me too.

Another man approaches, and Lutz introduces us both. Oskar Voss. I've been here less than fifteen minutes, and I've met the man I most need to meet.

"And *you're* Day Shabillée," Voss says. He leans toward her, lowers his voice. "I subscribe to a very secret newsletter, sent around by a colleague of mine. About American jazz in Paris. You've been in it."

Does he mean to flatter her, or threaten her? I don't like the sound of it. Just leave her to that little stage in the bordello cabaret, please. Don't take so much interest.

Though I'm not much of a wine drinker these days, I know, with only a sip, tasting only with the tip of my tongue, they've been duped. The champagne's more than a little off, a half bubble off plumb, in a way it wouldn't be if it was the '28. It's *so* off, I wonder how someone so proud to pour it wouldn't know the difference. I've heard that the Nazis have been robbing the vineyards, so the vineyards have been robbing them back, passing off the bottles from recent weak crops as vintage, slapping on dummy labels, rolling the bottles in dirt to give them some dust, even tossing spiders into the crates to spin some deceptive webs.

The wine tastes like a wet dog.

"She had that song," Voss says to Lutz. "It was so popular, nobody could ever get away from it. My wife and I, we had the record, we had the sheet music. We even had the music roll for our pianola." He raises his glass to Day. "Whatever happened to you?"

Day smiles, and she raises her glass too. "Your guess is as good as mine," she says.

Voss then looks at me, and I'm about to say something when he begins to sing. He snaps his fingers, suddenly remembering a few lyrics of "Where Were You When." He turns to Day. *Where were you when I first sang this song? It's my love-call to you, will you soon be along?*

Lutz slaps Voss on the back. "You're in fine voice," he tells him, in a gesture that's much overdone. Lutz is just sugaring Voss with sweet talk.

I'm about to take another shot at introducing myself when a gong strikes, calling us to the chairs for the fashion show. I fear I've lost my chance to weasel in close, but Voss turns to me as we walk through the salon. "And you're *le nez*," he says. "The nose of Paris." He takes my arm. "You'll sit with me."

A seamstress with a pincushion on her wrist hands out folding fans to help us suffer through the heat of the room. The chairs are situated in a crescent moon, surrounding a doorway with a blue velvet curtain pinned with foil stars.

Voss is younger than me, I'd say, but not by all that much. Mid-sixties? His only wrinkles are at the corners of his eyes. He puts on a kind face, and he's attentive, the sort of thing people fall for. "Won't you tell me about your perfumes?" he says. "Lutz tells me you fashion your fragrances specific to the lady."

"Or the gentleman," I say.

"And that's the way of things in America, as I understand it," he says. "Every local druggist has his own brew . . . mixes together his own mishmash of . . . toilet vinegars." I don't think he means to condescend, despite the pause and the country twang he gives *druggist* and *mishmash* and *toilet vinegars.* I think he means to be charming. And he does indeed put on a good American accent.

"Maybe years ago," I say. Just earlier today, I stood in a corner of the bookseller's to skim Voss's body of work: three guides to Paris, bound in violet-colored cloth, the titles in gold foil on the covers. His was a sensory tour, outlining the city's flavors and aromas—the cafés, the patisseries. The fashion houses where the couturiers swamp their vents with perfume before every show in their narrow, musty salons.

"What are the best perfumes?" he asks me.

"New?" I say. "Old?" I'm tempted to rattle off any modern perfume that might sound treasonous: *Indiscreet. Scandal. Shocking. My Sin. The French Touch. Nostalgia.* Instead, I tell him my favorites of all time, some that have come and gone: Houbigant's Violettes San Remo, Penhaligon's Hammam Bouquet. I've always been fond of Guerlain's Eau de Cologne Impériale, if for no other reason than the constellation of 18-karat gold bees that swarm up the glass bottle, upping the price with every inch. The perfume is quick, evasive, flitting away the second you catch its scent. It was designed to latch on to the royal headaches of Empress Eugénie and spirit them away.

"Not No. 5?" he says.

"I can only smell the touch of cruelty in it," I say. "Chanel uses civet. From some brood of mongooses. Kept in tiny cages in Abyssinia. They don't even have room to pace around. The farmers grab the mongoose by the tail and scrape up the oil from its ass." Again, I regret saying anything at all. I'm probably insulting him. Mightn't someone like Voss consider cruelty a virtue?

The curtains part, and the fashion show begins. All wartime fabric restrictions have been ignored for this show—not only ignored but flouted—the gowns saddled with more bustles and trains and overpuffed sleeves than I've seen since the turn of the century. Some of the fashions are inspired by the occupation, by the war. One gown suggests the ripples and billowing of a downed parachute, another a canvas tent, with its triangular shoulders. One model wears a khaki skirt-and-jacket set with a number of pockets, and pockets within pockets, for the management of official papers and passports.

The men chuckle at the sight of a scarf patterned with ration tickets. Another model wears a blouse printed with newspaper headlines from the Nazi invasion of Paris. The blouse gets a round of applause. I applaud too, at the wretched rags, so I'm not conspicuous.

I notice Zoé St. Angel among us, sitting across the way, next to Lutz. Voss notices me noticing her. He snaps open his fan with a sharp flick of his wrist, like an opera gossip, and leans over toward me. "Poor little Lutz loves too hard," he says. "He lets that showgirl run roughshod over his heart."

I straighten in my seat so I can peer over the fan's paper-lace trim. Zoé's wearing her hair so it falls forward over half her face. And a veil too. Lutz, in the chair next to her, is pouting. They seem in the thick of a tiff. I think I see a gray shadow beneath her eye. And is that a cut on her lip? I survey and analyze, and I see what I wouldn't otherwise pay any mind to—the snag in her stocking, the loose thread at the seam of her blouse, the scuff at the toe of her shoe.

I say, "He should let her go then." I worry that Voss can hear the tremor in my voice, the irritation.

Voss shrugs. He snaps shut the fan with another sharp, quick click. "He can't live without her," he says. He shrugs again. "That's why all of that's forbidden, you know."

"What is?"

He returns the fan to his lips, and he opens it just an inch. Raises an eyebrow. "Canoodling with the ladies of the captured nations." He returns the fan to his lap. "Isn't he handsome, though? For a while he was an actor in the movies. Horror movies, in Germany. He got a corpse pregnant with a demon. But he wasn't *always* the hero. Usually the victim. He was devoured by a pack of werewolves once. Got his blood sucked by a vampire. Rumor has it that his director was in love with him, so it thrilled him to kill Lutz in terrible ways."

Voss laughs a laugh he keeps in his throat, like a mild cough, amused by this director's infatuation. But I wonder where this director might be now. The homosexual camp in Alsace?

And why is Voss confiding in me? Would he be gossiping with *anyone* he sat beside?

The show has ended, and all the models return, to allow their gowns to be inspected. But Voss and I stay seated.

"But the sweetest perfume of all?" I say. "Mûrier Blanc." I pick up where we left off, dropping the name of one of the most famous of the scents from Zoé's family estate. The scent has been around longer than Pascal has; it was created by his father.

And Mûrier Blanc truly is one of my favorites. *White mulberries.* It speaks of southern France. It's one of those scents worn by many, but it can still catch you off guard. It's everybody's and nobody's all at once. At the heart of it is a lush honeysuckle, echoing the vine that creeps into every corner of your garden.

But the main reason I mention it is because Voss mentions it himself, in his published diaries of his walks through Paris.

Voss gasps at the mention of Mûrier Blanc. Clutches at his heart with melodrama. He stands. "Come with me," he says. He taps his finger on my champagne coupe. "We're leaving this swill behind. It's not what it's supposed to be. I do believe we've done been hornswoggled. Isn't that what *you'd* call it? Isn't that a word from back on the farm? *Hornswoggled*?"

The farm? I laugh along with him, but I wonder what he knows about my childhood. And why he knows anything at all.

Voss is dressed as a civilian, a dapper one, in a gold sweater and rose-colored pants, his shirt collar open, looking ready for the golf links. He even has tassels on his loafers. But I assume it's just a uniform of a different kind—a lure. It gets him things a Nazi might not get when dressed in his polished buckles and pressed jackets.

When I stand from the chair, he takes me by the arm and leads me away. I glance at Day, who glances back as I pass. She's leaning against a wall as a few officers fall over themselves to flirt with her. She has shed her fur; she wears a long black gown patterned with zeppelins that twinkle when the light catches on their silver sequins. She's become a bit of a favorite with the boys who haunt Madame Boulette's, and not just because of "Where Were You When." She writes original songs for them. They buy her a drink, tell her their stories of valor on the fields of battle, and their heroic tales end up in a ballad or a ditty.

Two soldiers appear at our sides. One places Voss's military greatcoat over his shoulders; the other drapes my synthetic gazelle over mine; yet another opens the door to the narrow balcony. Voss takes me by the elbow, and we step out.

"It's illegal for women to wear trousers in Paris," he tells me with a wink. We're handed two snifters of brandy. "The police outlawed it a hundred years ago or so, and it's never been off the books. A woman can only wear pants if she's attached to a bicycle or a horse."

"You like to mock me," I say.

"I'm not mocking you," he says.

"'Hornswoggled'?" I say. Our conversation is a fog of frost.

He leans back against the railing, stretches his leg forth, and pulls closed the casement door with his foot, all with the elegance of a dancer. I get the genuine sense he likes to be considered boyish.

"No, not at all," he says, taking a sip of his brandy. "Or maybe a little. I've never been to America, but I've read many American novels. The cheap ones. The dime novels. I should be ashamed to admit it. But I get a kick out of the Wild West. One of the first ones I ever read was about a Nebraskan such as yourself. *Nebraska Charlie*, it was called, *the Boy Medicine Man of the Pawnees.*"

I take a sip of the brandy too, just to send a rush of warmth to my cheeks. "How did you know I'm from Nebraska?"

He starts to say something, then stops. He says something else. He affects that country twang again. "Aren't all Americans from Nebraska? Or Texas?" When I raise my eyebrows, suspicious, he says, "I guess I've given myself away." Like he's been planning it all night, he pulls from his coat pocket a pulp paperback of *The Perfume Thief*, a detective's exposé about his career pursuing me. I've never seen this edition. It's clearly manufactured to titillate, with a buxom blonde in a silk robe sitting at a mirror, the vanity top covered with perfume bottles.

"I've been reading all about you," he says.

"You've been reading *nothing* about me if you've been reading that," I say. "He gets nothing right."

"Oh?" he says, skeptical. "You were never a thief?"

"I dealt in antiquities," I say, sly. "Artifacts. It's all a swap. Nobody can own any of that. Why should anyone keep a relic if they can't hold on to it? Anything old has a long history of getting lost, or being stolen. Just because you pay for something, it doesn't mean you came by it honestly."

But none of this rationale, which I've rattled off before, seems true to me anymore. I'm reciting someone else's lines.

His laughter lifts in a few clouds of steam. "Spoken like a true western outlaw," he says.

To be a crackerjack thief, you're always in character. You're always pretending. I would have made an excellent spy in one of our wars, or coups, or skirmishes; spying, like theft, relies on human fallibility. Little breaches. You romance, you seduce, you charm and promise—you dance small dances in tight spaces—and you manage to make people do things for you that they're not supposed to do. If every general obeyed his every order, every spy would be useless. You look for those squeaky hinges. You look for the people who need to connect. You look for egos—and sometimes the biggest ones are the weakest. To even the most discreet official, the sturdiest military man, a secret can seem worth having only if he can boast that he has it. And once a spy knows that someone has a secret, she's halfway to having that secret herself.

"I did actually work for a medicine show," I say, "like in your little western pulp. Some of my first work with perfume. Back then, we said it was healthy to smell pretty."

I wasn't famous until the detective's book. I was stealth. The detective, or the hack who wrote the book for him, made much of the metaphor—the ethereal thief of ether. The book became a bestseller, but certainly no one reads it today. For a time, everyone was crazy about me, though no one even knew what I looked like. The detective wrote the book before having been within a foot of me. He never had any idea where I was until I wasn't there anymore. But he got rich off me and that book and all that it inspired: a silent picture, a rose-infused gin, and, of course, a perfume that was all wrong. The Perfume Thief eau de parfum was not only obnoxious, it nagged at you, it cried for attention, it announced itself as it stumbled into a room. Anyone who wore it would never get away with anything.

"I'm going to call you Nebraska Charlie from here on out," Voss says. I don't like the idea of any "from here on out," or any nicknames, or any familiarity at all, but I'm encouraged by the suggestion of it. I need him to feel friendly toward me. He lives in Pascal's house, and I need to be invited in.

He returns the paperback to his pocket. "I know other things about you too," he says.

"That so?"

"You might be flattered to know you've left a trail of international dossiers in your path," he says. "Your holidays are kept in many scrapbooks."

I try to make light of it. "Vile gossip," I say.

"Now *that's* a name for a perfume," he says. "What should it smell like?"

Fresh laundry, I don't say. The common hausfrau here in Paris who has queued up for soap flakes might be paid in extra lumps of coal to eavesdrop and tattle. Even if you don't know how to spy, you know how to gossip. Gossip hasn't stopped with the war; as a matter of fact, war has turned everything into gossip. People go to the police to inform on their neighbors about whispers heard through walls. You can end up on a list if you so much as tune in the wrong radio show or read the wrong paper. You have to watch your tongue when standing in line for your rations.

Just going about our lives is illegal. I look out across the city, all the windows blacked out. You're all of you thieves now, every last one of you, for simply wanting to keep what's yours. I try to take another sip of the brandy, to settle my nerves, but I've already emptied my glass. I keep it at my nose, to breathe in its fumes.

Voss says, "Witches say the bark of the slippery elm wards off gossip. Put a pinch of that in our perfume, I guess." He then mutters something about *spice,* as he tries to wind his way around a quote. Shakespeare. He stumbles, fumbles words, finally settling on " 'And, in the spiced Indian air, by night, full often hath she gossip'd by my side.' "

With the mention of Shakespeare, I think of Ophelia. I think about the dangerous lines to be drawn between Zoé and the perfume her father bottled for her.

"You have all of Shakespeare at the ready in your head?" I say.

"Just *Midsummer Night's Dream*," he says. "I was Puck in a school production."

An actor. I believe it.

He says, "And what's the scent of Mûrier Blanc? If you were to describe it."

"It makes me think of New Orleans," I say. "It always takes me to a sidewalk café one afternoon. Drinking a cocktail of bourbon and sweet tea. The scent of pralines cooking in the candy shop next door." As I picture the cloth-of-gold roses vining along the twists of the ironworks, those ironworks twist into the shape of the insignia on the note from Zoé's father. I glance down now to study the balcony railing before us. I look over to the swirl of design in the silver buttons of Voss's coat. And I try to remember the exact fretwork of pewter that encases the milky glass of the bottles of Mûrier Blanc.

"And here I thought you'd think I was a sentimental fool if I confessed that I love Mûrier Blanc," Voss says.

"What does it make *you* think of?" I say.

"I came to Paris for the Exposition, the one in 1889, to see the Eiffel Tower when it was just put up," he says. He too looks out at the city before us, out toward where the tower stands lost in the dark. "I was still a teenager. I decided I wouldn't leave Paris until I fell in love. And I fell in love the day I arrived. The minute I arrived, really. Right at the train station. I bought a cigar from her. She worked in the tobacconist's shop. She sold me the cigar, I fell in love, then I bought a newspaper from her, just to linger. And then I asked her which perfume in the cabinet I should buy for a girl I'd only just fallen in love with, and she picked Mûrier Blanc. I paid for it. I handed it back to her. I asked her if she wouldn't mind trying some of it on, for me to smell on her wrist. She did. She let me take her hand in mine. Her skin was cool. And I brought the underside of her wrist to my nose." He pantomimes it all, the girl's ghostly hand in his. "It was perfect. Just when you think the scent's too sweet, you catch a pinch of its burnt sugar. Or maybe that bourbon you mention."

"Did the poor girl fall for it?"

He shrugs. He takes another sip of his brandy. "She might have," he says. "But I was too late. She was already engaged to someone else."

"Too bad you didn't think to ask her about that before you spent all of your money on the perfume."

"I'm glad I didn't ask," he says. "The money would be long gone by now, but I still have that scent of her wrist."

"Did you ever love again?" I say.

"Oh, many, many times," he says. "What about you, Charlie? Ever been in love?"

"Once," I say, which is what I've always said when asked that. I've said it even to those who've claimed to be in love with me. I've always talked about M to keep him with me. "I've probably loved more often than that. But I like the idea of having only loved him. It makes your whole life seem more romantic if you've only had one true love."

"*Him?*" he says. He smirks. He takes a sip of the brandy. He clears his throat. "I would have taken you for a ladies' man."

I hold the empty snifter to my lips again, and get only the burnt-wood scent. I wonder if Voss means to seem sophisticated, or if he's testing me. I hold my glass to my nose. I know that if I speak, I'll say what I shouldn't. I'm tempted to ask him about the camp in Alsace, where they've clipped the fairies' wings. *What are you all so afraid of?* I want to ask.

Finally, he speaks. "Did you ever know Proust, the writer? The greatest writer of France? Have you read his novels? Steeped in nostalgia. He had a séance in this very dining room. Came out on this very balcony during an air raid, during the war. Proust wrote about it, in *Time Regained,* how the German pilots were like Valkyries."

He turns his head toward me. In his pauses, and his lingering, I fear, more than a little, that he's only humoring me. Batting me around, cat-and-mousy. I fear he's about to tell me the jig is up, that

I'll be whisked away next. I'm the next to vanish. *My dossiers.* Has he brought them up to keep me in line? Do any dossiers even exist?

And even if he is amused by me, by my notoriety, what if others in his rank aren't at all? I have a long history of flouting the law, and I always thought I was only ever hurting myself. Never married, no children. But now it could all come back on me, if it put Blue and Day in danger.

I turn away and glance back inside. Day is once again the center of attention. She always looks as delicate as a piece of china in these rooms full of military men.

And yes, I'm a ladies' man. I think of all the women I made love to after leaving my man behind in Manhattan. I posed naked once, many years before I moved here for good, in one of these very hotel rooms, for a Dutch woman who'd gotten rich off the scandal of her naked portraits. Her portraits had shut down exhibitions. She'd been exiled from schools. Museums draped her paintings in velvet. *You have to part the velvet to get a peek,* she told me with delight.

There I sat before her, without a stitch on. No trousers or necktie to tell anyone how to see me. She served me cubes of sugar that had been soaked in perfume, to eat, a habit she'd picked up from French schoolgirls, who like it because it brightens their eyes. And they probably get a little kick from the alcohol in the perfume.

Voss finishes off the last of the cognac in his glass, and looks down into the snifter to see if he's left a drop. He then looks up, then up, then up, to where there are no stars, no squadrons, no bursting of shells. The sky is as deadly still as the street below. "Proust wrote that the sounds of the sirens in Paris were like the music of Richard Wagner. Like Wagner's 'Ride of the Valkyries.' " When he sees that I can't quite remember the music he's mentioned, he sings it for me, waving the snifter around as if he's conducting an orchestra: *Duh-de-duh-DUH-duh, duh-de-duh-DUH-duh, duh-de-DUH-duh, duh-de-duh-duhhh.*

He raises his empty glass to toast the pitch-black heavens. "To Marcel Proust," he says, then he quotes him, with actorly bravado: " 'The Germans have to arrive before you can hear Wagner in Paris.' "

···· 15 ····

Oskar Voss has invited me out for a winter walk. He seems to have no place to be. Even his wristwatch quits ticking only minutes after he winds it tight. "There's something about me that throws a wrench in the cogs," he says, tapping a finger on the glass. "And if it does manage to last all day, it loses minutes by the hour. By midnight, it's the middle of the afternoon." He holds the watch to his ear, shimmies his wrist, listening for a loose pinion or spindle.

"It's probably all that thumping and shaking you give it," I say. "You're knocking the clockworks all out of whack."

"That's the farmhand in you, Nebraska Charlie," he says, giving me a sidelong squint. "No-nonsense. But wouldn't it be more fun to believe in ghosts? Or that the marrow of my bones has some . . . some *voltage*? Magnetism? That there's something *otherworldly* that's dragging at the gears of my watch? Where's your sick imagination?"

He takes my arm. We've already fallen into an easy friendship, or so he thinks. I'm the polite and kindly old woman he's met on his holiday, the woman with the interesting life and perverse preoccupations. Harmless.

We walk arm in arm, with no destination in mind. This is our second walk this week. He fashions himself a boulevardier, like the vain popinjays who once wandered the streets of Paris just to flaunt their topcoats. The fops and coxcombs known for their knowledge of the avenues and alleyways. These days, however, such gentlemen would be scolded and fined. You're expected to use the streets only to get from one place to the next, and only when necessary.

These leisurely, meandering walks seem to be Voss's official assignment, somehow. He has an instinct about Paris. He's not just looking at buildings; he's peeking in windows. He's watching with his writer's eye. I sincerely hope he's not going back to his office to translate his lollygagging into marching orders. For all I know, he sits in his smoking coat and tasseled loafers as he sends his team out to kick in doors with their jackboots, to strip the city of all we've marveled at this afternoon: ornate brass work, velvet drapes, stained glass. Crystal chandeliers, lightbulbs and all.

But I sense that in his heart of hearts, if he has any heart at all, Voss is a true Francophile. Maybe he'd truly prefer to see the city move along as it always has. He knows that Parisians need to follow their own winding paths. He respects their eccentricities.

It has occurred to me, a time or two, that he might be corruptible. He has, after all, written three books about his devotion to Paris. So we'll have our little walking romance with the city, in case even a spark of sentiment can cast a shadow on whatever his intentions might be.

We hit an icy spot of sidewalk, and he lends me his walking stick. "But you'll be tempted to steal it, I suppose," he says, demonstrating that its handle, in the shape of a bulldog's head, twists off to reveal a flacon for cologne. Or maybe a spy's fatal dose, I think—a sneaky heart-stopper when you've been cornered by the enemy demanding answers. But I agree that it is most likely just a perfume bottle in that bulldog's skull; the stick is nothing but a dandy's crutch, a useless cane for spinning around gingerly. Too frivolous for suicide.

When we're discussing perfume, he asks my opinion but then does all the talking. He relates fragrance to music, and he's a little tickled with himself when he does so, as if he's the first to ever make such a comparison. He dismantles the classic perfumes for me, speaking of notes and undertones and echoes. Cadences, chords. Staccato, harmony, pitch, refrain. Even woodwinds, nocturnes, leitmotifs. I start tapping the cane against the sidewalk as he makes each point, like an old Russian piano teacher in a tapestry shawl, counting off the beats of the metronome.

We pass the stores with red signs in the windows. One after the other. Each time we do, I can feel the weight of it against our easy stroll. Is he at all distracted by them? Does he wonder if I'm distracted? Before the red card was taped up on the glass, there was a yellow one, communicating in both German and French: JÜDISCHES GESCHÄFT; ENTREPRISE JUIVE. A Jewish-owned business. The Nazis have been managing the sales of the Jewish-owned businesses to non-Jewish owners. The red signs go up when the Jews have gone.

We all know this has happened in Germany and in Austria. Some of the Jews who were robbed fled to France. But, in our sense of helplessness, we try to imagine distinctions between the troubles there and the troubles here. Here, we tell ourselves, the Nazis are unwelcome. In the end, they won't get by with their larceny. We'll take down those red signs soon enough.

But we have more theories than we have certainties. Every day that we wake to an occupied Paris, the more familiar we become with fear and disappointment.

Voss nods toward the café on the corner. We've been wandering the neighborhood in search of one that sells cigars and cigarettes. This one has TABAC emblazoned across the awning, and he sighs with relief at the sight of it. He says, "Can I get you anything, Charlie?"

I smile and shake my head.

When he steps back out from the café, he seems disgruntled with the cigar he's bought. He attempts to light it, but the wind keeps blowing out his match the second it sparks. I step forward to help cup the flame with both my hands. When our eyes meet, I'm not sure if I should keep looking or look away. I do a little of both, I guess, a girlish fluttering. But I can't deny there's some drama to it all—the flirtation and curiosity. I play into it.

When the cigar still won't light, I suggest the obvious: "You'll have to go back inside."

"Never mind," he says. He tucks the unlit cigar into his inside coat pocket. "The cigars you get here are too wet. The humidors are too humid. French tobacconists all work for the government, you know, so what do they care if their cigars get moldy? They'll never go bankrupt, and they'll never be fired." He speaks as if France is still France, our laws still law. He pops up his coat's lapel, buries his hands in his pockets, and hunkers down to walk forward. He wiggles his elbow at me, for me to take his arm, and I do. "The Führer insists we quit anyway. He thinks smoking is ruining us all. Giving us cancer. He's offered me, personally, a gold watch to give up the cigars. But what do I need with another watch that tells the wrong time, gold or not?"

A pack of children run past us, chasing after sheets of paper that have been spun along and around by the wind. Their faces are so filthy, it seems they've dirtied themselves with purpose for camouflage. At first I wonder why they're so determined to grab at all those loose Nazi leaflets, likely full of information we'd all rather not have, and then I remember that you can fashion a somewhat useful briquette from a wad of paper. Wet it down, let it dry, and it might burn just long enough to turn a cool cup of cocoa lukewarm.

My nose is running, and I've brought my handkerchief to my face, but I swear I can smell the peanuts that used to roast, only last winter, in front of the cafés. We pass beneath an optician's sign, a pair of wooden spectacles the size of a bicycle, and in the creak of its chains as the wind rocks it, I can hear the voices of vendors calling out, *Cacahuètes, cacahuètes, cacahuètes.* Their voices would fade, along with the smell of the hot peanuts, as you wandered farther, and it was all you could do not to double back, just for the rich scent so sweet and warm in the cold air.

"I've been reading your books on Paris," I say, to butter Voss up, though I've not glanced at them again since the skim I gave them before the fashion show. "I love all the scents you list, of course. It's sad how many we're missing this winter."

"Which do you miss the most?" he says, as if he's just another rueful Parisian.

"I've always looked forward to the kindling I would buy from the firewood shop," I say. "The shop hasn't had a stick of wood in weeks.

Usually, stepping inside is like stepping into the forest. Always so damp and dark, and fragrant with pine needles."

And at this very moment, we pass a shopwindow lined with bottles of perfume, a mirage in winter. In one of Voss's books on Paris, he claims there are ten thousand perfume shops in the city, so if it's true, it's not so whimsical that we would find the perfumes of the Parfumerie Chamberry at some point in our strolling. I stop Voss and point at the window, at a display of Mûrier Blanc, the perfume he bought when he first arrived in Paris as a boy. Next to it is Feuilles de Thym, which I happen to know was the first fragrance Pascal designed when he joined his father's company.

Voss thumbs his knuckle against the glass. "You know the owner of the Parfumerie Chamberry?" Voss says. "Monsieur Pascal? Someone told me you worked with him."

He's been tiptoeing around this question ever since we first met, and even now seems cautious. It's as if he's been circling me as I've been circling him. I wonder if he walked me this way just so we would pass this window.

"I sold some ideas to Pascal," I lie.

"The man abandoned everything," Voss says. "He's gone. As a matter of fact, I've been staying in his apartments. Rifling through his accounts. It's all rather tedious, if you want the truth. I sit at his desk, with a pen and paper, and I make note of all his pens and all his papers."

I play along, but I'm appalled. Pascal *abandoned* everything? Voss is *staying* in his apartments? He's counting *pens*? But I'm grateful too. This is the first he's spoken of any involvement at all with Pascal's business. "I'm dying to know what's in Feuilles de Thym," I say, trying to sound pleasant. "Do you know? Have you seen the accords?"

"I hoped *you* might tell *me*," he says. "I figured you'd have some professional insights."

"I suppose I have some ideas," I say. "But the scent's a little trickier than you'd think. The first scents of any perfumer tend to be overly complicated, like they fear they'll never have the chance to design another perfume again."

He takes the cigar back out of his pocket, but he doesn't try to light it again. He just puts it between his teeth. Chews on the end of it. "I have business I need to do, with a distillery, outside of Paris," he says. "And I need a day or two away from the war. I thought I'd visit Illiers. Do you know the place? A town from the childhood of Marcel Proust. He wrote about it in his novels. You'll go with me."

"Yes?" I say.

"Yes?" he says. I then realize his *You'll go with me* was a question, not a demand.

I know this moment all too well, this mix of satisfaction and agony as you swindle and cheat. You've gained their confidence, but now the real work begins. And the real trouble starts. In an instant, you've stepped from the shallows into the depths.

"Yes," I say. This is taking me farther from Pascal's house. And I'll be all alone with Voss, when I probably shouldn't be. But I can't deny the intrigue of it. There's something he thinks I know. I need to get inside his head to see what he thinks I have in mine.

16

I bring Zoé a perfume I'm calling Late Summer Plum simply because it's sweet, with a tart sting. I can still taste the garden plum M somehow came to have in autumn, its flesh like candy, its skin too bitter to eat. I had the juice all down my chin and wrist after only one bite. *This is why I gave it to you to begin with,* M whispered as he held my hand in his. He turned up my wrist to kiss me there, then on my cheek, and lips, with gentle licks at my sticky skin.

Zoé's apartment is cast in shadows, and she leans back deeper into them, out of the dim lamplight. She doesn't try on the Late Summer Plum; listless and wrecked, she just sprays at the air with it. My perfume is still a signal to Lutz that Zoé and I discuss only fragrance when alone.

"Are you all right, Zoé?" I say, thinking of her at the fashion show, hiding her eyes behind her veil. "Tell me the truth."

She says something, but I can't hear her. "I can't hear you," I say.

"I can't hear *you,*" she says.

The jazz on the record player doesn't match the mood of the room—it's frantic and brassy. You can't even tap your toe to it; the rhythm's all off. "Can we change the record?" I say.

She goes to the phonograph and turns it off, and that's when I realize how loud it really was—my ears are ringing from it. "Lutz loves jazz," she says. "The Germans can't decide whether they want to outlaw it or fill the streets with it. One minute it's too sinful, the next they think a little sinning keeps us all in line."

I say, "Is Lutz hurting you?"

She keeps her back to me. And she doesn't answer my question. "I could have any man I want," she says. "I've had proposals of marriage. From rich men. Handsome men. I could be kept in a gilded cage. Anything I wanted. I could ask for it, and I'd get it."

"Yes," I say.

"Is this my life, then? As a little girl, I dreamed of falling in love. I would fall in love and marry. And I'd be happy forever."

"I'll find the diary," I say, keeping my voice low. "I'll get the perfumery back for you."

She steps into the shadows and walks to her credenza, to her wooden alligator with its cigarettes. "Oh?" she says, weary, doubtful.

"I've spent some time with Oskar Voss," I say.

Zoé says, "Oh?" again, but this time with a lilt to it. She's impressed.

"I don't know yet what he wants from me," I say. "But I know he wants something. I'm playing along."

She turns to look at me, and she leans back against the credenza as she smokes. There does seem to be a bruise beneath her eye, but then it skitters away, then back, as the shadows shift when she brings the cigarette to her lips. "Lutz says Oskar Voss is sickly," she says.

"Sickly?"

"He has some kind of condition, some ailment that knocks him flat from time to time. Lutz keeps his eye on it. The Nazis don't have much patience with people falling ill, and Voss is on borrowed time. So Lutz keeps as close as he can get, ready to step in if Voss needs help." She raises her eyebrows at me. "Once Voss stumbles, Lutz will step on his head to push himself up in the ranks."

Has he thought about poison? I start to say, but I don't. But *I* begin to think of poison. I think of M again. He was a jack-of-all-trades, M was, and poison had its place in his sentimental education.

"Voss is taking me with him to Illiers," I say.

"Oh?" she says again. She says, "My father has a rose farm near there."

She gives me the whole history of the Parfumerie Chamberry. The true history, a humble one. "It's a love story," Zoé says. The perfumery was established decades ago by Zoé's grandfather, a barber in the Pletzl who stumbled onto perfume when experimenting with beard pomades of Irish moss and essence of rosemary. The barber's wife, a daughter of a kosher rum distiller in London's East End and an amateur botanist who grew herbs on her rooftop, brought some science to it. When they gave up the barbershop, they liked the idea of rhyming Chambéry with *parfumerie*, naming their new laboratory after the little Alpine village in southern France where they met and fell in love, when they were teenagers, when they both spent a summer killing aphids on a vineyard, spritzing poison on the grape leaves with perfume atomizers. Chambéry became *Chamberry*, because they failed to check it against a map.

I believe her, though it's nothing like the story the company tells about itself. The *official* story, like so much else about perfume, is fiction for the most part. Zoé's grandfather does come from a long line of barbers, but the company's history notes generations of chemists, of royal warrants from France's queens, empresses, all sorts of approvals and distinctions. Those of us who know perfume know that such storytelling is just part of the art. Secrets and lies are what people want. They don't want to see chemical formulas for synthetics and compounds. For cat piss and whale shit. They want to picture the perfumer bottling the dew off petals or brushing pollen from the wings of a sphinx moth.

They want perfume that links them to the bloodlines of royalty.

"Maybe I'll just tell Lutz myself who I really am," she says. "What difference does it make?"

I can't bear to ask about the details of her affair with Lutz, and the pain he causes, but I beg her to keep quiet. "I'll have something soon," I promise. And just saying it makes me feel a little closer to the diary.

I leave Zoé with a bottle of my azalea perfume, a scent that always soothes me. "I don't know why I didn't think of it before," I say. "Breathe it in, and it will calm you."

"Will it drop me into a deep sleep for a hundred years?" she says. *La Belle au bois dormant*. Sleeping Beauty.

I almost tell her of my fanciful notions about Voss, about how his infatuation with Paris might save us all. Voss with his love for perfume, Lutz with his love for jazz—they're enchanted, with our restaurants, our chocolate, our coffee, our wine. Maybe they're smart enough to realize they'll lose the Paris they love if they don't leave us alone to cast our spells.

···· 17 ····

In one of his books on Paris, Voss lists the scents Marcel Proust describes in his novels: myrrh, incense, hawthorn, lilacs, varnish, soot, unbleached calico, a moldy smell like that of stale toast, the heat of the barber's iron, *the baths that other people do not take.*

Blue and Day join me in my kitchen, where I've never cooked much, not even back when there was food at the markets. I converted it long ago to an apothecary, its cupboards stocked with bottles and jars of spices, florals, oils, extracts. I'll impress Voss with a perfume inspired by Proust.

Day sits on the kitchen counter, her sleeves rolled, her skirt hiked up. She has volunteered all her pulse points as I experiment and approximate. I have thirteen variations on a theme. I've dabbed at each of Day's temples, both sides of her jaw, her neck, her wrists, the insides of her elbows. I'm even sniffing at her ankles and the backs of her knees.

"Not enough lemon in this one," Blue says, tapping his finger on Day's jaw. "But a little too much of it on her right ankle." Blue can't volunteer his own pulse points, because perfume sometimes sparks a rash on him. Yes, my perfume apprentice is allergic to my art.

I pick up Day's hand, turn up her wrist, lift it to just beneath my nose. I look up and off, sorting out all the elements of the scent. "I think if I just back up on the fusel oil, a tiptoe or two, then it's definitely the left wrist."

"All you're going to smell in a minute is my rotting corpse," Day says, "because I'm about one tiptoe away from freezing to death."

"Frozen corpses don't rot," I say. I kiss her wrist before letting it go. Blue helps her down from the counter, and I drape her cardigan over her shoulders. And *such* a cardigan it is, a sweater of shaggy mohair in a shade of crème de menthe. "Reminds me of a goat's beard I combed out," I say, petting her shoulder. "On a farm, in Cyprus. The goats graze through the cistus shrubs, then the shepherds comb out the fur for the labdanum, which you can put in perfume for a little whiff of plum brandy." I put on some water to boil for tea. "Oh, you know, I think the one on the back of your left knee could use just half a drip of that labdanum."

"Do you even know what you're trying to find?" Day says, sniffing at her wrists, front and back, considering the scents. "Have you even read any Proust?"

"Heavens, no," I say. "It's hundreds of pages. Thousands, maybe." Voss arranged for a bookseller to send copies of his own guides to Paris to my shop, and with the delivery, he included all the thick volumes of Proust's novel. "If you're ever on a little boat, that's when it would be good to have editions of Proust. So you have something heavy to toss into the sea if the boat starts to sink."

"What does Oskar Voss want with perfume anyway?" Day says. "He works for the intelligence agency."

"Voss is a precious little fop," I say. "All he talks about is perfume. He says he wants to keep Paris Paris." I shrug. "He's like a boy with an electric train set, building a little tin village around the tracks."

I won't confess that Voss's affection for the city has made me just a touch hopeful. And now knowing that he's got some kind of sickness, some vulnerability, I feel like I might be able to sway him this way and that. But I don't want to seem naive or provoke any extra concern, so I don't mention it. If I see any doubt in their eyes, it might throw me off.

The copies of the guidebooks he sent me were in English, as if for my eyes alone. I'm desperate to visit the Paris he describes, if it still exists, if ever it did, its obscure little shops hidden by their own awnings and umbrellas. Between the wars, a hole-in-the-wall chocolatier could squeak by doing little business at all, living by its pluck, by its charm and character. But even those who saved for a rainy day didn't likely save for a rainy month or a rainy year. I've hardly seen any business myself, so I'm grateful for the ladies of Boulette's and their fickle tastes that demand I return again and again.

Voss writes of a Paris that I can't believe I've never visited: a shop that sells cubes of crystallized ginger so hot he hallucinated; a bistro that bottles its own pudding wine made from the juice of diseased apples. How did I ever miss the shop with the small bronze dolphin that dispensed a splash of perfume when you put your wrist to its spout?

While Blue, Day, and I wait for the water to boil, we sit in the cold room at the kitchen table, the three of us, our teeth chattering, suspicious of everything these days, suspect, as if the very air we're breathing is foreign, depleted, a threat to our lungs. The air is so ice-cold, we worry it's sprinkled with broken glass.

Blue says, "Félix says . . ." So many of Blue's sentences begin that way these days. *Félix says* . . . Félix, the scrappy little blood donor I found Blue with in the perfume shop that night. "Félix says that the perfume, the fashion, the cabarets, the dancing"—he tiptoes his fingers across the table, making them dance and kick toward Day—"we're all just fiddling while Rome burns."

Day slaps at Blue's little dancers. "Yes," Day says, "anything touched by women is frivolous."

Day's mocking Blue, but she knows she needs to seem frivolous indeed. She needs to be called upon to entertain the enemy, to pose herself in their lights, to stand just so to make her gown glisten just the way they like it, to be desired nightly. Every song she sings has to be approved, all the lyrics reviewed by the Nazi propaganda office, to ensure that the songs' sentiments ring hollow enough.

Sentiment. I keep thinking about Voss's quizzing me about my old love affairs. He appeals too much to my vanity. He listens to me, pays attention. Notices. These methods of his I know all too well; they've all served my own arts of persuasion.

"You think perfume and fashion can't be political?" I ask Blue.

"I'm just telling you what Félix says."

"Well, you tell Félix that . . . well, you should say . . . aren't military uniforms fashion? And those shepherds in Cyprus I was just talking about. Spending all their days, even in the hottest days of summer, combing goats. That doesn't seem like it could get political?"

The kettle whistles, and I go to it. I bring a meager tray of tea things to the table. No sugar, no cream. Just water in a pot, stained with old leaves from a tin at the back of the cupboard.

M was a tea-taster in Manhattan, testing for quality. That's how he learned about poison too.

"Of all the lovers you've told me about," I say to Day, "of all the lovers you've described to me for the perfumes I've made, who was your greatest one?" Day has never asked me this. I've never told her about M.

Day holds the teacup to her lips, breathing in the steam. "Guess," she says.

I suggest the ballet dancer (the scent of talc, sweat, leather, the sharp sour-sweet of roses turning to mold), and she says no. I suggest the journalist (typewriter ribbon, a struck match, the tart ash in the bowl of a hashish pipe), and she says no to that too. "You'll never guess," she says. "Because I haven't described him yet." *Ah,* I think. She, too, has more to tell. Why would I have suspected anything less?

Blue says, "I'm ready for my greatest love affair. I want my heart to be broken in a hundred different places before the end of it. Maybe you can make me a perfume that will conjure him up." I'm hoping this means Félix is not the great love that he seeks. That boy is too dangerous. I could see it in his scars. "I'll wear it on a handkerchief, since I can't wear it on my skin without itching."

"What should she put in this little love spell?" Day asks Blue.

"When have you been the happiest?" I ask him, and after the words are out of my mouth, I realize I'm peeking into the past of a short life overwhelmed by abandonment. I see in all of Blue's pursuits, even in his attachment to me, the orphan he was.

"The bees," he says, and I know he's talking about a few months at an apiary in Châteauroux, a bright spot in his sad childhood as he was shuffled among relatives. I think of the smell of clover in the fields, the sugar syrup that intoxicates the bees and makes them lazy. The hint of the smoke that stops them from stinging.

Day says, "If you could bottle a scent that fogs the memory, you'd make a fortune." When I find the diary, I'll need to figure out how to make it serve us too, for leverage. Maybe I somehow keep the diary for myself. To wriggle our way out of the things we might need to wriggle our way out of. Certainly if I ever had it, and had to turn it over, to save Blue or Day or myself, I'd tear out any reference to Zoé. I'd still be protecting her secrets. I'm no villain.

I sniff again at Day's wrist. I need to make the perfume complicated enough, perfect enough, and potent enough to distract Voss for the next few days. I need to jostle his senses. Even deaden them, if I can, so he doesn't detect the poison I'll be peppering his brandy with.

I don't intend to murder Voss. So *poison* might not be the right word for it, though poison it most certainly is. Some of it, anyway. It will sicken, but only slightly. And if he's sickly by nature, he won't suspect. I'll comfort him, and lull him along, and learn what it is that he wants.

Madame Roche keeps more than just sleeping powder behind her counter at the café. She has all sorts of prescriptions. The city's beggars go to the clinics, and then they go to Café Roche to swap their pills and potions for shots of liquor. I will bring to Illiers a few of these remedies, as well as some concoctions of my own.

···· 18 ····

In the little country village of Illiers, where the air is every bit as cold as it is in Paris, Voss and I huddle close, arm in arm, in the street. We're still in the occupied zone, so no one drives, though I suspect the villagers have always walked in the roads—the sidewalks are as narrow as a tightrope. I'm in a hooded cape of purple velvet that reaches my shoes. A fairy-tale hag, into the woods. I carry the walking stick Voss gave me the other afternoon. And in the bottle in the bulldog's brass head are a few swallows of something that, in heavier doses, might be a touch toxic.

Meanwhile, in my pockets are sachets of tea I've stitched together, a smoky blend of noxious herbs and pernicious weeds that would be fatal only to a kitten.

"It's a ghost town," Voss says with a sigh. "I mean, it's a ghost of itself. Or a ghost, at least, of what Proust described in his novels." Based on some notes from the town's mayor, we've found the house Proust visited as a child, his aunt's house, the heart of all his sentiment, and one of the settings for his fiction. "It's too small," Voss says as we stand across the avenue. He squints and holds out his hand, as if to block the house from his sight. "The family could not have been . . . *situated* in there, as he told it." He closes his fingers, closing his hand around it. It looks quite spacious to me. To make matters worse for Voss, the grocery store where the family bought their biscuits with pink sugar is now a bicycle shop.

And we've already been to the stream, which he declared murky and fetid. *Proust described the water as violet,* Voss complained as we gazed into the deep, dead green of it. *He said the floor of it was like Japanese cloisonné.*

In the hotel café, he's pleased that at least he can request Proust's cookies and tea. Voss picks up from the table the copy of *Swann's Way* that he's been carrying with him, with its ripped and raggedy blue paper jacket, its pages tabbed and marked and dog-eared. He reads me the passage about the madeleine, soaked in lime-blossom tea, and how the taste of it brought on a rush of innocent joy, of sweet nostalgia. He translates for me from the French. *"I had ceased now to feel mediocre, contingent, mortal."*

The waiter brings us the teapot and cups, and a plate of cookies, and while Voss again reads aloud from the book, from Proust's description of this madeleine in front of us, *those squat, plump little cakes,* I manage to slip a tea bag from the cuff of my coat, plop it into the pot, swirl its damage around. I let it steep for a long moment before pouring us each a splash.

Even the madeleine disappoints Voss. *Too rubbery,* even when he dips it into the tea.

"The girls at Boulette's always have memories they're hoping I'll bottle for them," I say. "A grandmother's powder, or sachets in a drawer. Pastilles their father kept in a tin. But if I give them exactly what they're asking for, they don't recognize it. They'll only believe it's true if it's better than they remember it."

I remember a day at Coney Island, with M, the two of us posing for an artist drawing cartoons seaside. He captured us perfectly in a quick sketch, with just a few lines here and there. The trick, he told us, is to depict only what's most distinctively our own. What makes our face our face. *The more I add,* he said, *the less it looks like you.*

"And what is that perfume you're wearing?" Voss says, sneering. "It's been watering my eyes all day. You've soaked yourself in it." He hasn't once mentioned it, so I doubt it's been such torture.

I hesitate to utter Proust's name under the circumstances. I say quietly, "It was something I was playing with. Inspired by . . . well, this trip. In one of your books on Paris, you describe some of the scents in Proust's novels."

He furrows his brow. "No no no no," he says. He picks up his book again. After a moment, he finds what he's looking for, and thumps his finger against the page. He reads aloud: ". . . *alone in ecstasy, inhaling, through the noise of the falling rain, the everlasting scent of invisible lilacs.*" He looks up to me. He raises one hand, shrugging, as if it were all so simple and obvious. "Rain," he says. "Everlasting lilacs."

He sweeps through the pages, seeking more scents to punish me with, but stops when the church bells chime. "Well, at least that's as it should be," he says. "The bells that chime every quarter hour." He looks at his watch, grimaces, holds it to his ear to listen for ticking. He then glances along the walls, seeking a clock. "I have an appointment," he tells me, slamming the book closed, standing from the table. "I'll be back before dinner." With a firm nod, he drinks the tea in one gulp, and he's off.

After he leaves, I retrieve the tea bag, in case there might be more sickness to squeeze from it. I tuck it into a wax candy wrapper. Can't he hear himself? Doesn't Voss realize he'll soon enough be as disappointed with Paris as he is with Illiers? In Paris, they've covered the eaves and awnings of the shops with banners in German. They've draped the city in swastikas. They've changed the names of the avenues.

They want the city's *every* essence, putting their filthy hands on even the untouchable—the scent of our ladies' necks, the bubbles in our champagne, the stout wallop of our black coffee, and the black exhaust of our cigarettes. The notes of jazz that lift from our basement windows. They'll filch the air from our soufflés.

Everything Voss loves will grow faint, then fainter. Paris will become everyone's old dowager aunt wrecked by opium.

···· 19 ····

We're to be here only a few days, but Voss packed for me a week's worth of new clothes. A day dress of black rayon, patterned with caramel-colored sparrows. An ivory evening gown with Madonna lilies. A blouse with a print of red feathers for one day, a skirt of paisley for another. I don't much like it, but I go along with it.

These dresses make me worry more about what he has in mind for me. The patterns are dizzying.

In the evening, we're alone in the hotel's front parlor. I'm in a dinner dress of pink chiffon, swirling with circus carousels in baby blue. I bring him a snifter of liquor.

"The old French colognes were made of brandy," I tell him. I've corrupted his with a sickly syrup of cherry laurel. "Some complain that the brandy crushes the violets."

"And what do the druggists use in Nebraska, Nebraska Charlie?" he says. "To make their colognes?"

"Fermented sugar beets, I reckon," I say.

He sniffs the brandy. Closes one eye. Looks up. Contemplates. Takes a sip. Takes another. And another. Drinks it down. He returned from his appointment even more irritable than he was before. He hasn't explained, but I imagine he visited Pascal's rose farm.

I take the snifter back from him, and return to the trolley along the wall. I pour him more poison.

"Did you see more of the village this afternoon?" I ask. We sit on opposite ends of a long sofa. I keep wanting to look down, to see if I've somehow left the room without my pants. And, of course, I have.

The dress—its flow and soft touch—makes me feel naked. But this dress helps me play a character, proper and doting, with its silky pinks and blues. I defer to Voss's authority, my dress fanned out, my legs tucked in, my ankles crossed.

He swirls the brandy around in his snifter. "No," he says. He seems to want to say more, so I wait, and he finally does. "You probably know that Pascal has a farm near here. For the perfume factory. Roses. I had a meeting with a . . ." He pauses, then says, with a pinch of disdain, "A *manager.*" He takes a drink. "But he was more of a farmhand, really. It was useless."

"Some people would say that bothering with something like perfume, in wartime, is just . . . fiddling while Rome burns," I say, but I say it in such a way that he knows it's *his* response that matters.

He's enlivened by this, as I knew he would be. "Well, it was the emperor who did the fiddling in Rome," he says. "And then he built his grand palace and gardens on the ashes of it all." He smiles, and he raises his glass toward me, like he's toasting the emperor's victory. But then he flinches. Squints. He presses a finger to his temple. "Spots in my eyes," he says. "I must have looked right into that lamplight." He sighs, and takes another sip.

"What does your wife wear?" I say, though he's not spoken much of the wife. In all the time we've spent together, including the few hours on the train to Illiers just this morning, he only ever answers my questions with questions of his own. I say, "What *perfume* does she wear?"

Dropping his voice an octave, Voss says, "When I mentioned my wife before . . . well, she's not my wife anymore. I'm not married now, but I've been married three times. It never keeps."

"It seems you'd be able to keep at least one of them," I say. "You're pleasant enough to be around."

"I'm almost inclined to say the same of you," he says, almost flirtatiously. We both smile. Is his smile fake too? He lifts his snifter in what I think is another toast, but he's signaling that it's empty. I'm happy to pour him more.

When I bring his brandy, I say, "Oskar, I sense . . . I sense that you want my help. And I want you to know that, without a doubt, I do want to help you. I do."

He takes the snifter and sips. "Why?" he says.

"Well, I'll be completely honest with you," I lie. "Pascal robbed me. He's a crook. We formed a partnership, to design some fragrances together, and he claimed them all as his own. He said he owed me nothing."

I'm feeling creaky in my old habits. I rattled that off too fast. Back in my youth as a thief, I knew I wouldn't get caught, and even if I did, I knew the consequences would be meager. I was expert at skirting the law. But if I fail at this, I'm done for, and not just me, but everyone in my orbit. I'm risking not just *my* neck but Blue's too, and Day's, and Zoé's.

Voss swishes his brandy around, and I wish he would say something.

"Ahhh," he says, finally, as if this is a revelation he's been waiting for. He says, his voice spiked with gossip, "Did you know Pascal kept a journal?"

The perfume diary. Suddenly, the book is in the room with us, and my heart picks up so much I worry it's fluttering the silk bow knotted at my chest. "Yes," I say. "If you mean the recipe book. With all the formulas and ingredients."

"That's the one I mean," he says. "Do you know where he kept it?"

"That I don't." I say, "I'd love to see it. I'd love to know if he credits me at all. If he confesses his theft."

Voss nods a slow nod. He nods and nods. "I'd love to see it too," he finally says. "There's work to be done. It will be a new age, Charlie, unlike anything before. A renaissance. The borders of Europe, all the different laws, the tariffs and taxes, haven't allowed for the exchange of ideas, and methods. And materials! The great perfumeries of Berlin and Vienna will now have for themselves all the fields and gardens of France. The roses. The best jonquil, the best jasmine. Carnations. Orange blossoms."

He leans his head back on the sofa. Closes his eyes. But he's not finished. "Fiddling," he mutters. "Fiddling! Perfume is not just vanity. Think of the spice trade. The Silk Road. Our desire to be intoxicated by the senses led to our very enlightenment. We wanted to get lost, so we found the world. Empires were built from cinnamon and cloves. And from all this, all this marriage of cultures, came science and medicine. The swapping of art. Dressmaking. Mapmaking. We wanted to take more and more and more from the sea, so the sea rose up around us for the taking." He swallows the last of his brandy.

He speaks like an explorer asking the queen for a fleet of ships and a royal charter. It's a lecture I'm sure he's delivered before, and it does seem it's exhausted him.

I touch my fingers to my hair, as if I'm tucking a curl behind my ear. "It all has to do with infatuation, I suppose," I say. "Opium. Gin. Cuban weed. African violets. We can be happy enough if we *think* we're in love."

Before I can ask him more about his work, he says he's feeling woozy, and he needs to go to his room and rest. Now I better understand our winter walks. The merest sniffle would send him into conniptions. A pinch of sore throat. A cough. Even a gentle stab of headache. He's terrified of falling ill but can't bear to stay in out of the cold. He'd suffer more, he says, if he couldn't walk the streets of Paris all winter.

I've always been frail, he told me. *But it's my frailty that gave me my sentimental education. I grew up reading books. Studying art. Long before I visited Paris, I knew its every corner. I knew its every luxury.*

···· 20 ····

We've left Illiers early, after only one night. Voss blames the moldy hotel for the dull thump in his temples. Or maybe, he says, some vapors rose from the green stream we walked along.

We're in our own compartment, on a train to Paris. He's wrapped in a heavy quilt, leaning back on a bank of pillows like a sultan. His eyes are bloodshot, his cheeks flushed a stark white. We've swapped sides twice already—he can't decide if it makes him queasier to ride facing forward or looking back.

I've overdone it with the poison. Or maybe he's even more frail than I imagined. But I lost track of things, meeting him brandy for brandy. The liquor went to my head. And then this morning, I served him drugged tea before I realized how sick he still was from the drugged brandy.

"You drank more than you think you did," I tell him.

"I did *not*," he says, his voice weak.

"You're used to cognac," I say. "That was Armagnac we drank last night. It's more stout. It's got more gumption when it comes to doing you in. Or maybe it was the elevation. We were much higher up."

He rolls his eyes, insulted. "I know cognac from Armagnac," he grumbles. "No, I caught something in that church."

"The church was empty," I say. We'd visited the Saint-Jacques, where Proust's characters worshipped.

"There was that old lady kneeling by the altar," he says. "She was sniveling and hacking. Probably crawled from her deathbed to beg God to end her suffering."

"She wasn't anywhere near us," I say. She'd been at the front, we'd been at the back, and the old church was lengthy, seeming like it might stretch through half the town, a vital artery of stained glass.

"That terrible, loud, death-rattle cough of hers echoed through the whole place, carrying all its infection with it. I only had to *hear* it to get it stuck in my own lungs."

I don't know why I'm trying to talk him out of his theories. Better he blame the old lady or the mold of the river. Or whatever illness it is that makes him weak from time to time.

He drifts off to sleep, then wakes only minutes later with a start and a gasp. He seems confused by the sight of me. I've gone back to wearing my own clothes. He directs his gaze to the scuff of my shoes, then up along the leg of my trousers. His attention catches on my necktie, but it's too busy for him to stare at. It's black and white, with a pattern of triangles that seem to throb and jitter even when you've not been overdosed.

"Can I ask you something?" he says, his eyes shut tight.

"If you have to ask me if you can ask me, then it's probably not a question I want to answer, is it?"

"Why do you dress the way you do?" he says. "The trousers. The neckties. And all that." His *all that* is delivered with somewhat of a sneer.

"If that's the tone you're going to take, then no, you *can't* ask me something."

Neither of us looks away from the other. And then we do. When I catch his eye again, I start to speak. "I'm . . ." But I'm interrupted by the train's porter, who has arrived at our door with the tea service I requested. He sets the tray on the seat next to me. He's brought no tea, only teacups, and boiled water in a china pot. I have a silk pouch of tea I tell Voss is medicinal, and I'm telling the truth this time. The porter leaves. I say nothing. I prepare the tea—the crushed leaves and leathery strawberry skins and dried pearls of rosebuds. I sprinkle it into a strainer held over the china cup. Pour the hot water through the strainer. I can sense Voss's impatience. He's waiting for me to finish the sentence I'd started. *I'm* . . . I'm what? I'd intended to say, *I'm neither one thing nor the other,* but I'm glad the porter interrupted. I'm not sure how I'd best explain myself beyond that.

I hand Voss the cup and saucer. "Drink up," I say. "This'll fix you."

"I didn't mean to be impolite," he says, shrugging his quilts away so that he can sit upright with the teacup. "I just want to introduce you to some people."

"And these people don't approve of ladies in pants."

"They don't approve of ladies in general." He squints again, turns his head away, holds up his hand. "Can you at least remove the necktie? It's throwing this compartment into a spin."

I take off the tie, and I shove it into my pocket. "This is how my mother dressed me," I say, in answer to his question about my clothes.

My mother attempted to prettify the hand-me-down britches and flannels of my two older brothers. Our tiny farm gave us little money to work with. She'd scissored some lace trim from a kitchen curtain, and she stitched it onto the hem of some pants, onto the cuffs of some sleeves, onto the points of some collars. She made cloth roses from burlap bags.

I was so desperate for love, and my mother was so stingy with it, I thanked her endlessly for the lace, until she finally insisted I stop. And she did no more sewing for me.

The church ladies, however, descended on our farmhouse in contraptions of silk and wool, suffocating bonnets and shawls, caged in hoop skirts, even on the summer days of desert-like heat. If you were a woman, it had seemed to me, you spent your whole life cloaked in your death shrouds. You were already in a casket of corsets and petticoats. I would later learn, at the turn of the century, that I was right—women's clothes were not only their coffins but also their killers. The getups that women wore would cinch and strangle, mangling our organs and stealing our breath.

But my family, we were the paving stones for the ladies' garden paths to heaven. By sharing their plenty with us, their tins of bacon fat and jars of pickled beets, they bought their spiritual redemption.

They needlepointed Bible verses, sewed them onto pillows, and gave them to us as gifts to rest our heads on—each parable was meant to remind us of their godly goodwill.

Give, and it will be given to you.

One gives freely, yet grows all the richer.

For where your treasure is, there your heart will be also.

I know they kept careful account of everything they gave us, but I don't know if they ever noticed all I took. My family's indifference to me was contagious, and I was a spectacular nothing in the presence of the church ladies. I didn't stir a breeze or muss a hair. The ladies couldn't be bothered with me—I was too strange in my lacy bib overalls and boy's haircut to consider for more than a glance. And when I did speak, my voice dropped into a foghorn, a bleat. An awful, unladylike croak. They didn't know how to unravel me, so they looked away, and just like that, I vanished. And like a sprite on tiny hooves, I pranced forth and back as they sat in my parlor humming Lutheran hymns, and I snatched what I could. A cameo. A stickpin. A widow's mourning ribbon of black silk. A tassel clipped from a shawl, a hatpin, a stone jimmied from the loose setting of a brooch.

I tell Voss just part of this, just a little, but it seems enough to please him. "Now you can ask *me* a question," he says. "So long as it's a simple one. I don't have the energy for anything complicated."

"What do you do?" I say. "What is your job, exactly?"

"Simple enough," he says. "I run a bureau, within the Abwehr. The Abwehr . . . the intelligence agency."

"What does that have to do with perfume?"

"The bureau is how I've come to have Pascal's house. And his business. I have a staff of two hundred. We manage . . . well, the particulars of the various . . . *things* . . . that have been lost in the war."

"Lost?"

"Lost," he says. "With all the upheaval. The new laws. Businesses changing hands. Things get lost." He shrugs. Raises his eyebrows. *So obvious, so simple.* But he's fumbling for words, which is unusual for him. His words tend to roll lightly along. "My people sort through it all. Valuables. Artwork, silver, furniture. Jewelry. Rare books. Rare wines. Some is sent to museums. Or to Nazi officials. But much of it is sold."

I lean back. Lift my chin. Cross my legs.

"I can just imagine the money to be made," I say.

"Oh yes. Even you, a thief since you were a little girl robbing the church ladies, could never imagine how very rich the world's very richest are." He lifts the teacup. "But I wouldn't trade this cup of tea for a castle. It's doing the trick. It's a miracle cure."

It's not a cure but an antidote. I'm glad he's trusting my tea. These little tea parties will help me slow him down. I'll thwart while I pretend to abet. And Voss has Pascal's house in Paris as his very own, so I'll make him sleepy, and I'll snoop.

I will find the diary.

"You're taking from the rich?" I say.

He shrugs. He looks out the window, contemplating, perhaps translating the truth, running it through the bureaucratic polyglot in the back of his brain. "My agency brings order to the upheaval," he says, clearly pleased with himself for coming up with this answer. "And we come to have the property of the enemy."

A number of Hitler's best gunslingers envy Voss his appointment, he boasts to me. These barbarians long for something civilized. If Voss took to his elegant feather bed for more than a day or two to convalesce, he'd risk having that bed pulled right out from under him. He absolutely can't be sick.

"It was my knowledge of Paris," he says, gazing into his teacup, "and my passion for France that helped me rise to this position. And now that same passion has made me suspicious to some."

Voss wrote the books on Paris, described the light, the sounds, the scents. To hear him tell it, he is among the men who talked Hitler out of bombing the city from the get-go. If it weren't for Voss, Paris would be ashes.

"Suspicious?" I say.

Voss looks up from his tea, quizzical, as if he didn't realize he'd said any such word. Voss doesn't like to talk about the war with me, in any practical sense. He cares only about the spoils. He seems to believe the war has been won already. Paris is his for keeps.

He sets his tea aside. He says, "Tell me your stories of heartbreak. I know you've got some. But you've been keeping them from me."

Just this suggestion of love brings the scent of cigar smoke and tweed, as M's spirit slips through the train. It was M who gave me my copy of *Odorographia,* which eventually sent me packing to seek the world's most impossible scents. The nests of the lost cinnamon birds of the Seychelles. The oil from the bergamot trees felled by the earthquakes of Calabria.

"You want to feed off my misery," I say.

"It *would* make me feel better," he says, smiling sly again. When I say nothing, he says, "I want to get to know *you,* Nebraska Charlie. I'm curious. I want to know all about your crimes. And how you got by with them. And *love.* I want to know *allll* about that lover . . . the one who ruined you." I'm startled for a moment. I've spoken of love? Of ruin?

He's depleted, barely able to sit upright. His eyes blink with sleepiness. He says, "I'm . . . I'm very sentimental. I'm the most sentimental man you know."

He gives me a wink and a smile, but not sly this time. I do believe he believes he's being sincere.

Voss never noticed in Illiers that I never took a sip from my own teacup. That's the first skill the poisoner learns—pretending to drink from the same draught. *Clink your spoon around,* M told me in Manhattan, all those years ago when this was all only hypothetical. *Make a production of sugaring it, or honeying it up, and nobody will notice that you've only poured yourself a splash. Blow on it. Smack your lips. Stir it some more. And let the cup sit with the same few sips you poured in. It'll look like you drank plenty.*

···· 21 ····

Luck and horses. That's what I told them in the train's smoking car when they asked what drew a western man like me to Manhattan. My lucky streak got me outlawed in Guatemala, I lied, even from the cockfights. "The cockfights aren't so brutal there," I said when they flinched at the mention. "They fit the cock's feet with steel hooks"—and I lifted my foot and wriggled my ankle—"so it's all over in a heartbeat, after a few deadly slashes. And the winning bird's wounds are stitched shut with kitchen string."

The silk of my swallowtail coat was patterned with galloping horses, and my carpet slippers were embroidered with horses of another color altogether—blue-gray Arabian steeds. I had a stiff, starched collar and a necktie with a tiepin shaped like a horseshoe. I was headed to the races of Coney Island to make a killing, I explained.

This was just before the century turned. Eighteen ninety-five, I guess. Or ninety-six. I was a few years short of my thirtieth birthday.

But, in truth, I wasn't following horses to Manhattan; I was on my way to sell rich women French perfume. I had developed two talents during my childhood on the farm, talents I honed further in the years after I ran away from the place: I knew flowers, herbs, and oils, and I knew how to deceive and steal. I was convinced I could fool the big city with my country concoctions. Perfume was the most exquisite fraud of all—a pretty little bottle of cheap fixings and alcohol that you sold for at least triple its worth. How could I, I pondered, with my counterfeit perfumes, be any more corrupt than the perfumers themselves? The expense of perfume hinges on a kind of false promise.

On the train, I talked giddily of horses and betting so the men would think me boyish. And with that, I was able to engage them in cards. I had actual aces up my sleeve, but I never once had to fidget them loose. The men were so confident that I was overconfident, they underplayed, and I beat them round after round. And the more bourbon they drank, the weaker their wits.

Luck. Fate. Winning those card games would lead me to M eventually. The money I won on the train inspired me to take a luxury suite at a hotel I couldn't afford, the Marie Antoinette, a frilly thing, a fat slice of let-them-eat-cake that took up one whole city block on Broadway, and it was there, in the tearoom, treating myself to a plate of sweet pickled mangoes and a cup of Turkish coffee, that I met a widow named Waverley.

I struck up a conversation with the old woman at the next table, the Widow Waverley—and that's exactly how she introduced herself, and how she signed her name to my bill for my pickles and coffee, the "Widow" serving as the honorific, and her signature the most extravagant collision of curlicue and dagger-stab I'd ever seen. She made the very most of the sharpest points of the *w*'s and the *v*, even as the vowels were fat, sentimental loops.

I joined her at her table and poured her more tea from a ceramic pot that I remember as having an open-winged butterfly as the handle of its lid, with a few other butterflies perched on the spout. But it seems more likely I'm wrong, that those butterflies flew in from the future.

"You say you're from Chicago?" she said.

"I lived there for a time," I said. "But I grew up on a farm in Nebraska."

"*Grew up* there," she said, astonished. "You don't mean to say there are *children* in the western states?" She spoke without an ounce of irony. She then tipped herself into my web, or tipped me into hers. She appraised me with a squint, and offered me not only a job but also a room in her house. She needed not only the protection of a gentleman, she said, but also a literary amanuensis. She was a poet, she explained, and needed someone to sort through all the little snippets of phrase she jotted down whenever overtaken by a whim. "They are all throughout the house, my phrases are," she said. "In kitchen drawers, in my sewing basket. I've even written on the wallpaper in places. You'll help me situate it all into proper poetry." Before I could say anything, she added, "You'll need a little something until you can make your perfume connections in the city."

That's how I had introduced myself: a dealer in French perfume. I would be working with department stores and druggists, I told her. Wholesalers. And that part wasn't a lie. Up in my hotel room, I had a suitcase full of counterfeit labels that I would affix to my own recipes.

And I did need a job in the meantime, and I needed an address. I needed the foundation of legitimacy and civility the widow would provide, so I could hide my illegitimate intentions for the island of Manhattan. And I needed a kitchen to brew up all that pretty stink.

"Judge," I said when she asked me to remind her of my name. "Judge van Horne." When I first ran away from the farm, as a teenager, I'd read about a jail sentence in the daily paper, and I'd thought "judge" was the judge's name, not his title, and I'd liked it. It seemed manly.

"Judge, darling, have you even ever *met* a poet before me?"

A poet? Yes. Many, many, many poets. But the poets I'd met in my travels were only scholars of burlesque and limerick, their every rhyme and reason corrupt and perverse. I'd worked as an actor in a medicine show; I'd manned a saloon or two. I'd drunk and sung with the lowest of outlaws and the filthiest of guttersnipes, their tongues untied when singing of entwined limbs and knocked knees.

···· 22 ····

At the Widow Waverley's club of widows, I announced I was a student of nasology, a bit of hokum I'd read about in *Le Petit Journal*.

I spoke of my insights into the gardens and farms of France, and the bedrooms of the ladies of Paris. I'd yet to step foot out of America myself, but I'd learned some French from a German actress in Omaha, and I would spend a little time every morning skimming *Le Petit Journal* for all its gossip.

"Tell me the perfumes you most admire," I told the widows gathered in the Widow Waverley's parlor, "and I'll tell you what it says about you." They attempted to outdo each other with their listing of the most exotic and expensive fragrances. These were patrons of the arts, these women; they were friends of composers and painters. They were the widows and daughters of robber barons, with their family names on the wings of museums. They paid small fortunes to smell like the Damask rose water of a Turkish harem, or the dried-up juniper twigs in a Russian steam bath.

After telling the women what they wanted to hear about themselves—*You're daring and adventurous, wicked and poetical*—I then prescribed for each of them a particular French perfume, a French perfume I'd bottled that morning in the kitchen. And they paid handsomely, and even slipped me tips.

"Give me some of this," one of the women said to me, handing me a pamphlet. It was all in French, but illustrated, step-by-step, with elegant sketches of women in kimonos collapsed in parlors, sticking themselves like opium eaters, their hair undone and tumbling to their shoulders. "In Paris, they inject perfume like morphine."

I had noticed this woman the moment she walked in. Like me, she wore a man's suit, her coat and trousers made of a papery silk that made every wrinkle seem part of a frantic pattern of crisscross and crosshatch. But unlike me, she wasn't pretending to be anything. She was simply the woman she was, despite the suit that she wore. Her long hair was pulled back, tied at the nape of her neck with a frayed piece of twine at the back of her starched collar.

This woman commanded the attention of all the widows, her mouth in a smug half smile, her eyebrows raised, a real grimace of arrogance, titillating the ladies with the rumors of the hypodermic mania of the Paris demimonde. "The women of Paris needle perfume into their veins," she said, "sweetening their sweat, enhancing their sighs, their moans, their whispers, with the scent of violets."

The women pretended to be scandalized, snapping their tongues, scolding. A few of them waved their embroidered hankies in the woman's direction, either in admonishment or as a white flag of surrender.

"You've not yet met Fanny, have you, Judge?" the Widow Waverley said, with a sly purr. At that, Fanny stood from her chair, bent at the waist, and took my hand to blow a kiss against it. She then produced a tin from the same pocket from which she'd taken the pamphlet. She opened the lid and offered me a candied violet. "They're even perfumed," Fanny said. "They smell a little like a flower, but they don't taste like one. That's the magic of potato ether."

Clearly this woman wanted to expose me as a fraud. *She* wanted to be the expert on perfume today.

The violet I took and put on my tongue was too slight to do much more than melt.

The Widow Waverley said, "Fanny was once one of New York's finest ballerinas."

"*Once?*" Fanny said, lifting an eyebrow. She then said to me, "*Once* you're one of the finest ballerinas, you're *always* one of the finest.

There are so very few of us." She then said, "Waverley here tells me *you're* a farm"—and here she paused a beat before saying, "*boy* from Nebraska. I had a farm too for a time, right next door, in Iowa. After the ballet."

"Why?" was all I could think to say.

"Civil War veterans were given certain benefits. If we still had our legs and our wits, we could head west."

"You were married to a veteran?" I said.

"I *was* a veteran, Mr. Van Horne," she said, having tossed in yet another pause before that *mister*. "But that's a story for another time. All these ladies have already heard it."

One of those ladies said, "Fanny is the subject of the novel I'm writing," a comment that led to debate among them all as to whether she had the right to boast of writing a novel that she'd not yet begun. *But I have all my characters and all my incidents,* she insisted.

In the flurry of that dispute, tea was served by the Widow Waverley. "The tea is from Holland," she said, "so you ought drink it as the Hollanders do." She took up a sugar cube to pop into her mouth. With the cube tucked into the pocket of her cheek, she slurred her suggestion that we do as she had, and that we keep the cube there for the tea to wash past with each sip.

Fanny leaned in toward my ear and slipped a card under the cuff of my sleeve. "I host a salon for people like us," she whispered. As Fanny stepped away to gather her hat and walking stick, thanking the Widow Waverley for lunch, I felt my cheeks go red-hot and sweat prickle on my forehead. I still had my sugar cube lodged in the inside of my cheek. I opened my mouth so it could roll in between my teeth, and I bit down. The cube wasn't as softened by the tea as I'd expected, and I hoped the crunch and crack of it didn't sound as loud in the room as it did inside my head.

After the others left, the Widow Waverley poured me a snifter of her home-bottled blackberry brandy and told me all she'd figured out on her own.

"What was the name you were given at birth?" she said. "You can trust me. I'm a poet. A lifelong student of human nature. I'm just curious."

I *wanted* to trust her, and I wanted to tell her, so I did. "Clementine," I said.

"Clementine," she said, nodding. "Do you wish you'd been born a man?"

"No one's ever born a man," I said. "Men are born boys."

"You know what I mean."

"Do I?"

"Of course you do. It's a simple question."

"But . . . I don't think it's a matter of simplicity," I said. "It's about the rightness of it, I guess. Or the wrongness. I mean to say, it seems to me the wrong question for the answer you want." I was talking in circles, but how was I to explain that I was born a boy, and I was born a girl too? Or, rather, how could I explain that *boy* and *girl* have nothing to do with birth?

She sighed. Took another drink. "One would think you'd have given more thought to all this," she said. She seemed disappointed that I couldn't reveal to her all the dimensions of my perversity. "Never mind," she said. "Fanny is part of the widows' club, but she rarely attends. I told her about you. I thought you should meet."

"She's a widow?"

She shot back the last of her brandy. She closed her eyes and let the liquor lead her elsewhere. She began Fanny's story: "A young man, knowing he was to be sent off to battle, attended every show in the city, to distract himself. Even the ballet. He saw Fanny dance onstage. He brought her roses. They fell in love at the stage door. Within a few weeks, they were married. And she was heartbroken when he left. So she enlisted to fight, as a man, alongside her husband. He died in her arms. And when he died, the man she was died with him. She shook off her coat, dropped her weapons, and stepped back into her old life. She even returned to dance, to ballet, but her heart wasn't in it. So she returned to the battlefront, as yet another man, a different one, and she fought until the war was over."

"And who is she now? An old ballerina or an old soldier?"

The Widow Waverley whimpered melodramatically. "What does it matter if she's a ballerina who doesn't dance or a soldier who doesn't fight?" She nodded at her snifter, inviting me to pour her more. She said, "All I can say with certainty is that she receives two war pensions—one as a widow, and one as a veteran."

After I poured us both more brandy, I took from my inside coat pocket the card Fanny had given me, and there was only a time, and a date, and an address, along with Fanny's initials. *For people like us,* Fanny had whispered in my ear.

Who? I wondered. Who are people like us?

···· 23 ····

I've learned from my mistakes in Illiers, and I will manage Voss's drugging better now, strumming at his health, easing him toward the brink of recovery, then pulling him back. Every teacup's aroma of flowers and herbs will convince him I'm helping.

Just pump the tea right into my veins, Voss told me when we reached the train station, *like with that perfume syringe the woman told you about.* I thought he'd been napping through most of my stories of Manhattan.

He insisted I bring him more tea in the morning. *Or any of your folk remedies from the old farm.* He's leery of doctors, he says.

So I arrive at Monsieur Pascal's house just after dawn. I know the house well from the outside, this *hôtel particulier,* a fat mansion not far from my house on the Left Bank. Pascal's house squats overstuffed on the corner, with two addresses, one for each street it runs along. It's a one-family house that could house five families. Five *rich* families, no less.

The concierge has not been evicted by Voss. She lives in a few rooms of the first floor, and Voss lives in all the floors above. She is hunched forward, a severe curve in her spine bending her sharp at the waist. Though I can't see her face past the hair that falls forward, she's intimidating with her brusque manner and bent back. I feel my own slouch in my shoulders, so I straighten up.

The concierges of Paris hold a place of authority and manage all the household contracts. They often seem irreplaceable, as if a concierge could steal the building right out from under you, simply by locking you out. And now here they all are in this ravaged city, still holding all the keys.

She fusses with hers on a metal ring at the end of a chain around her neck. She surely has more keys than the building has suites. "Too many keys cripples the keep," she tells me, and though there's a touch of singsong to her scratchy voice, I can tell she wishes I were elsewhere.

Her commitment, really, is to the house itself, and to the house's own long legacy of concierges at the door. I thought *she* might be the one to nettle for information, that Monsieur Pascal might have confided in her, that she might have an inkling about the best hiding places, or might recognize something about the squiggle in the note; she could be the very link I'm needing. But Zoé quickly cautioned me to steer clear. *Daddy inherited her with the house,* she said. *I think she was there even before my grandfather bought it. She's always been there, and she's always been old. She's probably just as happy to work for a fascist.*

Since Voss is expecting me, the concierge lets me in upstairs without a knock at the door. Her back is so crooked that her eyes are directed at my knees as she speaks. "Monsieur Voss is waiting for you in the kitchen," she tells me, but she's gone before I can ask where the kitchen is.

I've seen some very fine homes over the years, and this is certainly among the finest. But the second I step inside, I feel like stepping back out.

I take off my coat and gloves. The herringbone pattern in the tweed of my trousers matches exactly the woodwork of the parquet floor. I get a touch of vertigo when I glance down, but looking back up doesn't help. The house is full of open doors, and massive mirrors on the walls that double and triple everything, reflections of reflections of reflections.

What have I got myself into? I'm much too old for this. I run my eyes along all the mirrors, and I'm already worn out. I'm hoping to see deeper into the house somehow, hoping to spot the symbol Pascal etched onto his note to Zoé. *I write about you in my diary,* he wrote, but I'm certain the true message is in the squiggle at the bottom of the card. As I walk through the house, I study the carvings in the table legs, the crown molding over doorways. If Pascal was unable to take the diary with him, he would have needed to conceal it quickly. These old French houses, like my own, are riddled with secret pantries, trapdoors, narrow staircases.

I just want to find the diary and go, and never return. But I'm afraid I'm already in too deep. I fear I'm far beyond the point where I can just disengage when I decide to. A thief is at her most conspicuous when she's suddenly not around anymore.

Despite all the doors and windows I see around me now, it looks like there's no exit at all, like I'm in a mirror maze in a Chinese box.

Zoé told me Pascal had a spacious laboratory in the house, a studio, but she doesn't know if the diary was ever kept there. The diary was most often in his hands, she said. He might sit with it at the table at breakfast, or in the parlor in the evening, the journal open in his lap. He kept it on his bedstand, or on the kitchen counter, or on the library desk. He left it on the bench in the garden, or on the telephone table, or on the carpeted steps.

I follow the smell of toasted bread, and I find my way to the back stairs, and down, to the kitchen. Voss wears a spectacular smoking jacket—black velvet with gold leaves that shine and flicker in the light—but his pajama bottoms are a dull flannel. He's barefoot. I almost wonder if he has tried to brighten his face with cosmetics; there's a touch of rose in his ashen cheeks.

He's trying to seem alive, so I intend to instill some doubt about that. "You should let me call a doctor," I say, confident he'll reject the suggestion. He's still worried someone will find out he's sick. Survival of the fittest is a fine philosophy until someone poisons your tea.

"I just need a few days," he says. "I'll be up to snuff soon." He rises from the chair, and he does what he can to conceal his labored breathing. He steps up to me, and picks up the tea tin. Brings it to his nose. Sniffs. "How'd you come to know so much about tea?" he says.

"I've picked things up here and there," I say. I shrug one shoulder. "I learned a fair amount from that old lover of mine you were asking me about."

"Yes, I've asked you to tell me everything, and you've told me nothing."

Perhaps he *is* sentimental, as he said. Or maybe he means to play to my vanity. In any event, I'll tell him a little of what he wants to hear. But just a little. If I'm to find the diary in this massive house, I need him to have reasons to invite me back.

"He worked in the tea industry," I say. "And he gave me a manual once, something called *Odorographia.* A guide to raw materials, for those who bottle scents and flavors. I mapped my escape with it, after my heart broke. More than forty years ago. I followed the scents of the world, described in the book."

"To rob the world of its perfume," he says.

It was my guide to getting lost. I still have that very copy M gave me, with all my notes penciled in, my cursive inching out from the margins to tangle around the text. Tucked in the pages are my sketches on notebook paper of the flowers I discovered, and portraits of insects. Whenever I look at the book, I'm who I once was.

It's my own perfume diary, I guess. The doctored cardamom of a Lingayat priest. The magnolias of Himalaya. The star anise of Japanese temples. Orinoco sassafras. I've not carried around many things in my travels over the years, but that book has been with me always.

"And I knew a thing or two before that," I say. "From the farm. Old remedies. Marigold soup for headaches. Roasted lily blossoms to unclog sinuses. For an upset stomach, you chew on a clove."

Cloves, M said once, after kissing me, after tasting the spice on my breath, on my numb tongue, on one of our first nights together. I told him I needed to gnaw on a clove when I got nervous. *The clove farms of Zanzibar,* he said, *are worked by slaves. The slaves bat the cloves from the evergreens. Slavery, sweetheart. That's the spice that's settling your gut just now.*

Voss seems to get a lift from my discussing restoratives. His breathing has eased. He straightens his back. And I believe him when he tells me he needs me. "It's like every breath of scent you've ever breathed in is still somewhere in your very soul," he says. "I believe in fate, and I believe fate has led you to me."

He's standing too close, so I'm grateful for the kettle's harsh whistle. I lift the kettle from the stove and start the tea. "We'll work together, Charlie. Pascal robbed you, but I'll make you rich." He has dangled that bit of promise before. I listen, knowing there's more to it. And sure enough, before the tea has even steeped, he says, "I do need to ask a few things of you first."

I'm going to need a whole fistful of cloves to keep from getting queasy. But I nod. I raise an eyebrow. Still, he must see some hesitance. "You love Paris, I know," he says. "But you know that I do too. I *worship* Paris. And that's exactly why we should work together. My plans are a celebration of Paris, absolutely. You can trust in that."

I'm not sure why he feels the need to convince me of anything. I'm nobody.

After I've brewed his tea, he asks me to follow him back upstairs to an office. In the mirrors, as he leads me slowly through the rooms, I see myself turn every corner, and I practice my poise. I'm slouching again, so I straighten my back. I'm struck cold by the sight of my perfect poker face. Even the tea tray is mirrored. *Mirror silvering* is listed in my book of poisons, but it's too deadly.

In the evenings at my kitchen table, I study M's old book for symptoms and damage. In my cabinets, I have wolfsbane and devil's fig, and any number of sickening agents I collected from my spice merchants before the war. The various herbs and roots are sometimes bricks, sometimes cakes, sometimes nests of twigs.

But I'm most pleased to be finally using my pots of honey. The honey is not poisoned, it's poison*ous,* the bees having gathered it from gardens of yellow azaleas, or from rhododendrons, or other plants that might tip you into vertigo or double your vision.

Voss's plot for *me* this morning is far more banal. Desk work. "Surely you've faked a signature or two in your day," he says. I'm to post some reports to higher offices, mimicking his signature because he fears his hand's unsteady. He detects a shiver in his otherwise elegant penmanship. They all need to imagine Voss upright at his desk, in the pinkest of health.

As he rattles off instructions, he seems to grow weaker by the word. I pour him a cup of tea, and stir in the honey. When he finishes, he says, "Honeybees have bee dances. They communicate by touch." He reaches for the cup, and along the way he taps his fingers along my wrist, like the dance steps of an insect. It's the very lightness of his touch that causes me to recoil. I worry he's seen me wince, so I smile. I nod. I glance toward the desk and its stacks of papers and reports.

I sit down and practice his signature on a scrap of envelope as he watches over my shoulder sipping tea. After only a few tries, I've mastered it, though he signs his name with far more swirls of elegance than necessary; his signature is as pompous as the Widow Waverley's. He signs every form as if it's for posterity.

He decides not to linger. He asks me to carry the tea tray and follow him to the bedroom, where he'll rest. Like in most of the old houses of Paris, each room just leads into another, and that room into another, no hallways or corridors veining through the place. He says he intends to do some reading in bed, but he crawls in under the heavy quilts without a book. He sits up just enough to lift the teacup from the saucer I hold out for him. "When you're finished with the signatures," he says, "you're going to help me find the perfume diary."

And with those last few words, the house suddenly shrinks, the walls collapse, everything tumbles toward me.

Yes, let me help.

I make much of situating the tea tray, its spoons and cup and saucer, so I can linger. He'll be asleep in a blink. I listen for his soft snuffling.

I step away from his bedside and wander the house.

I get all mixed up in the maze of rooms, so after turning a few corners, I end up in the same place a time or two; but even taking that into consideration, and the doubling and tripling in the mirrors, I'm overwhelmed by the number of credenzas, bureaus, wardrobes, chiffoniers. I bump my shoulder on an armoire, knock my knee on a steamer trunk. Even worse, Pascal's tastes run toward the baroque, every cupboard door busy with scrolls and patterns and gilding, every leg and kneecap of a highboy etched with a doodad. It would take me days to find the squiggle I'm seeking among all this frippery.

I go up a set of stairs and down another, and I stumble upon the laboratory Zoé told me about, where Pascal experimented with the scents and synthetics, where he kept apothecary cabinets of oils and essences, bottles of dried roots and bulbs and pods, spices and leaves. A sink, hot plates, kettles, copper kegs. And along every wall: bookshelves. A towering library.

I walk through the room, running my fingers along the bindings. And on those bindings? All kinds of little code marks. A variety of squiggles almost like the squiggle I'm looking for, all of different twists and turns, like letters from foreign alphabets. A cataloging system of some sort. At first I'm discouraged, thinking the symbol I seek will be lost among all these similar ones. Even as I just glance at the bindings, the design I memorized begins to unravel in my head. But then I decide to be *en*couraged. It seems reasonable to think that I've at least narrowed the search down to this one room. So, with a pair of opera glasses I found in my meandering, I begin at the very top. I aim the glasses, turn the wheel to focus, and I look for that squiggle to bend back into shape before my eyes.

The laboratory smells like the wick of a candle just lit. Or one just blown out. But no, it's the scent of the books I'm smelling, the vanilla and cedar of their pages and boards. The stale wax of old leather. The salt and brine of the ink.

The autumn decay of a root in Bengal. A swamped field of sugarcane. Fresh ginger baked in the Jamaican sun.

Before I met M, I thought I'd already learned everything about flowers and spices. After we met, I realized I knew next to nothing. I read and reread the book M gave me until I knew all its arcane knowledge by heart.

···· 24 ····

In whatever city I was in, no matter the laws and ordinances, I wore my suits and collars, my oxfords and ascots, with a mix of confidence and fear. I strolled with a man's stride. I sat back in cable cars with a gent's jutting of knees and elbows. I robbed the rest of the world of every inch of space I could reach, of every breath I could take in deep and keep in my lungs, just as a man would.

I sometimes think I was more convincing then, even as my features were softer, more feminine. But the very notion of a woman dressing as I did in those days was so perverse, no one could fathom I was anything but an overly tender gentleman with a scowl to hide his girlishness.

But on my way to Fanny's salon, to the address on the card she'd slipped up my sleeve, I could hardly breathe at all. I curled in on myself, my shoulders low, the brim of my hat bent down. My heart beat fast. At the widows' club, Fanny had seen me. She'd caught me in the act. And so had the Widow Waverley. I was certain everyone I passed could recognize, in my furtive looks this way and that, that I was guilty of being a woman in wolf's clothing.

On the silk band of my bowler hat, I pinned a brooch shaped like a grape bunch, each grape a little round mirror, reflecting you back at yourself with a housefly's many-eyed stare.

When I walked into Fanny's parlor, all the many eyes that turned my way were turned back on them with my nifty pin.

There were probably twenty-some handsome, charming, chatty deviants in the room, all in suits and neckties, or men's smoking jackets. My anxiety lifted in an instant. Now that I was here, I wanted to be among them. Before I could step into this crowd, I was stopped by a young woman (in a velvet robe and silk trousers, a tasseled fez atop her head, her hair in a marcel wave) sitting at a makeshift desk, who demanded of me my alias. And I gave it: *Judge van Horne.*

She tapped at her typewriter, lining up the name on a paper card. Her desk wobbled on its skinny legs with each peck of a key. When she handed me the card, I saw that I was now a member of "The Brothers of the Sisterhood."

No sooner was the card placed in my hand than it was plucked away. Fanny was at my side, and she took the card and opened my suit coat enough to tuck it into my inside breast pocket. "It helps with the law," Fanny said, "having a club. On the advice of our attorney, Mr. Firth, over there." She nodded toward someone in a wing chair, who had a very convincing set of muttonchops. "We have to navigate these things." She led me to the sideboard to fix me a drink, chipping off a chunk of ice with a pick and dropping it into some bourbon. She handed me the glass, and I clutched it tight in my grip. "The police like to go after people like us"—again Fanny thinking she knew who I was—"when they feel like flexing a muscle. So they charge you under a law that forbids people from gathering in disguises—probably some old holdover from the Boston Tea Party. Mostly they just raid the basement bar down on Bleecker Street to round up the fairies who get all dolled up. But lucky for us, the law allows for clubs to hold masquerade balls. So we have a club. And masquerades." She did a little jig, a little vaudeville skip.

I'd had plenty of back-and-forth with big-city police in my day, and I doubted the paper card in my pocket would keep me out of the clink if the coppers came knocking.

I again scrutinized the facial hair of the club's attorney. "So there are some men here?" I said.

Fanny nodded slow and hesitant. She said, "Yes," then added, somewhat under her breath, "in a sense."

I started nodding my head in rhythm with hers. "But all of us here are women," I said.

"Yes," she said. "In a sense."

She linked her arm with mine and led me through the room, making quick introductions. Some members of the Brothers of the Sisterhood were clearly dressed only for the evening, as if this actually was just a masquerade. For others, the nights were extensions of their days—they likely wore their ties to work, to jobs as accountants and attorneys and shopkeepers. You could practically see the nicks on their chins where they'd cut themselves shaving. You could smell the sandalwood tonic that greased their curls back.

I was eventually introduced to a gangly fop named M ("Just the letter M," he said, speaking at a quick clip, his words rolling over each other, "and believe it or not, it's not short for nothing; it's even on my baptismal certificate that way"), and our eyes kept catching all evening long, even as we got drawn into other conversations. He had long, spindly fingers and a habit of tapping at the air as he spoke, making it look like he was always in the middle of committing a flimsy magic act.

I met so many astonishing people that night, I might not have made all that much of meeting M had the evening ended sooner. But as I spoke to a gent named Agnes, I noticed M was speaking to someone behind me. M began lightly leaning his back against mine. I leaned back too, but I was careful to lean only at the exact same level of lightness. But then he leaned more. And I leaned more. Suddenly, I couldn't hear a word Agnes was saying; I could only concentrate on the weight of M against me.

···· 25 ····

When Voss finally stirs, he finds me at the desk, dutifully forging his signature, sorting through the mess of papers.

"You're going to need to be paid for all this drudgery" is the first thing he says to me. Though he has slept for hours, he's still exhausted. He drops into a chair in the corner and rubs his temples. "Have you ever held a job? Did you ever get rich as a thief?"

"Not rich," I say. "At least never nearly as rich as the people I robbed. But I did well enough. It all afforded me my retirement. In the city of my dreams." Whenever I can, I bring up the charms of Paris. I know that will enliven him.

But he doesn't seem to be listening. "I'll have a secretary come up with a wage for you," he says. "Just until we get the perfumery up and running. When we get things going again, you'll be made a partner in that."

"You're being very generous to me," I say.

He nods slow. He says, his voice hoarse, "You were up in Pascal's laboratory," as if he can tell from the sight of me that I've been snooping. Or maybe he smells it on me, the dust of the book weevils twitching up a sneeze.

One of the gifts of a thief is to be able to lie without flinching. As a matter of fact, a good thief becomes more confident in her half-truths than she is in her whole ones. But I don't even need to lie—he has already mentioned the diary.

Before I can say anything, he says, "The bedroom happens to be right beneath the laboratory. And all the old floors in this house creak with every footstep. The noise woke me up a few times."

While Voss slept, I managed to inspect the bindings of every book in Pascal's lab. I never found the symbol. I say, "I glanced through some of the books, but I haven't found anything like a diary. They're all cookbooks, encyclopedias of botanicals, medical texts."

"Oh, I've had someone go through all those books already," he says, waving a hand in the air. "Surely you don't think I would need a thief to find a book on a bookshelf."

"I don't suppose you would," I say. He means to be condescending, but he has tipped his hand a little. He must be desperate to find the diary if he's already had all the books skimmed.

When I ask if he'd like more tea, he pauses. He says that perhaps a doctor is a good idea after all. He asks if I know of someone. "Someone discreet," he says. "Someone who will come to the house."

"Oh, well, yes, yes, of course," I tell him. "I know someone very discreet. I can bring him by in the morning."

But I know of no doctors. I don't even have one of my own. Like any criminal worth her salt, I almost never get sick beyond a sniffle. And when I do, I cure myself with my own pharmacopeia. I'll live to be a hundred and ten if no one kills me first.

···· 26 ····

Zoé reclines on a fainting sofa in her bedroom, letting her ladies-in-waiting attend to her costume and makeup. She's been sick for a few days, she says, and she looks it, so wispy-pale. This is the first time I've seen her since returning from Illiers. Her ladies are trying to keep her from fading into the ether, frantically pinking her pale cheeks, puffing powder onto her chin. They clip heavy earrings to her lobes, tighten the tiny buckles at the ankles of her shoes, weighing her down, strapping her in, before she floats away.

I hope to God she's not getting poisoned too.

Zoé sent me a message by courier this morning: *One of the girls here swears there's a gargle that'll put my notes back in my throat. It's a creaky old recipe but surefire, she says. Do you have these things in your kitchen?* Then a list.

No, I don't have an ounce of any of it. Oil pressed from plum stones? Ashes of bugloss boiled in mead? It's all the stuff of a witch's physick.

I tell her this, and Zoé tells me the recipe is from an elderly courtesan who lives in one of the bordello's back rooms, a kind of mascot who they prop up in the cabaret every night, with bright circles of red rouge at the tops of her cheeks. "The old woman says girls used to use it as a swift remedy for a syphilitic larynx," she says, her voice soft and low. "But *I'm* not full of syphilis, just so you know. I just cry all the time. Cry myself hoarse."

She dismisses her maids. After they've left the apartment, she moves from the fainting sofa to sit at her vanity, to finish painting her eyelids and her lips. Tonight she returns to the stage, and the cabaret has played it up in its posters and handbills: a portrait of her holding a white camellia, as if to suggest she's the courtesan of *Camille,* tragic and riddled with syphilis after all.

I take from my bag what I concocted for her throat from my own recipe, a mist made of steeped mullein leaves, vinegar, honey, horseradish. I've bottled it in a perfume atomizer. She opens her mouth. I squeeze the bulb, spraying the mist in.

"There you go, doll," I say, "good as new," even as Zoé cringes and shudders from the taste of it.

Zoé gestures me closer. I lean in. "The diary?" she whispers.

But before I can say a word, she shushes me. "The walls of a bordello are paper thin," she says. "On purpose. To keep the place noisy with love."

"Should I put on music?" I say.

"Lutz broke the phonograph," she says. "He gets very frustrated. Not with me. With the officers he serves. But I was playing a song he didn't like, so he dropped his fist on the record, and he broke the whole works."

I lean in more. "I *don't* know where the diary is just yet," I say. She nods, but I know it's not what she wants to hear. I add, "But neither does Voss. So that's good, at least."

Zoé looks in the mirror, squints, as if she can't quite see herself. When she speaks, her voice grows even weaker. "I read a friend's diary when we were little girls," she says, distracted. "I picked its little lock with a stickpin. There was nothing in it worth reading, but she was furious. We weren't friends after that." She starts to put on her lipstick. But then she stops abruptly. Glances up at my reflection in her mirror. "*You* don't keep a diary, do you?"

She doesn't want me keeping track of her secrets; she doesn't want to show up in yet another diary for the Nazis to steal.

"Never have," I say. But I did, for many years. Before I found Day, and Blue, I was a phantom. Whenever I felt lost or betrayed or uncertain, I simply became someone else somewhere else. For my every character I kept a diary, to keep my lies from tripping me up. I'd assign my aliases their own pain and heartbreak, and I'd commit them to memory. Sometimes my thievery required I linger, make friends, gain trust, so I needed stories to tell. I couldn't bear to tell my own.

Zoé gestures me closer again. "What is Voss up to?" she says.

I whisper back: "He plans on running the perfume company himself. Eventually. He told me about the office he runs, a procurement office of sorts. He's the head of a bureau that takes everything it can get its hands on."

She returns to her reflection, and her lipstick. She sighs, but it's not her typical sigh of glamorous boredom. She's frustrated. "Not *everything* it can get its hands on," she says, sharp. She tosses the lipstick onto the vanity table. With quick flicks of her wrist, she tugs a few tissues from the box, then dabs away some of the excess red from her lips. "Haven't you figured it out? They're not robbing *all* of Paris. They're robbing the *Jews* of Paris."

Of course this is true. But the uncertainty of it all, of the Nazis' plots for Paris, can make it sometimes seem as if we're *all* about to lose everything we own. They've turned out the lights. They've taken the food from our mouths. How can any of us be sure we won't come home some night to find the locks changed? What happens when the Nazis rob all the banks, and we're left with only our little account booklets of numbers in columns?

But "Yes," I say to Zoé, because there's no uncertainty about the Nazis' sentiments when it comes to the Jews. And, really, it's not just the Nazis' sentiments. "I've been thinking lately about my life in Manhattan," I say as I rummage through my bag, looking for the right perfume for the night. "When I was starting out as a thief, the women of high society were my clients *and* my victims. I spun around in their circles when I could. And I saw it happening there too. They didn't allow Jews in their clubs, or their resorts. Or their colleges."

"Do you have any camellia perfume?" Zoé asks.

"I have some that I *call* camellia, at least," I say. I take her upturned wrist, and I dab some on. "The camellia flower itself has barely a whiff of scent." That's something else I remember about the rich women—they often sought the perfumes of flowers that didn't smell. I guess it seemed exclusive to wear something so ethereal. "So many of the rich families in America consider their wealth a kind of royal bloodline," I say. "They were entitled to their every dollar, to hear them tell it. The Jews were from somewhere else, taking business that should be theirs. It's a wonder they didn't start taking everything from the Jews back then. They would have thought robbing the Jews would just be an act of taking their money *back*." I help Zoé with the clasp of her charm bracelet. "It's a wonder that things didn't . . . escalate."

"Yes," she says, standing, going to her full-length mirror, pinching wrinkles from her gown. "Aren't we lucky." She rolls her eyes. "Over there, kicking the Jews around is still just sport." She takes a deep breath so she can sigh again. She studies her reflection. She cocks a hip, bends her wrist, practicing the postures of fatigue. "Lutz somehow arranged to have the stage filled with bouquets of white camellias for the show tonight."

"Have you ever come across perfume injections?" I ask. "Subcutaneous perfume? Was that anything your father ever sold? Was that all just a myth about Paris?"

"To perfume the blood?" she says. "How gruesome. Don't give Lutz any ideas." She holds her wrist to her nose, to smell the scent I put there. She says, wistful again, "Is the house the same as it always was?" She looks over at me with those little-girl eyes.

I say, "I've never been inside before now."

"You can see so much of my mother in it," she says.

I never knew her mother, but at the mention of her, I, too, can imagine her in the house. The tapestries and wallpapers, the sofas and chairs, are all in powder blues and rose pinks and sea greens, like dusty meringues in a pastry-shop window. Zoé grew up among antiques, probably tiptoeing across the Aubusson carpets woven with portraits of unicorns in fields of thistle. She sat in the walled-in rose garden behind the house hosting tea parties of her own, with dolls with human-hair pompadours and satin ball gowns, with felt mice in bow ties infesting her paper macarons and glass candy. Such a life.

Before I retired to Paris, I never had a house. I lived in hotels. I lived in women's dormitories, or men's dormitories, depending on the city I was in. I've rented cottages and beach cabanas. I've slept in desert tents. The few belongings I had I kept in a steamer trunk in a locker at a railroad station in Manhattan. But if my house were taken from me now, I'd feel lost at sea.

···· 27 ····

At Café Roche late that night, Day arrives still dressed for the cabaret, in a pearlescent gown. "Oyster," she says, and at first I think she means the pattern of circles hammered into the satin, but she's talking about the color.

"In the American issues of *Vogue*," Day says, "they compare everything to something to eat. Nothing's brown, it's 'yam.' Or 'candied yam.' Or 'honeyed' something or other. A dress hasn't had a leg-of-mutton sleeve in fifty years, but all of a sudden they're back."

"The Americans are flaunting their riches," Blue says. "That's what that is." He peeks into the paper bag Day dropped onto the table. She has brought us food again, this time a roasted bird as paltry as a parakeet.

I left the bordello before Zoé's big return to the stage, so I ask Day how it went. "Her voice broke and cracked a time or two," she says, "but everyone's always so in love with her." Day smiles *and* rolls her eyes, both jealous of Zoé and charmed by her.

I wait for her to sit before I get down to business. I say, "I need a doctor."

Day goes completely still in the middle of taking off her coat, one sleeve off, one sleeve on. "Right now?" she says. "What's wrong?"

"Oh no no no, not for me. Oskar Voss . . . well, he . . . I guess he . . . he must have . . . well, he *caught* something in Illiers, you see. I need a doctor who might . . . who might be *persuaded* to make a diagnosis that will keep him in bed a while longer." I can't bring myself to admit to drugging Voss. No one needs to know all my methods. "I thought maybe the brothel has a discreet doctor it uses . . . one who is perhaps somewhat disreputable . . . who might be paid to tell Voss to stay in bed. To drink tea. A doctor who might . . . *overlook* whatever might be really wrong."

Day and Blue exchange a glance. A look of concern, I suppose. And though their concern should trouble me, I'm pleased that *they* might worry about *me* some. Day says, "Any doctor curing whores of the clap has the most integrity of all. He's keeping Paris sexy, even if he might be mocked for haunting a cathouse."

"I suppose that's right," I say.

"I'll do it," Blue says. "I'll wear my tweed jacket." He runs his fingers through his thick curls. "You can cut my hair."

"*You* can't be a doctor," I say. "You look like a schoolboy." But an actor isn't a bad idea at all. And Blue has made it sound like the whole troupe of them have dipped their toes in espionage. "What about one of the other actors?" I say.

"Monsieur Rémy," Blue says without hesitation, with a gasp of awe and respect. His mind on covert activity, he leans back to show off the bicycle chain around his waist, strung through his belt loops, something he learned about from Félix. "I don't know how to use it yet, but the idea is you pull on it, give it a few quick twists"—he pantomimes all this for me—"and you bring the chain before yourself, wrapped around your fists, and you strangle a German when you get half the chance."

Paris's famous *souterrain,* its under-city of catacombs and railway lines, and its underground veins of limestone quarries, is crawling now with covert Americans, Blue says. "There are doorways in the theater basement that lead right into it all," he says. He makes it sound like there's a whole other war down below, among the rats and skeletons, playing out in the light of lanterns and coal miners' headlamps.

Blue says that Félix tells him the homosexuals are at the heart of the Resistance. "We've been driven out of our nightclubs," he says, "so we lurk in the shadows."

I've not seen Félix at our house since the night I walked in on them together in the shop, but the boy is clearly much in Blue's thoughts. I want to issue a warning, but I don't know how to word it. I know Blue so well, and I know the twists in his romantic imagination. If I tell him that Félix is too dangerous, he'll just be all the more drawn to him.

"Eat," Day says to Blue, nodding toward the bird. "And don't let anyone see that chain around your waist. You're less apt to choke anybody with it than you are to *get* choked by it."

I'm glad she's being motherly so I don't have to. He might listen to Day but will think me a scold. And a hypocrite. I should never have spent all these years telling him my own stories of crime. He's far too tender for such a life, especially with so many enemies in our midst.

When I'm with Zoé, I'm ready to take on the Germans barefisted. But when I'm with Day and Blue, I fantasize about all the ways I could sneak them away, and maybe go with them. I don't know anymore what's bravery and what's cowardice. Maybe my brain has finally gone scrambled from all my shifting identities over the years.

But as I poison Voss's tea, I could be poisoning my own as well. If I'm caught, we're all caught.

"You need to eat too," I tell Day. "You're wasting away to nothing."

"Am I?" she says, smiling, kittenish, straightening up in her hammered satin.

"Eat," Blue says.

"I don't want to spoil my appetite for all the fine food we'll eat when the war is over." With that, she glances upward and begins to reminisce. "Ah, the ortolans, before the war," she says, speaking of the teeny-tiny birds served on paper doilies. "I'd sometimes order them if I was at the right place. I knew a chef who had them delivered alive in a cage, and he'd suffocate them himself by sticking their heads in brandy."

"Ghastly," I say. "I'd rather starve."

Day taunts me. She says, "Oh no, it's delicious. It's so delicate, you can taste its fear. You can even taste the fatal brandy that choked it."

"You're wicked," I tell Day, and she smacks her lips, blowing me a kiss.

"This isn't that kind of bird," Blue says. "This handsome fella died for his country, a hero. Feeding the hungry. Maybe I should eat him standing up, in salute."

"And besides, I'm *not* wasting away," Day says. "I still need to drop a size to fit into a new dress I spent too much on. A velvet dress. A red one. *Candy-apple* red, I guess you'd say."

"Kidney pie red," Blue says.

"Medium-rare filet mignon red," I say.

"Roasted wild boar red," Day says.

We go on for a beat or two more: *venison bourguignon red, ratatouille red*. Blue wields the little bird's drumstick like he's Henry VIII with a peacock leg.

28

The concierge knows me well already, though she's let me in and out only a time or two. And she never looks up, so she can't know my face. Her back's too bad. She recognizes the rhythm of my footsteps, though. She tells me I have an uneven step. My right foot falls lighter than my left. "I can even see it in the wear of your shoe," she says.

I suppose if you go through life doubled over, you learn your way around by the cracks in the sidewalk. I've long known I have one leg slightly longer than the other. But I've somehow never noticed the wear of my shoe. This worn-down heel seems like something that could have got me caught years ago, if there'd ever been an expert detective on my case. I wonder how many other telltale signs I've signaled without knowing. Every day of my old age, I learn I've been luckier than I've realized. I've been more visible than I thought.

I've brought along Monsieur Rémy from Blue's theater, an actor who has played Iago, Claudius, Caliban, all of Shakespeare's villains. But he brings to *this* stage a bedside manner and a stern finality to his diagnosis. "Get some rest. Drink some tea," he tells Voss, while packing up his stethoscope. "This flu that's going around won't give up. It holds on tight. And it'll get worse before it gets better. I've seen a hundred cases of it. But you'll be on the other side of it soon enough."

Voss isn't in bed; we're in a shabby room I hadn't discovered in my meandering. He sits on the house's most battered sofa, a threadbare camelback with flattened cushions. The velvet, a shade of dusty peach fuzz, has been worn to a sheen.

This room, where all the furniture went when it fell into decline—

the chairs and settees with broken springs that poke, a chifforobe with drawers that won't close, a lamp with a shade of stained-glass roses, its petals chipped—*this* was the room Pascal liked best, according to a magazine article Voss read. Leaning against the walls are paintings and prints that once hung elsewhere. Weevil-eaten books with brittle bindings are stacked here and there. On one patch of wall not only is the wallpaper peeled away, but the plaster's gone too, exposing pink bricks.

Despite the lab with cabinets full of bottles and vials, and shelves full of books, and sinks with running water, Voss imagines that it was here, in this humble space, that Pascal liked to contemplate his art. "He must have enjoyed the room for its light, and because its windows looked out over the Luxembourg Gardens," he tells me.

I'm inclined to believe it. A wicker basket full of origami sits in one corner. Zoé told me that whenever her father was stumped by a scent he couldn't quite capture, he folded paper cranes, bats, swans. Or he cut out paper dolls and made little dresses for them with soap wrappers. Or he'd shuffle around a deck of cards, creating a complicated game. Games, puzzles, folding, cutting, they all sent his mind clicking along. The scents and synthetics for his perfumes would occur to him, all adding up, as he fiddled with something else, as he played music, as he smoked a cigar.

I see the doctor out and fix some tea. I return to the upstairs room and set the tray on the low table before Voss's sofa. I sit in the chair across from him. I lean forward and push his cup and saucer toward him.

He leans forward to push the cup and saucer back.

"I'm sick of your teas," he says. He squints with a twinge of pain.

The pockets under Voss's eyes are growing more plump and more gray. His pallor is pale yellow. He works his jaw around, his tongue clicking with a dry smack. He's unpresentable.

I lean forward again. I push the saucer forth with my fingertip. "The doctor said you must," I say.

I could never kill anyone, no matter what my dossiers might say. I know I couldn't. I'm *not* a murderer, but we are at war. And if Voss died, would anyone know? Has anybody else but me been around?

I fantasize. If he were out of the way, could I linger on, live as Voss, find the diary, rescue Pascal's perfumes? I sign Voss's name better than he does. I could come and go in his oxfords, with their heavy heels, and the concierge, with her eyes always to the floor, wouldn't flinch. I'd just be sure to walk without favoring one step over the other, since she seems to know my uneven missteps so well.

Voss finally picks up his teacup, and he glances down into it. "Proust writes about those little slips of Japanese paper you drop in a bowl of water or cup of tea," he says. "They unfold, open, bloom . . . into flowers or birds. Or houses. Have you ever seen such a thing?" I shake my head. Then, out of nowhere, he says, "Proust's mother was Jewish." He offers this with a lilt in his voice, as if to defend himself. "And so is Monsieur Pascal, of course."

"Where *is* Pascal, anyway?" I say. I've been too worried to ask. I haven't wanted to seem too invested in the answer.

He says nothing. He puts the tea down and picks up a basket from near his feet on the floor. He overturns it atop the coffee table between us. Bottles of Pascal's perfumes spill out. He says, "You've probably been asked, in your shop, by a lady or two to copy Pascal's perfumes. And sell it to them at half the price. Hm?"

"Yes, I've been asked," I say. "I *can* do it, but I don't. I have some pride." He raises an eyebrow at me. "Sometimes I will copy a perfume that isn't made anymore. For old ladies, mostly." I add, giving my voice a sting of bitterness, "And I'll happily copy the perfumes *I* invented for Pascal. Because that's not really copying Pascal, is it. If I invented it?"

I've already told him I worked with Pascal on three scents: Escroquerie, of course, but also Bien Adoré (wild plum, sweet willow, curdled sugar), and Envoûté (fire, white thyme, dark loam). Though I had nothing to do with them, they are my very favorites of his, and the most defining of his genius, so I'm happy to steal the credit.

None of these on the table are any of those perfumes. I'm to hold each bottle beneath my nose and recite what's in it. Or what I think is in it. I toss in a few things that aren't, just to keep the recipes out of reach. *Ylang-ylang, cicely,* I say. Voss writes it all down in a stenographer's pad.

"I can't take another sniff," he says, though he hasn't put a nostril to any of it. He's been sitting upright, but he now slouches down, the back of his head against the back of the sofa. When he opens his eyes again, he looks over to the side, lifts his chin, gesturing toward the wall.

"What do you think of *that*?" he says. I twist around to look; on the floor, leaning against the wall, are paintings, some with frames, some without. He seems to be asking me about the famous one, of two women from the waist up, naked, their skin milk white.

One of the women pinches the nipple of the other.

"The women are taking a bath," he says. "Together. Why do you think that is? To save bathwater?"

I turn back around to face him; he's smiling at me, amused by his joke. "Yes, I suppose it's only a matter of bathwater," I say, smiling too. "But I don't know anything about the painting. I know it only from Gabrielle." Though it's a woman's name, Gabrielle is a fragrance Pascal designed to be worn by men. The image of this painting adorns the box. The bottle, clear glass, is in the shape of an armless torso, resembling the woman whose nipple gets pinched.

Her frosted-glass head is the bottle's lid, the stopper. To apply the scent, the gentleman beheads the lady and daubs her severed neck at his jugular.

"When I first saw the painting here," he says, "I actually wondered if it might be the original. Certainly Pascal's rich enough to own such a thing. But no. The original's owned by the Louvre. And the back of this one has a stamp. It's a registered copy, by the students who set up their easels in the museum."

"It's a very good copy," I say.

After a moment, Voss says, "Do *you* . . . wear Gabrielle?" He raises an eyebrow.

Even sick, he's being sly. I know what he's getting at. Ever since the scent first appeared in shops, in that box with the tweaked nipple, it's been a secret message whispered among the lesbian women of Paris. And eventually the lesbian women of America too. And elsewhere in the world. If you're out and about, and you smell this gentlemen's scent on a lady, you know that lady is a ladies' lady.

And if you fancy a lady who *isn't* wearing the scent but you hope she's the type who *would*, you simply lean in toward her neck and say, "Is that Gabrielle you're wearing?" If it isn't, and she *is*, she'll say yes.

All of this code, which was never Pascal's intention as far as I know, was revolutionary in my little world. Suddenly, we could all hide in plain sight.

That is, until we were all found out. By the mid 1930s, it had become a euphemism used against us. *Ohhh, she wears Gabrielle*, people will say with a sneer, when they can't bear to wrap their tongue around any other words for it.

"You're not answering me," Voss says. "I asked you if you wear Gabrielle. It's a simple question."

"That's not a question a gentleman asks a lady," I say. "And if a gentleman does ask, a lady doesn't answer." I take a sip of my own untainted tea. "And it's *not* a 'simple question.' "

"That's all the answer I need," he says.

My heartbeat picks up. I try to swallow, but my throat's gone dry.

Voss leans forward to pick up the cup. It's a relief to see him drinking the tea. He trusts me after all, it seems. "I simply want to know," he says. "That's all. I mean no harm. I'm your *friend*, Charlie. You should know that by now." He takes another sip. "And I'm drinking your tea, like you asked." He returns the cup to the saucer, and the saucer to the table. "And we're not so unalike, you and me."

"Oh?" I say.

"You can't see it in my face now, perhaps," he says, "but when I was young, I was as pretty as Lutz is. Prettier. When I was a boy, people mistook me for a girl. Long eyelashes. Soft eyes. Gentle voice. I was teased, but I'm grateful for the taunts. Gave me my fighting spirit."

His voice weakens to a squeak when he says *fighting spirit.* And I feel my confidence spike again. He sees in me a kinship. I suspect he's never told anyone of growing up girlish.

I can settle in.

"We should get back to the perfumes," I say, and I reach for the next bottle.

But Voss takes from the pocket of his smoking jacket a bottle of Gabrielle. He hands it across to me. I know he's got his eyes on me, so I'm careful in how I handle it. I don't want to give him any reason to mock me further, so I'm mindful not to even rub my thumb over the bottle's breasts.

I open the bottle and hold the head-shaped stopper to my nose. The bottle is clear, but the liquid is green, to suggest absinthe, Paris's most beloved and most outlawed addiction. In the perfume, I smell myrtle pepper, black currant, burnt coffee, with only an afterthought of something floral: linden and peony.

"And a hint of poison," Voss says.

My throat closes again, and I can't swallow. Has *he* poisoned *my* tea? But then he takes another sip of the tea I served him.

He says, pleased with himself, "The woman in the painting behind you. Gabrielle d'Estrées. She was poisoned."

I return Gabrielle's head to her body. I hold the bottle in my open palm, and I study the cold serenity in her glass face.

He says, "And here's where it gets interesting," and I pray, *Please, God, don't let it get interesting.* "Some say she was poisoned by perfume." Voss sits up straighter. He's newly invigorated, some pink spotting his cheeks. He holds out his hand, wiggles his fingers, wanting the bottle back. I pass it over. He removes the stopper and puts it to his nose. He dabs the stopper to the skin of his wrist. "Gabrielle was to marry the king of France. In 1599, or some such. But instead of marrying the king, she died a horrible, violent death. On the very night before her wedding, no less. That chalk-white skin in the painting? It went black and blue in an instant. Like thunderclouds rolling through. They say she was poisoned by a wedding gift. A pair of perfumed gloves. The perfume was poison, and it seeped into her skin when she tried the gloves on."

"Seems unlikely," I say.

"How so?"

"Why would she open her gifts *before* the wedding?" I say.

"That's what you think this story is about, Nebraska Charlie?" he says with a pitying tilt of his head. "A breach of etiquette?"

"Who poisoned her, then?"

"Actually, now," he says, *"that . . . that* is where the story gets interesting. Our king could not marry our dear Gabrielle, of course, because she was dead, so he married a Medici. Did the Medicis, the world's great poisoners, commission the poisonous perfume to begin with? Of course they did. And, now, wait, wait, *here's* where the story gets interesting, actually: the perfume was created by Pascal's ancestors. His family is a family of perfumers that goes back generations. They had royal decrees; they bottled perfumes for monarchs. They had access to rare materials." When I say nothing, he says, in a lower tone, "I know what you're thinking."

Does he? I won't suggest that it's all a myth, that the fragrances of the Parfumerie Chamberry began in a barbershop less than a century ago, that all the perfume houses of Paris have fictional histories that work them into the warp and weave of kingdoms and queendoms.

"You're thinking it's an extravagant theory," he says. "You think it's precious. But Pascal must have had it in mind when he created Gabrielle. And if it *isn't* fiction, and Pascal's family actually was involved, what if there are clues in the perfume? Clues to the past?"

Certainly some of Pascal's perfumes delighted in riddles and something called a *calembour,* a French pun. My French is too feeble to fully appreciate them all, but his very simplest is his perfume Allô, a play on *à l'eau,* at the water, a scent that suggests mist and linens in a seaside hotel.

"What do you want from it?" I say. Is he striving for a specific connection between perfume and power, something to prove? Hitler may not be moved by perfume, but poison will touch his very soul.

Voss holds his wrist to his nose, and he grimaces, the scent of Gabrielle overwhelming him, dropping him back into his slouch. He falls into a funk. He lets out a heavy sigh. "I'm just asking for a minute of your imagination, Charlie," he says. He sighs again. "Anyway, it's more likely it was her unborn child who murdered her. Gabrielle was pregnant. It went wrong." He adds, "And they're sisters."

"Who?"

He nods again toward the painting. *"Gabrielle d'Estrées et une de ses soeurs.* That's what they call the painting. They're sisters, not lovers. So Gabrielle . . . she doesn't likely *wear* Gabrielle, if you know what I mean."

"I do know what you mean," I say.

He pushes himself up from the sofa, his hand at his stomach. "Enough of that," he says, with a groan of disappointment. "I'm going to do a few hours of work at my desk." He cringes again with a jolt of pain. He holds up one finger, signaling for me to wait for it to pass. We wait.

I put my own teacup aside. "I'll help you to your office," I say.

"No, I'll be fine," he says, but he nonetheless takes my arm as we leave the room. I lead the way down the stairs, and he puts one hand on my shoulder.

After I've left him in his office, I turn, then turn again, and I walk right up to a reflection of myself, in a mirror in a gold frame. I notice I need a haircut. My hair is standing on end in places, from the gusts of wet wind, I guess. I lick my fingertips and attempt to pat it down. *My sweet farm girl. I love all your cowlicks and rooster tails,* M told me as I sat up naked in bed on what was most certainly a Sunday morning, the sunlight filling the room and stirring the dust.

I lift my chin. Tug on my necktie, tightening the knot. I smooth out the wrinkles of my shirt. I was never a pretty girl, but when I set my square chin just so, with my lips at half a smirk, I'm not a bad-looking chap. And other than those years that my mother stitched ugly frills onto my secondhand overalls, I've always had a handsome wardrobe. I've never been without the town's best tailor, whatever town I happened to be in. A glance in a mirror almost always ups my confidence.

I walk to the stairs holding Voss's bottle of Gabrielle that I picked from his pocket. He won't suspect me. He's in too much of a dither. I run my thumb over Gabrielle's smooth breasts as I tip the bottle to dampen the dauber. I pluck off her head and touch the dauber to the back of each ear. I touch it to my wrists and to my neck, filling the air with the scent of my theft.

29

Zoé has her own dressing room backstage at the cabaret, and I can't quite find her among the bouquets and baskets of camellias.

The socialites of Manhattan I knew long ago had read French novels in which women killed themselves through floral asphyxiation, by filling a room with lilies and gardenia, shutting the door, and stuffing the keyhole with a handkerchief. My clients longed for someone to bottle such a delicious death.

I find my way through the flowers to Zoé at her vanity. Day's here too, sitting on the vanity top, legs crossed, leaning back against the mirror.

Neither says hello. They both seem morose. Zoé is even touching a hankie to her eyes, like she's wiping away mascara after a crying jag.

So I'm even more eager to please, I suppose, and to report some progress. "The painting of Gabrielle d'Estrées," I say. "How did your father come to have that?"

"You've been up in his room," Zoé says. Her voice is even more feeble and scratched than it was yesterday. But maybe she's just wrestling with a bout of hay fever. She's even decked out in camellias herself now, with corsages pinned across the bust of her white gown, and more flowers flouncing down the length of it. The virgin bride of the brothel.

"I'm getting to know the house, yes," I say.

She shrugs. "I don't know where the painting came from," she says.

"And the perfume," I say. "Gabrielle?"

This perks them both up. Zoé looks up and over to Day, to smirk, to give her a wink. "I know nothing about *that*," she says. "Do *you* wear Gabrielle, Day, darling?" She drums her fingers on Day's knee.

Day winks back at her. She says, "Well, I don't wear Gabrielle myself. Not regularly, anyway. Known lots of girls who have. How about you, Clementine?"

I play along. "I knew the girls who wore Gabrielle even before there was any Gabrielle to wear."

I take the bottle from my pocket. Off with her head. I breathe in the perfume. The scent takes me back to the lives we led, in the years just after the War Before, when you could pitch a revolution by dancing with too much leg. We were the degenerates of the twenties. We didn't take to the underground to resist; we took to the streets, and even to the movie screens, in silver, where girly men kohled their eyes and fluttered their lashes. Sure, we got our own black eye or two, but we refused to believe we were building the scaffolding toward our hangman's noose. We were looking back at our war dead and remembering to live life. Their brave souls possessed us.

Now we creep and whisper. Every risk seems either too weak or too fatal.

I tell Zoé about Voss's giddiness over the Medicis, his speculations about her family's ancestors, and the perfumed gloves. I tell her his theories about how the Parfumerie Chamberry found its path to success: political assassination. I'm a little giddy about it myself, but I only manage to drop Zoé back into her foul mood.

"Don't be ridiculous," she snaps. "All that poison and greed. He's just shylocking."

I didn't expect her to take offense, though I see now why she might. *Shylocking.* I've never heard the expression before, and I'm not sure I've heard her right. But it makes sense. Shylock, Shakespeare's Jewish villain. Yes, perhaps Voss wants to believe the perfumery got to where it did by taking pounds of flesh along the way. Oh, the *corruption of Jews.*

I certainly won't defend Voss, but I do think he's at least somewhat moved by the romance of the intrigue, and by this tantalizing key to

French history. And it all draws me closer to the diary, though I won't defend that either, these instincts of mine. I can't always convince people of my sixth sense. When you have a special talent, you like to think it's God-given, some bit of magic that can't be taught. You have an ear for it. A tingling in your bones. I've certainly boasted of my instincts to Blue over the years. You can learn the tricks of a cardsharp, but a con game calls for a bedevilment you need to be born into.

Like my little birth defect—the crooked hip that gives me that uneven step. All these years, I've been walking through rooms with one shoe lifted slightly off the floor.

Zoé begins to weep. The sobs come upon her with a sudden shiver that works up her spine. She lowers her head, puts her hands gently to the flowers at her chest. At first I wonder if this talk of Shakespeare has reminded her of Ophelia, the perfume her father bottled for her, his apology. Maybe she's feeling sentimental, or afraid, maybe thinking again of what will happen if her father's diary tells everything about her.

Day puts her hand on Zoé's shoulder. "We've been crying most of the day," Day says to me. She then tells me a few of the girls have gone missing from the bordello. Girls who were Jewish, who thought they were keeping it secret.

"Which girls?" I say.

"Charlotte," she says. "Pauline."

I can't quite picture them, but I know the names.

When I start to say something, I realize I've clenched my teeth. I open my mouth, and my jaw trembles. If I speak, my voice will tremble too.

I thought that Boulette, in all her dastardly conspiring, was at least keeping her girls safe.

Sometimes when you're cornered, when you feel your most defeated, is when you're at your most invincible. You're angry. You're suddenly able to see around corners and to peer into the dark. I've weaseled out of many impossible predicaments when heady with an adrenaline rush.

I can't let anything happen to Day, or to Zoé, or to Blue. That bicycle chain around Blue's waist makes him seem even more delicate. But maybe I *can* teach him instinct. At the very least, he can practice my steps.

I will beat Voss at whatever game we're playing.

Though I don't quite recall the girls who've gone missing from Boulette's, I do know them by the scents I made. For Charlotte, apple and chamomile. For Pauline, pear and almond.

···· 30 ····

When I first met M at the Brothers of the Sisterhood meeting, he sidled up to me at a sideboard. He took a cigar from a box, among plates of glazed apricots, gingerbread, candied pecans. He had a cutter in his pocket shaped like a woman's legs in mother-of-pearl bloomers—he put the tip of the cigar in the blades between the knees and squeezed them together.

"Let's skedaddle," he whispered in my ear, chomping on the end of the unlit cigar. "Snip-snap."

He gave me his arm, and I took it.

M was very boyish with his long-legged strut. I suspected his trousers were purposefully cuffed an inch or two too high to show off a pair of dazzling socks—they were a lumpy lamb's wool dyed tomato red, woven with strings of tinsel, to give them snippets of flash.

"So tell me who you are," he said once we were outside in the cold autumn air. "What do you do with your time, when you're not on my arm? How do you while away your days without me?"

"I write poetry," I said.

"Is that so?" he said, a lilt in his voice, as if I'd said I tatted lace or played whist.

"Well, no, not really. I write down the poems that someone else recites. I'm a poet's secretary." I waited, and I said, "What do *you* do?"

"I drink tea," he said.

"That's not work," I said.

"It absolutely is," he said. "I'm a tea inspector. A taster. To assure quality. To prevent deceptive leaves from blowing into the country." He stopped for a moment to touch a match to the tip of the cigar at his lips, huffing and puffing at it to get the fat end of it smoking.

"I would think cigars would be bad for a tea-taster's taste buds," I said.

"Yes, you might think that, but you'd be wrong," M said. "Good tobacco stimulates and refines the tongue." He gave me a wink, then led me around a corner and into Washington Square Park.

"I'm picturing you in your office in a white linen suit," I said. "With your best china. A peppermint-striped tablecloth."

"No, no, no, it's all too dreary," he said. "A dim, damp room near the docks, much sipping and spitting. The oldest of us are jittery and peaked." M explained that to reject a foreign tea tainted with lead and wormwood, or with Venetian red, French chalk, Prussian blue, the taster had to taste it first. Even if you only dipped your tongue in, the poison took its toll. "I'm doomed," he said.

Then he said, "They say that this blue haze you see in the streetlight"—the smoke lifting from his lips, mixing with the frost of our breath—"is the spirits of the dead that got rustled up. This used to be a graveyard."

I memorized everything along the way. The cinnamon-pepper smell of dry leaves still barely on their branches. Apples freshly pressed for cider. The glow of a church's illuminated cross.

The south side of the park was lined with tenements and cafés, while just across the way were the grand manses of old families. There seemed to be a party winding down on the rich side, the end of a wedding, a crowd of men in black coats and women in puffed sleeves spilling from a house on the corner, and a line of carriages, cabs, trotting up to the door to carry them off.

"We're in luck," M said, his words tumbling forward again. "We need a ride to the Bowery. I'm too feeble to walk. Poor me, I've got bones in my legs." He looked at me, then took his cigar from his lips and put it to mine. "You need this for your costume. You're going to get us arrested, in that man's suit, with those beautiful eyes and those beautiful lips." But M was being playful. He tugged down on the brim of my hat. "No one can trust a man that pretty."

We wove in and through and about the elegant crowd, M shaking men's hands with a firm grip, tipping his hat at ladies, pretending to know everyone. As a tipsy old couple was about to step up to the next carriage in line, M tugged the wife into a waltz and spun her dizzy as the husband wheezed with laughter. ("A girl with a cigar!" the old man said, laughing in my face, before taking the cigar and smoking it himself.) Finally, M dropped the wife into the husband's arms and insisted they finish the dance themselves. We then leapt into the carriage. M barked out to the driver the cross streets, and the horses capered off.

"They're all smashed on fizz," M said, and he took from his coat a half-empty bottle of champagne he'd somehow lifted in the hullabaloo. He took a swig from the bottle, and I took one too.

And then he kissed me.

···· 31 ····

The Bowery, at that late hour, was a particularly wicked neck of the woods. We elbowed our way into the music hall, and up a rickety set of steps to stand in the upper gallery, to look down at Thistle Bishop, billed as a "female impersonator" who was "pretty enough to kiss."

That may have been so at one time, but Thistle had had a long career of farewell performances, milking his retirement well into old age. He once-upon-a-time sang with a warbling falsetto, M told me, but his voice was now coarse and husky.

But before we even saw a single hair of Thistle's wig, a buxom woman in a tuxedo and top hat took the stage to rattle off an introduction. *Ladieeeeeeees and gentlemen,* she sang out.

M leaned his shoulder into mine. He put his lips to my ear. "Which are you?" he said.

"Which *what* am I?" I said, *my* lips at *his* ear.

"Lady? Or gentleman?"

I paused in thought, but I wasn't thinking about what the answer was so much as what the answer should be. What would M want to hear?

I put my fingers on M's chin, and my mouth to his ear again. "Lady," I said.

He pointed his thumb at his own chest, and he said in my ear, "Gentleman." He then kissed my ear, and my cheek, and my neck.

In between some of the bawdiest bawdy-house hymns I'd ever heard, Thistle made about twenty costume changes behind a curtain, in and out of dramatic opera gowns of velvet and satin and crepe, fringed with ostrich feathers and chinchilla and lace quilling.

At the end of the show, he lectured on dress reform for women, discussing the treachery of corsets and bustles, defining the weight and restriction of women's clothes as a masculine tyranny. His speech was impassioned, and convincing, but it nonetheless stirred up giggles. As he spoke, he began undoing fasts and buttons, until he stood only in corset and petticoat. His last gesture was to pull off his wig with a defiant and victorious yank, to boisterous applause. Everyone was shocked, though the shock was what they'd come for.

Outside the theater door, a small boy in a cap sold paper boutonnieres. M bought one for a coin. He put his hand to my breast pocket to pin it on, and he concentrated, his brow furrowed. His eyelashes were thick and dark, and I wanted to feel them blinking against my cheek.

But when he finished with the pinning, M turned away, to step into the street. He waved at an approaching cab, a fairy-tale surrey drawn forward without a single horse. The driver stood at the back of it, perched, watching over the cab's canopy, but with no whip in hand, no reins. A phantom carriage. A magic carpet.

"Electric," M said. The electric cab company wasn't even yet licensed, and it had only begun to usher its battery-powered surreys and hansoms into the streets, one by one, with their low hum, a *bzz-bzz-bzz*. I'd heard rumors of people seeing the cabs, or even catching a ride, but they were mostly a wonder. I somehow wasn't surprised M could summon one from the night. Eventually I would think of M as part of the city's machinery, one of its very engineers. He was so in time with its ticking that I suspected he had never followed a map; I imagined Manhattan's map most likely followed *his* paths and ramblings.

M took my hand and helped me up into the cab's seat, and I sat back, like in a rickshaw, nothing before me but a footboard. M kept hold of my hand and asked for my address, then called it up to the driver. As the driver eased away, M walked alongside. "I'll write you a letter," he said, "now that I know where you live."

"Will you remember?" I said.

M began to compose a catchy song on the spot, my address the only lyrics. "I'll sing it all the way home," he said.

He stepped up his pace. His fingers unlinked from mine only after the cab sped up.

I had time to settle into a swoon, and to marvel at the night, and to watch the stars overhead get jostled with every crack and bump we hit in the road. M's song caught in my head, and I sang it too. I put a blanket across my knees as the night got colder. I held the paper flower to my nose, and I could swear it blossomed with the scent of M's burnt tobacco and warm whiskey breath. I licked my lips and still tasted his kiss—sweet from the sugared tip of his cigar.

I also had his ring on my finger, a gold snake coiling around four times, little rubies for eyes. I'd slipped it from his hand as the cab pulled away. I did not steal it. I only borrowed it for the night.

···· 32 ····

I tug the coiled snake from my ring finger, my knuckle swollen, my skin baggy on the bone. I'm in the kitchen alone. I place the snake next to Oskar Voss's china cup—*plink*—on the saucer, and I fill the cup with untainted tea. I've been easing him off the poison again, so that I can give him more later.

It's been a few days since he spoke of his interest in Gabrielle. I've quickly grown impatient and weary. But telling him about M has been an unexpected tonic. For him and for me. Instead of dreading it as I did when he first asked for stories from my past, I've come to appreciate their effect on him. When I'm talking, Voss is in *my* dominion.

I carry the tea set from the kitchen to the room upstairs, the spoons clattering, my hands shaking from the weight of the tray. I keep stepping on the backs of my trouser cuffs; my pants are sagging and loose. I wear a bulky old sweater the color of smoke, and I've pulled the sleeves up over my hands because of the terrible cold. The Paris winter has gotten so bitter, it's even biting the Germans in the homes they stole.

I'm afraid for Voss to get better, but I'm afraid for him to stay ill. I've gone back and forth on this. One day I'll dose him just a drop or two, to steal just an hour or an evening from him, and the next I'm convinced unless he's well, he's of no use at all. The poison has made him comfortable. He's quite at peace here at Pascal's house. And though I want to steal the house out from under him, I don't want the Nazis to take it from him first.

I set the tray on the table before him. "We deserve a drop of sun, don't we?" I say. I walk to the window.

The heavy velvet drapes have been kept closed every day, to smother the drafts. They're so thick, like carpets, that I have to put some shoulder in to part them. And there, hanging over the window, is a screen of tatty—a curtain of blinds woven of vetiver grass. In the summer, it soaks up the heat. Your maid sprinkles it with water to release a sweet musk, the cool, thick scent of freshly turned soil.

I open the tatty, and I press my forehead against the cold windowpane. I have a knock of pain in the back of my head, a headache settling into my skull. Maybe *I'm* the one getting poisoned this go-round.

Last night I dreamed of butterflies, their flapping wings as loud as a sheet whipping on a clothesline. I could feel them caught in my hair and tiptoeing across my cheeks, and my neck, and the backs of my hands. It seemed they might try to lift me with their sticky, spindly legs. I could smell their perfume, a scent of sea salt and gardenia.

"Look at that," Voss says. "It's even more handsome than I pictured it."

I turn to see Voss attempting to put the snake ring on his ring finger. He can't get it past the middle knuckle, so he moves it to his pinkie. He holds up his hand to admire it.

"You've kept it all these years," he says. He twists it around and around. "It's priceless."

Yesterday I made the mistake of telling Voss I still have the ring. So today, I had to bring it to show him. *It will take my breath away,* he insisted.

"Yes," I say as I step over to sit in my chair.

"And M never knew that you stole it?"

"He knew," I say. "After I told him."

In Manhattan back then, letters arrived at your door five or six times a day, and the mailbox on your street corner was emptied twice as often as that. The city was in the process of building underground pneumatic tubes to send letters hurtling with a proper gust, so that a note sent from downtown could reach its uptown recipient within the hour. Everyone wanted every word every minute. A love affair by letter could intensify in a week. M's first letter arrived at the Widow

Waverley's the very next noon. It was unsigned, but the red wax seal of the envelope had been stamped with a simple, unadorned *M.*

I remembered your address, M wrote. And that was all.

In my response, I confessed my theft. I told him he'd have to invite me out again to get the ring back. In his next letter, M suggested I not give it back, that I wear it when we met, and he'd steal it himself when I least expected it. *And we'll just have to keep meeting, until it's on my finger again.*

Voss says, "Oh, let's do that too. I like that. You can have the ring back if you steal it back."

My head begins to pound again. I say, "I'm not a thief. Anymore."

"You stole my bottle of Gabrielle."

"I just did it for fun," I say. "To see if you'd notice." Indeed, I've even worn the fragrance every day since. I hold my wrist to my nose now. I can almost get lost in my own fictions—the perfume so reminds me of M, with its sulfur-sting of a struck match, its hint of bitter plum, that I wonder if somehow Pascal stole this one from me too.

"I didn't notice it stolen," he says. "I just noticed it gone. And I just now tricked you into confessing."

"I *had* to take it," I say. "Your bottle is the only bottle in town. There's not a drop of it to be had anywhere in Paris."

"Ah, *that* you noticed," he says, nodding, impressed.

"Yes," I say. "I know all the ladies around here who wear Gabrielle. And none of them can find any Gabrielle to wear." I only know this from Blue, who knows it from the theater. There's already so much anxiety, with the homosexual camp in Alsace and the closing of the nightclubs, that something like the sudden disappearance of a notoriously lesbian perfume is as ominous as it is puzzling.

"I can't wait until I first notice it's gone," he says. At first I'm confused, then he begins to twist twist twist the snake ring around and around his finger. "I wonder how long it will take me to realize you took it. Or maybe I'll catch you in the act."

"You'll catch me," I say. "You certainly will. I have no knack for such things these days."

Voss examines the ring again. He says, "M had small hands. The hands of a lady." He pauses, looking at me. "Were you ever genuinely fooled, at any point at all?"

"Fooled?"

"You never really believed M was a man, did you?"

"M was a gentleman, always," I say.

"Scandalous," Voss says, with a sigh that sounds like boredom. "You were never naked with your lover?"

I won't dignify that with an answer, but the question brings me back to that music hall in the Bowery, in Thistle Bishop's sprawling dressing room, full of gowns on dressmaker's mannequins, and hats in cabinets, and a wall of wigs on faceless burlap heads. Thistle had many admirers and received gifts of many kinds. There were vases of roses and orchids and tulips. A sideboard of bottles of champagne and brandy, and pastries under glass. Thistle loaned M the room for an evening.

Everywhere were silk hearts dangling from ribbons, little sachets of dried fennel, to disgust the moths. But it didn't seem to work—when M raised the wick on the kerosene lamp to light the room, the shadows of moths rushed and sputtered.

In thinking of it all now, I see the insignia I seek, the symbol from Pascal's note to his daughter Zoé, in patterns on velvet. I see it everywhere it most certainly never was, in Thistle's every gown. I see it in the fretwork of lace, and the filigree of a sleeve, and the embroidery of a boot. And then all those designs begin to twist into swastikas, everywhere, on silk, in metallic stitches, in the icing of a cake.

I close my eyes tight.

M undressed me, uncuffing my cuffs, unlinking my links, unknotting my necktie, unclipping my wingtip collar. Unbuttoning my suspenders and the fly of my trousers, unlacing my boots. He stayed entirely dressed himself, keeping on even his topcoat and waistcoat and derby, while my naked skin goose-pimpled in the ice cold of the music hall attic. M removed my socks, first one, then the other, rolling the silk down my ankle, over my heel, and off my foot. Then he delicately draped my suit and underthings over a wooden valet stand.

M carried from Thistle's wardrobe a dress of satin, its color shifting with the angle of lamplight, fluttering between a faded rose and a silver gray. He held it in his arms as if it were a lady who'd fainted.

M seemed a master of the costume's busks and lugs and elastic cords, the shanks and rivets, spring clamps and screw buttons and clinches. And I enjoyed watching him fuss over and around me, his tongue at his lips as he strung me up with ribbons and laces. He shifted me around, situating me correctly within the gown and its trappings, taking my hips, my breasts, my waist in his hands. I let him lead me, like in a waltz.

And no sooner had he dressed me than he began to undo all he had done. He took no time to gaze. He didn't hold me up to a mirror. Instead, he unlaced, unbuttoned, unhooked. It was clear that he had only dressed me to undress me. Once I was naked again, I touched the buttons of his shirt, but he took my hands, kissed my wrists, shook his head. He ran his kisses along my breasts, down my stomach, across my naked hip. He lowered me to Thistle's fainting sofa. He gently pushed my knees apart and kissed the inside of my thigh.

I tell Voss none of this.

···· 33 ····

I coerce Voss into getting out and about. I insist we go to the cabaret. I'll even wear a dress, I tell him. And by the time I get back to my shop, a dress has been delivered. Blue holds it up; the gown is likely a wink toward the weather—floor-length white silk patterned with penguins. A long white coat has arrived with a note pinned to its lapel, dictated by Voss to the shopgirl. Hearing his thin voice in the girl's jumpy cursive is peculiar. *Does your heart bleed for the cashmere goats too?* it asks me. *Please don't worry. They have a pastoral life, and their hair just falls off in handfuls.*

Voss has also sent a wig, pinned to a faceless burlap head. I'm to have platinum curls that practically shimmer like tinsel.

In the evening, Blue brings out his toolbox of theatrical cosmetics, his brushes and pencils, and he paints a face on me as I sit on the settee in the shop, my hands folded in my lap. He sits on the table before me.

I concentrate on his face as he concentrates on mine. He chews on his lower lip as he brushes blush across my cheeks. My cheeks flush from the attention. When I was his age, girls would rouge their cheeks so they'd seem always blushing, always innocent. Blue's cheeks are naturally rosy.

The night's cold has already settled in my bones. I can hardly bear to think of leaving the house. And I still worry that I'm inviting as much trouble for Blue as I am for myself. I should be using all my talents as a sneak-thief to keep us hidden in all the many nooks and crannies of our home. Instead, I court disaster.

When Blue finishes with my makeup, he leans back and clicks his tongue, pleased with his work. "Devastating," he says. "My femme fatale. My Mata Hari." He pats his chest, miming a fast-thumping heart.

"Mata Hari was executed," I say.

"But she went in style," he says. "She blew a kiss to the firing squad. The suit she wore was tailored special for her to get executed in." He does some last-minute teasing of the wig's curls with a tin comb. Every story of caution I ever tell him he interprets as romance.

Blue opens a compact mirror and holds it before my face. "Look at yourself," he says, and at first I don't think he means to be literal. With his mention of execution, I was pulled into the fairy tale of vanquishing witches. *Look at yourself,* Blue says, and I see the powder-and-paint mask and platinum wig of a poisoner-of-Nazis.

I take the mirror and stand from the settee. I touch my pinkie to the corner of my bright red lips. "I've done some of my best work in a woman's clothes," I say. "Men expect you to be fidgeting with all your clasps and buttons. Your lipstick. Your eyelashes. They think I'm looking at myself when I'm looking in a mirror." I snap the compact shut.

As I hand it back to Blue, I notice he's wearing a ring I've not seen before. I've never seen him wear any ring at all. I reach out for his hand and cradle it in both of mine. I run my thumb over the ring, like rubbing it for luck, making a wish, wanting M's ring back on my own finger.

Blue's ring is thick and heavy, unadorned, no stone. "Brass," Blue says. "Félix gave it to me, from his own finger. He wears a fistful so he can shatter a guy's jaw if he comes at him." Blue takes his hand back to run his own thumb, adoringly, over the ring. "He says it's from melted-down gun casings, from the battlefield. It's patriotic, really, to knock a nose out of joint with it."

I give his nose a playful knuckle-thump. "You do worry me, my boy," I say.

"I worry about *you* every minute. Be careful tonight."

"Everything's dangerous everywhere," I say. Too little food for the people of Paris, no coal for their stoves, icicles on the inside.

"Let me wear that wig," he says. "I'll go instead."

"I'll take you up on that later," I say. "Perhaps you can stand in for me at my execution." I give him a wink with false eyelashes so heavy they make my eyelid feel like it's thick with infection. I peel both strips of eyelashes off, and Blue scolds me by clucking his tongue with disappointment.

He comes to me to do some last-ditch straightening of the wiry curls of my wig. In our nervousness, ready too early and waiting for my car, we sit on the settee and count the pearls in my necklace that's a mile long, then count again after Blue concludes there are only 318 while I came to 330. But we never do reach the same number, even after counting the pearls two more times, rolling them through our fingers as if they were rosary beads, with a hiss of whispers, nuns numbering sins.

···· 34 ····

Voss sits slumped in the back of the car, and I'm alarmed at the sight of him. I've made a mistake in insisting on an evening at the cabaret.

"You look like you've seen a ghost," he says to me.

The driver, a Nazi attendant in uniform and cap, gets back behind the steering wheel after helping me into the car. I catch his eyes in the rearview mirror.

What if Voss just collapses at the cabaret? I don't know how much of my poison can be traced in his blood while he's alive, but an autopsy will surely do me in.

"Are you even up for a night out?" I say.

"I'm not," he says. "But they need to think I am. They need to see me out and about, having a wonderful time, just like you said." He forces a smile. "So we'll go out and about, and we'll have a wonderful time." He drops the smile. He takes another painful breath. He says, with a whimper, "We'll just stay for a minute or two."

He's wearing a black dinner jacket and a white silk scarf. Without asking permission, I unravel the scarf from his neck and begin wiping the sweat from his face and hair. I give him a rigorous toweling until the scarf is nearly soaked, then drape it over the back of the seat in front of us to dry. I open my handbag to get at the cosmetics Blue used on me, and I begin to resurrect Oskar Voss.

First I hand him a snuff bottle of scent, a mix of lemon, lavender, and rosemary, a formula passed down to me by Fanny all those years ago, from her days as a retired ballerina in New York—she'd suck in a snort to revive herself after a performance. He takes in a deep breath of it, then another.

I touch my fingertip to the tip of a lipstick, and dab some of the red lightly on his lips. I dab some more. I lean back and pucker and smack my own lips, telling him to do the same, to spread the red around. I then tap at the rouge in a pot and rub it into his cheeks with my thumb. I lean back, consider. He looks fresh from the undertaker's. "Forgive me," I say, and I work at his cheeks more with my knuckles, practically beating a rosy glow of health into him. I crank open the car window in hopes the winter wind will cool his skin, to keep him from sweating all his paint down into his white collar.

Not only does he look like he's got more blood in his cheeks, but he acts like it too. He's breathing easier, sitting up without a slouch.

I open my compact and hold the mirror out so he can see himself. He looks past the mirror, to me. "You haven't mentioned your dress," he says. "It's a Schiaparelli. It was in *Vogue* magazine."

"It's clever," I say. "I like the penguins. I'm not so fond of the wig."

He shrugs. "Take the wig off, then," he says.

I don't hesitate. I drop the wig onto the seat between us, which kicks up an electrical storm of static, tiny blue lightning bolts snapping. With my comb, I try to fix my hair in my compact mirror, but I just stir up more voltage. There's a tin of putty in my purse, so I take a plug of it and grease all my hair back, like a croupier at a casino.

Voss says, "Much better." I use some of the putty still sticking to my hands to slick a wave into his forelock. He gives me his handkerchief so I can wipe the putty from my hands.

"Aren't we a pair?" he says. He angles my mirror up and around his head, to inspect his greased curlicue.

Aren't we a pair?

I ease over to my side. I pretend to rifle through my purse, rummaging among the lipstick, candy tin, cigarette case. *Aren't we a pair?* It is what I intend for him to think, what I *need* him to think, but the sound of it, with such sincerity, does send an honest-to-God shiver along my spine. Because it's just the sort of thing you want to hear from the people in your life.

He doesn't have all that much charm, but he has an easy way about him, which has likely served him well in his climbing up. Every now and again, he provokes a minute of my sympathy. And I do believe his fascination with me is genuine. I've spent so much of my life thinking polite society couldn't bear to know a single truth about me that I fall victim to those who show me a nod of respect. Around Voss, I let myself think my life hasn't been as unspeakable as I thought.

Once we've arrived at Madame Boulette's, Voss has enough vigor to saunter among the tables, slapping backs, shouting greetings above the squawk of burlesque on the stage. I can tell he's trembling, but he manages to make his weakness intimidate with a slow air of elegance. The grim composure of authority.

Lutz stands from his table and elbows in on that composure, giving Voss's hand such a hard shake it seems he might topple the old bloke. Yet at the same time, with that bone-rattling handshake, Lutz is clearly eager to please. He wants to both defeat and surrender, I suppose, whichever might better his rank the quickest. Kowtow or leapfrog. I watch Lutz. The way he stands, the lift and set of that square jaw, the smile—none of it is unrehearsed. He and I, we've practiced our lives in front of a mirror.

They do that thing that men do, holding the handshake, pulling each other in to speak right into each other's ears, a tug-of-war of camaraderie. But this back-and-forth seems to embolden Voss. He won't allow Lutz the last word.

Lutz looks over at me. "I didn't recognize you," he says, and he takes my hand and leans forward. But he does not kiss the back of my hand when he brings it to his lips. He turns my wrist and holds it to his nose. He acts overtaken by the scent of my perfume. "Is this yours?" he says. "This perfume? A creation of yours?" Before I can even answer, he says to Voss, "This is why I led her to you. Her perfumes are purely from the garden. She captures the exact scent of the flowers."

It's all more performance—he wants Voss to think I'm his own discovery. If the perfumes of Paris are what carry Voss upward, he wants to be sure he's tethered to that.

Voss gives Lutz his nod of dismissal, then takes my arm, and we walk away. I say, "Surely you're not fooled by all of that."

He pats my hand. "You know I'm not, of course," he says. "I never even hear half of what he says, because I'm so fascinated by his face. The architecture of it. What's it like, do you suppose, to walk into a room knowing you'll stun people dumb with your beauty."

"What makes you think I wouldn't know from personal experience?" I say, pretending to be playful, though I have to force a smile. "Why do I have to *suppose*?"

He pats my hand again. "You're beautiful in a number of ways," he says. "An infinite number of ways. He's beautiful in one way only."

We slip into a banquette at the back of the cabaret. I say, "Does he work for you?"

"Not quite."

"You should do what you can to be rid of him," I say. "Send him elsewhere."

Voss raises an eyebrow. "My heavens. You put on a designer gown for an evening," he says, "and you become one of those women who tell it like it is."

"He's destroying that poor girl," I say. "The cabaret singer. And you shouldn't trust him yourself."

He reaches across the tabletop to squeeze my hand. "You have a good heart, Charlie," he says. "When I meet people with good hearts when they're young, I tell them to be careful of people taking advantage of their kind nature. It's my standard line of advice. But you're the very type of person I'm warning them against."

I squeeze his hand back. "I don't think I've taken advantage of kind people," I say. I squeeze one more time, as a signal that we should stop holding hands.

He takes his hand back. "There's a new wave of Nazi officers already rising up," he explains. "They're *more* German than the rest of us, don't you know. Lutz is part of that new wave, but he's staying friendly with the old guard. He'll use me until he can destroy me. At least, that's what's rattling around in his pretty head. But he's going nowhere, accomplishing nothing. He'll not get the best of me. I'm not a little torch singer in a whorehouse."

"Why has he picked you?" I say.

"He knows all my business."

"Hm," I say. "Does he know more than I do?"

He pauses, and just as he's about to say something, Madame Boulette brings us a bottle of champagne. She pours some for each of us, then puts the bottle in a silver bucket. Voss smiles and takes her hand. But she seems startled by the clamminess of his sweaty palm, so he drops his hold quick. "My next book about Paris will have a whole section devoted to Madame Boulette's," he tells her.

She flutters her lashes and fans her fingers at her cheeks, pretending she's cooling the heat of a blush. I like to think she's mocking him by acting so girlish. After she leaves our table, swinging her hips in her snug velvet gown, the band strikes up loud, and Day takes the stage. The German soldiers in the audience shout and whistle shrilly because these are the songs they love the most, the songs Day writes especially for them, off-the-cuff operettas using their girlfriends' names, and the names of their towns, and all the bliss of their lives before the war.

But the song Day sings now is bawdy, about a fräulein named Sigilwig with nipples as pink as a possum's tongue. The pink, pink tongue of the *Beutelratte*. The men roar at the mention of the girl's name, as if they all knew her when.

Voss says something I don't hear. When I ask him what he said, he scoots along the bench of the banquette to sit right next to me. "You don't like her," he says. He gestures his thumb in the direction of the doorway. "Madame Boulette."

"That's not true," I say. We're leaning toward each other so we can keep from shouting but still be heard.

"Like it or not, I've gotten to know you, and I know every face you make." But he's not looking at my face. He's dropped his eyes down to the tabletop, watching the bubbles pop in his glass. He touches a finger to the stem. "You don't like her, because you disapprove. You disapprove of her . . . service . . . to the German military."

"We're all doing what we can," I say. Then I say, "Maybe I disapprove of her flirting with you, right in front of me." I must be possessed by the bullet-holed soul of Mata Hari. "I mean, look at this." I *ting* my fingernail against the side of my champagne coupe. "It's pretty much emptier than it was before she filled it. She could barely be bothered enough to pour me a sip."

He smiles and pushes his glass over. "You can have mine," he says. "And I *will* write about Paris again, you know? My new diaries for the new Paris. And the new Paris will be just as good as the old one."

"You didn't answer me before," I say. "When I asked you if Lutz knows more than I do."

"You've grown bold as I've grown weak," he says. He smiles. "But *you* I trust. There's honor among thieves. Is that the expression? Or is it that there's *no* honor among thieves?" I don't answer, so he continues. "All Lutz knows is that I know what I'm doing. And he knows I have plans for the perfumery. The perfumes of Chamberry will give everyone's memories back to them. Every girl they ever loved, every man who ever loved them. In the flowers of those bottles, you'll find the gardens of your childhood. The altars of your church. Your weddings. Your funerals. We'll convince Parisians to spend their money, as soon as they have some again, to buy back the lives they had before. And they'll seek the nostalgia of our perfume. The way I see it"—and here he points at me—"Berlin can get rich soothing all the pain it caused."

Ting ting ting. I tap my fingernail on my half-empty glass again. "Forgiveness is the fragrance that flowers yield when trampled on," I say.

"Is that from a poem?"

I shrug. "I read it in a magazine for rose gardeners."

"Well, there you go," he says.

"What does Lutz know about Pascal's perfumes?"

"He knows we have all of Pascal's properties. The laboratories. The shops. The mills. The distilleries. The farms in Grasse."

"But you don't have Pascal?"

He shakes his head. "His every factory was ransacked by its own workers," Voss says. "It's like he had them all hypnotized. All he had to do was whistle and they threw their own wrenches in their own cogs. Hundreds of people worked for the Parfumerie Chamberry, but there's not a single list with a single name. They shoveled all their papers into a furnace. And all the workers, they're all gone. He had an army of girls who did nothing but go in every day to sit at a bench and pinch together the little silk rosettes." He flutters his fingers around, pantomiming the ruching of roses. "And another army of girls to tie those rosettes to the long necks of the bottles of Le Cygne. All of them, every one of them, nowhere now."

But they did find one gentleman who couldn't quite vanish. When Voss mentions him, my heart skips ahead. *Jean-François.* It worries me that Voss knows his name.

Jean-François has worked in the shop in Paris for decades; he's as famous around town as a cinema star. He could never just disappear. His every signature suit is a distinctive clash of plaids, a collision of color and checks in his vests and trousers and sports coats. He's not even passably handsome and has the presence of a field mouse, but it's him women imagine when they make love to their husbands. In his soft, low voice, Jean-François recites lists of spices, litanies of bouquets, as he cradles your hand in his and stirs the air above the wrist he's just spritzed. He looks at you knowingly. And know, he does. He knows how you want to seem to others. He selects a scent for you, and even if you don't much like it, you're convinced *you're* the one who's wrong. So you tell him you love it, and you outline all the reasons why, because you want to impress him with your sophistication. As you tell him what you like about it, as you bring words to it all, you discover its finest qualities. And you get to know yourself a little better.

"He told me that the recipes mean nothing without Pascal," Voss says. "Because the scent isn't just about the flower. It's about sunlight and shade. Soil and insects. Inspiration. Romance. At least, that's what he said at first. As we questioned him more, he became more generous. He said the perfume diary is everything we want it to be. The diary has all the recipes, and everything about them."

"But he doesn't know where it is."

"He *says* he doesn't know."

I somehow doubt it was a polite inquisition. It perhaps hasn't even ended yet. I imagine Jean-François stripped of his plaids and stuck in a cell. A gun at his temple. A flashlight in his eyes.

"You'll help us re-create the scents," Voss says, "but you're going to invent new ones too. Fragrances of your very own. We'll even call one of them Perfume Thief, don't you think? Voleur de Parfum. You'll have all the ingredients you've ever wanted, no matter the expense. Once we've won the war, the victors, with their riches, will demand the luxuries they've been deprived of. Your perfumes will be how the women of Europe communicate their power to each other. You'll be creating the language of their influence."

Those women will just be sniffing at each other's slashed throats.

As much as I yearn for Voss and his villains to lose everything in the end, there's no way of knowing how things will play out. So I can see how someone like me might fall into the snare of someone like him. The promise of wealth, influence, notoriety. A place of legitimacy in the New Europe. My very character linked with elegance. I know what he's thinking: I'd have to be a fool not to sacrifice my flimsy principles, when the stakes are so high.

Some would cast *me* as a villain already, for my years of robbery, but was I ever so crooked as all that? Compared to these devils, I'm an angel of mercy.

"Even alcohol," I say. "For perfume. Even that's a luxury in wartime."

And there must be more to Gabrielle than Voss will tell me. You can still find Pascal's other perfumes if you look long enough; at the very least, you'll find remnants from the secondhand dealers along the quai. But every last bottle of Gabrielle—those armless torsos—must have grown legs and run off.

Voss sits so close to me, listening so carefully, I can feel him jump when the cabaret is noisy with applause.

Whenever Zoé takes the stage, the spotlight is lowered to a faint glow, draping across her like a veil of gauze. She fades away night by night. Her ballads have become even sadder; they're sung in a whisper, and the men cheer the grand tragedies—stories of jilted lovers who end up dead, or next to dead, in every song's last stanza. A sailor's girl who walks into the ocean, rocks in her pockets. A broken-down dope fiend done in by one last swig of absinthe. A hopeless widow leaps from a widow's walk.

Zoé opens her mouth and leans into the microphone, and everyone quiets.

"I'm losing my voice," she whispers, and just like that, her voice is gone. She continues with the song nevertheless, and we try to read her lips. We swear we can see the details of our own sad stories take shape. Our lies, our confessions. Lovers lost or forsaken. We even hear her sing their names.

···· 35 ····

In the morning, I'm in the very back of a long black car. I've been driven before, but never by this man. I tell him he's taken a wrong turn. And when he says nothing, I fret. We take another turn, then another, each twist in the path angling me farther from home, and farther from Pascal's house.

"I know you can hear me." I'm raising my voice above the scratch of the tinny, hectic music from the dashboard radio. This time the driver responds, but only with a shake of his head. And then I say it in German, or I hope I do. I don't know the words well enough to know if I've used the right ones. And again. *I know you can hear me.* He begins to sing along to a song.

Voss is onto me. I'm to be registered. Fingerprinted. I've heard these stories. You report to an office, you sign a paper, you check a box, and next you're arrested.

My first instinct is to think back, to stumble over all my missteps, but that's an amateur's trap. Was there something I said last night, at the cabaret? Could he read my disgust on my face? Is he closer to Lutz than I thought? I'm frightened for a moment, but a moment of fright is all you can allow yourself. At the first bristling of fear, you turn it useful. Because it's fear, not fearlessness, that gets you to let go of the good sense that keeps you still. Sometimes that means running away even if a gun's at your temple.

But, of course, I'm an old woman. I won't get far on foot.

And what if this is nothing at all? What if I'm *not* being abducted?

Leaping from a moving car—I can think of no more efficient admission of guilt. How would I explain my fear to Voss?

So I sit and I wait and I wonder about all the people of Paris who've fallen victim to common sense, all those who've gone along without struggle, because it's illogical to expect the worst. It's crazy. You'll hurt yourself. *Just follow.*

Then I see that I couldn't tumble out even if I wanted to. There's no handle on my door.

I say, or try to say, *I can pay you something if you take me home.*

The driver just tosses a box of cigarettes into the backseat. And some matches.

I decide this is a good sign, these cigarettes. If I were his captive, what would stop me from dropping a match down his collar? Sticking the hot end of the cigarette on his neck?

I consider lighting a cigarette, to fall into a coughing fit. Turn it into a production. A collapse. A raspy, wheezing cough, an old crone choking on her own tongue. He'd have to stop. He'd have to let me get some air.

I light a match, let it burn. But that's all I do. It burns to the tips of my fingers. I blow it out.

And the car stops, with the puff of my breath.

36

We're stopped in the middle of the street, but since there's no traffic anywhere around, it makes no difference how close we are to the curb. To our immediate right is a towering furniture store I've visited only a time or two. Greenspoon's. A Jewish-owned business that has been shut down.

Closed or not, it's Greenspoon's we've come to visit, it seems.

The driver opens the door for me, still humming along to the song he was singing, though the radio's off. I step from the car, and he hands me a sealed envelope; I recognize Voss's extravagant handwriting, shivery with his shaky hand.

Give them, the driver says in English, tapping his finger against the envelope. He points to the store. And then he says, *I wait,* and I try to feel relief. He will wait, because I'm returning. He will wait because he is taking me home.

I decide to tear into the envelope before I even reach the doorway; I don't care if the driver sees me. I remove the folded sheet of paper.

Oskar Voss is all Voss wrote. With the number 8 squiggled in an upper corner.

Though the store is clearly closed for business, the door is unlocked. When I open it, a little bell jingles a tiny ring—one of those snippets of music from daily life, once upon a time, that now seem a fairy-tale sweetness long lost.

Inside, there is a scurrying of industry like in the hours before a sale. A man walks along an aisle, balancing a tower of tasseled pillows. A woman pushes a squeaky-wheeled pram overflowing with dolls. And, at a slower pace, there are those who seem to be shopping, women in coats and hats, handbags in the crooks of their arms, strolling, glancing, clucking their tongues. Some of these women are German, but most are French.

Though I only catch a glimpse of the dolls in the pram, they stay with me, their goldilocks and the pink cheeks of their porcelain faces.

No one notices me. The store is massive, the ceilings stretching up three stories. The main floor before me resembles the nave of a cathedral, with short partitions throughout, like two rows of pews lining a center aisle. Within these sections, furniture was once arranged in homey little settings—sofa, love seat, wing chair. Beds and nightstands. Floor lamps, cocktail tables, wine cabinets. At Greenspoon's, you'd have been invited to be seated, or to even lie down, and to imagine the better life you'd have if all your belongings were new.

A Frenchman steps up to me, grunts, holds out his hand for my paper. At first I think he might be handsome, but quickly all his features shift, and his stubbled chin, his piercing eyes with a touch of bloodshot, his jet-black hair greased into a movie-star swoop, all become sinister somehow.

He grunts again. Nods sharp at a man at a desk with a long scar that seeps down his cheek from the corner of his eye like the trace of a tear. That man stands, takes the letter, tells me to follow him. *Suivez-moi*. Another Frenchman.

In this cavernous space, I can hear echoes of laughter, of coos, of conversation. I hear the wings of a bird caught inside, high up, fluttering at the panes of the broad arched window that lets in the gray winter light. I hear shoes click-clacking quick on tile, and the rolling of a cart's wheels that sounds like a billiard ball across felt.

In the sections where there'd been furniture, there is now a variety of goods—one cubby holds only pictureless picture frames stacked and leaning, another holds shelves full of clocks, none of them ticking, all of them telling a different time.

At the end of the nave, where an altar would be, is a grand staircase of marble steps and gilded railings. We go up up up, my knees popping, and we're passed by two women coming down, another pair of French ladies in fashionable coats and hats, discussing the play of light on the diamond in the ring on one's finger. One of them wears a cologne I know, Heureuse. Happy. Another scent from Chamberry, but one I never much liked—somehow oversweet *and* dusty, like a piece of old marzipan spoiling in a confectioner's window.

And the lady's been freshly blasted with it, heavily, so much so that I can feel it scratching at my throat, tickling up a hack. I cough. My eyes water. I dab at them with the end of my scarf as I trudge up.

When we near the top of the stairs, some hyacinth enters the mix, then some orangey-lemon, some polished cedarwood. The air's noisy with scent.

The second floor looks down on the main floor, and it's lined with archways that lead to more departments; my guide escorts me closer to a pea-soup fog of floral stench, into a room with the number 8 spray-painted on the wall. Inside are glass cabinets and barrister bookcases, and mirrored trays arrayed with squeeze-bulb atomizers, and women spritzing and spraying and waving at the air. They sniff toward each other like truffle pigs.

The man who has led me here hands the note with Voss's name to a woman behind a counter. She was expecting me. She seems to know more about why I'm here than I do. "This is for you," she says, handing me a canvas bag. "Monsieur Voss invites you to take what you want. The perfumes you don't know, or don't know well. Perfumes you'd like to study more closely. For research."

The shoppers notice me, and I note their disdain. I take from my pocket my black woolen stocking cap, and pull it onto my head, over my ears. I look like an old salt from the pier in my peacoat and dark trousers. I know those bottles and boxes—expensive and fashionable perfumes, colognes, talcs. And I know these women.

These are the perfumes you wear when you want people to know you're wearing them. Delicate oils weighed down, anchored, burdened, by the glands of caged vermin. These scents are the ones I think of when I think of old-moneyed matrons at the opera, their face powder crackling their dry cheeks, their droopy earlobes stretched taut by fat pearls dangling on diamond-studded strings.

The fact of the matter is, so many of my wealthy clientele who hired me to steal never understood what was truly worth having. They were like the fisherman's wife in the old fairy tale; they didn't care what they got, they just wanted *more*. The perfect clients, the rare ones, were those who listened to me, who let me seduce them with the fable and poetry of fine essence. They believed me. I stole for them what I wanted to take. They recognized that scent should ghost away at first dab, that all you'd need was to breathe it in once, let it move and inspire. You don't wear perfume; you interpret it. You apply it. It shouldn't matter whether anyone knows you wear anything at all.

Of course, so much of my disdain for the rich was because they always knew I wasn't one of them. No matter how expensive my perfume, they could smell my tawdry soul.

This building, it seems to me, is peopled with the wealthy French, with Nazi officials, and with the gangsters of Paris and their molls. It's an operation, clearly. I step closer to the shelves, and I realize all these bottles belonged to someone. Most of them are less than full. I touch my fingertip to a frayed silk knot at the neck of a rose-colored decanter. I pick up another bottle, a clear one, and breathe on it, frosting it with my breath, and I see the swirl of fingerprints, maybe those of the woman who'd worn this scent last.

I don't want any of this, but the woman behind the counter is very interested in my selections. And some of these *are* perfumes that I've heard of but never tried. Some are from whole other generations. I start filling the bag.

I decide Day might like this charming bottle shaped like a dancer in a pirouette, her arms lifted, a somewhat drooped feather tied to her back with a ribbon to resemble an angel's wing.

I find myself gently cradling the dancer in the palms of my hands, as if it were a wounded bird, as I leave the department. I hear the squeaky wheel of that pram again, echoing, and I try not to think of those dolls, and the children they've lost.

···· 37 ····

In Pascal's upstairs room, Voss sits on his sofa, and I sit in my chair. I've gotten to know well all the old chair's discomfort. You sit too much *this* way and you've got a wild spring jabbing your ass. Sit too much *that* way and you bump your elbow on its rickety arm. The whole thing is falling apart, right out from under me. The chair is covered entirely with a blanket, so I can only imagine what a true wreck it is. Pascal, so rich, sought solace here, in this broken-down room. Zoé told me the house reflected her mother's eye for elegance, so I wonder if this space was Pascal's retreat, a place he could leave cluttered and dusty. Or did he need this room only after his wife's death? Did he need someplace that didn't remind him of her?

Together, Voss and I examine the perfumes I brought. But I can't concentrate on any of them.

Did I ever truly believe more could be taken from Voss? More than just the perfume diary? How could I have thought that his corruption was within reach, that I could turn him against his own country and its crimes? That I could convince him that Paris can only survive if the Nazis don't?

He hasn't really been waylaid by my poison, I realize. Not at all. He's so very familiar with the sinister habits and methods of these monsters that he's been able to navigate with ease, even from his bed. He's kept his corner of the black market thriving, his stolen department stores well stocked.

"I thought you would enjoy this assignment," Voss says. "But you seem distracted. You even look a little green around the gills. I hope you haven't caught my flu."

"Actually, it's *you* I'm worried about," I lie. "I feel just fine. But, Oskar, you don't look at all well."

"That's sweet of you to worry," he says, "but—"

"Could it be something else?" I say. "Maybe it's not the flu."

This does what I'd hoped it would—he wilts before me, weakened by my diagnosis. He's been hoping he's better. He eases back deeper into the pillows of the sofa, holding a black bottle of perfume to his nose. "I'm fine," he says. "I've had a long, long life of doctors telling me I'm on the verge of death. The closest I ever came to it was when I was a little boy. I was in the hospital for a month. I'd start to kick whatever it was that ailed me, then something else would swoop in to take me down. My immunity, it seems, is the culprit. Any bug that comes along can just tippy-tap at it, and the whole thing shatters. It falls apart and lets all the killers in."

"I'm sorry to hear that."

"But I'm a master at hiding my illnesses," he says. "I've been doing it for so long." He manages an office that provides endless reams of accounting, hatch marks and scritch-scratches, to demonstrate his efficiency, to demonstrate the effectiveness of the pillaging, to provide staggering lists of the wealth acquired since the Nazis took Paris. And it was Voss who facilitated, on his arrival, a very simple trick: the ballooning of the exchange rate, sending the value of the deutsche mark upward to crush the downward spiral of the franc. Voilà.

All he needs is to show Hitler how rich he's making them all and he can stay in bed until his dying days.

I pick up one of the bottles of perfume I've brought from Greenspoon's, one from Parfumerie Chamberry. Enjôleur. Beguiler. They haven't sold it in many years. It's only half empty, but whoever had it last likely kept it on her boudoir table for decades. It was never terribly expensive, and it was much adored in its day. Maybe it was an anniversary gift from her husband. Or her children bought it for her when they were small, impressed by its grand and elegant label, its name in raised letters beneath gilded swirls. Maybe she treated herself to it. She wore it sparingly, on special occasions, so that it would never become common to her. She wanted to always associate it with only the best days and nights of her life.

Voss might *want* to save Paris, but his idea of *how* to save Paris is a perversion, and has nothing to do with the people of this city and their livelihood. He has no interest in giving anything back. He wants to take more and more. He wants to get rich off the things we love the most, not caring whether we're alive to love them.

He tells me as much. It's not even a confession. It's merely an explanation. *There's honor among thieves.*

All his years of strolling the city, of committing its every meandering avenue to memory, of writing book after book revealing its secrets, leading everyone down its lovely wrong turns, made him the culprit best suited to rob it blind. His sense of the people who lived in all the houses he passed aided in the Nazis' plundering of the wealth of the city's Jews. He could tell what kinds of lives were lived behind the closed curtains by assessing the curtains themselves. He mapped out an elegant blitz, at street level, his first summer here.

"Everything's for sale," Voss tells me, and you can always get the asking price. Every division of the occupation—the police, the intelligence agency, the military, the cultural departments—has its own corner of the black market, its own department stores and dealers and procurement agencies.

"We can pry the gargoyles off Notre-Dame for the right price," he says. "And it serves the gargoyles right. For years, they've watched over the city with dirty greed in their eyes."

"Are you planning to sell my ring too?" I ask. "M's snake ring."

"You're supposed to steal it back," he says.

"You never wear it."

"The bottle of Gabrielle that you took from me," he says. "Have you spent any time with it? Have you considered its scent?" He takes from his pocket another bottle of Gabrielle he has come to have. Maybe he has every bottle in town. He leans forward to put it on the table between us.

Gabrielle changed everything for the lesbians of Paris. The subtleties of perfume I respect in my shop didn't apply. Such gentle scents reminded us too much of the women of the last century, who sprinkled their respectable hankies with rose water, only to fade away into the stench of the streets. Instead, we would announce our presence. We wanted to leave our scent lingering in every room we left, and on the clothes of every woman who embraced us. We wanted our lovers' eyes to water. We wanted to wear our perfume on our skin, not our silk, to carry the scent of our nakedness everywhere.

Voss says, "The concierge has a package for you, for when you leave. It's your very own copy." He lifts a pinkie to gesture behind me. I don't have to turn to know he's gesturing to the painting of Gabrielle d'Estrées.

"Where did you find one?" I say.

"They're all over Paris," he says. "Don't tell me you haven't noticed."

"Well," I say, "thank you."

"I want you to study it," he says, "along with the perfume. I want you to figure out what Pascal was up to. The painting itself is full of riddles. Nobody knows what any of it means. And Pascal loved a puzzle."

Now I do turn to look. There's more depicted in the painting than just the sisters in their bath; there's a woman sewing at the back of the room, and even farther back, a painting on the wall of a man posed with his bare legs parted. There's a ring, pearls, silk. And that nipple getting a pinch.

Voss says, "I want to find out whatever it might be telling us. About the perfume diary. About the history of the perfumery." He pauses. "About poison."

What *I* want is to tell Voss I've been poisoning *him*. The truth is itching the tip of my tongue. Will I ever have the chance to look into the yellowed whites of his eyes and tell him I've been spoon-feeding him his aches and pains? Will I ever be able to boast of my betrayal?

He might even be amused that I've kept him sick with the recipes M collected.

M not only kept books about poison, he had a book from Tibet that had poisonous pages, its paper spun from a tree's bark that chokes the beetles that infest libraries. M had a whole poison collection: an antique teacup made of a jade meant to crack if poison's poured in; a lock of hair clipped from a wig powdered with white lead.

He knew of butterfly traps.

"Boil some sugar with some rum, some beer," M explained. "And put it down with some flowers, with a lantern. The butterflies come drink, get drunk, collapse."

M told me this in the parlor of a bug collector. The collector had opened his home to the public for an exhibit, *Beauty, Ugliness, and Oddity,* and we strolled among the displays of insects, living and dead. We wore matching suits, right down to our neckties, patterned with strawberries and houseflies. We carried the magnifying glasses a young girl had handed us at the front door.

And that was the first time I saw M's own broken heart.

The world is made up of eaters and eaten, came a voice from across the hall, where a ladies' club had gathered to hear a gentleman's lecture on the exhibit. And it was an *old* ladies' club, which the lecturer seemed to take into consideration. He seemed to think he flattered them by talking about butterflies in their last stages of life, and how *that's* when they have powers of flight they've never had before.

M gave me my own lecture, on butterfly poison, as we studied the bugs.

"After you've poisoned it," M said, "you have to keep it poison*ous*. You create a little poison house for its corpse, with an inkstand in a corner full of turpentine. You have to kill the tiny mites that will . . . that will . . . the mites will feed . . ." M stammered. He stopped speaking. He cleared his throat. I leaned forward to look through his magnifying glass, to see what he was seeing. Was he concerned about the fly tiptoeing along the teeth of the Venus flytrap?

"I need some air," he said. I could tell he was on the verge of tears.

As we walked down the block, he spoke of a lost love. "I'm being foolish," he said, wiping at his eyes with his shirt cuff, like a little boy crying. "A naturalist," he said. "She could have stayed here and chased butterflies, but she left me to travel the world. The world she most longed to see was one I wasn't in."

"Oh," I said.

"She's why I was first drawn to you, to be honest," he said. "Perfume. She loved perfume too. She went off to seek the perfume of butterflies."

I stayed silent, to punish him, but he didn't even seem to notice that I wasn't speaking. So finally I said, "And that's why you're with me? Because I make you think of her?"

"*Everything* makes me think of her," he said. He then appeared to realize how that must have sounded to me. He cleared his throat. "Don't get your feelings hurt," he said. "Don't be sentimental. She's gone. You're not. We're together now. Surely you have old lovers you can't get out of your head."

"No," I say.

We walked without speaking for another block, and by the next block, we had fallen in love with each other again. I forgave him for still loving, with such passion, someone else. We held hands despite the fact that we were both in men's suits. It was dangerous—we risked ridicule, or much worse—but I needed his hand in mine, and he needed mine in his. We needed it more than ever, this simple affection.

Back in my room, in my bed, he said, "I almost forgot," and he gave me a single bonbon from his pocket. "That's Schweinfurt green," he said of the paper wrapper. He cupped his hand at his mouth and whispered: *"Arsenical."* He described for me a steam chocolate factory in Darmstadt, and the rows and rows of maidens in kerchiefs wrapping the candy with bare fingers, sitting beneath glass lampshades greened with Schweinfurt too, the lamp's heat gassing the air with the dye. *"Arseniuretted hydrogen,"* M whispered. I felt his breath hot on my ear as he unbuttoned my shirt. "The little darlings," he said into my neck, his thumb rubbing against my nipple, "were dropping like flies."

···· 38 ····

Madame Boulette takes the stage. She blows kisses to the audience, and they cheer for her. They applaud. "At Madame Boulette's," she shouts above them, "we use only Aryan talent onstage," and she's met with more cheers and more applause. She then gestures upward, to the bedrooms upstairs, "*And* Aryan talent offstage!" Even more cheers, more applause. "And all my girls are in the pinkest of health." She winks when she says *pinkest*. "While *you* pay handsomely for the finest champagne, your comrades who frequent the cheap places empty their pockets on doctors' bills." The men laugh to assert their authority. *They*, they want everyone to know, would never think of canoodling with the floozies of cheap houses.

But the crowd seems sparse tonight, and her boasting just draws attention to the raggedy trappings of the joint. Either the cabaret has fallen into rapid decline over the last week or two, or I somehow never noticed the thin air heavy with must, the stained and frayed tablecloths, the threadbare carpet. A few frazzled lightbulbs shudder and buzz.

It's pajama night at the cabaret, and all the waitresses are wearing negligees and serving cocktails with names like the Sleeping Pill and the Knockout Drop, full of syrups and sodas to hide the hair-tonic aftertaste of bad gin.

I order an Ether Dream, and it arrives in a martini glass, the gin turned cloudy with sugar-water flavored with rosemary and mint. The clever bartender floated atop it a cloud of beer foam. My barmaid, like all of them, is in a night-slip that's as slight as a dream itself, practically an illusion. She carries, in the crook of her arm, a rag doll done up to look just like her. The doll, like the barmaid, has long false lashes heavy on her lids, and a heart-shaped pucker of red lipstick.

Those little lost dolls at the department store. I can't stop thinking about them. When I saw them, their hats and skirts were askew, their delicate cheeks and limbs scratched, but I like to imagine they were loved when they were with their girls. I imagine each one was propped up, pretty and coy, on plump, lacy pillows like a bedridden princess.

Day takes her place at the microphone, in a silk dress printed with the signatures of French girls' names, a mesmerizing scribble, all in different penmanship. *Sophia, Manon, Margaux, Léonie.* Each signature, each name, suddenly seems a plea. A chorus. Before singing, she thanks the soldier who bought her the dress. "I wrote this song for him," she says. "And about him." The men in the room whoop and bellow.

Day whisper-sings her song. All these villains open their hearts to her, and with just a few lyrics, and some sharp turns of phrase, she makes their tiny lives into something worth singing about.

Her voice soothes me like nothing else. It's *necessary,* Day's voice.

After her number, I coerce her to sneak away, to skirt the curfew. "Do you know how many songs there are about the night?" she asks me as we walk to Blue's theater. "And about dreams? And the moon?"

"I don't know," I say. "How many?"

She takes a breath. She looks up and off. "Almost all of them," she says. Despite the cold and the dark, she carries a paper parasol of a dandelion yellow.

We step up to the stage door.

After Blue's play every night, the cast and crew gather in the basement. Day has an interest in the *stoppeur,* a tailor who takes your torn coat or ripped dress and mends it so magically, with such intricate stitches, you'll never find the tear again. He has a shop of his own but also works as the theater's costumer. "I've been to umpteen fashion shows this month already," she says. "The Nazis can't stop demanding dresses to send back to their wives. Or their mistresses. Or whoever. All the shops toss up a show in a heartbeat." She taps her forehead with her finger. "I memorized the designs I want stolen. I can describe them to a T."

To a T. Voss wants to re-create Pascal's perfumes, but even if he does get all the recipes and formulas, could any of those roses ever smell as sweet again? Even when summer comes, *if* it does, even if we're allowed to sit at the sidewalk cafés, won't we just long for our last summer in Paris, before the war? Everything, even the sunlight, will have the Nazis' fingerprints all over it.

Down in the basement, everyone's still in costume, still in makeup, so when a woman in trousers passes by, a woman near my age, I assume she's still in character. She wears her hair like a girl, long tresses that fall straight, and past her shoulders. A thousand strokes with a hairbrush. Only a few wires of silver coiling among the nut-brown locks.

Day whispers, "She didn't seem to be wearing any perfume at all, but I certainly got a whiff or two of Gabrielle."

Day takes my arm to lead me deeper into the party. At first I assume we're heading for the makeshift bar in the corner, but then we angle back toward the woman in pants.

"What part do you play?" Day asks her.

"I'm not in this one," she says.

"You're not an actress?" Day says. Her elbow is in my ribs, giving me a gentle nudge. "You're not in costume."

"I *am* an actress, but there aren't a lot of parts for a woman over sixty," she says. "I'm a printer by profession. A bookbinder. An artist. I do the posters for the show. And the programs. And some set design."

"Oh, well, my, my, how about that," Day says. Then she says, "Maybe you can point out the *stoppeur.* Which one is he?"

"I've not seen anything of him," she says. She takes a sip from her martini glass. "Why are you asking, anyway? Who are you?"

She's asking who we are, but she's not all that friendly, this one.

"I'm Clem," I say, holding out my hand for a shake. "This is Day. We're friends of Blue's." I see him in the corner and point him out. She won't shake my hand, so I lift it to wave at him. He waves back, and starts working his way over.

"Then you probably know we keep getting arrested," she says. She means to impress us. "The *stoppeur* has been taking up . . . *covert* activities. Someone who can make a dress might stitch some secret code into a skirt. Or sew in some extra panels, where you can tuck away papers." I glance over at Day, who drops her eyes. Were those her plans all along?

The woman continues, leaning toward me more, her voice lower, speaking out of the side of her mouth almost. "A printer might do some quick-sketch passports and forged papers. If somebody were in need of such a thing." She winks. "I'm Annick," she says, and now we have our handshake.

Blue steps in, and he hands Day and me martinis of our own. "Annick is the one who loaned me the books," he says. A few days ago, he brought me books on the grammar of ornament, of shapes, designs, motifs, in the hope that it would bring me closer to the design Pascal drew at the end of his note to Zoé. I read the books looking for insights into the house's patterns, that I might unlock a room just by knowing better the source of the curlicue. Egg and dart, bead and reel, Celtic knot, quincunx, acanthus, Egyptian patterns inspired by lotus flowers and egret feathers, the mathematical latticework of the Moors.

Annick is called over to the piano; the actors need someone to play so they can sing along. "They're feeling sentimental," she says. The basement is full of props and set pieces, all the old sofas and chairs from different eras and decades, the theater's crew relying on donations of castoffs, or haunting the flea markets.

I like to imagine that the war will end soon, and the people who've lost their homes will return to Paris, to stroll through Greenspoon's. *This one,* they'll say, touching the black scar on the piano lid from where an uncle rested his cigarette that day, when he sat down to accompany the girls' singing. *And this one,* they'll say, knowing a china horse by the chip in its hoof. They'll know a silver teapot by a dent in its spout. A fur coat by a rip in its lining. A wristwatch by a scratch in its glass. A doll by its torn dress. They'll be newly grateful for all the old flaws, for the damage that left these precious things overlooked and unbought and distinctly their own.

"I'll bet you had dolls as a little girl," I tell Day. We sit on a divan with a lush pattern of roses, a piece from a nineteenth-century play.

"I had a beautiful doll from Paris, actually," she says. "My father bought her in Marseille when his ship was docked there. I cut off all her hair, not because there was anything wrong with it, but because I found a pair of scissors. I went around cutting up everything. That's one of the great discoveries in a child's life, the power of scissors. The damage you can do. My mother was mortified, and took her to a dollmaker to have the wig replaced, and then the thing got put up on a shelf. I never touched her again."

I never had a doll myself, but I loved seeing them clutched in the arms of other girls. And I loved seeing them seated in store windows, in their hats and pinafores. I never much wanted one myself, but I wanted to *want* one like those other girls did.

"The hair on my doll's head was just painted on," Blue says. "A little sailor doll I got one Christmas at the orphanage, when I was in between relatives to stay with. I got the doll, and a little sack of oranges. Me and my sailor boy, alone in the world."

I ask Blue about Félix, his lover. He's an actor in the troupe too. But Blue hasn't seen him in a while.

"He goes looking for trouble," Blue says. He touches his fingers to the ring Félix gave him. "I'm worried about him." His voice has shifted, slips deeper. He's gone serious, and sad.

I'm waiting for him to sigh, to gasp, to swoon, to balloon it all up into melodrama, like he usually does, which so often works to carry the despair away, to let it float out of reach, and comfort us. *It can't be as bad as all that,* we get to say to him, the grand tragedian. Instead, he droops lower, slowly stirring his martini with the toothpicked olives, leaning closer and closer to his glass, like he might just slip into the gin and drown.

Day reaches over to squeeze his hand. "Blue's inconsolable," she says, with a pout. "Clem, tell us another story. About M. About New York. Immediately."

As I've told my stories as part of my plot to keep Voss close, I've repeated them to Day and Blue. I haven't spoken of any of it in so long, if ever, that I can't bear for Voss to be the only one in Paris to know me so well.

This mere suggestion works to perk Blue up. He takes a deep breath, closes his eyes, lifts his chin, as if taking clean air into his lungs. "I *live* for your stories these days, Clem," he says. "You have to remember everything, so you can tell me, or I'll fade away." Ah, thank God, there's his theatrical flair. I wonder if he learned it as a child, shunted from relative to relative, tossed from one pack of cousins to the next. He threw fits to insist his way into their families.

"Why did you never tell Clem about Annick?" Day asks Blue.

I should object to this line of inquiry, but I know Day has caught me looking Annick's way. I've decided I like watching her play the piano, though she's graceless about it, hunched over the keys, her hands in claws, her hair in her face. Gracelessness can be a kind of grace, after all.

Blue shakes his head, dismissive. "She's trouble," he says.

"*She's* trouble," Day says, pointing at me. Then she says to me, "Tell Blue to stay out of your love life."

But I do like that Blue is looking out for me.

"It's *your* turn to tell a love story," I tell Day.

"I've already told you all my love stories," Day says. "You've turned them all into perfume."

"So of all those perfumes, which lover did you love the most?"

"It's the perfume I *wear* the most," she says. "My music man."

The varnish of a violin, phlox, the smoke of a blown candle. He was an American too, here in Paris, Day says. "I was twenty-five, twenty-six. He wrote songs for me, about me. He would pencil in the notes, then change them all around, then change them again. So his sheets of music were full of these ghost notes, half erased."

"There's a word for that," Blue says. "*Palimpsest*. When something's erased but you can still see it on the page." Blue, my librarian.

"Palemsest," Day says.

"Pa-limP-sest," Blue says. "P-p-p-p-p-p."

"I would run my eyes over the song, and hear all the other notes too," Day says. "His was the only marriage proposal I ever accepted. But I took too long actually going to the altar, so he fell in love with someone else." She raises her glass to us. "To palemsests . . . palim*p*sests," she says. "You can still see all our old lost lovers just by looking at us."

Day hands me her martini glass, and I put my lips to her lipstick print to take the littlest lick of gin.

···· 39 ····

I proposed marriage to M, with his own ring. I put the snake ring I'd stolen on his finger, but then he took it off, and he put it back on my finger. He said he wanted me to keep it. And he said he couldn't marry me.

He was already married.

M had a husband. M was twenty when they met, but the man was in his forties. Walked with a cane, because he had taken a bullet once. From an oyster pirate. Poachers. He owned a long stretch of oyster beds in Long Island, and a number of oyster cellars throughout the city—little basement saloons where oysters were served raw with lemon and vinegar. He always boasted that he'd shot more pirates than pirates had shot him. An ugly cuss, but M was living in a cramped flat with six girls, so he didn't seem so bad. Especially since he promised M could live however M wanted to live. Within reason.

How can you survive on what few pennies I likely pay you? the oyster farmer asked. I can picture M then, with braids coiled up, pulled back, and gathered in a net. A long black dress, a starched white apron. M worked as a waitress in one of the oysterman's all-you-can-eats.

And that was when M first dabbled in poisoning. To keep you from eating all you can eat at those all-you-can-eats, they eventually slipped you a bad oyster. It was up to M to keep track of who was next up for a rotten one.

The oysterman, quite smitten by M's tomboyish swagger, took M aboveground, to the Murray Hill Hotel, for top-notch bluepoint oysters, and sweet cider, violet beans, pheasant pie, baked deviled lobster. M had never eaten so good.

In the cellars, you have your oysters with beer, he told M. *Up here, you have them with champagne. But let me tell you something, Miss M. I'd sooner own the cellars. The rich will make you poor, and the poor will make you rich.*

M only told me all this some years later, in a letter, when I was traveling, when I was following the paths of things worth thieving. After M refused my proposal, and told me we could only ever live apart, that he could only ever see me on the sly, I couldn't bear to hear any explanations. Or promises. Or alternatives.

I went to work for the widows. The young ones and the old ones. They were in great need of a gentleman thief. When you can afford to have anything you want, you only really want the things you can't have. In my months of serving lunches to the Widow Waverley and her club, I'd stoked their fascination for perfume. All I had to do was tell them a scent was priceless, and they were prepared to pay anything.

Unlike the widows and their children, I'd not won any prizes just for being born. Even the blanket they swaddled me in belonged to a neighbor and had to go back, cleaned and pressed. I had no heirlooms looming in my future, to be passed down. Not even a needlepoint sampler. I left the farm with only the clothes on my back, and I outgrew even those within weeks. I have nothing from my childhood, or from my ancestors, whoever they were and wherever they came from.

When M told me he was committed to the old man for as long as the old man lived, I felt, again, bereft of everything. The floor left my feet. The city I was in slipped out to sea. I was a thief, and I'd been a thief since girlhood, and yet I somehow had nothing of anybody's. Once again I was as empty-handed as the day I was born.

I was lighter than ether. Fainter than glass. I could slip through keyholes. Shimmy through pipes.

I met with each of the widows privately, plotting my disappearance, assignment by assignment. They gave me newspaper clippings. Pages torn from books. Pieces of correspondence, all outlining what they most coveted. And they had the names and addresses of other rich women in Manhattan who'd hire me too. And from them I learned about women in cities all across the country. They requested not only the rare but the impossible. I promised I'd bring them both.

The Widow Mott craved an ancient perfume bottle from Athens, in the shape of Aphrodite on the half shell, carved from alabaster, housed in a museum with weak locks. The Widow Burnham had read Casanova's memoirs, and wanted the small crystal bottle he wore on his watch chain, in which he kept cotton soaked in otto of roses. The girlish Widow Henry was inclined toward a tabletop guillotine, from the age of the French Revolution, that beheaded dolls and sprayed a pink mist of orange-flower perfume.

They wanted colognes that sat on the floor of the sea in shipwrecks. Soaps dredged from the ashes of Pompeii. The fragrant, holy tears of weeping statues. Fumes captured from rare orchids.

When the Widow Hazzard said she'd heard tell of a lepidopterist's collection of butterfly scent, I knew she must be talking about that old lover of M's. I knew that fate was pitching me out, casting me away, with this divine coincidence. I wrote down everything the Widow Hazzard could tell me about the lepidopterist, and where I might find her, and the next day, I left Manhattan determined to steal every drop of that butterfly perfume.

···· 40 ····

Our covert cocktail party isn't the only one in the city tonight. As we walk home from the theater, people stumble out of pitch-dark bistros and sway down alleyways. We're none of us much worried about the curfew and the cold. The risk of madness from constant lockup is starting to seem every bit as troubling as the threat of citation, I suppose.

Blue and I drop Day off at Café Roche along the way. We're arm in arm and tipsy from martinis, and we can almost convince ourselves we're above it all. The confidence we get from the gin gives us vision, and an end's in sight, we've decided. We love seeing people out and about at this late hour, as if we're striving backward, to the way it was.

Tipping me more into tipsiness is the thought of Annick at that piano, and her surly charm. She hunkered down over the keys like she was pounding out something all blood-and-thunder, but the melody she played was featherlight.

But when Blue and I turn the corner, I'm struck sober. Even with the streetlamps off, I can see by the moonlight the car in front of my shop. I see someone leaning back against my front door smoking a cigarette. At first I wonder if there's time to turn on our heels and head back. But then the man catches sight of us. And I see that the man is Lutz.

I take my arm from Blue's. "Keep walking past the shop," I tell him. "You're only walking me home. You live somewhere else."

"No," Blue says. "I'm not leaving you alone for this."

"Be a good boy and go," I say.

"Forget it."

As we get closer, the inside of the car lights up with a flash. Zoé is in the backseat, and she's lighting her own cigarette, signaling to me that she's there.

"There you are, old chum," Lutz says to me. When he pushes himself up from the door, he makes himself dizzy. He grabs hold of the doorknob to keep from falling over his feet, and then he just swings there, back and forth, playful. He takes no notice of Blue at all. "I've come to ask you a very important question."

I'm relieved that he's drunk. He's not here on official business. "I hope I can answer it," I say.

He points toward the car. "Why doesn't Zoé St. Angel love me with all her heart?"

"I would have guessed that she did," I say.

"You spend all that time with her"—and now he's poking his finger at my chest—"filling our rooms with your stench, but . . . but you probably don't know her any better than I do, do you?"

"I certainly don't," I say.

"So what *do* you know?" he says. He glances over at Blue but still doesn't quite notice him. He says to me, "Do you know anything about love potions?"

"I only know perfume," I say.

"Then make a perfume that will make her love me," he says. He looks again at Blue, and this time he sees him. "Who are you?"

"He rents one of my rooms," I say. "That's all. He's a boarder. He lives upstairs."

"Then run along," Lutz tries to say, but his slurring prevents it. He tries to say it again, then again.

"Yes," I say to Blue, "go on inside."

"We'll all go inside," Lutz says. He goes to the car window to tap against it. He gestures for Zoé to come out. She's in a pale green nightgown and a white fur coat, her hair tied up in a scarf. She's got on high-heeled bedroom slippers, with a wispy riot of green feathers at the toes.

Once we're inside the shop, I nudge Blue in the ribs. I whisper that he needs to go upstairs and stay away. He whispers back that he'll be nearby.

"There are so many things I do that annoy her," Lutz says. He picks up a bottle and holds it in the lamplight. "This is an ink bottle," he says. I only ever use secondhand bottles I've bought at the flea markets: old cologne bottles, whiskey bottles, aspirin bottles, bottles for snuff, iodine, salt, vanilla, buttons, matches, arsenic. He opens the lid for a sniff. "God-awful," he says, recoiling, squinting.

Zoé takes a seat on the settee. "Ignore him," she says to me, but she's looking at him. "He becomes maudlin when he drinks."

"What did I tell you?" he says to me, looking at her. "Everything I do annoys her. Everything. The way I drink. The way I talk. The way I breathe. And she thinks I do all these things that annoy her *only* to annoy her. That all my little habits are just performance. To torture her. My every thought. My every gesture. My every move. It's all about her, and her misery."

His spite and bitterness seem to be sobering him up. He's speaking clearly now, standing up straighter. But he nonetheless returns to his mission of finding a perfume that will cast a love spell. "What's the most intoxicating scent?" he asks me.

I once stole, from a lemon farmer in Pasadena, the hypnotizing stink of a rare beetle that blasted its enemies with a gust of fog. The farmer was an agricultural genius who'd somehow bottled it. But that bottle is long gone. I want to send Lutz home, so I hand him a potent perfume that always brings to my mind the smoke of a toy cannon at a garden party, on Bastille Day, a pop that stopped our hearts. I wore seersucker and flannel sandals.

Lutz doesn't like it. As he looks at the shelves and tables of perfume, he finds his way to the copy of *Gabrielle d'Estrées et une de ses soeurs* that Voss had delivered. It's still mostly wrapped in butcher paper and twine, leaning against the wall, but some of the paper is torn away. Lutz lifts the flap of it and peers inside. "Huh," he says, with a note of suspicion. He looks over at me, his eyebrow raised. "How'd you come to have this?"

"It was a gift," I say. "It's just a cheap copy you can buy . . . well, you can buy it at the flea markets."

"Oskar Voss sent it to you," he says.

"Well, yes," I say, unsure if I should lie or not.

"You and him," he says, "you're very good pals. *Very* good pals." And now he seems to be slipping back into his drunkenness. "I would say very, *very* good pals, even. I'd say you were even *more* than good pals but for the fact that he's not to your liking. In that way." He tilts his head toward the painting, lifting an eyebrow.

"We both appreciate perfume," I say.

"Gabrielle must have something in it that's . . . that's a little titillating, doesn't it?"

I ignore the pun he's batting around. "I suspect the liquid's tint is from *Cannabis indica,*" I say. "That's often used to color perfume a pale green."

"What else?" he says, and now he *is* all business. "What else is in it?"

"I wouldn't know," I say.

"You wouldn't know," he says. After a moment, he says, "And how is Voss, anyway? He didn't look well at the cabaret."

I cross my arms, feeling protective. Voss is a villain, but he's *my* villain. If anyone takes him down, it will be me. "He works too hard," I say. "That's all."

At the suggestion of Voss's hard work, Lutz's shoulders droop; his head drops. He's suddenly exhausted. He walks over to sit next to Zoé. He leans against her, puts his head on her shoulder. He says to me, "Well, I hope you don't catch whatever he's got," and then he nuzzles his nose into Zoé's neck. I try to catch her eye, but she won't look at me. She shuts her eyes tight as Lutz begins kissing her neck and her ear. When he notices how tense she is, he pulls back. He says to me, "They sent us a report on gonorrhea. Did you know that more claps are caught from kept women and actresses, and from shopgirls, than from prostitutes? More actresses have it than both public prostitutes and clandestine prostitutes combined."

Zoé stands and walks toward the door, clutching her coat closed around her. "I'll wait in the car," she says.

Lutz says to me, "Now look what you've done." He stands to leave but asks me again for perfume. "Give me *something,*" he says. He's pleading with me now, his eyes wet, his voice soft. "So I can at least tell her it's something you recommend."

I give him a simple perfume of May roses, to hint at Gabrielle d'Estrées, though I don't tell him that. I tell him only that it's one of the oldest perfumes of Europe.

Oskar Voss so wants to believe Gabrielle was poisoned by the Medicis, and this recipe is one devised by Catherine de' Medici's own private perfumer. The perfumer would access her chambers through a secret passageway so that he couldn't be abducted and his recipes stolen. Some believe he concocted her poisons for her too.

After Gabrielle's death, the king of France married a Medici to settle a *war* debt, no less. And now here's Lutz, drunk and slovenly, begging for love potions. All the swagger of generals and dictators so often leads to rose fields.

And I'm awake the rest of the night, restless over the sight of Zoé in such despair. I feel further from the diary than I've ever been.

···· 41 ····

In the morning, the concierge lets me upstairs, where I'm to wait for Voss. Our little room has been disturbed: drawers opened, cabinet doors flung wide, everything in disarray. I walk through, straightening up. The bell-shaped birdcage where Pascal kept the origami birds he used to fold, fidgeting them together as he puzzled out his perfumes, has been tipped over, its gate unlatched, the birds spilling out. In among those uncaged are many unfolded ones, as if Voss were looking for words written inside their wings.

The only thing he seems to have handled with care is the painting of Gabrielle d'Estrées; he has propped it up on an easel of its own. But he has turned it, so that Gabrielle-and-her-sister's nipples face the wall. It seems he might have been studying the marks on the back—the stamp from the Louvre museum, and the registration number of the student who painted the copy.

Across the floor are sketches Voss left open; they're all blueprints, all signed by Pascal, for the design of his perfume bottles, marked with lines and dimensions and notes. Erasures. *Palimpsests.* Here's the bottle, artichoke-like with frosted-glass leaves, that contains Cœur de la Conscience (chamomile, pine). Here's the little sphere that holds Pénélope (apple, primrose). I roll them back up and place them atop the Japanese cabinet.

And the blueprint for Gabrielle. The bottle really is quite beautiful, even on the page. Pascal treats his designs as if he's intending to hang them framed in a gallery. Ink and watercolor on a page of parchment. Gabrielle's every line, every curve, is perfect. I get caught up in his notes that run along the side of the page, details about the frosted-glass stopper (*the mold-pressed head*), and some that didn't end up in the actual bottle: the nipples, particularly. The bottle for sale has smooth breasts, but the blueprint indicates nipples colored pink with applied patina (*cupric nitrate, nitric acid*). At the bottom of the page, he explains that the bottle is a nod toward the perfume of ancient Rome, when bottles sometimes took human shape. *Perfume was an aphrodisiac,* he wrote. All of it, even the flow of his handsome handwriting, is seductive. *An aphrodisiac.* For women who love women. He doesn't mention anywhere in his notes that the perfume was intended for men. Was that always a lie? Was the perfume always a gift to the lesbians of Paris?

"You don't have to pick up after me," Voss says.

He startles me, and I jump. I even gasp.

"I'm too antsy to sit," I say.

"Are we *both* on edge?" he says. "I've been frenzied all morning myself."

Frenzied? I've never seen him anything but unruffled, comfortable in his quilts and luxury, high on my poison. Despite managing a grand larceny, he daily makes time to play games of chess in the parlor alone, on the telephone with a chess master in Russia.

I begin to roll up the blueprint, to return it to its cardboard tube. "I'm glad you saw that," he says. "I was going to show it to you. I'm not interested in Pascal's bottles; only what's in them. But it's certainly a curiosity."

I put the blueprint away. "What are you frenzied about?" I say. We both remain standing, on opposite ends of the room.

"One can be frenzied without reason," he says. "I was just having trouble focusing my attention on any one thing." He walks to the sofa, sits, picks up one of the perfume bottles scattered across the coffee table. "And as I sat in here, sniffing at perfume, looking around, the room suddenly seemed full of secrets." He nods toward the chair across from him, gesturing for me to take a seat. "What are *you* frenzied about?"

Instead of sitting, I walk to the window and look out, down into Pascal's garden. To judge from the brittle, winter remnants of the bushes and shrubs, Pascal might've been as interested in the insects he lured as in the flowers that bloomed. In the summer, he'd likely see the red-jacketed gendarme beetle. He'd see Tiffany-blue dragonflies. Praying mantis. Moon moths with wings like pale green opera cloaks. And butterflies, of course, would flock to the flowers of the tulip tree.

"Lutz came to my perfume shop late last night," I say.

"Lutz?" he says, and his surprise is either genuine or very well rehearsed.

I walk slowly to my chair, well rehearsed myself, my hands in my trouser pockets. I pull out a cigarette tin. I sit on the very edge of the chair's cushion and light up with a gold lighter. I reach up to hook a lock of hair behind my ear, a habit I've always had even though I've never kept my hair long enough to have hair to hook back. Until today. I've not been to the barber, and my hair is growing out of its boyishness.

I picked up the habit as a kid, watching the schoolgirls, memorizing their every quirk of femininity.

"He was there to punish his girl," I say. "She was with him. He was demanding a love potion." I hold the open tin out to him, and he leans forward to take a cigarette for himself. He then leans in for a light. "He was mostly drunk," I say.

I tilt my head back toward the painting of Gabrielle d'Estrées. I say, "He saw the copy of the painting in my shop. Your name came up."

"The poor boy can't get me out of his head," he says. He breathes the smoke in, then out. He fusses with a loose thread on the sleeve of his pajamas. He's trying to seem indifferent. "What did he say?" he finally says.

"He suspected the painting came from you. Made him curious. He wondered about the work I've been doing."

"And you told him nothing."

"I told him nothing," I say. Voss might finally be useful to me.

Maybe if I can convince him Lutz is a threat, he'll make Lutz disappear. "But for all I know, he'll be back to the shop."

He keeps his eyes on mine. He says, "That little bawdy house of yours stirs up plenty of Sturm und Drang."

And now I fear I've made a mistake in making too much of Lutz. I don't want Voss to be suspicious of my entanglements with Zoé. For all I know, he has more loyalty to Lutz than he's letting on. I get even more nervous when he changes the subject.

"You've taken up smoking with a vengeance," he says, holding his cigarette before himself, squinting at it. I buy the cigarettes from the nuns who collect tobacco from stubs they find in the gutters. They roll it into new cigarettes and give them to the men and women living in the streets of Paris. But they sell them too, and the money goes toward their own efforts of resistance.

"You don't have any idea what it's been like," I say. "With things the way they are."

"Well, neither do you," he says. "I've looked after you very well, I'd say." When I don't respond, he says, "Wouldn't you say so too?"

"Would I?"

For cigarette paper, the nuns use the onionskin scritta from a monastery's printshop, where the monks churn out Bibles for soldiers. The world's history of war is full of stories of men saved by Bibles in breast pockets, bullets stopped by the thick book of thin paper, a fraction of an inch from plugging a heart.

"Other than Lutz's drunken spat with his little bird last night, have you been bothered in any way?" he says. "Have you had plenty of rations? That's not by accident, Nebraska Charlie." He thumps his thumb against his chest. "I'm your fairy godmother."

I even have a document Voss gave me, all in German, indicating that I'm under assignment, and that any questions of my status should be referred to him. I'm both glad for the paper and terrified by it. Should I get in a pickle with the Nazis, it'll do me no end of good. But in every other sense, it'll be seen as a damning piece of proof as the French tally up who was faithful to France and who wasn't.

He says, "And I should also point out, I've made no trouble for the pretty boy you keep in your attic." He watches for my reaction. "What is his name, anyway?"

I wonder again about Voss's loyalties. Does Lutz report to him? This is the first time Voss has made any mention of knowing anything about Blue. I don't want to seem alarmed, but I nonetheless stumble over my tongue. "I think . . . well, I guess you must mean my . . . my . . . my shopkeeper . . . Blue, is his name. My assistant. In the shop. His . . . his heart is . . . broken. I mean, he has a bad heart. A heart ailment."

"Little boy Blue," he says. "With the broken heart. Precious."

He almost sounds wounded. There's a tone of lonely in his voice, like I've kept a secret from him. But I won't give in to it. "I'm an American," I say. "You can see how that might make a girl nervous."

"Well, lucky for you, it seems the Americans might not lift a finger to help," he says, "so we're all still very good friends." This has cheered him up, this shift into war talk. The vulgarity of Americans inspires him, always. "Besides, none of you have much business passing judgment, do you? If you're to believe the pulp westerns. No one over there lives on an inch of land that wasn't got without gunshot. But in defense of your countrymen, how can anyone really own something they can't carry with them. Hm? Didn't you tell me something like that once?" He flicks his ashes into an empty teacup. "Are the Germans any worse than your neighborhood bank foreclosing on a mortgage? If you don't pay, the banks will call in the hired guns too, to throw you out. Real estate isn't *all* about money. It's also about brute force. Sentimental attachment, however, counts for nothing. Not in my country, and not in yours."

"So many of *our* spats end with you patting yourself on the back," I say. "Have you noticed that?"

"*Spats?*" he says, cheering up even more. "Is that what we're having? Have we turned into an old married couple?" But he doesn't mean for me to answer. He shifts his tone to a serious one. "Yes, I know about your boy Blue, but I'm not having you *followed*, really.

I'm having you *looked after*. There might be those who think they can get to me by getting to you. Since you've been in and out of the house so much. They think they'll see into *my* mind by drilling a hole in *your* head. So we have to be careful."

"Who do you mean?" I say.

"The men of my men," he says. I take him to mean his partners in crime—Lutz and such. "But I don't want to tell you anything more," he says. "Because I don't want *you* to ever have anything to tell about *me*." He offers this as some kind of generosity, some protection, but to me it sounds like I've been thrown to the wolves. He wants to be sure I have no secrets to confess when it's confess or be killed.

I pick up the bottle of Gabrielle from the table. "This is somehow the key to something, isn't it?"

"Charlie," he says, then pauses for a long moment. "I need something from you. I need you to describe, on the page, how Pascal might have used poison—poisonous gas, war chemicals—to create perfume. To create Gabrielle, specifically. I need evidence, formulas, that show how Pascal would have diluted the poison, to make it wearable, on the skin. Breathable. It needs to look convincing."

What is he talking about? I can't follow his logic. Is Hitler hoping to slowly poison the lesbians of Paris? But no: "Gabrielle went into production in the early twenties, a few years after the Germans lost the war. In its scent, there's something like strawberries about to go bad, wouldn't you say? Sweet and rotten, same reek as the gas I smelled hanging over the battlefield."

"I wouldn't say so," I say, sniffing at the perfume, though my mind does cast back, considering the possibility.

"Your *imagination*," he says, drawing out the word, sighing, tossing the rest of the cigarette in the teacup. "That's what I'm asking for. And your expertise. Just make up a formula, but one that would be convincing to chemists who might look at it closely."

"Why?" I say, and I toss my cigarette in the teacup too.

"The French fought with a deadly gas, and so did the Germans," he says. "And the war was won before all the gas was used. Those poisonous clouds came late into the battlefield. And somehow such warfare seemed more vicious, more deadly, than all the other vicious, deadly warfare, so the treaties that ended the war forbade the use of chemicals ever again. By anyone. Anywhere in the world. Can you imagine? There are laws in war. Rules. Like it's a card game, some rounds of Doppelkopf. Anyway, the Allies took every drop the Germans had. Added it to all their own vats of poison."

"And you think the poison went into perfume?"

"We believe Pascal worked for the French government," Voss says. "Or, at least, he was in service to the government. For him to experiment as he did, for him to manufacture his perfume formulas, to manage trade secrets, to license, to protect, he had to strike all sorts of deals with the law. The world of fragrance no longer operates on gentleman's agreements as it did centuries ago. There are no more gentlemen. So we have reason to believe the government approached Pascal to assist in ridding itself of the gas that was against the rules of war to keep. But rather than just letting it loose, why not make a little money at it at the same time? Pascal was to dilute the gas, to juggle its chemicals around, deactivate it, render it harmless. And then bottle it, sell it, send it faintly into the air." He waves a hand lightly, up and up and up. "All the German gas designed to choke the French would instead be sweetening the air with the scent of flowers. And the money made from it would strengthen the French military."

Voss speaks of it all with such admiration, such infatuation for Pascal's genius, I can tell he's overtaken for a moment.

"But Hitler," Voss continues, "thinks France did not do what it was supposed to do. That is, rid itself of the poison. He believes there are tanks and tanks and tanks of it still. He has plans for it all. He has factories building weapons. But I don't think it's just for practical purposes that he wants it. It's retribution. He wants to take back all that was stolen from Germany."

"And that's why all the bottles of Gabrielle have gone from the stores," I say. "He thinks that's where the poison is, and he'll extract it all?" I genuinely hope this is true; it's such madness, and I'd like to see Hitler finally undone by his ambitions.

"No no no," Voss says. He sighs. He slouches deeper into the sofa cushions. "*I* have all the bottles. *I'm* creating the intrigue around it. I'm glad to know that Lutz was curious about the painting of Gabrielle d'Estrées. I need his curiosity. And I need Hitler to think I'm onto something. I've told him that we just need to find the factories and farms where Gabrielle was produced, and we'll find the tanks of gas. And I've promised him that there's even more in the perfume diary. I've promised him formulas that will assure him of winning the war. I'm close to finding it all, I've told him." He tilts his head. Shrugs his shoulders. He smiles, but it seems to pain him. His voice drops. "But I'm not. I'm not close. I'm just painting him a picture of possibility because I *know* there's something to all this. I'm getting him invested in my theories, to allow for more time."

So now I'm embroiled in a plot to *trick* Hitler? I'm to compose a formula designed to deceive, to tinker with the very mechanics of this war, by suggesting the scent of rotten strawberries? "I'm not sure I can help," I say. Voss is out of his head. When all my deception was confined to these rooms, then we could just sit here sipping tea and talking scent. I just needed to keep to this house, so I entertained his flights of fancy. But now he's taking on a task that's beyond him. It's ridiculous, even for Voss. I can't trust his hunches.

"You *can* help," he says. I can see the sweat on his forehead. "If I don't show Hitler that I'm . . . that I'm . . . *discovering*, that I'm integral to winning all of Europe, then I won't have his ear anymore. He'll trust someone else. He'll listen to Lutz, or some other lug with big ambitions. I can't leave all this behind, Charlie. I'm too far along. This . . . *this*"—and he gestures around, signifying the house, the perfume—"I could lose it all. I could be sent to a tent, to tally munitions. Or, worse, I could be sent to a desk back in Germany. Signing stacks and stacks of papers until I'm crippled with arthritis."

I'm realizing he's not quite so chummy with Hitler as he might have always let on. But outlining his own demise for me just now seems somehow to embolden him. His voice grows stronger again. The threat of an ordinary, lackluster fate truly terrifies him. And he has gotten this far, after all.

"And I do think I've excited him about the historical connection," Voss continues, sitting up a little straighter, lifting his chin. "I think it amuses him that perfume might have assassinated Gabrielle d'Estrées, and that Pascal's family made the perfume. Because it's not enough that I'll rebuild Paris, Charlie. Hitler doesn't care about perfume in and of itself. He hates perfume. For all its musks. For civet. He thinks of perfume as a kind of slaughter. Hitler gets very emotional about animal cruelty." He rolls his eyes.

I'm not at all convinced, but still, I tell him I have ways to make a page look aged. I can make an ink of rotten mushrooms and oil of cloves that will fade the very moment it touches paper.

This effort to buy Voss more time is a way to buy more time for myself. And the more I become involved in the deception, the more I can deceive. "But what happens when it all leads nowhere?" I say. "We don't know where the gases are."

"We'll deal with that when we have to," he says.

···· 42 ····

I spend the evening alone in my kitchen, contemplating recipes for Gabrielle, and experimenting with inks and other agents for aging the page. And I get lost in thoughts of M. The scents: shoe polish on leather, the sticky vanilla of old books, sprigs of spearmint he'd grind with his teeth after a day of poking his tongue into cups of tea. The winter wind on his skin when he came in from the cold. The cedar scent of the mutton tallow the barber tugged through his hair.

I smell sulfur and gunpowder, fire and ash, hell and brimstone. M and I lie back on a blanket in a park to watch the fireworks shift and tumble the constellations. We're angels fallen to earth from the plaster frescoes of the band shell.

Sometimes I wore, for him, what he wanted me to wear. Back then we dressed for winter even in the summertime, so I wore the full overskirts and underskirts, the petticoats, the corsets, the whalebone rib-killers of a virtuous lady, all the better to stash all I picked from pockets; I hid under a mile-wide hat, its straw brim wilting and weighed down with armloads of wool roses and silk chrysanthemums, casting shadows across my face.

I was the story the fairgoers would tell for years, of the pilfered pocket watch, Mother's lost mother-of-pearl opera glasses, the earring clipped right off your lobe. One second you have everything you brought, then there's a rustle of my endless skirts as I brush past, a bump of my elbow as I'm hustled by the crowd. After a heartbeat or two, you feel that jump in your gut, that panicked flip-flop when you sense your pocket's too light or your finger's ringless. You feel the rush of a breeze where your bracelet should be. The pearl choker at your throat has been replaced by a lump in your gullet. I was only just there, and you can still smell the sting of the caraway I chew on, swear you can hear the seeds cracking between my teeth. In an instant, every innocent face in sight is slapped with aspects of guilt.

When we were in bed together that summer night, M and I studied our loot in the moonlight. He slipped the stolen rings onto my toes, draped a watch chain between my breasts, pressing the clock to the beat of my heart. I took in the salt and pepper of his sweat, in my nose, on my tongue, and his skin's hint of ginger and dirt.

But anytime I try to bottle any of it, M scurries away. He throws me off his scent.

I do, though, sell in my shop a cologne I call *M.* It's the perfume of our correspondence. The wood pulp of paper torn by the nib of a pen. The burnt wick of the sealing wax. A hint of cinnamon oil, from an ink that flickered red, glowing in the dark.

A touch of lime, from a wash that erased any words you wanted to take back.

My leaving Manhattan wasn't the end of the affair. M and I wrote to each other for years. Sometimes I even stayed longer in a place than I needed to, or wanted to, just because I knew he'd be writing back.

I kept every letter. I've carried them around the world with me. In a sense, the *letters* were the affair.

Clementine,

Read this letter every day, and every day, it will remind you that I still love you. Even if I never write again, these words will always be true.

M

Clementine,

I am angry at you for being angry with me. Every day, I will mail you a blank page, to punish you with silence.

M

Here's my silence. In all the empty space below.

M

Clementine,

Unless you know I've written you in a secret ink that's see-through, you're not seeing these words. You can't see these instructions: heat the page with a match, and my sentiments will rise up in ghostly pale green, then fade away to nothing again when you take the match away.

But please know, even if you can't read a word of this, that anything I could possibly say says nothing at all. I'm no poet, so I don't know how best to tell you all the secrets in my heart.

M

···· 43 ····

I dream my bed is crawling with winged spiders. I wake with a start and see Day beside me, tiptoeing her fingertips over my arm. I bolt upright, and Day jumps too. She holds her hand to her chest. "I'm sorry, I'm sorry," she says, cringing, whispering. "I was trying to wake you gently."

I might still be lingering in my dream, for at the foot of my bed are two shadowy figures I can't quite make out in the pitch-dark of the room.

"Is there someone else here?" I say. Lutz and Zoé, back for more? I pull the cord of the bedside lamp. I'm both startled and relieved at the sight of them: two young women—or tall, lanky girls, really—who could be twins.

Day snatches at the lamp cord, turning the light back off. "No light," she says, though the curtains are heavy, and no light could get out. "We might have been followed."

"Yes, you might have been followed," I mumble.

"You're going to have to keep the girls here," Day says.

"*Here?*" I say.

"Yes," she says. "Just for tonight. Or for a few nights. Or maybe more."

Before I can say anything at all, Day grabs at the cord again, turning on the light with a hard tug, nearly knocking the lamp over as she rushes to the end of the bed. The lamp wobbles, sending dark, dusky wings flickering through the room like bats in a belfry.

I reach over to right it. I tip the shade to lean the light toward the end of the bed. Day grabs the chin of the girl on the left, to aim her face right at me. The girl on the left looks just like the girl on the right, except she has a shiner and a split lip.

"They're practically children," Day says. She's scolding *me.* "You're going to leave them another minute in that brothel? They can't live there."

"Of course they shouldn't live there . . ."

Day folds her arms across her chest. Her wig is off her head and stuffed into her coat pocket, the curls partly peeking out. "You've got all kinds of hiding spots in this house," she says, but now she's not scolding, she's pleading. "All kinds of space. In a time like this, your house isn't just yours." She pauses. She's thinking. She says, "It belongs to Paris."

"But I . . . Yes, yes, I know. But I . . ."

Day pulls open the girl's coat. She pokes at her ribs. The girl's wearing a flimsy peignoir of chiffon and silk. And what I took to be blood on her chin, from her split lip, is actually smeared lipstick. Day says, "They're starving."

The girl doesn't seem that thin to me. And of all the places in Paris, I suspect Madame Boulette's is well provided for. I begin again. "You see, I have to be careful, because the work I'm doing . . ." But I don't continue. How do I explain the danger I've put *her* in, and Blue, by spending my days plotting to deceive Hitler? That I've been poisoning a Nazi to gain access? All I've told Blue and Day is that I've been curing Voss's flu with cups of tea. I've just innocently kept him company, I've told them. I search the house for the diary as he naps.

"Clementine," she says to me, her voice cracking, "we're always wrong if we think we've done enough. In times like these."

The girls shiver. The one's teeth start chattering.

"What are your names, girls?" I say.

They seem stumped by the question. They look at each other. They look over at Day.

Day's pleased that I've asked. "I've told them they can't remember their old names," she says. "I gave them new ones. I named them in your honor. This is Rose, and that's Violette. Flowers of the garden."

Day returns to the lamp to turn it out again. She tosses aside my bedcovers. "They can just crawl in with you for tonight. The bed's plenty big."

"Oh, Day," I say, but I scoot over to make room. The girls get in, coats and all. Day covers them up.

"They'll just be here a few days, Clem," she says, "or maybe a few more than a few. There are some nuns in the country taking in . . . well, taking in girls like Rose and Violette here. So we just need to get things arranged." She comes around to my side of the bed to kiss my forehead. "I have to run," she says. "If they notice I'm gone at the same time they notice *they're* gone, we're in for it."

"*We're* in for it?" I say.

At the bedroom door, she turns back to say, "In a few days, I may bring by a few others. But only a few." I *must* tell her the house might be watched, but as I'm trying to find the words, she says, again, "Only a few." And then she's gone.

I look over to the girls. One holds the other, the other holds a rag doll, both of them close to the bed's edge. Their backs are to me. "Get some sleep, Rose. Violette. Unless you'd rather I called you by your real names? Which would you prefer?" They mumble: *Rose. Violette.* "Okay, then," I say. "And tomorrow we'll make a nice room for you." And Day's right; there are any number of ample nooks and crannies in this house. And there are mattresses in the basement left behind by the academy. The cellar seems to have been a makeshift dormitory for the schoolboys. *Or a dungeon,* as Blue has suggested.

"Thank you, ma'am," the girls mutter.

"You'll call me Clementine," I say. "Or Clem."

"Yes, ma'am," they say. "Good night, ma'am."

And then I recognize them by the perfumes they wear. *My* perfumes, from when I conjured scents for the girls in Boulette's house. I smell pine needles and fire. I recall how the one girl described being lost in a storm alone, a little Gretel in the woods, and the hot, intoxicating smell of lightning striking a tree.

I scoot down beneath the blankets, turn my back to them, lie on the edge of the bed to leave them plenty of room. Though I'm certain I won't be able to sleep, I begin to drift off. But then I wake to the sound of weeping. One of the sisters is crying, and it sounds like she's trying to muffle her despair with her pillow. The other tries to coo comfort, whispering. She begins to sing to her sister, a lullaby, a song about sleep. When that doesn't work, she begins to beg. *We have to be quiet*, she whispers. *Don't cry, don't cry, don't cry*, she says, and that chant drifts into a lullaby of its own.

···· 44 ····

In the morning, the girls are gone from the bed. Did I dream them? When I go downstairs, I see that Blue is tending to them. He's brought out his makeup kit. Rose-or-Violette's bruises have been expertly blushed away, and the pink of her lips hides the cut. Blue did such a good job, I can no longer tell the two girls apart.

"I let the girls paint my face too," he says, fluttering his eyelashes. But his cheeks are always pink, his lips always pouty and red, so I can hardly tell. He says, "Ladies, this is my darling Clementine," parroting my tenor and cadence. He tries again, adjusting an octave or two here and there, a little higher, a little lower. "My darling Clementine." And then he says it again, inching his voice closer to the sound of mine. *My darling Clementine.*

He's been practicing my voice, my stride, my slight slouch, upon my insistence. Young men have been plucked from their homes and sent to Germany, thrust into the labor force. Blue, despite his bum ticker, is otherwise able-bodied. So, if needed, we'll drag out his makeup kit, dress him in my most ladylike, and shove his pockets full of my documents and identification. We'll send him off.

Blue isn't one to take it all lightly. He's an actor. He doesn't want to just pass for a little old lady. He wants to *become* me, specifically, down to every whistle between my teeth and every hitch in my giddyup. He follows me around the house, practicing the fall of my shadow.

He has even started *adding* to my character, to have more to borrow. He bought a pair of crochet roses, one for him and one for me, to pin to our matching lapels. And upon his request, I designed a perfume for myself, for him to steal from my skin.

This project seems also to distract him from Félix's absence. He's become a scholar of holes in the plot, ever since Félix up and left. He goes back and forth: one minute he's certain Félix is lying low because of the danger of his missions; the next minute he's certain he's dead; and then he's *wishing* for his death. One minute Blue's heart is broken; the next his heart's unbreakable. *Take a dagger and drown yourself,* as the actors say: Say one thing, mean another.

"How old are you girls?" I ask them. They tell me they're seventeen.

Blue says, in his own voice, "I told them to tell you they were fifteen, so they'd seem even more tragic. But that shows how good they are, that they wouldn't lie." He's clearly trying to convince me that the girls should stay. With his cheeks so rosy-hued, I can't help but remember when he first showed up here at the house, lost and pathetic, like a fairy-tale waif.

"Bring them each a mattress up from the cellar," I tell Blue, "and put them in the library. That's where you girls will sleep."

I imagine a houseful of refugees, all of them rehearsing my voice and my gait, wearing my clothes, walking in my shoes, escaping the city one by one by one.

···· 45 ····

"Let me read your leaves," I tell Voss. Reading tea leaves always seemed to me to require little skill or instinct. You just hold the cup by the handle, rock the last drops back and forth, swirl and agitate, letting the wet sediment clump in telltale shapes.

After he's drunk the tea in a few long gulps, I take the cup back, and I see what seems to me a flock of blackbirds.

He sits there, looking at me, expecting more. I tip the cup forward. I point out the birds.

He's twisting M's snake ring around and around his pinkie. This is the first time he's worn it since that day he took it. He's wearing it to taunt me, I suspect. He's frustrated I haven't given him a recipe for Gabrielle yet. I've assured him that it's not as easy as he might think, that I can't just do it overnight, that in order for it to convince, it needs to be able to withstand careful scrutiny by chemists. It must be impeccable. *And we have to be careful of Lutz,* I say, hoping to tip Lutz toward a bad fate. *He's already suspicious.*

In truth, I'm taking my time, dragging it out. I need more hours in the house to see if there's even anything to find.

"What might these blackbirds mean?" Voss says. He twists twists twists that snake ring around and around and around.

I want the ring back.

I put that ring on M's finger myself, and M took it off and put it back on my finger. *I want you to keep it,* he said.

Of course we can't really be married, I said. *I know that.*

You know nothing about me, he said, which is a very cruel thing to say to someone who loves you.

I swirl the tea around some more, knocking the birds apart. I remember a little magpie who brought me scraps of things when I was a child on the farm, the little trinkets and beads he stole and left in the crook of a tree. "The French here have a folktale," I say. "The blackbird's feathers were white until he tried to steal gold dust from the Prince of Riches. A demon came after him, breathing fire. The blackbird escaped, but he was forever soiled by smoke."

"Demons," Voss mutters.

"I can read your palm too," I say, offering more magic. I hold out my hand.

After a moment of hesitation, and a sigh, he offers me his palm.

This, I know *nothing* about. I don't know love from logic in the lines of his hand. But he's not very interested anyway.

Holding his hand in mine, I decide to take the ring back. It will be very easy. He's only indulging me, after all, with some impatience, glancing around the room.

I feign a ritual, holding my palm pressed down on his open hand, slipping my fingers in and among his.

And though I do take the ring from his finger, I fail to do so without his noticing. I clumsily fumble it, and it falls to the floor and rolls away.

Any other day, Voss would have been amused by my failure. But today he's annoyed. He takes his hand back, sighs some more. "I don't have time for this, Charlie," he tells me. Scolding me, really. He waves his hand at me, dismissive. "If you can find the ring, you can have it," he says. "And then you can go."

I nod, and I stand. Is he upset with me only because I'm slow with the formula, or does he already know about the girls in my house?

I kneel down, to look for the ring under the chair. The enormous wool blanket that covers it has tassels so long, they touch the floor. I stretch my arm under, reaching past the legs, and when I toss the blanket back over the arm to see beneath, there it is. Right in front of my eyes.

Not the ring. The insignia I've been seeking. The bit of flourish on Pascal's last note to Zoé. Over and over and over and over, a hundred of them repeated again and again in the pattern of the fabric of the chair I've been sitting on for weeks.

46

I squirm in the chair whenever I'm in it, twisting my spine, feeling for the diary's edges and points with my back and my ass. Digging my shoulder blades in. My elbows. Three days have passed since I discovered the insignia.

Voss is no longer quite so owly with me, now that I'm reading him my love letters. I swore to myself I'd never share them with him, but I need something to keep me in this chair, to keep him inviting me back, and they've had quite the effect.

He won't let me fix him tea anymore. He has seen a doctor that the concierge arranged, and this doctor dismissed my teas as folk remedies that do more harm than good. So Voss is always awake, and I'm never alone. But the letters keep me here, in a rickety chair that might very well be the vault where Pascal's diary is kept.

I can't just go tearing into the chair, tugging at the seams. Yesterday, when I knew that Voss would still be asleep, I arrived early to investigate the chair more closely, thinking the concierge would let me in. She wouldn't. *But come sit in my kitchen with me and wait,* she said, shuffling along the way that she does, bent at the back, her eyes on the floor. *You've never had coffee as strong as mine. You won't sleep for days.* And though I was grateful for the coffee, real coffee, a flavor that eased even as it sent a jolt, the concierge just sat not speaking, repairing a button on a blouse.

I've even asked Voss to let me roam the house alone, emphasizing again my keen criminal intuition. I could practice a kind of water witching; I would listen for loose floorboards underfoot. Press my ear to the wall, tap around for hollow spots. I would need complete silence and concentration. *I have instincts,* I told him.

Idiocy, Voss said.

And it is idiocy, really. How have I ever gotten away with anything? It's humiliating to sit here, the diary likely within reach as I read these letters that I've not read in years, and never wanted to read aloud. And though the paper has grown fragile, and the words faint, seeing M's handwriting makes me feel exactly as I did when I first laid eyes on them; I'm that same tender wretch. Whenever I first opened a letter from M, I wanted to read every word at once, to know his every sentiment in a glance. And at the same time, I dreaded reaching the end of the letter, because I knew there wouldn't be another one for weeks.

I couldn't at first smell the perfume on your last letter, M wrote me. *But I read the letter all the way through, and when I got to your signature—that faint scribble of yours, always looking like it was written with the tip of a feather—there, suddenly, was what I expect might be lily of the valley. It'd been there all along, but I was too much of a brute to notice it, it was so gentle, so pretty.*

When I finish reading, Voss is looking up and off. He says, "How did you prepare the paper?"

He's still caught up in the documents I gave him this morning. I concocted what I consider an excellent approximation of the Gabrielle formula, and created a few exquisitely antiqued pages along with it. I was afraid if I didn't come up with something, he'd hire someone else to do it. And since I've hooked him on these letters that I've been carrying with me for decades, I know he'll keep me around. For whatever reason, he listens close to M's words, though they can't offer him any kind of insight into the damage he seeks to do. Though I've no doubt his soul is corrupt, I know he's prone to sentiment and nostalgia. He loves the lovelorn refrain of my life with and without M. He's a romantic at heart.

All that sensitivity just makes him all the more disturbing.

I tell him I took an old journal, tore a few pages out, bleached them, scratched at them with powder of alum. I don't tell him, though, that I visited Annick in her printshop. I wanted papers to go along with the recipe, vaguely official-looking documents, to hint at Pascal's involvement with the government. I think I gained a great deal of her respect when I told her I needed to mock something up that might suggest a secret agency of licenses and approvals.

You're up to no good, she said with a wink. But she had everything I needed, including a whole cupboard full of surreptitious stamps and embossing seals to choose from.

"No," Voss says, "I'm talking about the perfume that M mentions. You wrote M on perfumed stationery. How darling."

"It was more about the play of it than the romance," I say. I feel the heat of a blush in my cheeks.

The etiquette books of the day advised young ladies against perfuming their letters. It was believed to be a bit vulgar, so the stationery shops, more often than not, kept perfumed paper behind the counter. You had to ask the clerk for it, sheepish, as if you were requesting picture postcards of naked ladies.

One letter I sent M had what they called a "kissing spot," where the perfume was confined to a little heart-shaped blot in an upper corner. Or I wrote on paper with scent worked right into the pulp. Or I would perfume the paper myself, using rice I'd soaked in heliotrope cologne then sprinkled over the linen stationery, in layers in a box.

And M would respond on scented paper too, but not stationery. He'd write on soap wrappers, or on prayer papers that priests burnt like incense, or on paper torn from the lining of a cedar box of cigars. He wrote me a short note on the singed paper of a torn-up firecracker. You could still smell the gunpowder on it. All M wrote: *I'll bet you're so handsome in your light summer suits.*

M wrote me once on a page that fell out of a crumbling book of love poems, his words weaving in and around the poem's references to honeysuckle and stolen kisses, the paper's scent tickling my nose, smelling of toast and mildew. *I write soft,* M wrote, *keeping the tip of the pen as far from the paper as I dare to, or it seems the whole page will become a cloud of dust. Wish I were there when you got this, so I could warn you to open the envelope without touching it much.*

One of his letters, too fragile to show Voss, was written on a wax wrapper that, when it arrived, still smelled faintly of peppermint, a particular sting of mint that was on M's breath when he kissed me sometimes, the candy freshly cracked between his back teeth. The letter had only one sentence: *Every day, I carry the weight of your absence.*

···· 47 ····

I've refused any rides home this week. The weather is changing, and though it's still cold, it's warmer than it was, and even a few degrees above freezing feels like spring. Instead of walking home, I walk farther away, taking wrong turns. I stumble back, Alice-like, into the wonderland that I love. Paris, where I live. The shopkeepers have stepped out to stand beneath their awnings. They clean their windows, sweep their walks.

"Clementine?" I hear someone say. The curiosity shop is run by a dotty old woman named Yvonne, and she's often sitting out in front of it in fair weather, on a stool, repairing an alarm clock or some such, her apron riddled with little springs and tiny cogs.

Today she's got a tin mermaid with a rusty key in her hip. She winds it up, and all the scales of her fishtail shiver and rattle. "I'm getting my summer window display together, to rush the season," she says. "It's so good to be out and about, isn't it? Here it is only February, and the air smells like spring." She breathes in deep. "Damp and earthy. Like peat moss."

I envy her the air she's getting. I suddenly can't catch my breath. I feel like there's a strip of cellophane across my mouth, and I'm having trouble keeping steady on my feet.

Yvonne's arm in mine makes me want to fall, helpless. I lean on her as she leads me inside. The shift in light puts spots in my eyes, and the spots in my eyes put pain in my head, and I swear I can't see. My heart feels like it's stuttering.

"I'm . . . I'm . . ." *I'm suffocating,* I'm trying to say.

"Just sit for a moment," Yvonne says in a singsong. She lowers me to a bench along the wall, and she speaks with such confidence, I trust that she knows the clutch in my chest better than I do.

I sit on Yvonne's bench, twisting M's ring on my finger.

The shop is suddenly alive with the chiming and striking of all the many clocks on the walls, and cuckoos clucking as they snap in and out of their coops. I look up and around, and I realize the shop is full of puzzles. Games. Cabinets. Tables with tops that swivel and shift to become something else. There are chests with springs and triggers. Even the bench I'm sitting on has a little hinged door on its arm. All around me, all I see are hidden things.

I think about Pascal's love for puzzles.

And I can breathe again.

"Yvonne," I say. "I need to know about how a person might hide a book. In a chair."

"I get a lot of that lately," she says. "Everyone wants everything under lock and key." I think of my own house with its false doors and trick stairs and the girls I've been hiding.

"Could you bring me a piece of paper?" I ask. "And a pencil." When Yvonne returns with it, I quick-sketch the chair in Pascal's parlor. And next to it, I illustrate the insignia in the fabric. "Does this look familiar to you?" I say. "Do you think it might have a drawer somewhere inside?" I remember once hearing that gentlemen employed chairs with secret compartments to hide their photographs of naked ladies.

"Well, I guess there'd be no way of knowing, unless you happened to know who made it. There's no factory line for such things. If it's truly to be a secret, then it's got to be one of a kind, doesn't it?"

But then Yvonne nods. She has an idea. She takes me by the arm again, and we head down the street, just a block, to a furniture dealer. Yvonne introduces me to the owner, then asks him: "If you were going to hide a book in your run-of-the-mill wing chair, how would you do it?"

I hold out to him the sketch I drew.

He harrumphs, rolls his eyes, and leads me across the shop floor, grabbing a silver letter opener from his desktop along the way. He grumbles and gripes as he walks. "Everybody thinks chairs are full of fluff. Or that they're solid wood, or something. Nobody ever thinks what it might look like under the upholstery. Never give it a single thought. People pay so little attention to the world around them, to the design that makes the world work. Don't care a lick about the things they can't live without."

He selects a chair, pulls it out from along the wall, and turns it around so its back faces us. He begins to pry at the fabric backing with his letter opener, loosening the nails of the trim. "You're wanting secret drawers, like in a dime novel, but a chair's practically hollow. It's all framework and air. What do you need a trick chair for, when any chair will do?" He pushes back a flap of the fabric, and Yvonne and I peer in.

"Well, look at that," Yvonne says. "I could crawl up in there myself, if push came to shove."

···· 48 ····

On slow afternoons, Madame Boulette invites the painters of the Latin Quarter to the cabaret to paint her ladies lazy and naked. The girls nap on settees that are carried onto the stage for them, and the painters set up their easels. And those girls who stay awake stay lost in their own vanity.

Those girls who've not fled, that is. The girls we called Rose and Violette have left us for nuns in the countryside of southern France, and an Ivy and an Aster popped up in their place only minutes later; then, when they left, a Tulip and a Clover and a Pansy. Day had promised me I'd house only a few girls for a few days, but my perfume shop is now practically a train station.

There's a whole path in place, a network. The nuns who make the cigarettes for the poor of Paris have gained a flair for it. They pepper the tobacco with crushed candy lozenges, with shavings of chocolate, with peppermint sprigs. All of Paris craves their smoke. So the nuns have expanded their operation beyond charity, selling their cigarettes to fund their efforts to help people out of the city. Rose, Violette, Ivy, Aster—all our flowers have benefited.

Blue, who knows his way around a costume, helps to buckle and knot the girls into nuns' habits, which are not unassuming at all. Our girls sneak out of town in starched headwear that's as gangly as a white crane lifting from a lake, wings outstretched. They lower their heads, penitent, while their wimples flap with each shuffling step.

I've called a meeting with my conspirators, and we join the artists at Boulette's. Zoé is convinced that Lutz somehow hears her every word in her apartment, that he has somehow posted listeners at her walls, or hidden microphones in her vents, so we tuck ourselves into the back of the cabaret, hiding behind our easels and canvases, to whisper. Zoé sits at the easel to my left, Day to my right, Blue in front of me.

Madame Boulette provides the painters the best paints, from the best color shop in Paris. She likes to spoil the artists because she was a model herself in her youth, and she boasts that she hangs naked in garrets and ateliers all across the city. She worked cheap, so in those portraits you'll see all the finest artists coming of age, finding their style as they shape her breasts and curve her hips.

I confess everything, my voice low, as we sketch and paint. The poison, the recipe for Gabrielle, the perfume diary within reach for days. I'm glad to make my confession here, out in the open, our eyes on our canvases, so they can't scold me for not telling them sooner.

"What do you know about your father's work for the government?" I ask Zoé as I paint, as I attempt to approximate the exact pink of the model's skin. "About any formulas he might have concocted? For the military?" On the one hand, I'm hoping she might know something somewhat useful. But on the other, how very aggravating if she kept any such information from me.

"My father was a perfumer," she says, all wispiness, as she dots the canvas with purple, with a lazy *tap tap tap*, for the grapes in the bowl next to the settee.

"Yes, of course. And a perfumer is a chemist."

She puts down her brush. "My father's entire life was about beauty. What would the military want with his attar of roses?" She looks over at me. "The diary. How are you getting it out of the house?"

Together we all consider what possibilities there might be for nabbing the book.

"You've been making Voss woozy for weeks," Zoé says. "Just turn his lights all the way out."

There's the concierge at the door, I tell them. She takes my coat when I get there, and puts it back on me when I go, always certain to send me off empty-handed. Whatever her many setbacks—her severe nearsightedness, her hard of hearing, her hooked spine that pitches her forward, her eyes on the ground—she makes up for with her efficiency and service and pride in her work.

"You could give them *both* a little nap," Day says. "Sneak the book out, then go back in and pretend to have fainted too. Could blame an ether leak."

The suggestions become more and more ridiculous, until we finally settle on the most ridiculous one of all.

"Get Voss out of the house," Blue says, "and I'll pretend to be you." He's mimicking my voice and does manage to capture something particular about the way I talk.

I know that the actor in him has been hoping to put his impression of me to some dire use; he's probably even longed for me to become somehow incapacitated.

I would just need to convince Voss to walk with me again, like we did in the early days of our twisted courtship. Ever since our night at the cabaret, he's been squeamish about leaving the house. He has become content with his imprisonment in Pascal's mansion.

And then, of course, fate steps up onto the cabaret stage. Another model takes her place on a bench, and when she undoes the belt of her robe and lets the silk fall from her shoulders, I mistake the swirl of a blue and purple birthmark across her shoulder and arm for tattoos. They look, at first blink, like a constellation of butterflies.

···· 49 ····

There's something depleted about Voss when I see him again, but it's a different kind of depletion than when I drugged him daily. I wonder if my recipe for Gabrielle has done its work for him. I wonder if his mission might be shifting, the pressures altered.

"What's M up to?" Voss says, soft, lazy, practically purring it.

But he knows that M rarely tells us what he's up to—few of his letters ever said much of anything about his life. He wrote most often of how little he had to say and how inarticulate he was and how much he regretted that he hadn't a way with words. His letters were lovely apologies for themselves. Or he'd write about the ink he used, or the pen in his hand, or the wax he'd melt to seal the envelope. Nonetheless, over the years, I've read each one over and over, like they were lyrics I was committing to memory. There was sweetness and sentiment in his insistence that he wasn't the sentimental type.

I wish my letters were like yours, I read aloud to Voss. M had written on a paper cone that had held roasted chestnuts he'd bought from a cart in Central Park. The paper is still dotted with oil spots, and though it no longer smells of the chestnuts, I remember that it did, so richly, that scent of cooked sugar and burnt wood. He wrote the letter on a Sunday afternoon in 1907, a decade since I'd last seen him in Manhattan. *I never say all the things I want to, because it'll all fall flat on the page, and you'll think me a fool, so if you'd do me the favor of reading between these lines, then I'll only feel half as inept. I always was better in your imagination.*

Voss says, "He doesn't feel foolish at all. He's playing *you* for the fool. He sends you these sweet nothings, and you respond at once, with your heart on your sleeve, and he can go on, happy-go-lucky, knowing he's still on your mind. He's again aglow from your admiration. And you won't hear from him again until that glow begins to dim a little. I'm quite frustrated with him, honestly. I hoped these letters would be better."

"Well," I say, "M has to be careful, doesn't he."

"How's that?"

"He was the vulnerable one. He was married."

Voss rolls his eyes. "*You* were the vulnerable one," he says. "You. You were all alone. For M to court your affection . . . it was irresponsible."

I had wanted to stay aloof in my letters, but I couldn't. You never know, when you're waiting, if you're waiting in vain. While I waited and waited for M to respond to whatever letter I'd last sent, I'd become determined to punish him. I would decide I'd make him wait too. But then his letter would arrive, and I'd forgive him everything. And I knew I'd just be punishing myself. If I sent no letter, I couldn't enjoy that irresistible treachery of anticipation.

I could *feel* the anticipation. It was like another sense, a sixth or a seventh. It could be intoxicating, that fear that he might never write back. I'd indulge it, like self-pity, and be wasted by it. So when his letter would finally arrive, it needn't have said anything at all. Just the sight of my name in his hand—it gave me life.

Were these love letters? Was this love? Infatuation? Preoccupation? Did it matter? Even the possibility of devastation appealed, to be haunted by him should he never write again, to spend the rest of my life interpreting meaning in his silence. Reading between his lines. Above all, I believed in M's gentle nature and kind soul, despite his fascination with poison. Even that had a harmless, gothic charm. I always believed he deserved true love, even if he couldn't have it with me.

I'm about to speak. "Don't defend him," Voss says before I can. "He owed you more respect."

I want to believe Voss is capable of this flicker of compassion, since he's telling me what I want to hear. But that will be the mystery that haunts me, if I survive all this: How can he be so moved by beauty, and by tales of love, here in this room with me, while his agencies consume the very soul of Paris? How can any self-respecting man profit from cruelty? What if I led him to Greenspoon's, and showed him those lost dolls in that squeaky pram?

I want him to explain it to me. That's how I'll punish him. I want to hold the tip of my knife to the bob of his Adam's apple, and I want him to sing to me every sick note of his wickedness.

···· 50 ····

In Costa Rica, I tell Voss, the grasshoppers look like chimney swifts when they take wing. They collect on the limbs of the coffee trees and weigh them down, break them off. They don't have a taste for the cherries, but they wreck the fields nonetheless.

It's the spring after I left New York; I'm not yet thirty. I'm sitting on the front terrace of a coffee baron's pink house, with the fields just across the road. I watch as the workers run among the trees banging kettles with metal spoons, and rolling mallets up and down the ribs of washboards, to rattle the locusts, to send them up and off. The noise starts to come together as something like a song when a few men arrive with instruments—a little wooden fiddle with horsehair strings, a potato-shaped flute. They form an orchestra, marching in the shade of the leaves of the banana trees planted among the rows.

A maid lowers a bamboo blind at the edge of the terrace, which doesn't do much of anything to muffle the thrum of the insects and the racket of the workers.

"That plague of locusts makes me think of the farm I grew up on," I tell those on the terrace. I remember standing among the grasshoppers, their feet pulling at me as if plucking me apart, their footsteps sticky, like they'd marched through syrup. They stepped across my eyes shut tight and tugged at my lashes. I pictured them stripping me bare, stitch by stitch, casting me naked into their new world.

"It's hardly a *plague*," the baron says. "They'll rest a minute and be on their way."

The baron's wife refills everyone's cup with coffee from a pot of glass and copper, spilling nearly as much as she pours. Her hands are gnarled with arthritis and riddled with heavy gemstones; it seems as if her knotty fists have begun to grow around her rings. "In Costa Rica, we worry over the volcanoes and earthquakes," she says. "We don't fret about the garden pests. We can scare them off with whistles and spoons."

There are seven of us on the terrace, sitting at iron tables, and on teakwood benches, under parasols and Panama hats. We're part of what they've called an "olfactory club," an international cabal of sensualists. It's not just about perfume, but about anything pleasantly scented—we inhale and analyze the fragrances of fresh flowers, herbs, wine, sweets, supper. We attempt to be poetic about it, but we're at a loss for words most of the time, no matter the language we speak.

I'm new to the group. They're thrilled to have me, because the olfactory club is aging toward oblivion. They're all of them old, but for me and one other. She's new too. They're thrilled even more by her, because of her strange scholarship.

I catch her looking my way, more often than not. I become a scholar of the scholar's glances, and the blue of her eyes, which I decide are a mix of midnight and ocean sky, until I decide that's not right at all—they're lapis lazuli and turquoise. Dutch china and sapphires. Bluebell and bluebird and blueberry. But maybe it's not the blue doing me in; maybe it's only because her eyes are finding mine that I find them so pretty.

I see why M fell in love with her.

I wear trousers, a vest, and a pocket watch with a chain. My hair's cut short. And hers is too, though it falls a little lower than mine, past her ears. She wears trousers, a whole suit, a touch too heavy for the climate—a cheviot tweed, of gray chalk. And it needs tailoring; it's too broad at the shoulders, too tight at the chest. Wrinkled and trunk-battered, a professor's cheap getup. Her brown oxford shoes are scuffed bone-white at the toes. On her lapel is a ladylike touch, a butterfly-shaped clip with wings of silver lace. "I wish I'd been given your liberties when I was young," one of the wives tells us on the terrace.

"Nobody's given me nothing," I say. To them, I'm the very picture of the Wild West, and the smell of it too, the spice of a gunfight still caught in my clothes.

I cross my legs, revealing a woman's boot with a woman's heel.

I get the scholar's attention and hold her eyes in mine for a beat or two too long. She obviously wants me to catch her looking.

Maids bring out platters of scents particular to Costa Rica—balsam flowers, breadfruit, a thorny, blood-colored pitahaya. We hold the objects to our noses, roll our eyes back in our heads. We sigh, we moan.

The maids then bring out a few trays of empty ruby-red cordial glasses, and I fill them with my contribution to the club's lost afternoon—an herbal liqueur I claim to have bought from a swamp pirate of the bayou. Everyone sniffs at the stuff before they take a sip. *Do I smell licorice? Molasses? Pineapple? Sweet onion?* They drink the shot I give them, then ask for another. It's at the tip of their tongues, they say, a specific scent that's escaping them. Just when they think they're at the edge of discovery, it flitters away. *Dill? Marigold? Anisette?* They stare off in contemplation.

Sandalwood? Almond? Fig? Their voices are growing fewer, and their jaws are growing weak. They're slurring their words.

I ease into the house, and up the stairs. I have to hurry. Now that the herb has kicked in, I won't have long before it wears off.

The liquor includes an elixir made from the crushed leaves of a hypnotic weed I bought in Oaxaca, on my way down by train, a local concoction that fishermen pour into the sea to stun the fish just long enough for them to stick their hooks in.

In the library at the end of the hall, the blue-eyed lepidopterist, M's butterfly chaser, has set up for her presentation later in the evening. She has plucked off the wings of butterflies, soaked them in alcohol.

She has extracted the scents they give off in their efforts to find love. In her glass bottles are the perfumes of their mating calls.

She has already made a display of little framed boxes of pinned butterflies, and next to each box is a corked bottle of essence. Each bottle is marked with some scientific-looking collision of letters. I take all the bottles and place them in a satchel. I turn my ear to the hallway, listening for silence.

I leave the room, and step easy across the terrace, trying to keep my heels from clicking too loud against the terra-cotta tiles. For now, the olfactory club is out like a light, slumped in their chairs, their mouths fallen open, their eyes shut tight, their snores buzzing like a swarm of houseflies.

Suddenly, the scholar's blue eyes are piercing right through me. I stop in my tracks. "Look at you," I say.

"*Shhh,*" she hisses, her finger at her lips. "They need their sleep."

She can't possibly know that my satchel is full of her butterfly juices. I just need to keep walking. But I don't.

She remains seated. She picks up her cordial, still full. She crosses her legs. She sniffs at the liqueur. "For such experts," she says, "they don't know much. I couldn't tell you exactly what you put in this, but I could smell right away that you were up to no good." She swirls the liqueur around in the glass. "There's the faintest hint of . . . corruption."

"I have to go," I say, not going.

"I'll go with you," she says.

"*You're* the one who most needs to be asleep," I say. "You're the one I'm robbing." I nod at her glass. "Take your medicine."

"It's not a robbery if I go with you," she says.

One of the old women—the wife of a candle-dripper in Tijuana—on this side of sleep, bats at a grasshopper that's trapped itself in the curls of her ox-hair wig. She then thumps her knuckle on her nose. She rubs at her eye.

"We'd best leave," the lepidopterist says, standing.

We walk down the road to where I've arranged for a coach to wait. The giant grasshoppers light on the lanterns of the carriage, in its curtains, climb through the manes of the horses. The driver up top swats them from the sleeves of his uniform. He kicks them from his boots, jimmies them from his laces with his riding crop.

On our way to the hotel, the bugs thumping against our roof, I tell the scholar I was hired by the wife of a railroad tycoon who keeps an acres-wide garden in New York state, every plant planted specifically to lure butterflies. She's a butterfly fiend. She'd heard of the scholar's research, and she coveted her vials of scent. "You may remember her," I say. The woman had offered the scholar a handsome sum herself, but the scholar declined in the name of science. So the woman hired me. She so longed to go to the opera, or the races, with the scent at her neck. *I'll pay anything.* And she would. She was rich, and there was nothing else she wanted more.

I don't tell her that I know M, and that he still cries for her, still loves her.

I can feel a grasshopper alive under my boot, rustling its wings, sounding like the papery *th-th-th-th-th-th-th* rattle of a rattlesnake.

At the hotel, in my room, the scholar puts the scent at *my* neck, in a finger dab. She has come to Costa Rica not just for the olfactory club but to find the scent of the *Heliconius cydno,* the longwing butterfly that hovers in tropical lands. "But this is the *Hamanumida daedalus,*" she whispers in my ear. She has stripped me of my trousers, and my suspenders, and my shirt. The *Hamanumida daedalus* smells of toffee. Butterscotch. She dabs a dot of butterfly between my breasts. "*Mycalesis safitza,*" she says, looking up at me with those blue eyes. The blue of a bruise? Of forget-me-nots? She kisses me where she's placed the scent. Licks at my nipple.

I know these ways. The whispers that make everything she says—science, chemistry—sound like seduction. She leads, and directs, but with a touch so soft I can barely feel it. I close my eyes and imagine M.

The *Mycalesis safitza* smells of chocolate and vanilla bean. The scholar touches her fingertip to another bottle, then puts her hand between my legs. She slips one finger inside. Then another. *"Ixias cingalensis,"* she whispers, her arm around my waist and beneath me, arching my back. I take the bottle from her and hold it to my nose. I breathe in its scent of meadowsweet.

···· 51 ····

I tell Voss about the butterfly hunter, at some risk, I suppose. I've left out almost nothing. Not the sleeping potion. Not the sex. He could so easily connect the dots between my drugged olfactory-club fellows and the spiked tea I was funneling down his gullet for days.

But I also know it's my corruption that has kept me here. He appreciates my depraved logic. My sick pursuit of beauty.

After finding the blue-eyed butterfly hunter, I stuck with her, hopping from jungle to jungle. I was with her for almost a year, almost as long as I was with M. I honestly thought I could fix my broken heart by being with someone M loved so much. By knowing the butterfly hunter intimately, I reasoned, I was getting to know M better too. It was as if I was now somehow part of M's yearning for the lepidopterist. And maybe there was some element of revenge. Maybe I thought I could have the love affair with her that M longed for. I would confess it all to M in long, detailed letters, and he'd be broken with regret and jealousy.

But I never mentioned any of it in my letters to M. For years after, I looked back at it all in embarrassment. I'd been naive. Childish. From then on, butterflies mocked me.

I didn't thieve a single thing in my travels with the lepidopterist, though I made myself useful by negotiating with guides and hoteliers on the prices of donkeys and hammocks. I typed reports on typewriters that weighed half a ton, in Ceylon, in Singapore, in Trinidad. And though I'm not named once in the book she published later, I'm everywhere in it.

"She could never quite figure out the scents on her own," I tell Voss. "She had no language for it."

"You made it all up," Voss says.

"She'd write in her little notebook whatever I told her," I say. "If it hadn't been for me, her every butterfly would've smelled only of sugar or spice." I gave her heath mold and sea salt, Turkish steam, Texas firefly, scarlet trumpet creeper, Russian hedgehog. Fanciful descriptions, I suppose, but I only ever had my own instinct to draw from.

No matter what I said, she'd hold the bug to her own nose, and she'd nod slow. *Yes, yes,* she'd say. *Yes, I can see that.*

She left me for a missionary's wife we met in Tongatapu. The preacher had left, and the wife stayed behind. She lived on the beach in a thatched hut and smoked a meerschaum pipe. Her dresses were just sheets of hibiscus bark hammered thin and wrapped around and around her middle. She smelled of coconut oil. The lepidopterist never knew she'd never loved me until she fell in love with the missionary's wife.

"You never mentioned M to the butterfly killer," Voss says, "in that year you were with her?"

"No."

"Why not?"

"The longer you wait to confess," I say, "the guiltier your secret."

He seems annoyed by the mention of guilt. He sighs. "How so?" he says, with a pointed tone of boredom.

"She might have thought I was only with her to punish M."

"And didn't you *want* to punish the butterfly killer with that? When she left you for the other woman in Tongatapu? You could have said the only reason you were ever with her was to punish M. And then you could have told M about the butterfly killer, to punish *him*."

"She lives in Paris now," I tell Voss.

"*Who* lives in Paris now?" he says. "Not the lepidopterist?"

"Yes," I say. "The lepidopterist."

"How dare you keep this from me?" he says, but with bemusement.

"I haven't kept it from you," I say. "I'm telling you now."

"You've seen her, surely."

"Yes," I say. "A time or two."

"A time or two? Is she still with the missionary's wife?"

"No, no," I say. "She's alone." I explain how we became reacquainted. Before the war came on, I had a supplier, a spice vendor, who traveled the world and brought back to me rare scents and flavors. The squeeze from green lemons, the peel of sweet pomegranate. Myrtle berries, Turkish rhubarb, de-pipped raisins, radish seeds. One day he arrived with glass vials in paper tubes, and on the tubes were labels marking the species of butterflies the scholar collected, and the descriptions of their scents I'd invented years before. The *Mylothris agathina: candied cactus.* The *Papilio polydamas: tanned penguin leather.*

"You smelled your own nose on them," Voss says. "Does she have any of her research left?"

I shrug. "She'd fallen on some hard times," I say. "So she'd been selling it all off. But she might have kept some of it back. I can't imagine there was much of a market for it." I stop speaking for a moment, and pluck at a puff of lint on my trousers. "She doesn't live far from here, now that I think about it."

I don't need to nudge any more than that. *We'll go in the morning,* he insists. *We haven't taken a stroll in days,* he says. *No, it's been weeks,* I tell him. *Perfect,* he says. *That's that.*

···· 52 ····

I have no idea what became of my butterfly hunter. I haven't seen her, or bottles of her butterfly scents, since she left me for the missionary's wife over forty years ago.

We are off to Annick, the printer and bookbinder. And actress. She is French, while my lepidopterist was American, but I revised the story accordingly when telling it to Voss. I gave her a French name. I revised her eyes too. They're brown, with such warmth.

"I'm wearing your favorite," Annick says when she opens the apartment door to us. She waves her hand at her throat, stirring up the scent. "The *Catophaga paulina*. You always said it reminded you of Irish-moss lemonade."

She's laying it on thick, this one. She's been tasked with making as little impression as possible. I just needed a lure to get Voss out of the house. My script calls for her to be distant, absentminded, and lovelorn. She's to be the lepidopterist as I prefer to picture her: full of regret. Wounded. We would sniff at the vials of fraudulent butterfly juices I'd concocted from my perfumery's collection of oils, satisfy Voss's curiosity, then move along.

Annick gestures us into her apartment. "Oskar Voss," I say, nodding an introduction. "My partner in perfume." And to Voss: "And Professor Baptiste here is a scholar of the mating tricks of butterflies."

As Voss shakes Annick's hand, he sniffs toward her and her Irish-moss lemonade. She hooks her finger around the knot of her own tie to tug it down, to bare her throat. She arches her neck.

"Not unpleasant," Voss says after taking in a full snuffle. He then leans back to examine her attire. "You seem to share my lady friend's taste in tailors."

"You know," Annick starts, then stops, leading us to the sofa by the window, with that swagger of hers. She's waving a finger in the air, strutting her long legs, and I swear she kicks up an electrical spark with the whisk of her corduroy trousers. "I wore what women wore well into my twenties," she says. "Then one day, at the fair in Vincennes, I'm bustled up tighter than a trussed pig, can hardly breathe from all the gut-strangling of all my straps, and I look up on the stage and there, among the clowns, is a man in a silk dress and a wig, fluttering a fan around, doing somersaults, showing off his bloomers. Dancing. Spinning. Light as a feather." I sit on the sofa; Voss sits in the chair across from me. Annick still stands. "And I thought, well, isn't that the way it is. When you're wearing a woman's clothes, you're either a tragedy or a comedy. And I wasn't having it. I've worn trousers ever since."

I catch Annick's eye and try to signal she should ratchet it back, this performance, but I get caught up in those eyes. She holds my gaze, and my heart speeds up. I haven't been smitten with anyone in years, and here Annick comes along, in the worst of times, to surprise me.

She keeps going, and I'm enchanted: "There are even butterflies that take on a costume, to throw off the enemy. 'Mimickers.' They take on the flight patterns, and the wing colors, of a more disgusting variety of bug. If they seem like insects that will stink and stain, and taste bad, they'll be unbothered by their predators." She winks at me and tightens the knot of her necktie.

I'm taken in by the spectacle of the character she's created. She really does seem to be someone I invented. She drops onto the cushion next to me, her legs open, her knee near mine. She stretches out her arm to rest against the back of the sofa, and I lean back, and we're touching. And when we touch, she doesn't move her arm an inch. I feel the weight of it against me. And I feel inclined to tilt in her direction, her energy pulling me in. The eye of the storm, sucking in ships.

And I know that fair in Vincennes she mentioned. I've mocked up perfumes based on people's memories of it. A few have come to me with their nostalgia for the fair, fearful that they'll never be able to visit it again. The gingerbread pig with your name in icing across its back. The hot axles and grease of the carousel, with its giant hares in mid-leap, bobbing up and down as you sit in the saddles on their backs, breathing in the fumes.

"Go ahead," she says to Voss, pointing in the direction of the veneered box next to him. "Look inside the humidor."

He lifts the lid, and the glass vials jingle. He removes one, uncorks it, holds it to his nose.

"What's the label say?" she asks.

"*Ornithoptera darsius,*" he says.

"Ah, *that* butterfly," Annick says. "Smells like the musk of the wolverines that infest wrecked castles."

Voss scrunches up his forehead, purses his lips, considers.

Annick pats my knee. "Clementine devised descriptions for the scents, way back when," she says. "She breathed them in, then put her words in my mouth." She looks at me, smiles, winks again. As Voss fusses with the humidor of butterflies, she keeps her hand on my knee. Her eyes are steady on mine. She doesn't look away, and I don't either.

She then pats my knee again, smiles again, pulls her hand back to her own knee, and looks to Voss. "What's that you've got now?" she says. *Pinacopteryx charina,* he says. *Ah,* she says, *evaporated apricots in coffee jelly.*

This goes on for a while, this back-and-forth, of butterfly species, and what those painted ladies smell like when they're looking for love. Because that's the upshot—the lepidopterist's cabinet was bottled flirtation.

···· 53 ····

Across the street from Pascal's, when we left the house to visit Annick, Blue sat waiting in the two-seat buggy of a *vélo-taxi*—one of the bicycle-drawn cabs that we ride in, in these days of the gasoline bans. The driver remained in his bicycle seat patiently smoking one of the cigarettes Blue had bribed him with. The buggy had no top, so Blue hid behind a parasol, keeping one eye out, watching for us.

Here's what was supposed to happen:

Blue and I wore matching trousers of a light cashmere; they're bell-bottomed like a sailor's blues, and they flow as we walk, not at all unnoticeable with their flutter and flap.

Blue had been practicing to be me for weeks, reciting my lines, in my voice. He would tell the concierge, as me, that he had doubled back for the cigarette tin. *Cigarettes . . . we're absolutely addicted.* Blue was to rush by the concierge, assuming she'd follow but not giving her a moment to object; he'd wave a paper fan beneath his chin, sending up some of the perfume I've been blasting at my neck for the last several days, just for this moment, so the concierge would know it was me, my new signature, a scent that quotes the rosemary and clove of a concoction called thieves' vinegar. Legend has it that spice merchants warded off the plague by dousing themselves in it to plunder dead bodies for their watches and rings.

Blue had squeezed his feet into a pair of my shoes that have been worn down by my misstep. The concierge, she of the bent back, her eyes always cast downward, knows me best by the slant of my heel.

Blue was to creak the steps exactly the way that I do, and his cashmere trousers would move with my particular rhythms of pace.

The concierge would unlock the door, then wait while Blue went up to the upstairs room.

Once there, Blue was to take from my coat the kidney-sticker I've had since my days in the Wild West. He would simply go to the back of the chair, and use my dagger to pry at the trim, loosening the nail-heads further, cutting whatever strap might sit in his way. Blue, an expert tailor from his backstage work at the theater, had secreted a zipper in the lining of my coat, where he would hide the diary once he found it. And then he'd be gone.

···· 54 ····

As Voss and I stroll away from the butterfly hunter's apartment, taking advantage of the spot of sun and lack of wind, we meander like we used to.

"You haven't told me," I say. "What happened with the formula for Gabrielle I gave you?"

He doesn't answer for a while. "Nothing," he says. "Nothing yet. I don't know how much time it gives me. If any. And now there's something else . . ."

I wait for him to tell me the something else, but he begins chattering on about the shops we're passing. A milliner's shop, and a shop with lingerie. *Cheap,* he says. *Poorly cut*. A shop that sells rebuilt typewriters sends him into a long-winded reverie on the stately beauty of the machine and the music of its racket.

"You say there's something else," I say. "About the Gabrielle."

"Oh yes," he says. "Yes." But then he pauses again. He looks around, as if seeking some other shop to go on and on about. Finally he says, "There's some indication that Pascal was even more involved with the war effort than I had guessed, beyond the excess chemicals . . ."

All I can think about is Blue, and the concierge, so all I see anywhere are the keys above the doors of locksmiths. There's a locksmith on every block and around every corner. Keys lit up with electrical bulbs or neon, or wooden, painted gold, hanging from chains. There are so many apartments in the city that the locksmiths have always done swift business, every little niche of Paris shifting on every day rent is due.

And then I realize Voss has been leading me to my street. "I've never been to your shop," he says. "You never invited me. I was beginning to think it was a figment of your imagination."

"There's not much to it," I say.

"We'll see," he says.

The rest of the way, I fret, afraid to walk in on Blue in my clothes. At the house, I twist the key in the lock with enough rattle to echo, sending the tumblers this way and that, unlocking the lock, then locking it back up. But my hands are shaking, so my difficulty with the lock isn't entirely fake. I mention Voss by name, my voice close to the glass of the door—*You'd think a thief could get into her own house, eh, Oskar?*—doing what I can to let Blue know that if he's in there, in my costume, he shouldn't be.

And he isn't. And neither are any of our girls. Or rather, Madame Boulette's girls. Our latest batch of lost trollops typically sit in the parlor upstairs, collapsed on the sofa, lazing around in kimonos and ratty silk stockings.

I open the drapes and blast the room with light, the sun playing off the mirrors along the wall.

"Precious," Voss says.

"I'm sorry to disappoint," I say, and out of the corner of my eye, I catch sight of the necktie I'm wearing. Without a neck. Wriggling unknotted across the rose-patterned chaise beneath the window. A snake in the garden. It's the tie Blue wore as part of his disguise. The one difference between his and mine is that his is now spattered with blood.

I step around and turn my back to Voss, so I'm between him and the necktie. I pretend to fuss with some unstoppered bottles, then sweep up the tie as he runs his eyes across the shelves opposite me. I shove the tie in my pocket.

"I'm not disappointed," he says. "It's charming. It's like the fashion industry here in Paris, isn't it? Composed of a million little craftsmen. A miracle, really, that a single dress gets made at all. Lace made in one shop, buttons in another. Someone else, even, for the button-

holes." He picks up a bottle to smell the perfume. "It can only exist by its very fragility."

And then I begin to think I'm breathing in the fumes of a drug I sent along with Blue. Were he to get caught, by the concierge or anyone, a quick, carefully positioned spritz from the perfume bottle could make the person take a seat, if not conk all the way out. The useful aftereffect is a lost hour or two, the fumes robbing your victim of recent memory. So if someone catches you, you're not caught at all. You just make her forget you've run into each other.

And I'm thinking the fumes are doing their number on me too, slight as they are. I feel dizzy as I sit on the chaise, but with Voss's back to me again, I manage to slip the tie from my pocket and drop it back behind the cushions, just in case it is somehow holding on to the scent.

When Voss turns to look at me again, his expression is serious, perhaps sad, as he fiddles with a bottle, twisting its lid.

"I've not lost faith in any of this, Charlie," he says. He pauses. His eyes sparkle with some emotion, it seems. "This is a beautiful shop. I mean it," he says.

"Thank you, Oskar."

"Have I ever told you I had sons?"

Had sons. A peculiar way to put it, but no, he hasn't told me any such thing, and he knows it. I just shake my head.

"I have a son who is a military man too," he says. "I'm very proud of him. And I want to protect him. Nobody wants their children sent to any battlefronts in this war. And my son has sons of his own. So you see, this is . . . this is why . . . well, I fear everything's going to fall apart in Paris before I find anything I need."

I'm so surprised by his vulnerability, and so desperate for him to leave, I say nothing. But he goes on.

"My other son," he says, "would be my oldest. If he'd lived. When he was a little boy, he jumped into my arms, and . . . it was like he fainted. Like he fell asleep. He died after a few hours in the hospital. A heart condition. Very rare. And even more rare in children so small. To have your child stop breathing in your arms casts a pall of loneliness over the rest of your life. You never recover." He returns the perfume bottle to the vanity. "And you spend the rest of your life counting birthdays. Wondering what he'd be like now if he'd lived. A little terrible, tragic indulgence you allow yourself every now and again."

"I can only imagine," I say. But I'm trying to analyze. Might the loss of that child have thrown a shadow through his brain? *Casts a pall of loneliness.* Can such terrible grief deaden you to the grief of others?

"You can't imagine at all," he says, but not unkindly. He's not scolding me.

Voss then straightens his back, puts his hands in his coat pockets, and gives me a sharp nod of dismissal. "I have no need to see the rest of the house," he says, as if I've invited him to.

"Oskar," I say, "if you don't mind too terribly, I'll let you go back on your own. It's been . . . well, I've had a lot on my mind this morning too. Old acquaintances, and all that."

"Ah," he says, cheering. "Your old lover made you sentimental." It always returns him to his best spirits when he can remark on my perversions. Though he says nothing to mock me, I can hear the notes of ridicule in the lift of delight in his voice.

···· 55 ····

Voss summons a car by phone, it arrives, he leaves. It takes minutes, maybe seconds, but seems endless.

I call out Blue's name even as I pull closed the drapes in the shop, to shut out the street. When I turn back from the drapes, he's there. He says, "It's much worse than it looks."

"How could it be worse?" I say. I'm startled at the sight of him. He's still in the clothes that match mine, but his shirt and trousers are blood-spotted, like his necktie. His sleeve is torn. His hand is wrapped tight in a bloodied silk scarf. He had put on some makeup this morning, to actually downplay the pink of his own cheeks and the pretty flutter of his thick eyelashes, and it's a smear across his face now, all horror show.

"No, no, no, no," Blue says. "I meant to say . . . *it looks worse than it is.*"

"The dagger," I say, and I go to him, to cradle his wounded hand in both of mine. "It's got a mind of its own." But, of course, what I'm really thinking is that I should never have given Blue anything more blunt than a butter knife.

But no, not the dagger. Blue went right to Pascal's upstairs room, with no problem at all, he explains. The concierge was convinced by Blue's costume and demeanor and let him pass. But no sooner had he dipped his hand into the back of the chair than he pulled it back out, away from a sharp sting. He'd cut himself, scratched up against a staple, or a sliver of wood. Maybe a nail.

"You'd think I'd opened a vein," he says.

It was one of those slight, shallow cuts that won't stop bleeding, out of all proportion to the damage done.

And he bled for a bit before even realizing he'd bled on the fabric of the chair, on the blanket, on the rug. He attempted to sop up the blood with his necktie, but he was terrified too, that he'd somehow severed something vital and his body was too shocked to feel it. In his fussing about, he knocked into the chair, which dislodged the book from its nest and sent its corner poking out.

"But the diary wasn't just a little pocket thing," he says. "It wasn't one of those girls' diaries with a heart-shaped lock. It was a long, fat ledger book. Overstuffed. Some pages falling out, others crammed in. And while I was trying to smuggle it into my coat's lining, where it didn't fit at all, the concierge walked into the room. To check on me. I was on my knees on the floor, and she saw me. And she saw I wasn't you."

Sometimes, when you're caught, you don't have time to contemplate the best defense. And sometimes that *is* your best defense, to rely on instinct. Any thinking is overthinking. Let adrenaline work your tongue and talk your way out.

But all I can do is overthink. My mind darts around, considering the damage done. I should never have entrusted this task to anyone.

"Where's the book?" I say. I sit on the edge of the chaise. My knees together. My hands folded atop them.

Blue shrugs. He tilts his head, on the verge of tears. "I don't have it," he says.

"You don't have it."

"She said . . . the concierge said . . . she said she would call someone unless I left it on the table in the studio," he says. "So I did. And she escorted me out. She didn't say another word to me."

The goddamn concierge.

"You used the drug I gave you?" I say.

"Oh," he says, nodding his head, jittery, "oh yes, yes, I used it. I used it. I *spilled* it. Down the front of myself. But it must not work anyway, because I remember every stupid thing I did wrong. It's all

I can think about." He tilts his head, his lip shivering. "I've made a mess of it," he says.

"No," I say. "You didn't make a mess. *You* didn't. This was mine to make a mess of."

The important thing is that Blue is here, with me, and that the concierge did not try to have him arrested. And since she let him go, that gives us room to maneuver. There may be ways I can convince Voss that the attempted theft was an act by Lutz. That I've been watched, and followed. Or maybe I can convince him that the concierge is lying, that she herself is working for someone out to discredit him. I will play to his every insecurity.

But for now, we do nothing. The phone will ring when it rings. Or there will be a knock at the door. Never go chasing after people to tell them your lies. Your lies have to wait for the people to come asking for them.

"Pour us both a shot of whiskey," I say, nodding toward the cabinet in the corner. "Something American."

Blue and I sit side by side on the chaise, twinned in our costumes, letting the bourbon and smoke tingle and burn. I cross my legs. He crosses his. He puts his head on my shoulder. I put my head on his head. We see ourselves in the tilt of a mirror on the wall.

I pat Blue's knee, and I send him upstairs. He needs to hide for the time being. For all I know, the house is thick with the ladies from Boulette's. I've lost track of who's here and who's left.

The phone rings, and I yelp from the shock of it. I've never heard it ring this loud. The closet beneath the stairs is a kind of phone booth, with a door of stained glass hinged in the middle, and an ivory telephone with gold bands. I lean against the door, and answer.

"This is Madame Vachon," she says, and it takes me a moment to remember who that is. I only ever call her *the concierge*, which has always seemed to be her preference.

"Yes?" I say.

"I thought you might like to know that I found the perfume diary," she says, and her voice is so strained, so tense, I fear what she'll say next. I look to the front door, waiting for a shadow to cross the glass. I cower against the wall. "And I gave it to Monsieur Voss myself. I know *you* would have liked to have found it, but you didn't. *I* did. Because I know this house better than anyone. I've been in this house longer than anyone else alive, since long before Monsieur Pascal was even born. And I'll die in this house, so help me God. I don't care who owns it; it is *my* house."

She finally pauses long enough for me to ask, "What do you want?"

"Nothing," she says. "*I* found the diary. It had nothing to do with you." She pauses again. "You'll be fine."

And she slams down the phone.

···· 56 ····

I'm nearly turned away from Boulette's in the early evening, by a pinkie-ringed thug leaning back on the door, in a beret and neckerchief. I've dressed to the nines, or so I thought, but now I notice that my tuxedo has lost some of its shine, and my top hat's without polish. "Do you have your membership card?" he grumbles, one of his eyes bulging, the other swollen shut. *I do,* I think, and I consider bringing out the brittle card I've carried in my wallet since that night in Manhattan, decades ago, when I joined the Brothers of the Sisterhood.

"I'm not sure, but I don't *be-lieeeeve* I'm *technically* a member," I say, furrowing my brow, needlessly fumbling at the inside breast pocket of my tuxedo coat.

"You have to be a member to get in," he says.

"I've never been a member before, and I've always gotten in," I say. He ignores me. I take off my top hat, hold it at my chest, and lean forward on my walking stick. "How do I go about becoming a member, my good man?"

"You fill out an application."

"How do I go about getting an application to fill out?"

"By being invited to apply," he says.

I put my hat back on. "Any reasonable person would find this situation untenable," I say.

"You could complain to management inside," he says, shrugging, sucking on a very thin cigar, "but you can't get inside if you're not a member." He shrugs again. "I'm just as frustrated about it as you are.

Bureaucracies can be very crippling." With his half smile, half sneer, he flashes a gold tooth.

The door then opens a crack, jostling the thug from his perch, and Madame Boulette is there to usher me in. "*Merci*, Albert," she tells him, gesturing past him, welcoming me.

She puts her arm in mine, the two of us suddenly friends, and leads me toward a hallway I've not been down before. "Albert's helping a bit because our locks have proven weak, you might say," she says. "A few of our birds have . . . flown the coop . . . without paying their rent. And a few of the other houses nearby have lost some of their girls too. So we're . . . troubled." She sighs. "A few of my best virgins, no less." She forces a smile. She touches the tassels of my silk scarf. "But it's good having Albert at the front door, and he's working for peanuts."

"For peanuts?" I say. "Because he belongs in a zoo?"

"The poor thing's a mobster," she says. "So many of them have lost their way since the occupation. With the new bullies in town, the old bullies have to beg for alms."

We turn a corner into a little jazz salon where someone I've never seen before sings a song I don't know. Her voice has a hiccup to it, one that comes ticking around like clockwork, or like the squeak of a porch swing.

"We're using the cozier club lately," Madame Boulette tells me. "The soldiers are busier than they've been." And indeed, the place seems to be serving only locals tonight, and very few of them at that. Though the girls are wearing as little as they ever have, and even less, the men they're sitting with are slack and slouched and intent on not leaving a drop in their highballs. At a table nearby, three girls sit by themselves, stirring their drinks with their cocktail umbrellas and chewing on the ends of cherry stems.

Madame Boulette talks in my ear: "The Resistance fighters are finally ruining the soldiers' evenings just a touch."

I spray perfume in Madame Boulette's direction. "Narcissus," I say. "With a little kiss of ambrette, to land it. I hope Zoé likes this one. I've been a disappointment, mostly."

She taps the bridge of her nose, blinks her eyes tight. Stops just short of a sneeze. A rejection.

She leads me to a table in the corner. "Champagne, Mr. Charlie?"

"We're having gin," Zoé says, suddenly here, a martini in each hand. I barely recognize her because she's chopped her hair short. It's not as short as mine, but it's certainly short for her. Her curls bounce like springs.

Her gown is tiger-striped, and on each shoulder strap is a rhinestone-studded panther, stalking, creeping down over her clavicle.

The singer onstage has moved on to another song I don't know, but with the same squeak in her voice. "You don't have the diary, do you?" Zoé says the very second Madame Boulette's out of earshot.

We both sit with our hands in our laps. I can't take my eyes off our martinis sitting untouched between us on the tabletop, the gin perfectly still. "It did not go smoothly," I say.

Zoé picks up her martini glass and takes a sip, swallowing hard. I see her hand tremble as she sets the glass back down. She licks her lips. "So where is it?"

I pick up my glass, my hand shaking too, and take a sip. I put the glass back down. "I believe Voss has it now," I say.

Zoé nods slow slow slow, her eyes downturned, then she tilts her head back, her eyes closed. She puts her hand to the back of her neck to rub there, as if massaging out an ache. She takes another sip of gin, then says, "So you get it back from him." She shrugs.

"Zoé," I say, "sweetheart . . . it's over. It's over now. *That's* what I'm telling you." I shrug too. "I told you from the beginning that I couldn't possibly . . . that I . . . Zoé, I'm a small-time crook. That's all I ever was. And I'm an old, old woman. I had no business even thinking that I could—"

"Oh, for fuck's sake," she says, leaning in, hissing. "It's my own fault? For trusting you?"

"No, no . . ."

"And you don't even believe that yourself," she says. "You don't think you're that. You don't think you're small-time. You can still get it. You can still go back and get the book."

"I . . ." But instead of denying I can do anything, I find myself saying, "I'll try. I'll try, of course," and a plot starts to creak together in my head, in spite of myself. "What more can you tell me about the concierge? Madame Vachon."

"She terrified me when I was a little girl," she says. "She slammed doors all the time, even when nobody was going in or out. She rattled around like she was a ghost haunting the house. I always thought she was listening in, to every room at once." After a moment, she leans back and crosses her arms. "Don't tell me *she* found the diary for Voss."

"She caught Blue in the act of taking it," I say. "In my clothes. She demanded the diary and told him to leave. And then she phoned me to insist that *she* had found the diary. It sounded like wounded pride, really. She's not going to tell Voss anything, she says. It was some kind of victory she refused to let me have. But she's also trying to keep herself there, I suppose. Voss is the master of the house now, so she wants to make herself useful."

Zoé reaches over to touch my hand. She holds it. Squeezes my hand tight. I squeeze back. "*Don't* go back to the house," she says now. "You need to stay away, don't you? What if Madame Vachon *does* tell him something? Or he figures it out? If he has any inkling, any suspicion, you're doomed. You need to hide, Clementine."

I take my hand back to bring a cigarette tin from my jacket pocket, set it down, push it toward her. "*You* need to hide," I say. "The cigarettes on top are ones you'll want to smoke. But the next layer, under the parchment, is instructions. Unroll the first cigarette, and you'll find a map, detailing where to go when you leave here. Unroll the next one, and there's an itinerary." I explain it all, cigarette by cigarette, this blueprint of her escape to the nuns in southern France. There, she'll join an effort by the Americans to help artists and intellectuals out of the country.

The cigarettes I packed in Zoé's tin are like sticks of candy—so sweet, they'll numb your tongue, with hints of chocolate and toasted coconut.

I push the tin a little farther toward her. She still doesn't touch it.

"I'm dead," she says.

"Maybe you're not actually in the diary," I say. "Or maybe there's no way of recognizing you."

She takes another bracing swig of her gin. She leans back in the chair. Looks around the cabaret. "Can't we just have Paris back?" she says. "Why should I have to leave it?"

It was either our Rose or our Violette who told me: *Sometimes an open door to the outside seems scarier than being under lock and key.*

"You just *do,* sweetheart," I say. "It's best not to get philosophical about it."

She takes one of the sweet cigarettes from the tin. Leans into the tabletop candle to light up. "Lutz knows about the diary," she says. "He found out somehow. He thinks the diary's going to lead him to something else Hitler will want. And *I* should care, he says, because he'll be rewarded, and he'll put me up in any castle I want."

"What does he think is in the diary?"

Zoé says, "He won't say. He may not know much at all. He thinks Voss is weak. He thinks he should just take whatever it is Voss is after."

And we drink some more. And some more. And a new singer takes the stage. The gin lets every worry, every terrible fear, take wing for a moment. Fly away. "What castle did you pick?" I say.

"No castle," she says. She fidgets with the clasp of her charm bracelet. Twists the bracelet around her thin wrist. "I told him I'd take the Notre-Dame cathedral. I want to haunt the bell tower, like the hunchback, among the gargoyles."

"Leave tonight, then," I say. "He's not here. Leave with me." I glance over at Madame Boulette, who's sitting at the bar. The club's so dead, she has her wig off and in her lap. She wears a silk cap tight on her skull as she teases her wig's human-hair curls with an olive fork.

"It's not as easy as this," she says, tapping her fingers against the cigarette tin. "I can't just get away." And she does sound too exhausted to go anywhere.

"It *is* as easy as this," I say, pushing the tin closer toward her.

The evening's master of ceremonies, who appears to be another of the thugs Madame Boulette newly employs, takes the stage and announces Zoé's name, introducing her.

Zoé stands. "They told Day not to come back," she says. "Everyone's so concerned about the girls from upstairs getting away, they're letting hardly anybody in." She drinks the last drops of her gin. "And since I'm the bird in the cage, I have to sing." She walks away, leaving the tin behind.

"Please, Zoé," I say, but I'm thinking of Day now, and my voice is so weak, I doubt she can hear me above the saxophone on the stage.

But she does hear me. She stops. She pauses, her back to me. "Zoé," I say again. She returns to the table, crushes her cigarette in the ashtray, and picks up the tin from the tabletop.

···· 57 ····

It's a literal itch, Day says, when she's not singing for people. It tingles her skin, like an allergy, when no one's around to lend an ear.

She's been fired from the cabaret, now that the bordello is in a quick downhill slide, so many of its girls having run away, the management in a frazzle.

I've stopped at Day's on my way to see Voss. He called me early this morning to tell me he was sending a car. I told him I'd rather walk. *Don't dawdle,* he said. *You'll want to see what I found.* And I do believe he's genuinely enthusiastic to show me the diary. At the very least, I know his moods. To be honest, I think I might be his only friend. I'm certainly the only person he can confide in. *That,* at least, is something I might still be expert at: tricking people into trusting me.

Or I could be wrong. I could be expert at nothing anymore. Did the concierge even notice that Blue bled all over the chair I sit in every day? Could that old woman be capable of any kind of deception at all? If Voss is in any way suspicious, then I'm waltzing right into his snare. He would most certainly want to toy with me before he carted me off to the camp in Alsace. I'm terrified at what he might be like at his most diabolical.

Or he doesn't suspect a thing. And I have one more chance to lift the diary right out from under his nose.

"The café was open way past curfew last night," Day tells me. I've brought her a tray of breakfast from downstairs. "It was full of happy drunks sick of staying home." She sits up in bed, and keeps her sleeping mask on. Over the eyes of the mask are eyes of silk with long lashes, one open, the other closed in a flirty wink. "Nobody can stay in anymore. Not another minute. So we sang all the songs we knew, then made up new ones when we ran out." She tilts her head, pouts, looking at me with those embroidered eyeballs. "Can you do something about the sun so I can take off my mask?"

I place the tray across her lap, then adjust the drapes the best I can. This corner room has four windows, each with a window seat, each seat cluttered with department-store mannequin heads used for hat displays. Each head props up one of Day's wigs.

"We made up a sad little song about the elephants that get killed for their tusks for piano keys," she says. "It was a jazz funeral." On a plate on her tray is a deck of cards, so Day can tell her own fortune. Day insists on a fortune daily, and Madame Roche always stacks the cards so they predict the best. Day's never once objected to their sunny forecast.

"I wish you could get away," I say. I sit on the edge of the bed and help myself to a wiggle of bacon.

"Actually, I *am* going to be gone for a bit," she says. "A couple of the musicians from the cabaret are going on a short little tour, for a week or two. They need a singer." She pushes the mask up on her forehead and inspects her breakfast.

"Tell me the truth," I say.

She won't meet my eyes. "What *truth* is there to tell? I'm singing, that's all."

"Just promise me you'll be careful," I say. "Even singing all the old songs makes everyone nervous." I pour more coffee into her cup. "The girls of the bordello. The oldest profession. There's a new word for them now. *Horizontales.* Horizontal collaborators."

"Collaborators?" she says. She looks up and off, a gaze of despair. "They've done nothing wrong. They just sleep with the bastards." She takes the top card from the deck, then tosses it aside without even seeming to see what's on it. She plucks up the next one and tosses it aside too. *"Collaborators,"* she says, looking at me, rolling her eyes.

It's stuck in her craw. "*All* of Paris is a whore. We're all *horizontales;* that's why we're here to begin with. We're here to get too much of everything nobody needs. Thank God we have those big beautiful churches where we can drop off our sins." She picks up the deck of cards and shuffles them fiercely, with a hard snap and flutter. "If men liked to fuck more than they like to kill, we'd all be better off," she says.

"I'm scared for you," I say. I can't bear to tell her that I've lost the perfume diary.

She puts her hand to my cheek. She smiles that smile of sweet pity she likes to give me. And she's about to say something when the sound of somebody striking up a tune on the piano downstairs, even at this early hour, distracts her. "Maybe they never left at all," she says. "Maybe they slept in the café." We hear someone banging a broomstick on the ceiling. She interprets this as a summoning. "I'm being called to duty," she says, pushing the tray aside. "Grab me the copper-colored one, won't you, love?" Day takes a seat at her mirror. "You know," she says, looking over at my reflection, "in all these years, you've never asked why I'm always so poor. You've never asked what happened to all that money from 'Where Were You When.' Don't you ever wonder how I kept from getting stinking rich?"

"I figured you'd tell me if you wanted me to know."

"I *do* want you to know," she says. "I figured I'd tell you if I was ever asked."

"Then I'm asking," I say.

She shrugs one shoulder. Gives her head a little shake. "I was fleeced." She shrugs that shoulder again. *Simple as that,* that shrug seems to say. "By crooked contracts. Crooked managers. That's why I left the US to begin with. They'd book me into terrible dives, then pay me nothing. Less than nothing, sometimes. I'd end up owing them, just to warble in some dump." I hand her her wig. She rustles it around, looking for the front of it. "*You're a Negro act,* they'd say. *You're lucky you get any work at all.* And the thing is, I think they believed that. They thought they were doing me good. I was their charity." She pulls the wig on over her head, tugs on the curls to shift it into place. "But they never convinced me of that. They didn't, Clem. I never believed them. And that's why I came to Paris. And I'm here, and I sing, and I never take more than I need."

Next to her vanity is a trolley, all its glass shelves covered with bottles of perfume, some I've made, some she's bought, some she's been given by admirers. She asks me to pick the day's perfume for her, then rejects what I hold forth. "No, the blue bottle. Today I want to smell like a French whore." The blue bottle is one of mine, inspired by some descriptions in an old edition of *Le Guide rose,* the pink-jacketed pamphlet that provides an annual rating of the city's brothels. For the perfume, I tried to capture some haggard courtesan: a hint of crushed bedbug, and the smoky patchouli from an incense lamp hanging off a bedpost, and stale coffee.

"I'll write a victory song," she says. "A song for the liberation."

I help her pull her dress on over her night-slip. I know I need to go, that Voss is expecting me, but I can't bear to leave her side. If *I* am arrested, this is the last I'll see of my sweet, darling Day.

She kisses me hard on the cheek to blot her lipstick, then hands me a tissue to wipe it away. But I leave her sloppy kiss there.

···· 58 ····

The concierge answers the door as she always does, her eyes on my shoes. I've worn a pair meant to surprise her: harlequin-checked smoking slippers with metallic threads of blue, green, yellow, pink. Playful. Friendly. "Nebraska Charlie," she says. She's never called me that before.

"Madame Vachon," I say.

She leads me in and up the stairs, fiddling with her keys. Always fiddling fiddling fiddling with the keys, though of course she knows exactly which is for what. She likes the music of it, I suppose, or she's working a hex, like each key's a chicken bone.

"How's the mood of the house?" I ask her.

"You'll see," she says. We've reached the landing. She unlocks the door and taps it open, setting it to squeak on its hinges.

I don't move. "Are you friend or foe?" I ask her.

She twists her neck around to actually look *up* at me for once. "We're all friends here," she says. She waves me in.

I find Voss in the laboratory. He stands at the tall table, drumming his fingers on the journal in front of him. The perfume journal, most certainly. He glances around, gesturing toward the bookshelves. "Every book in this room is about the senses," he says. "Perfume. Color. Music. Food. The perfumeries of Shakespeare's time must have been as gory as an abattoir. Goat's blood. Pigeon blood. The gall of an ox. The membrane of a mollusk."

"Oskar . . . ," I say, but I don't know what to tell him. I don't know what to ask for.

"I haven't slept," he says, as if it weren't obvious from his wild eyes. "I keep getting distracted. I shouldn't be in here, among all these books. I don't have time to read them." I suspect his sleeplessness has been spiked. He's taken something. Then he says, "We found it." He giggles, actually. Drums his fingers faster. "We found the perfume diary. Guess where it was."

"How should I know?" I say.

"And that's the thing, isn't it? You *should* know. *You* should. You're an international crook." He giggles again, a giggle even more lunatic than before. "It was right under our feet. The concierge, with her eyes always low. She found it. She said the chambermaid was up there dusting, knocked over our whole tray of perfumes, shattered the glass, spilled all over the rug. The concierge had the rug swiftly removed, and she noticed something off about one of the floorboards. Just a feeling she had, she said. 'I know the bones of this house better than I know the bones under my own skin,' she said. She lifted a board, and there it was."

He is talking so fast, he's tripping over his tongue, which I suspect is weighted, furred, with whatever jolt of pep his Nazi druggist has prescribed. He explains that he had put the concierge to the task of finding the book before he even met me. She had boasted even then that she knew every inch of the place. "When she gave me the diary yesterday, I offered to pay her, but she said it was her duty to the house. The poor thing was embarrassed it had taken her so long to find the diary. Finding lost things was part of her job. *But,* she said, she had always had her eye on the crystal candlesticks on the mantel. The girandoles with the little brass cherubs. So I gave her those."

She swapped all the perfumes of Paris for a matching set of gewgaws.

He pushes the diary toward me, across the countertop. The book itself is nothing special—as a matter of fact, it's battered and faded, its canvas cover warped and torn. They'll put it in a museum case someday, and you'll marvel at its simplicity.

But I'm stunned by it. I run my fingers over the cover, which is either pale black or dark blue. There's a block of faded red, the word *journal* across it in scratched-up gold leaf. There are copper plates at the top of the spine and at the bottom of it, and at the tips of the corners of the front cover. I run my thumb over them, rubbing at the tarnish.

And I open the book. Just inside are marbled endpapers, and a card tacked there with the name of the shop the journal was bought from: *A. Roussel: Imprimerie, Librairie, Papeterie.*

I turn to the first page.

There I find a lined ledger of household accounts, specifically what's been paid to the butcher, and the meats received. Veal, kidneys, lamb, brains, *bœuf, gigot, saucisses, graisse,* all written in a fine hand, at an elegant slant.

The next page is more of the same, and so is the next, and the next, a complete history, week by week, month by month, dating back to 1903, of every shank, filet, rib, tenderloin, *araignée, basse côte, gîte à la noix.* April, May, June, *juillet, août, septembre,* 1904, 1905, 1906, '07, '08, '09, page after page after page chronicling one family's penchant for flesh and gluttony.

"Can you believe it?" he says.

Has he not found the perfume diary after all? Has whatever drug he's on tipped him into madness?

"Imagine how frustrating it was as I first turned these pages," he says. "Can you believe that he just took an old book of household accounts, and turned it into a collection of some of the most valuable recipes in the history of France?"

Voss reaches across to turn the pages for me. Finally, the kitchen cupboard is bare.

We arrive at a perfume recipe.

Essence de néroli fin, 46 grammes. Esprit de romarin, 8 livres. Fleurs de lavande récentes, 4 onces. Sommités d'absinthe, 2 onces. Racine sèche d'angélique de Bohême, 125 grammes.

I realize I've been grinding my teeth, but I don't know for how long. Maybe for days. Or weeks. But now it stops. So does the tingling I've had in my funny bones, and my wrists, as if a doctor has been knocking his mallet at me, testing my reflexes. My fists unclench too, and the pinch in my neck and shoulder goes away. There was a low whistling in my ears that I didn't even know I was hearing nonstop, until now that it's sputtered out to nothing.

I'm like a fairy-tale hag, shuffling off her curse.

Pages of perfume recipes. And with each one, there are notes. Influences listed, titles of songs and symphonies, and lyrics, and lines plucked from poems. Quotes from philosophers and geniuses and clever debutantes. The names of characters from novels, and operas. Mostly, there are flowers. They bloom around me, a sudden garden. Spring.

And code. Tacked onto the end of every recipe is a symbol. I don't know if Voss has noticed, but it's quite apparent to me that Pascal has left ingredients off. Somewhere there's another book, a key to the codes.

As the pages flip before me, I keep an eye out for Zoé's name, and for the recipe for Ophelia, but Voss rushes ahead, leaping his fingers through, to bring me to a page he has marked with a tattered dirty little feather, as if he'd just reached out the window and into a nest.

"Read it, read it, read it," he says, tapping his finger on the page, but he won't let me read; he keeps talking, telling me what's there.

Poison. Voss is thrilled that he was correct all along about the unused gases of the War Before. Pascal writes of his engagement to prettify the phosgene, the benzyl acetate, all the deadly breezes from military tanks. He tamed them into *sympathetic fumes.* He was tasked by the government with bottling the diluted poison, selling it to the women of the world, and paying a tax to the military based on the percentage of bottles sold. The French were then meeting both the peacetime requirements of disarmament and the demands of a public still reeling from the violence of the war.

Pascal worked with his own chemists, and with executives of the military, and a cabal of professors from elite universities worldwide. He made use of the poisons and other war excesses as well: the lubricating oils of airplane gears, the slicking agents for rifle chambers. He created Possédée, *possessed,* a violet perfume; he created Serrure et Clé, *lock and key,* a jasmine mix.

"What about Gabrielle?" I say.

He shrugs. "That's where I was wrong," he says. "The recipe is in there, but there's nothing particularly revealing in it. Unless there's something in the little code that he's peppered the book with. Did you see that?" He turns some pages back, to note the symbols I've noticed. He stops on the page with Gabrielle, and taps on its symbol at the end of the list of ingredients. A circle with a dot in the middle of it. A nipple. He shrugs again. Sighs. "Clearly he's left things out. Maybe he kept a code key, or maybe he didn't, but it doesn't matter to us. We . . . *you* . . . will have enough to work from here to re-create the perfumes."

"But is this enough for *you*?" I say. "Is any of this useful? Does it say where the gases are kept?"

"No," Voss says, but with no note of disappointment. "It doesn't tell where the gases are kept. But it tells us something better." He turns more pages before me. "Read, read, read," he says again, and again he won't let me.

While frolicking in the laboratory with his chemists, who'd all danced with war and its gases and oils, Pascal summoned from his flasks and test tubes a poison of his own. Accidentally. He'd simply been after a synthetic, an artificial additive, for his perfume. The synthetic turned out to be absolutely poisonous, and therefore nothing Pascal could use. This perfume, with its hint of orange slightly turned, a scent of oversweet spoil, wreaked all kinds of havoc in the test labs, killing all its rats, its cats, its birds, its dog, its ravens.

Through his associates in the government, he offered the formula to the military. He didn't see this as a contribution to war and destruction. He saw it as an act of loyalty to the country he loved.

Regardless of any international treaties prohibiting research of chemical warfare, Pascal wrote in his diary, *France must protect itself from those nations that ignore such prohibitions. For France to rely on a mutual trust is foolhardy. We must be at the ready. We can't allow ourselves to be poisoned by our own efforts toward peace.*

Further testing by the military found the perfume to approximate war gas so closely, it surpassed anything the French had ever produced before. This was the poison the warmongers lusted for, a liquid that turned to fume.

It wouldn't contaminate the battlefields the way other gases did. Once it killed, it dissolved. Mustard gas stays on the ground for weeks, Voss explained. Armies must often march through the lands they've just poisoned, among the vehicles and equipment, among the corpses, all still smoldering with gas. But Pascal, without even intending to, had created a weapon that could fade away minutes after felling its victims.

Pilots could fly low over the fields of war and strafe the enemy, clearing the way for the advance of their own soldiers.

"It's a *clean* annihilation," Voss says. He speaks as if entranced by the beauty of it. He even draws out that word: *cleeeeean.* "Unlike anything else anyone has. The Wehrmacht can attack with the chemicals but keep on marching through. Can you imagine? A lethal perfume, gentle and sweet, that kills then turns harmless, a coy, lovely vapor. And knowing Pascal as we do, isn't it likely that the scent remains? Perfuming the battlefield? I'm desperate to know the scent. What do you suppose? Sage? Leather? Or something gentle, like fresh laundry?"

I'm turning the pages backward through the book.

He says, "I know, I know, it's grisly war talk, my dear, but the war is going to rage on and on and on, regardless of what we do here in Paris. The important thing is that Hitler's listening to me. He's trusting me."

I look for Ophelia. If there's any mention of Zoé, I'll rip the page out. Right in front of Voss. He'll believe me if I tell him it's my favorite fragrance, that it's the puzzle I most want to solve. "He's trusting you?" I say, to keep him talking.

"When Hitler writes about the condition of the world," Voss says, "and its cultural demise, perfume is his metaphor. For suffocation. For eroticism. But I've been changing his mind, Charlie. Me. He's listening to me." He thumps his finger on his chest. *"I've* saved Paris. When he moved his armies in, he considered it a city of whores." He shrugs. He throws his hands up. He's wide-eyed and giddy. I've never seen him so happily agitated. "Whores who cared about nothing but their own romantic collapse. Their morbid sentiment. Their nostalgia. He saw Paris as a city of the pampered, a people who were cruel to the poor."

Horizontales.

"The formula for this gas you're talking about," I say. "It's in the book?"

"Well, no," he says, and here he reaches across to slam the book shut and pull it away from me. "He only describes how he came to discover the gas. The formula, it would seem, is recorded elsewhere. *But,* it's enough to have the book for now. Hitler will commit resources to me. Support. Mostly he'll give me time to find the formula. He'll be patient with me. He'll trust that I'm on to something. And this will lead to the support we need for our perfumes."

I nod. I lean forward. I hold out my hand. Wiggle my fingers at him. "Give me the book," I say. "I'm ready to get to work." He stays still.

I nod. I smile.

He shakes his head. "I need more time with it myself," he says. "When I can give it a sober eye." He then admits that his doctor gave him something so he could stay up all night studying the book, orchestrating his mission. "It's some sort of miracle pill. It not only keeps you awake but adds hours and hours to your night. You can accomplish everything in a blink." He begins drumming his fingers on the book again. "I've even planned a party already. For tonight, for all our best men in Paris. Very formal. It's here at the house. *My* house. I need to be seen. Now that everything's falling into place. They need to recognize my standing." He takes my elbow and leads me toward the door. "You'll come to the party," he says. "And you'll bring the boy in your attic, won't you? I'd love to meet him."

"He's not . . . I don't think that he can . . ."

"You'll bring him," Voss commands, with a twitch in his brow. "And I'll send you something to wear."

By the time I've gotten back to the house, my gown for the night has been delivered, with a note from Voss: *Illegal silk from Lyon,* he writes, meaning the hosiery, complete with garter belt and buckles, in the thin, peppermint-striped box delivered with the dress. All silk is supposed to go to the war effort, but it seems some legs must be deemed essential.

···· 59 ····

To amuse himself, I suppose, Voss has sent me a gown with the faintest pattern of butterflies, as if some bug-catcher dusted their wings with sugar and sent them fluttering against the pink satin.

Voss even arranged a tailor's appointment for Blue in the afternoon, and by evening, he had a sharp new tuxedo so flattering and stately it almost seemed as if the tailor somehow tailored Blue to fit the suit, not vice versa.

I don't know what Voss wants with Blue, if anything, unless perhaps he's interested in Blue's work at the library. Voss keeps a librarian of his own within the intelligence agency, a woman even older than me, a German librarian who dismantles libraries. She catalogs and evaluates the collections and archives of the enemies, helping the Nazis go spelunking into the mindset of Jews, of Catholics. She determines which books to save and which to burn. *She reads by the light of a match, so to speak,* Voss says.

I put on some lipstick, and I can see how just the act of it can lend a lady confidence. A few swipes of wax and you've masked yourself. Barely a twist of the wrist, this way then that, and you've armed yourself with artifice.

I smack a kiss toward my reflection in the mirror, and this seems to summon a knock at the shop door. Our driver. I take a deep breath. Straighten my back and drop the lipstick in the evening clutch Voss delivered—a little pearlescent box of Bakelite. The Nazis are crazy for Bakelite; they made cheap radios from it so they could pipe their propaganda into every German living room.

But it's not the driver who's at the door. "Félix," I say. Of all people, of all times. For a moment, I wonder if he somehow knows we're off to a Nazi's cocktail party.

"Félix," Blue says too, standing right behind me. It's been some time since Blue has heard from him. "You're . . . you're alive, I see."

"For a minute or two," he says. He puts his hands in his pockets. Smiles with what looks to me like pity. Or apology. "How handsome you look."

That's all it takes. I look over at Blue, who forgives Félix everything with that *how handsome.*

Félix is spruced up too, like he has dressed for the occasion of breaking Blue's heart. His hair is mussed in the tidiest way, a few of his curls greased with pomade so they'll droop fetchingly over one eye. He's got on a fine coat, one busy with buckles and pockets, probably something he'll claim to Blue was snagged off a drunk German's back.

Blue invites Félix in, but Félix invites Blue outside.

I stand back in the shadows, so I can watch through the window without their seeing me, but I needn't worry—they're completely caught up in each other.

On these late winter nights, moonlight keeps the streets lit in pale silver. We haven't had streetlights since the Nazis arrived, when they painted the bulbs a blackout blue. They hoped it would stop us from creeping around come midnight.

Outside, Blue and Félix stand in the bit of light that falls from the shop's window. They talk in clouds of fog, their hands shoved into their coat pockets. They bounce on the balls of their feet, from the cold. Rock from foot to foot.

As I watch them now, I imagine Félix in close-up on the cinema screen, his wet eyes looking right into ours, the snow collecting in the fur of his coat's collar, in his newly grown beard, in his long lashes, like soap flakes on a movie's soundstage.

Félix seems to catch me looking, so I step away, deeper into the shop. I fuss with my dress as I check my reflection in the mirror again.

Only a few moments later, Blue comes back in alone. He's sniffling and coughing, from the cold and from crying some, I suppose. He rubs at his face with his sleeve. "He's off on another mission," he says. "He doesn't know when I'll hear from him again."

"I'm sorry, sweetheart," I say.

He comes to me and leans his head on my shoulder. I hate it when Blue's wounded, but I do love comforting him. "Fix this," he says. "Bring him back. Make him love me so much he can't leave my side."

Only a few years after I left M, America went to war, and my career in thievery thrived. During the Spanish-American War and the War Before, women longed for love potions, to cast lasting spells on the men who left their sides to fight. Ladies sent their soldiers off with handkerchiefs doused in their scent, or they tucked little bottles into their men's pockets, pretty perfumes to suck up their snouts like smelling salts.

And if it was a potion so rare and coveted it had to be stolen, that made it seem all the more magical. Love and desire is as much the thief's dominion as the witch's. A stolen cure for sadness. People need to take things because they lose things.

"He'll never forget how you looked tonight," I say. "How could he?" I turn him so we can see ourselves in the mirror. "For so so long, I've wanted to shoehorn you into a suit that fits you." The wealthy widows who rent him like to see him in the expensive clothes left behind by their dead husbands, whether the suits fit or not.

My gown is too young for me. I tug at the top of it, hoping I can tuck my shoulders down into the off-the-shoulders bodice. I had first decided against wearing the stockings and garter belt, since the dress is floor length and full-skirted—a ball gown, nearly—but I can just imagine Voss demanding I give him a cancan-dancer flash, to flaunt my violation of the silk restrictions.

"You look beautiful," Blue says, but he says it with a note of despair. He drops his attention to his hand, to the ring on his finger. "Did you see him kiss me just now?" Before I can say I didn't, he says, "That kiss was something, though, wasn't it? That was a real kiss."

"Some people go their whole lives without getting kissed like that," I say.

"I hope he's careful. I just want Félix to grow old, even if it's without me," Blue says, with a sigh.

"Let's go looking for our own trouble," I say. "Take your mind off things."

"Yes," he says. "*We* actually have a mission, don't we?" And I like the note of scorn in his voice.

He helps me on with the jacket Voss sent. It's a synthetic fur that looks like white ermine, and I'm determined to keep it on all evening, to hide my naked shoulders in it, my freckled chest, but a maid lifts it away the second we arrive at the party, and the place is so packed, she's gone before I can object.

Blue and I move through the crowd arm in arm. I don't recognize anyone. I look out for Day, for Zoé. Not even Lutz is here.

Blue says, "I can see the appeal."

"The appeal of what?" I say.

"The appeal of getting spiffed up," he says. "You sure can get noticed, can't you, when you're just a tad natty? It even does your posture some good."

"Yes," I say. "Even if you're *not* getting noticed, you think you are. Because you look so fine, you tell yourself. How could they *not* notice?"

How can you simply fade away if all eyes are on you?

I hear Voss before I see him. "You must be the boy with the bad heart," he says to Blue.

"I must be," Blue says, shaking Voss's hand.

"Charlie has told me almost *nothing* about you," he says. Being among this crowd, and these cocktails, has made him cheerful. "You don't have a drink," he says, looking around for a tray. And in the looking around, he spots someone else. "I need to step away for just a moment," he says, "but, Charlie, I insist you take Blue to our upstairs room. You have to show him the loose floorboard." He puts his hand on Blue's arm. "For weeks, she and I had been talking about Pascal's perfume diary, and all the time it was hidden right beneath our feet. Did she tell you that?"

I still can't tell if his taunting is playful or a coy signal that he's onto me. Or is he hoping to pump Blue for information? And Blue is unsure how to answer. He shakes his head slightly, raises an eyebrow, looks quizzical. He's smart to play dumb.

But as I lead Blue from the room, he leans into my ear and whispers, "Is there a trap up there? Is the concierge waiting? So she can point me out as the man she caught wearing your clothes, stealing the diary?" And I realize I haven't seen the concierge all evening.

I had intended to sneak up to the room anyway. I can't shake the feeling that Voss was right all along about Gabrielle, that the perfume is some sort of clue. And when Voss opened the diary before me, turning to the page about Gabrielle, I caught sight of a few hints. For one, the ingredients included pennyroyal, a toxic plant with the faint scent of mint. And water iris, also poisonous, and completely *without* scent, therefore pointless to include unless you simply wanted to list it.

"Hand me your lighter, and a cigarette," I tell Blue. "And stand at the doorway. Keep an eye on the stairs." After my meeting with Voss today, I went directly to Annick's printshop to get her opinion. I have a theory about Pascal's copy of the painting of Gabrielle d'Estrées and her sister.

I put the cigarette to my mouth, and hold it there with my lips.

I light the cigarette lighter, but I don't light the cigarette. I run the flame close to the canvas, studying the shine, the reflection of the light.

I look for signs of something hidden, for a wrinkle in the placid rose-milk of the women's skin. Annick speculated for me, considered how a document might best be concealed on a canvas, how a sheet of paper might be treated or coated, how a page might be safely painted over without causing any ink to smear. Maybe he wrote the secret formula on a piece of paper that he then concealed in the painting. You would treat the paper with egg whites, let it dry so it's like shellac and won't absorb the oil of the paint.

I take a razor blade I have tucked into the strap of my brassiere. I'm looking for the paper in the painting, for a shine along the paper's edge, or a raised border, to cut at, to release the page from the oil paint.

Paris is full of forgers who could have done a special copy for Pascal, Annick said. Every bordello in Europe has at least one copy of the Gabrielle d'Estrées painting hanging in its rooms. Gentlemen's clubs, low saloons, the social halls of other, more private societies.

"You've brought us champagne," I hear Blue say, signaling that Voss is coming near. As he walks into the room, I turn away from the painting and bring the flame of the lighter to my cigarette.

"The night Charlie and I first met at the Ritz," Voss says as he hands Blue a glass, "they tried to pass off some kind of swill as a fine vintage." He hands me his other glass. "But not tonight. Tonight you get the 1923 Veuve Clicquot." He takes the cigarette away from me. "But you can't taste its gentle nature if you're burning your tongue with this." He puffs on the cigarette himself.

I taste the champagne, nod with approval.

Voss says to Blue, "One thing that Charlie did tell me about you is that you're an actor," though I don't quite recall that I ever did tell him that. Voss then tells Blue to follow him; he wants to introduce him to someone, someone important, in the theater world. "Are you coming, love?" Voss turns back to ask me.

"I'll be along in a minute," I say. I take a seat in my chair. "I just want to linger for a moment. For old time's sake." I put my foot to the loose floorboard and tap my toe against it. "I want to figure out how I missed that floorboard."

"Ah, in your throne of humiliation," he says. "We'll be back to work very soon, Charlie. We'll finally put all our plans into place."

After he leaves, I turn around in my chair to glance back at Gabrielle d'Estrées in her bath. I didn't see anything suspicious when I held my flame near the paint. I sit and stare at the canvas, flicking my thumb at the lighter, sending up sparks, thinking, stumped. I turn away from the painting to take another sip of the champagne. The concierge did a careful job of cleaning the room after Blue bungled his theft. There's no sign of blood or a break-in. And though she claimed the chambermaid broke bottles of perfume, there are still some on an end table. Pascal's perfumes. Such beautiful bottles, as beautiful as their scents. And Pascal designed those too. The architecture of the bottles was part of what made the perfumes so divine.

The blueprints. The day I came into this room and everything was in disarray, the origami birds rustled from their cage, I looked at the sketches Voss had taken from the cabinet. I now put down my glass and lighter, and I walk over to open the cabinet's bottom drawer. Each cardboard tube is marked with the name of a perfume. I take out the blueprint for Gabrielle.

Because now I remember. When I was reading the notes on the blueprint, about the materials and processes used in the manufacture of the bottle and its stopper, I saw a reference to silver nitrate. It caught in my mind but then quickly escaped when Voss startled me.

If you used silver nitrate on glass, you'd create a mirror. I had wondered at the time if Pascal had originally meant for the Gabrielle bottle to be reflective.

But no. He was simply providing a clue. He didn't mean to create a reflection with that silver nitrate. He meant to conceal something.

I take the blueprint from the tube, and return the tube to the cabinet. The beat of my heart is skipping along so fast as I unroll the paper, I hold my hand tight to my chest, as if I can slow it down with the press of my palm. In the upper corner is the nipple-like mark, the code, the round circle with the dot that I'd seen in the perfume diary's recipe for Gabrielle.

M wrote me another letter in invisible ink. It arrived in a beautiful little porcelain box painted with cherubs. The letter was wrapped around a bottle, and the bottle's label read only, *Solution for making the invisible visible.* When I treated the paper with the solution,

M's handwriting took shape, and his whole letter was about invisible ink, about methods old and new that he'd practiced over the years, including one recipe from forever ago, made of pressed marigolds, steeped pansies, bruised violets. But silver nitrate was key to the formula of the ink he'd used for my letter.

Just think of all the secrets hiding on blank pages, M wrote. *Years and years and years of invisible ink in letters from men to their mistresses. Or bawdy poems written by virgins. Or lesbian confessions.*

The paper of the blueprint is rough, which helps to keep the ink hidden. And when I tilt the page just so, I can make out the little specks of silver across the front and back of it.

I step behind the chair to hide myself should anyone walk in. I lift the bottom of my gown, gathering up all the rustle and frill of it, up up up, past my knees. I'll clip the blueprint to the hook of my garter belt, and I'll waltz right on out with it. But as I fuss with it all, I realize the clip's not strong enough to hold the stocking and the paper both.

I roll down my hosiery, wrap the blueprint around my leg, and pull the stocking up over it. I clip the stocking in place.

I return to the party. I have a drink, and another, and I'm at ease, everyone's chatter in foreign words a dull throb in my ears. Voss finally tells me I look tired, and he'll send me home. "You know me so well," I tell him.

A Nazi officer drives Blue and me, so I keep mum about my theft in the car. But once we're inside the perfume shop, I tell Blue to lock the door and to make sure the curtains are drawn tight. I drop my fake fur to the floor and pull up the bottom of my dress as I walk to the counter. I unbuckle the garter, roll down the stocking, and unwrap the blueprint from around my leg. I shove aside the bottles atop the counter, and switch on the table lamp. I point out to Blue the silver I'm seeing, the etching on the page from the nib of a pen. But he doesn't see it. I tell him to trust me. "I've got a good eye for seeing invisible ink," I tell him.

In the morning, I go to Annick. I suspect her shop might have the solutions that will lift the letters from the vaporous ink, and, of course, she knows all about these things. Within a few minutes, we've tested a patch of the page with a sponge. There are notes on reactions and impurities and processes of manufacture, on character, properties, syntheses.

This is indeed the formula for the poisonous gas Pascal discovered. Voss was right about Gabrielle hinting at poison, but wrong about the poison being the perfume itself. It's pleasing, really, that Gabrielle, such sweet nectar, is entirely innocent. Never was there an ounce of chemical warfare in its Sapphic fog. Gabrielle was only ever her mysterious self, naked and pale, just a clue in Pascal's game of hide-and-seek, tucking the formula away in the story of her bottle.

"I'll be damned," Annick says, and she sounds truly impressed. She gives me a pat on the back. "I'll be damned." She shakes her head. "You snuck this right past the Germans. And they were the masters of invisible ink in the last war."

She tells me about the spies who would dip their neckties in liquid to make the ink to hide their plots. "If the spy was a lady," she says, "she'd sneak around with her invisible ink in a perfume bottle."

···· 60 ····

Everything you once were turns to smoke, says one of the nuns, smoke rising from her lips as she speaks. We're in my courtyard, and she weaves among the girls, my house flowers, inspecting their costumes, as if they're all on their way to take their vows. Some of the ash from her cigarette spills onto the shoulder of a girl we named Pansy, and she pats the habit hard, to brush it off. *We lose our names,* she says. *We lose our clothes.*

Our painted ladies always leave us in nun's habits before sunup, their faces scrubbed raw and cinched tight with starched, linen wimples. They escape penitent, in disguise. Blue and I rub their tears away with our thumbs, and we coo-coo and we tut-tut and we cry a few tears of our own, as if we've raised them from hatchlings in a dovecote.

The nun's habits come from the basement wardrobe of Blue's theater; the troupe once did a play about a convent overcome by mass hysteria, all the nuns done in by stigmata fantasies.

We only ever *loan* them to the ladies we escort from Paris. The nuns, the genuine ones, launder them and bring them back, for the next batch of escapees. They deliver the habits starched and folded tight in makeshift shirt boxes, with little silk pillows tucked in, sachets of cedar shavings and powdered sassafras that somehow make the clothes smell more worn than before, with a hint of flesh and stale sweat.

Though I was fearful of harboring them at first, and the girls are never with us long, we do grow attached. Even to the worst of them, even to that noxious weed we called Myrtle, who liked to change all the clocks and wore jingle bells on her ankles, a jangling bracelet that announced her every step.

I haven't been called to Voss's for a few days. I haven't seen Zoé either, so I entertain the hope that she made her escape. Day is gone too; a few days ago, she left town with her musicians. I'm picturing her singing in the unoccupied zones, perhaps in the south, a fresh rose in her hair, finding a new lover for me to capture in perfume. And Blue is here with me, the play having ended its run. When he's not working at the library, he's at my side, fully dedicated to the city's courtesans.

Blue has taken to making note of our girls, jotting down a history of each and every one, in Bible-paper *carnets de croquis* the nuns give us. He interviews them and documents their lives by listing the things they've lost: their real names and the names of their mothers and the names they gave their dolls, the streets they grew up on, the songs they sang as children. Or the things they *wish* they could remember: the candy their grandmother kept in a cut-glass bowl, or the tune their father whistled on Sundays, or the flowers of the sachet in the linen drawer, where the pillowcases were kept in the summer cottage, a scent that could drop them off to sleep in a blink. If only they could smell that scent again.

Go ahead, go ahead, go ahead, whisper the truth under your breath or drop it down a well. If you tell the truth, even if only in your heart, someone will hear it. That's one of the miracles of existence, like radio waves or the *tap tap tap* of electrical signals. Science is designed to perform these magic acts, to carry our voices, one to the other, so that if I speak down here, as low as I can go, my words will echo up and out.

Take these girls, for example. Somehow all the harlots of Paris know that the old boys' academy is now a halfway house for brothel refugees. And though we have no intention of turning away anyone who *isn't* a lady of the evening, only ladies of the evening arrive, as if the whistle is pitched in a key only their ears can hear.

Finished examining them, the nun stands back. Citing the writings of a mystic, she says, *The nun's black habit should help her remember that someday she'll die.*

···· 61 ····

Blue and I relax after the long day of sending ladies south, on the settee in the shop, our feet up on the same ottoman. We have snifters of brandy.

"One of the widows in Manhattan hired me to steal a mask that was two hundred years old," I tell him. I haven't thought about that mask in years. "It had been made for a courtesan in Venice, who wore it to look like the society women. Only eyeholes to see out of, but no hole for the mouth. There was a button you'd bite, to keep it on your face."

"Seems it would keep you quiet too," he says. "Button your lip."

"A face of blue velvet, with a silk lining inside. She would perfume the silk and walk the streets inhaling the scent." I think of the old perfume called Holy Basil, a serene and heavenly blend of geranium, jasmine, Tonquin bean, tolu. So very calming, and a calming scent can put you in ecstasy almost, if you let it. The right scent is all you need to slip away into tranquility, into that part of your brain where all the awful things get hushed.

My pulse slows now just thinking of it, this notion of sprinkling some silk with Holy Basil, holding it to my face, and breathing it in. Waltzing through Paris without a care.

Just as I lose myself to the thought, I hear a rustling in the house. I bolt upright and listen closer, my ear turned to the hall. Blue looks at me, puzzled. He hasn't heard anything, so I decide I just know this house's creaks and complaints all too well. I think again of the concierge: *I know the bones of this house better than I know the bones under my own skin.*

But no, the random racket comes together in the sound of footsteps. I stand, my heart fast. And then the women step cautiously into the shop from the back of the house.

"There's four of us," one says. Another one says, "We heard there was a key under the gargoyle's foot."

The gargoyle in the courtyard behind the house. "And a few more are coming too," the first one says. "Or maybe a few more than a few."

These are girls from Boulette's. For one, I made a perfume of bitter almond, acacia, frangipani.

One of the girls says, "The Nazis have shut down Madame Boulette's. Even the cabaret. Especially the cabaret. Because of what happened with Zoé St. Angel."

"What happened with Zoé St. Angel?" I say. "I just saw her sing the other night." But even as I sputter it out, I know how pointless it is, how impossible it is to know anything about anyone who's not standing right in front of you. I know how quickly everything can change.

"It happened yesterday," one of them says. And then the girls tell me all they know.

···· 62 ····

Here's how it goes: Zoé's alone with Lutz, in her glass apartment atop the brothel.

He walks up behind her. He kisses her neck. He whispers in her ear. He traces his finger along her throat, following her swallow of whiskey. He says, as he often does these days, "Why don't you love me anymore?"

"What a thing to ask," she says.

"*What a thing to ask*?" He takes a step back. He leans his hip against the credenza. "What a thing to say, 'What a thing to ask.' "

"What is it you want me to say?"

"You might insist that you *do* love me," he says.

"Then I do," she says. "I *do* insist." She pours another shot of scotch for him, and he leans back to sip it. Lutz is so arrogant, Zoé always manages to comfort him eventually, to convince him she loves him more than life. Her *I do insist* is hardly insistent at all, but it makes him stop pouting.

He brings his hand to her throat again, but this time it's to run his fingers gently over her neck. She realizes, as the scent rises, there's perfume on his fingertips. The scent of Ophelia. *Her* perfume.

Is he toying with me? she thinks. Is this his way of telling her she's caught? He knows? He's read about her in her father's diary?

He presses his fingers in, like he's taking her pulse. "Your heartbeat picked up," he says. "Do you like it? The perfume?"

Zoé puts her hand to his, to lower it from her throat. She holds his hand open, before herself. She traces her finger over the lines in his palm. She doesn't look up. "Why?" is all she says.

"Oskar Voss thinks he's onto something," Lutz says. He's looking down now too, and he runs his fingers soft over hers. "Somewhere in these perfumes of Pascal's is something useful. Something we can take to Hitler. And to the fields of war. It will help us win."

She starts to say something, then stops.

Lutz turns her hand so that *her* palm is up before *him* now. He runs his fingers over the lines in her palm, then along the veins in her wrist. He says, "I just need to find the answers before Voss does." He looks up at her with those beautiful eyes, that beautiful face. "I need to be the one to bring these discoveries forward. Whatever they are."

"So find the perfumer," she says.

"Pascal?" he said. "If only we'd thought to keep him alive. But we have an assistant of his . . . helping us. He claims not to know anything, but I predict his memory will improve."

Zoé takes her hand back. *If only we'd thought to keep him alive.* She turns her head away from Lutz. She lowers her face. She clutches the lace shawl at her shoulder and brings it to her cheek.

"Nothing," she tells Lutz when he asks what's wrong. *Why are you crying?* "My eyes are watering, is all. The perfume's a little . . . strong for me."

"It's not the perfume, it's all this god-awful smoke we can't get enough of," he says, pulling a cigarette from his shirt pocket and lighting up.

Zoé and Lutz have stocked the credenza with all the fixings for cocktails and smokes. There are crystal decanters of scotch and bourbon, and matching highball glasses, and a silver ice bucket with tongs shaped like a wishbone. There is a humidor of polished cedar, and a table lighter of pink onyx. There is the novelty box with the wooden alligator that opens its jaw and fishes out your cigarette for you.

Zoé opens a drawer and takes out the tin. The cigarettes I gave her: a top layer hiding a second layer, with a plot of instructions printed on the cigarette paper. She takes one, lights it with the onyx lighter. She likes bringing out the tin in front of Lutz, her liberation right there at her fingertips.

She has smoked nearly the whole top layer. If she starts smoking the layer under the parchment, she'll be burning away the map of her own rescue.

Lutz leans toward her again, nuzzling his nose against her, taking in more of her perfume. In the jostling, she nearly burns his hand with the tip of the cigarette.

"Be careful," he says softly.

Be careful. Zoé's fingers begin to tremble. And she lifts her cigarette, and she touches its burning coal to his neck.

Lutz yelps, stumbles back, slapping his hand against his wound like he's been stung. Zoé reaches over for the statue of a horse rearing up on its hind legs—it's a stomper Lutz brought home one day, meant for crushing your cigarettes out with its heavy brass base.

Zoé holds the horse at its middle and swings it with all her strength, knocking the base hard against Lutz's left temple. The blow doesn't knock him out, but it knocks him over, and he stumbles on an ottoman. He's on the floor, facedown, too shaken and winded to stand.

She knows she can't let him get up, but she can barely stay standing herself. She can't bear to hit him again. The first act was instinctual. And now her heart beats fast, and she can't breathe.

She steps over to him. Covers her eyes with one hand. She lifts the horse above her head and gives Lutz another whack against the back of the skull. When she opens her eyes, she sees his blood across the rug.

She doesn't want to stay and investigate his stillness, but she does linger long enough to listen for a whimper. *Is he alive?* they'll ask her later. *He was alive when I left,* she'll be able to tell them. She picks up her cigarette tin, and its blueprints for her escape. Some of the drapes are closed, some open. Anyone might've seen her up in her glass box. Anyone might've witnessed her hitting Lutz. But she manages to make it out, and down, to the corridor behind the cabaret; she stops when she hears men's voices. German. She turns another corner. She comes face-to-face with Madame Boulette.

Zoé sees Madame Boulette glance down, and it is then Zoé realizes she is still carrying the bloody horse, gripping it tight. She drops it to the floor, and as the thud of it echoes down the hall, Madame Boulette takes Zoé's wrist. She leads her past a curtain, and past another, and down some stairs. They enter a wine cellar. This frightens Zoé even more; she's made a mistake in following her, into a basement trap. But Madame Boulette yanks on one of the cabinet shelves, loosening it from the wall with a few hard tugs. Some hinges squeak, and the cabinet rolls away, revealing itself as a secret door to a hidden room.

Enough light leaks into the back room that Zoé can see there are more racks of wine—we've all heard of people building false walls in their wine cellars to keep their best vintages from the Nazis' gullets. But this room also has a window, up at street level, just big enough for someone small to shimmy through. Madame Boulette walks to the other end of the room to open the shutters. She unlocks a wrought-iron grill with a key she keeps in an empty bottle in the cabinet. She pushes the window open. And she unfolds a stepladder, and helps Zoé up and out.

That's exactly how Madame Boulette snuck us out too, the bordello girls tell Zoé, when she's back among them, in the nuns' sprawling villa in unoccupied France, miles south of Paris, near the sea.

···· 63 ····

Within a matter of hours, the story of Zoé's escape is passed up from Marseille, through the convents and churches and rectories, snippets of gossip working back to us.

Zoé told the tale of her escape on the night of her arrival. There at the nuns' villa, winter ended weeks ago, but the nights get cold, so they all dragged the quilts from the beds into the garden, to wrap themselves in.

The nuns offered what they could, over candlelight; they brought her a plate of snails plucked off the grapevines on the garden wall and cooked in the butter churned from the milk of their own scrawny cow. There was a saucer with a few sardines alongside a spindly sprig of rosemary.

One of the girls from Madame Boulette's poked a toothpick at a burnt-out glowworm that inched across the ironwork table. Zoé wondered if she meant to spark up its glow or to skewer it, for a canapé.

The cupboards were bare, the villa a wreck.

This was where Zoé was to wait, in a house of crumbling stonework, just a pile of rocks rolling slow down a hill.

She will meet with the American man with his list of people to save, intellectuals and artists, inventors, dissidents, poets, to see how she might be added to it, so she too can hope to board a fishing trawler after midnight in the outer basins. She'll pray the storms won't toss the boat against the rocks before they get to Gibraltar.

"How could you do it?" a Sister Eugénie asked her. But Zoé knew the nun wasn't condemning her. She wanted to know; she wanted immoral instruction. But before Zoé could answer, the nun asked, "Is he dead?"

An older nun slapped at the younger nun's shoulder. "Don't be so rude," she told her. She told Zoé, "You don't have to answer that." But her eyes stayed on Zoé's, waiting for an answer nonetheless.

"He was alive when I left," Zoé said.

He was alive when I left, sang a redhead from the bordello, a protégée of Day's, one who fancied herself a songwriter now, *alive when I left when I left when I left,* as she uncorked a bottle of the convent's own brew. She poured the beer into a champagne coupe for Zoé, over twigs of juniper berries and shavings from a fennel bulb.

···· 64 ····

I'm being followed as I walk to Café Roche, I'm certain of it. The street's busy with people going about their day slow, less frantic in the warmer weather, and I can't say I like the sight of it much. The last thing you want to see is everything back to normal before anything's back to normal at all.

I didn't sleep in the night, but I didn't dare walk the streets after curfew. I need to check on Day somehow. I just need Madame Roche to assure me she left her apartment days ago with the musicians.

I slip away from all the bustling, and I wind around, then back, then around a corner I don't know, onto a narrow street with a tricky curve to it, the buildings casting their shadows against each other, creating a too-early twilight. One building looks like it's been singed by centuries of flames, an armless angel perched near the door leaning out like the wooden sibyl of a ship's bow. Her stone cheeks are streaked with lime.

My shoes echo on the cobblestone walk, just heightening my sense that there are men close behind. I pick up my pace.

And maybe Day is back already. She wasn't sure how long she'd be gone. If she's back, I need to convince her to move in with Blue and me. Why haven't I insisted on it all along?

When I open the door to the café, Madame Roche looks up, giving me her one good eye. She's sitting at the bar, telling the bartender's fortune with a deck of cards. "They ransacked her room," she says before I've even opened my mouth. She's always been no-nonsense, Madame Roche has, always speaking low with a voice that has a wet rattle, like a clogged spigot. But I detect a crack of worry in her voice just now. "Late last night they came by. A few Nazi soldiers."

"Was Day here?"

"No."

"Did they know she wasn't here?"

"They knew she wasn't here," she says. "And they said she won't be back for a while."

A while. Somehow this offers a moment of relief. I'm so grateful for any bit of promise. She won't be back for a while is much better, of course, than she won't be back at all. That's the nature of optimism now.

"Did you recognize the soldiers?" I say.

"No," she says. "But one of them was the most angel-faced of anyone I've ever seen, I hate to say."

Lutz? *He was alive when I left.* "Anything wrong with that angel face, by chance?" I say. "Maybe a welt? A goose egg?"

"A bandage when he took off his hat," she says, tapping her finger on the side of her head. "Right in the thick of his curls." She then tapped her finger on her neck. "And a little something here too," she says.

"A cigarette burn," I say.

"You know your Nazis," she says.

Her bartender hands her a cordial glass, and she holds it out to me. "A little swallow to settle your nerves a touch?" I shake my head, refusing it, even as I reach to take it and toss it back. It burns going down, and doesn't settle a single nerve.

Madame Roche gives me the key to Day's room, and I go up. Day was never one to own much more than what she could carry with her in a pinch, but Lutz made as much of a mess as he could with what little he had to work with. Her wigs, particularly, are strewn everywhere—on the floor, across the bed—as if she suddenly had hundreds.

All her dresses are off their hangers, but that's not so unusual. She's never been one to put her clothes away. She wears them, then drapes them over chairs or the bedposts. Not only was it costly to have her gowns laundered the way they should be, but she hated for the patterns to fade, or for the dresses to wear away with the soap and steam and the press of the iron. *They don't get dirty,* she says. *And they smell better after I wear them, because they get doused in my perfume.*

I pick up a wig from the floor, and its shade of blond is typed on a label sewn to the inside cap: *pineapple ice.* I sit on the edge of the bed, the wig in my lap.

I feel my hands shaking, and then my shoulders are, and I'm crying. I take a deep breath and assure myself that Day is more savvy than I am. Maybe she knew trouble was brewing. She didn't want me to worry, so she told me she'd be off making music. She promised she'd be back soon. I hope she's with Zoé, and she's finding her way to the fishing trawler to carry her to America. I can't bear not knowing. It gnaws at my gut.

I twist my finger through the curls in the wig. Often as I prepare a bed for someone new at the house, I find the husk of someone old. A stocking that's lost its match. A slither of ribbon. A pair of underwear with a line of silk rosettes around the waist.

I decide to return some wigs to their heads; I put a dress on a hanger. I fold some silk. I remember the days years ago when I'd dress up proper, in satin and ruffles, wherever I was, to buy gifts to send M back in Manhattan. I'd stand there at the haberdashery, playing the little lady selecting something special for her gent: a shaving brush with bristles plucked from a badger's back, a Hungarian mustache wax, a lizard-shaped tie pin, bloodstone cuff links, slippers of teddy-bear cloth, a menthol aftershave of rectified spirits.

With every gift, and every letter I sent M, no matter how little I said, I feared I'd said too much. I even learned the particulars of recalling a letter you'd already dropped in the mail. If you presented to the post office proof the letter was yours—a description, an example of your handwriting—and you did so within an hour of posting the letter in the letterbox, you could get it back. You could take back your words. Though I never actually went so far as to go to the trouble, it was on my mind each time the letter slipped from my fingers and down the chute. It felt like a magical promise of protection: make a mistake and undo it.

···· 65 ····

After straightening Day's room, I go home and put on a suit I never wear. It's ball-of-fire orange, or "dragon-fruit red," to hear my tailor tell it. It tends to draw attention. A wool suit, flecked with shimmering threads of yellow, with a matching waistcoat, all of gabardine houndstooth. I wear my collar open, no necktie. It's been long enough since I've been to the barber that my hair's just an inch or two short of somewhat feminine. I slick it back with pomade, and you can see the rake of my comb through the silver and gray.

Or, I should say, Blue slicks my hair back. He puts makeup on me too—a little black for my lashes, and some lipstick made of sumac berries; a red that's the shade of a rusty scythe. But I like that I don't quite recognize myself when I look in the mirror.

"Day is fine," Blue says, though I can hear the lack of conviction in his voice. "She's like a nymph, really. She's always been able to stay above any misery that's nipping at her ankles." The fact is, Blue has never been a good actor, not even onstage.

Any confidence that any of this high style gives me is gone the moment I discover that the concierge is not the concierge anymore. This woman now at Pascal's door is someone I've never seen. But she seems to know me. "Monsieur Voss is expecting you," she says. But there's no reason he would be.

She leads me upstairs and through the front rooms, making no mention at all of the fact that the house is wrecked. Chairs are upside down, lamps broken on the floor. When I look into the rooms we pass, I see that every desk, every chest, every cabinet, has had its drawers pulled out and overturned.

In the kitchen are footprints of men's boots in the sugar and flour that's been shaken from the bags. Cupboard doors hang open on their hinges, dishes having spilled out, as if we're on a listing ship.

Voss sits at the kitchen table in silk pajamas, powder blue, the color of a clear sky. He's doing nothing at all.

"Where's the concierge?" is the first thing I ask, once the new concierge has left.

"Oh," he says, waving his hand in the air, "she's off . . . explaining herself."

"No one loves this house more than Madame Vachon," I say. "Not even you. She didn't have anything to do with this." It's a feeble defense of her, I suppose, but I have to say something. I don't need her *explaining* anything about me.

I move to the counter to make some tea, plucking a couple of teacups from among the broken shards. One is missing its handle but otherwise fine.

"Well, we'll see," he says. "She did at least provide a useful description. Of the cyclone that hit this place."

The stove *click click clicks* when I turn the knob, then *whoosh,* the fire lights beneath the kettle. At the sound of it, he says, "No no no no no no. No tea." He holds up two cigarettes. "We'll have these. Hungarian tobacco, rolled in with some coffee grounds and table salt."

I smoke with him, but I don't sit with him. I stand at the window, and perch myself against the ledge. "So who did this?" I say, knowing full well.

And he knows I know. "Zoé St. Angel fluttered off, and everything went topsy-turvy," he says. "She didn't just *leave* her pretty officer, she gave him a few thunks on the melon on her way out. The concierge said there's a grisly scar, which, frankly, he was needing. He was just too lovely. It'll give him a touch of rough-and-tumble."

"Did he find what he was looking for?"

Voss shrugs. "If he found what he was looking for, it must have been in the last place he looked. There's nothing in this house he didn't bust into. And I was only out for a few hours this morning." He looks me up and down. He then waves his cigarette in my direction. "Well, look at you," he says, with a sigh of boredom. "Dressed like a true swell. You're up to something."

"I need your help, Oskar," I say.

"Oh, I should say so," he says. "You definitely need help. You've raised some . . . you've raised suspicions, Nebraska Charlie. And that's made some folks suspicious of me." He pauses, and I feel the need to speak, but he interrupts. He says, "You seem to run in all the most vicious circles. Madame Boulette's. The cabaret singers. Oh, and you'll find this interesting. There's a very peculiar thing the concierge revealed. About the perfume diary. She lied, as it turns out. There was no chambermaid who made a mess. She didn't just find a loose floorboard. Someone claiming to be you was the one who found the book, it seems. But you know that already. You knew that all along." He draws in a drag from the cigarette. "You've played me for a fool, my dear."

"Oh, Oskar, no," I say. "Oskar, I just . . . I just wanted it, that's all. I wanted Pascal's perfume diary. Why wouldn't I? You know me. You know me probably better than anybody else by now. Monsieur Pascal's perfume accords? All his recipes? It was irresistible. I wasn't *stealing* it from you. I was just . . . taking it."

He seems to accept this. He even seems pleased with it. I allow myself a moment of relief. I bring to my nose a tiny vial of that calming Holy Basil.

He smiles just a little, and he flicks the cigarette toward the ashtray on the table. I take a step to lean forward, to flick my ash in too.

But then he says, "My ascent was short-lived. We discovered one of the farms we didn't know Pascal had, in southern France. They found tanks there. But they're practically empty. And until I can actually produce the formula for the poison Pascal discovered, then it doesn't much matter that I know of its existence. As it turns out, the time I thought I was buying was only minutes, not weeks." He pauses. "Why are you here?" he says. "In that suit?"

"I need your help," I say.

"Yes, you said that."

I say, "My friend Day . . . the singer . . . her place was torn apart like this one. She's completely innocent, but Boulette's has been shut down, and . . . well, I'm wondering if there's a way you can check. If she's . . . if she's been arrested, then maybe you can help her. It's all a mistake."

"Day Shabillée," he says. "Yes. There's been no mistake. That little lady has done a lot of damage."

"That can't be," I say.

"I'm afraid it *can* be," he says. He then goes on to describe Day the spy, and it all starts to fit together. Without even leaving Boulette's, Day weaseled secrets from the Nazis she sang to. She played to their vanities, promising to write songs about them—about their heroism and handsomeness. She poured them drinks, and tousled their hair, and they often gave her more than she needed, and more than they realized. The men told her where they were going and where they'd been.

She wrote charming, harmless lyrics; but the notes she plotted on the pages of staff paper were a code that told everything else. Every clef, every sharp and flat, every quarter note, every eighth, every sixteenth, all a musical cryptogram. Her notes weren't to be played; they were to be decoded.

And the musicians that performed at Boulette's freelanced, moving among the clubs of the occupied zone, slipping in and out of stage doors. They performed for soldiers of all stripes. The music Day placed on the stands of her saxophonists, her trumpeters, her drummers, her ukulele pluckers, every time she took the stage, had foiled more than a few nefarious plots.

"Day's only a singer," I insist, nonetheless. But I'm proud of her victory, of her using music, and everyone's fascination with it, to confound. "She sings, that's all. You remember the song she sang.

You said you loved it." And I start to sing "Where Were You When," though I haven't much of a voice for singing. And to make matters worse, my voice cracks only a few verses in.

I stop. I say, "I took care of you when you were sick. I looked after your work for you." I hate that my voice is shaking. But maybe it's exactly what I need.

Voss won't look at me. He runs his hand over the tabletop, as if clearing it of crumbs. He then begins drumming his fingers. He's thinking it all through, and I don't interrupt.

"You took care of me," he finally says, nodding, still looking at the tabletop. "You did." He looks up. Pauses. "And that's why I'm letting you go, Charlie. I'm letting you get away. That's what I'm doing for you."

So that's when I say, "I have the formula."

His smile comes on slow. He raises an eyebrow. He's either skeptical or impressed. Or both. He drums his fingers some more.

"Is that so?" he says.

I nod. I suck in some smoke. Blow it out. But then I regret it because the puff of smoke shivers with my breath. My whole body is trembling.

He leans the kitchen chair back, and rocks it on its back legs, like a schoolboy. He contemplates me. Me and my suit. He says, "And how'd you come to have it, if I may ask?"

"You basically handed it to me," I say.

"Did I?"

I shrug. "You insisted I show Blue the room of my defeat. At the party. You wanted to boast of my failure at finding the perfume diary. The bottle blueprint, from the drawer in the cabinet. Pascal's sketches for the Gabrielle bottle. He tucked the details in with all the measurements and numbers and notes. I've worked with chemistry long enough to recognize it. I snuck out with the diagram and took it to a chemist I know. It's the formula, we're sure of it. And other information you've been looking for too."

Voss rocks in that chair for a moment longer before dropping the front legs back down to the floor and tucking his cigarette into the side of his mouth to free his hands to applaud. "Brava!" he shouts through the other side of his mouth. The slam of the chair, the slap of his hands, his shout, startle me enough to make me jump.

He says, "I've been outwitted by the great Perfume Thief." After a pause, he says, "So? Where is it?" Before I can say anything, he says, "Oh yes, of course, of course. This is the deal you're making. You give me the formula, and I arrange for Day's release."

"Or the other way around," I say.

"Or the other way around," he says. *"Or,* I could have *you* arrested too, and you could give it to me then."

"I need your help. I'm desperate, Oskar. I'm supposed to keep her safe."

He grinds out his cigarette, though it's only half smoked. He stands, and steps toward me. "I should just believe you?" he says. "That you would collaborate? That you would just hand over to me such a weapon? Oh, but that's right." He reaches over to button up my jacket. "You've killed before. I've known that for a while. Your reasons for leaving America. It's all documented, Charlie. The dead and how they died. Your part in their murder."

"That's not how I see it," I say.

"I don't suppose you would." He takes my cigarette from my fingers, and puts it to his lips. He leans back to sit on the tabletop, exhaling smoke. "Confess to me," he says. "It's one of the stories you've never told me. Of how you finally got caught. Confess to me, and I'll confess to you. I'll tell you a secret of my own."

"If I tell you, will you help me?" I say.

He shrugs one shoulder. Half nods. "Tell me, and we'll see."

···· 66 ····

I returned to Manhattan in my fifties, during the twenties, the Modern Age. We all thought we'd finally got the world the way we wanted it. The war had ended. I thought I could find good work, since the release of a silent movie about my crimes had become a sensation. I sat through as much of the film as I possibly could, every heist committed with a giddy hiccup and a kicked-up heel. The actress playing me was always in dresses except for one scene, and the silk pants were so billowy, so ballooning, it was like the most extravagant skirt of all.

But I did like the clever gimmick: with admission you were given scented cards, and whenever the theater's organist called out a number, you were to hold the card to your nose, and the perfume was to carry along with it some of the drama or comedy of the scene.

When I first arrived again in the city, I shopped all the men's boutiques and haberdasheries and bought a season's worth of new suits and shirts. The stores displayed their silk neckties on a tray, coiled like anchovies in a tin. At Tiffany & Co., I bought a lapel pin shaped like a golfer in mid-swing, studded in diamonds, with sapphires where the golfer's socks met his knickers.

The whole cityscape that had risen up in my absence looked like it had taken its cues from the Tiffany window displays, the Art Deco architecture resembling solid-gold cuff links, platinum brooches, sleek wristwatches of titanium and rhinestones.

I snagged myself a job. And to my mind, this was something within a razor's edge of legitimate. I became an executive for a perfume company, a place called Minx & Minx Ltd.; I drew a paycheck. A salary. I had a wardrobe allowance that afforded me the finest tailors—I wore suits of ivory linen in the summer, and in the winter of a cashmere so pure and frail it was doomed to collapse by April from the first nibble of a moth.

And we *did* sell perfume. God-awful, here-today-gone-tomorrow concoctions peddled to down-on-their-luck flappers in drugstores, sold by the quart, practically, with kicky names. Jazzmina. Gin Lizzie. Zozzle. Hotsy-Totsy. Eau de Lollygag.

But Minx & Minx had derelict reasons for hiring a derelict executive. They knew they could make far more money from their legal access to alcohol than they ever could from the perfumes alone. Among my responsibilities was to help them produce perfumes *without* alcohol, so they could sell their allotted alcohol for thousands of dollars a day. At a meeting of the Aroma Club, an industry organization, perfumers insisted to the prohibition commissioner that perfume was a necessity, not a luxury. The commissioner assured perfumers that reputable, law-abiding businesses would have all the alcohol they wanted.

My appointments were not with department stores and advertisers; my name was not stenciled deep in any brass nameplates. My meetings were with the city's most moneyed bootleggers and mob bosses, with the saloonkeepers of Harlem's most elegant speakeasies. It was a tough gig because we weren't the only ones out there. So many of these reputable businesses with vats of alcohol dabbled in this secondary market. The flavoring companies that dealt in extracts for your apple pies. The hospitals that sterilized the scalpels they cut into your gut. I even knew of an optician with a spectacles shop who cleaned lenses with a violet-scented alcohol spritz—even he did rumrunning on the side.

But at Minx & Minx, we did the best business of all. The city's underbelly invited me in, and we crooks brokered honest deals. And I lived the life. These were fine-living fellows, these Manhattan gutter rats, and they gave me tickets to the opera, to the ballrooms; they sent limousines to deliver me direct to the city's best T-bones and frog legs. And they were tickled, not troubled, by my taste for suits, and they liked to impress me with their own insights into style; they gave me gifts: a Rolex Oyster, a pair of chamois driving gloves, a diamond stickpin for my necktie.

Minx & Minx got so flush toward the end, it hosted a lavish New Year's Eve party on the ice rink atop the Biltmore Hotel—the outdoor Ice Gardens. It'd been a cold winter already, and the men had stopped shaving weeks in advance so they'd sport a heavy beard to warm their chins at the open-air party. The women had spent months haunting the furriers for the healthiest mink and ermine and lynx, for fur capes, fur caps, fur slippers. And the night of the party, the rink itself was alive with white fox, tamed by a circus upstate. The dray horse that lived in the hotel was there too, off-duty; his job, on a normal day, was to drag the ice-scraper across the rink. But that night there was no room for skating, so he stood still and endured us petting his nose and shoving apples in his teeth.

We all stood elbow-to-elbow even to eat, and most of us simply grazed at the banquet table decked out in roasted partridge and quail. We tongued oysters out of their half shells. We plucked up sugared plums and brandied figs, then licked the syrup from our lips and fingers. And from the lips and fingers of others. And we drank. Hot cocktails in copper mugs. Buttered scotch. Cocoa and cognac. We guzzled hooch without worry, because the party was packed with senators, both state and federal.

Blue lights twinkled on strings strung overhead, and origami cranes, folded from perfumed paper, were tied to the lights; they fluttered hard in the wind that kicked up late, sometimes snapping free and dropping like from a hunter's gun.

As midnight neared, the temperature plummeted, and the waiters dragged out iron kettles of burning cedar to warm us, and scent the air. We huddled close. The waiters salted the bonfires with crystals that spat sparks and tinted the flames pink and purple.

I was shivering in my white tuxedo and crimson cape and sipping some eggnog from a snifter when I finally met the detective who had been pursuing me for the entirety of my career. I didn't recognize him. He tapped me on the shoulder. "Clementine?" he said. He held out his hand for a handshake. His eyes were damp, either from the wind or from emotion. He said, "You're under arrest," and he said it with such a mix of relief and heartbreak, and infatuation, that for a beat or two I was almost happy for him.

In those last days of December, everybody who scrambled to keep the country dry had been frantically tallying up numbers, for some grim holiday statistics. The prohibitionists hoped to reach a thousand dead in time for the New Year's Day headlines. A new annual record. And thanks to a vacant-lot shantytown in Hell's Kitchen, and a tent of frozen hoboes just at the last minute, they won their sweepstakes.

Bootlegging was cold-blooded murder, they said. But not so. I'll tell you: this was a government sting. The feds started sneaking wood alcohol and other contaminants into the industrial stuff they provided us and others. One cocktail of bad booze isn't going to blind you, but the drunks who can't get enough? They started dropping like flies with this government plot. The prohibition agents were doing double duty with that booze—they were able to portray alcohol, and its friends, as negligent, while also ridding the city of its drunks. And *that's* what they were finally snagging me for: they were shutting down Minx & Minx, and taking me in.

My lawyer posted bail, and made a hell of a stink in the night court. It was as if my detective knew he'd lose me, so he'd already left me behind. He was nowhere to be found in the courtroom. *All this insanity will either work in your favor,* my lawyer told me as we had coffee in an all-night diner after my arraignment, *or it'll nail your coffin shut.* At the very least, he advised me, I'd best start putting on a dress when meeting a judge and jury. Grow my hair out and twist some curl into it. *And would it kill ya to put on a little lipstick?*

So I booked my passage overseas, carrying a suitcase full of phony passports.

···· 67 ····

After I've told Voss enough of the story to suit him, I lean back against the windowsill in the kitchen and feel my fists tighten. From the kitchen table where he sits, he asks, with a playful spike, "Do you *feel* like a mass murderer, my love? *Were* you guilty?" I want to leap for his throat.

"No more guilty than a hostess at a cocktail party," I say. "I was just pouring drinks."

"So you have no ghosts at all?"

"It's terrible what happened," I say. "But I was only selling perfume spirits." He keeps his eyes on mine. Waiting for more. "It was the prohibition agents . . ."

"Ah, the prohibition agents . . ."

"*Yes,* the prohibition agents . . . they were the ones who tainted the well. All those dead people are *their* ghosts. And no one even knows whether any of those who died had a sip of anything that I had anything to do with. Most of the alcohol that I . . . I *managed* at the perfume company, it was sold to the clubs. The speakeasies. And a lot of times, they did their own extra distilling of it. To keep it clean, so it tasted clean."

"And none of *those* people died?"

"I don't know," I snap. I'm so tired of Voss and his curiosity. But I'm trapped, hoping for mercy. "I doubt it. Even with the wood alcohol in the mix, there wasn't enough to kill a baby." The moment the words are out of my mouth, I want them back. I think of Voss's child, dying in his arms. I'm so afraid of disappointing him, of pushing him away just when I need his help the most. "That's what the government said," I add, as if to give my words to someone else.

But Voss smiles. "How many martinis *does* it take to kill a baby, do you suppose?" he says.

"The fact is," I say, "they were setting me up so I could take the fall for a whole pit of vipers."

And I *do* have ghosts, I don't tell him. Not only did I quit thieving when I reached Paris, but I quit drinking, and didn't tipple so much as a glass of wine until the occupation. Those last days in Manhattan, I was stupid with greed, and lazy from the ease of dealing with those who deal with the devil. I wondered if my own soul was too dark to even see the dark around every corner I turned. So yes, ghosts I've got.

Voss says, "The drunkards shouldn't have drunk so much. They died by their own hands. That's what your prohibition agents would say, I suppose."

I still want to defend the dead drunkards, and to praise their lusts, all these years later. I want to defend their every sick whim. They should have wanted a better life for themselves, we'd say. But why should their love for their own addictions be something so shameful? They should have wanted a long life of dead-quiet churchgoing, in a gray village, on flat land? Is that life so much better lived than a shorter one always hot with trouble?

"Did you see M during those years you were bootlegging?" Voss says.

"I didn't see M," I say. But we kept writing to each other. *Can't we meet?* I wrote once. *Hasn't it been long enough? We're just old friends now.* And when he wrote back that we weren't just old friends, that it had not been long enough, that it could never be long enough, and we could never meet, I fell in love with him all over again.

In the quiet, I say, "I need your help."

"You've said that," he says softly. "Charlie," he says after a moment, his eyes turned downward, his voice even softer. "You and me, we're not enemies."

"Of course not," I say.

"We're a lot alike," he says. "I've always thought so. And I think you admire me as much as I admire you." Here he looks up. He catches my eye. I nod. I nod vigorously. "I've been inspired by the life you've lived," he says. "In the stories you've told me . . . I can imagine myself. And how different my life might have been. I have no regrets—I'm not a man with regrets—but I sometimes think about parallel lives. You do too. What if you'd gone to M, when you were back in Manhattan? How different would everything be?"

We described these parallel lives, M and I did, in the letters we wrote to each other after my return to Manhattan. We were only a subway ride away from each other, and we wrote letter after letter about where we would meet, if we could. We pictured ourselves together all over the city.

"And how different," he continues, "if you'd even just *dressed* as a woman should. If you hadn't spent your life . . . deceiving."

"A life in a dress would have been the deception," I say.

"*I've* been in love," he says, as if he hasn't heard me. "With people I shouldn't love. That's the little secret I said I'd tell you." He repeats himself, saying, "I've felt inspired by you. By your stories. I've been admiring . . . I've been envious. A little infatuated." He's not looking at me. "My family had the means to keep me out of the military, but they put me in, to cure me. After a boyhood affair, with another boy. But I *wanted* to join the army; I was attracted to the camaraderie. Not just to the men and their beauty, but to how they spoke to each other. Their friendship and intimacy. I wanted to be a student of . . . of what it meant to be masculine, in a natural way. In a way that wasn't performance. I wanted to be among men who were simply who they were. And I fell in love again, like I thought I might. With a soldier . . . and *he* loved *me*. I often think about him, even though we had a very short time together. How ridiculous to long for him still. But we do, don't we?" He looks up at me. "We long for them. Our longing becomes part of who we are. If we let it fade, if we get over it, then we lose that part of ourselves. And we don't get it back."

Am I supposed to be moved by this? Stunned? Does he feel that he's confessing? I refuse to give him the satisfaction of being shocked. But if I open my mouth I'll scream. *We* don't long for anything. *We* don't share any hurt at all.

I have no reason to doubt his undying love for his young soldier, but that doesn't make us the same. For weeks he has condescended to me, belittled me, for my suits and neckties; he has regarded my affection for M as precious. And now he stands before me, claiming my sentiments and sorrow as his own.

But I do bring myself to smile. And I nod in case my smile is too twisted or too pained or too glum. I'm willing to do anything that might bring me closer to finding Day.

He squints, and though he's been looking at me, he seems only just now to be seeing me. He tilts his head. "You've painted your face," he says. He stands. He brings his hand up, and I hold still, with a kind of curiosity, I guess. He presses his thumb hard across my lower lip, and I let him. I let him rub the red off. He then puts his thumb to his own lip. He turns his head, to and fro, against his thumb, working the red in, almost subconsciously. When he drops his hand to his side, he's distracted, as if he's already forgotten about the lipstick. It leaves him with the faint trace of a fresh kiss.

···· 68 ····

Voss insists I bring the blueprint to him in a few hours, and when I return with the paper rolled up and tucked into a cardboard tube, there's a long black car in front of Pascal's house. And it's raining. The driver takes my umbrella and opens the door to the backseat. I slip inside the car to sit next to Voss.

Blue tried to discourage me from going off with Voss; he said he would deliver the blueprint for me. But I can't have that at all. And I guess I'm feeling under the influence of Voss's stories this afternoon. After our conversation in the kitchen, I truly believe he does admire me. For so long, alone in Pascal's stolen rooms, Voss has surrounded himself with illusion. He is not what he is; he's a gentleman of Paris, he supposes. And I'm certain now that he can't imagine the city without me. I *need* to believe that's true. And I can't imagine the city without Day.

The driver moves slowly through the mostly empty streets, though the streets aren't quite as empty as they were all winter. The Nazis now allow some traffic so long as it doesn't require fuel. Parisians taxi by horse and carriage, or in cars converted to burn wood, their exhaust pipes sputtering out black clouds of charcoal.

I open the cardboard tube, and I pull the page out. I unroll it and hold it across my knees for Voss to see Pascal's illustration of the bottle of Gabrielle. On both sides of the bottle, in French, are notes and numbers that have nothing to do with the bottle itself, or the perfume, all in silver. I point out also the notes and numbers that seem to tell the story of the formula Voss is seeking.

Voss doesn't touch the paper; he only glances at it. "You're giving this to me," he says. His voice is weak. Tired. "You're committing a war crime against your own country. Did you know that? All this time, I would have taken you for a pacifist."

I want him to believe we're on the same side to some degree. I say, "There are American generals who say that pacifism is more dangerous than chemical warfare. With chemicals, you end things. You cut things short. Pacifists, though, get their emotions wrapped up in it all. They can't see straight." I'm not very good at this song and dance anymore. I just want to see Day safe.

Voss laughs without smiling, without laughter even, just a little puff of a snort through his nose. "You Americans and your keen sense of logic." He begins to recall a play he saw, in Paris, before the war, the War Before, called *The Perfumed Death*. "A woman suffocates in garlands of roses," he says.

He reaches over to touch the blueprint. "It is interesting that Pascal named a perfume after Gabrielle d'Estrées," he says. His voice lifts, upping the volume, but only a notch. "The king preferred she wear no perfume at all. He didn't even want to smell soap on her. He wanted to smell only her stench."

He tells me to put the blueprint away, and I'm happy to. I'm ready for him to be satisfied by it. I wasn't worried all that much, as it is an impeccable fraud. Annick had no trouble dummying up a copy in no time at all. And between the two of us, we know enough about chemistry that I was able to rework the formula into convincing nonsense. Voss will wring no poison from these equations.

I knew he wouldn't fall for simply some sheet of notes handed to him. But *this*, this all fits his sense of mystery, and his fascination with Pascal's genius. And, honestly, he likes the idea of me, the sneak-thief, finally coming through with something deliciously covert.

Voss says, "I'm taking you to her. To your friend. I've arranged for her release."

On reflex, I grab hold of his forearm. He pats at my hand, gently, but I know he means for me to let go. I do. "Oskar, I . . . I . . ." I look away. I look down at my hands. "I don't know what to say."

"I've done it at some risk," he says. "To myself. Like I told you, you've kicked up a fair amount of suspicion."

"I know," I say.

And now that we've moved on to the next steps, I'm frightened of where they'll lead. I don't know how long it will take Voss and his cohort to diagnose the blueprint as a hoax; but when writing the narrative to string in and around the formulas and instructions, Annick and I stuck in twists and turns, and false leads, and red herrings—I even incorporated an outdated shorthand in a few places, a shorthand taught in a book long out of print.

I needed to tempt the Nazis, to make it seem worthwhile to unlock all the blueprint's secrets and codes, but also to keep them unable to unlock anything at all. This will give me time to get Day out of Paris. Maybe *I'll* leave too. Voss doesn't want the blueprint to disappoint anyone either. He too is still jockeying for time.

"Did you describe your crimes to M, in your letters?" he says.

"I did," I say. M was the first person I told about moving to Paris, after my arrest. I wrote a letter in the middle of the Atlantic. Once I was settled, and had an address to give him, he wrote back. *It was all my talk of poison,* he claimed, *back when we were lovers. It became your destiny.*

The rain, which had been light, only sprinkling the car windows, falls harder, a swift and sudden downpour, sending the few people out on the street running for cover, splashing through puddles. Voss raises his voice above the pounding of the rain against the roof.

"Do you think that's what drove you to commit the crimes in the first place? Would you have had such a life if you'd not had M to describe it to?"

I find myself confiding in Voss. I tell him that my whole career rested on a sense of invisibility, an invisibility I believed in. I'm not trying to convince him. I'm simply telling the truth. I *was* vapor. In my letters, I wanted to describe to M the exceptional life I lived without him, a life in shadows, me always slipping out of sight the second anyone looked my way. I wanted to seem exceptional so he would regret losing me. And yet, at the same time, I wanted him to think I was nothing at all, less than I'd ever been, nearly nonexistent, *because* of him. He'd ruined me; he was my damage. I wanted him to always carry the weight of that guilt.

The car turns a corner and slows to a stop. As if she were expecting the car to come, a woman steps from beneath an eave, where she's likely been waiting for the rain to let up. She can walk between the drops now. She wears a raincoat, belted at the waist, and a silk scarf wrapped around her head. She has her hands in her pockets. And I know her by the tick-tock of her hips.

But before I can say anything, before I can thank him again, Voss says, "I was very much hoping we could work together, Charlie." The driver is driving slow enough to go slower than Day. She's moving farther down the empty street, her back to us. "You're *such* a disappointment," he says.

It takes a moment for me to realize exactly what he's said. His English, normally quite light on his tongue, is so heavy with accent, I at first think he's speaking German to me. But the word *disappointment* untangles itself.

He says, "I needed very much to trust you."

The car slows again to a stop. Day moves on along.

"You *can* trust me," I say, but I can't swallow, and my words get caught in my throat.

He knows I'm not innocent. I concentrate on my rapid heartbeat. I lose myself in the rush of blood in my veins. In the silence of the car, I slow my pulse. *This is how I'll die,* I think, running the words through my head, again and again, a mantra. I think my pulse might slow to nothing.

I see there's no handle on this side of the door. No way of getting out without being let out. And no crank for the window.

The car begins to inch forward again, without Voss instructing the driver. The car moves, but Day stops. Someone has called her name. I hear the clop of heavy shoes on the pavement, and I look out the window as two men in patterned suits and damp hats pass the car, walking toward Day.

My pulse speeds back up, and I feel sick. Day turns away from the men, picks up her pace. "You're *not* disappointed, Oskar," I say. But I keep my eyes on Day. "I know you. And you know me." I sputter something about the formula on the page, that he'll need me to decipher it. I claim there are keys I didn't give him. I'm trying to negotiate.

Though I can see only the men's backs, I can tell from the jut of their elbows that they're pulling their guns. I scratch at the door. At the glass.

I scream Day's name. I pound my fists against the window. I hear the gunshot, and I feel the noise of it in my spine. I see Day fall to the ground. Our car picks up speed and drives past the men, who now stand over Day's body, their guns still drawn. I can't stop clawing at the door. I press my cheek against the glass.

Voss tries to speak above my sobbing, above the noise of the rain again on the roof. *You have only yourself to blame*, he says.

69

Roses, Voss says. *That was my boyhood. My mother worked in the rose fields, and all the children of all the mothers worked in the fields too, every July. You snap the rose off the stem, right at the calyx. Rose after rose after rose. In the mornings, and in the evenings, when the flowers won't spoil from the summer sun. The petals feel lighter than the press of heat on your skin. Every petal even lighter than its scent. Hundreds of acres. Thousands of pounds of those petals that weigh nothing.*

Voss won't stop talking. He's told me that he's driving me home, and that we'll say our good-byes, and that will be that. I won't be arrested. I won't be watched. He wants nothing more from me. Day, he tells me, took my bullet. Her death is my punishment for my betrayal.

But don't be so hard on yourself, he tells me. *She's better off this way. Day's musical notes have sunk ships and bombed buildings. Men have died from her interventions. Her death might have been gruesomely prolonged otherwise.*

I want to protest, but every time I open my mouth, I can't breathe. My words skip. I lean against the door. *She just wrote down things that men said,* I try to say.

···· 70 ····

I spend day after day in bed, but I don't know how many, altogether. There's a day-by-day calendar on my nightstand, but I haven't torn a page away since summer. When the war came, I forgot all about it, it just left my mind entirely, my nightly habit of tearing the day's page off and dropping it in the drawer, for scrap paper for when I wake in the night, or in the early, early morning, with an idea for a fragrance, or a solution to a scent that's not quite come together yet. My brain's sometimes better when it's still halfway caught in a dream, when I'm lying there puzzling over what's real and what's not, a nightmare turning to mist and slipping away before I can even describe it to myself.

Sometimes, sleepless, I remember things I've long since forgot, or things I've never forgotten but haven't remembered in years, and everything comes back doubly vivid, or triply, and it's even more alive than when I lived it, all the colors filtered through bottle glass. There's the gentlest clicking of locusts, the creaking of crickets' legs, the thick scent of lilacs scratching the back of my throat. The wine tart on my tongue. A kiss, a taste of lipstick and powder and the flat lick of its red wax. An insect tickling the back of my neck, and the acrid smell of its crushed husk on my fingertips after I pick it off my skin.

But when I wake now, I'm terrified. The night sits on my chest like a demon. It holds me to the bed. I couldn't even write a note if I wanted to. I couldn't sit up, couldn't lift a pen. The nightmares won't fade away. And the days are too sick with pain. Morning comes, and I can breathe a little. But only a little. Some days I dress, some I don't, but I never leave the room. It seems I'm barely awake a minute and it's already time for bed. I sit with my cigarette lit but unsmoked. The paper burns away to my fingertips, the ash finally tumbling into my lap. And the sunlight burns away just as quick. People bring me things I do not eat. They say things I do not hear.

For a while, Day lived on a ramshackle houseboat. Some mornings she'd wake in the fifth arrondissement and sometimes in the sixth, depending on the ebb and flow of the Seine. Her boat sat afloat on the line between the two districts, moored at a dock off the Île de la Cité, the little island smack-dab in the middle of Paris. If you asked her where she lived, she'd tell you she was shipwrecked. *I'm capsized in the river*, she'd say. With a potbelly stove fueled cheaply with corncobs dipped in kerosene, she kept the cabin not just warm but hot, so hot it seemed she'd boil the water of the river away, right out from under her boat. And yet her teeth were always chattering. She was always cold.

Nonetheless, one winter night a few years ago, we sat on the deck bundled up, lighting the skirts of little paper men in Chinese robes, fireworks disguised as dolls. We touched a match to their red dresses, and they flitted up and away, their skirts turning to smoke, kicking up the powdery perfume of incense as they spun out their flames, then popped, a last crack before disappearing in the dark, the quick, sharp scent of gunpowder tingling in your nose, working up a sneeze. The river and the night were so still, we swore we could hear the sizzle of the hot doll when it hit the water.

"You sing your songs, and they sing them back at you," she told me of her nights at the cabaret. This was before the Nazis arrived; these were the gentlemen of Paris she sang for. "Your words are in *their* mouths, then their words are in *your* mouth, and you're swallowing their smoke with every note you're trying to hit. You've swapped your pretty little love songs for dragon's breath breathing down your throat." She refilled her glass, with a brandy that smelled of butterscotch and pine needles, like the fir liquors they drink in ski lodges. "The devils," she said, lighting the paper dress of another doll.

I can't stop myself from picturing it. Her death. I see it in different ways, my imagination twisting. There's a raincoat but no rain. It's a tree-lined street, sun-dappled. As she falls, her coat opens, and the sheets of music she's smuggling are caught by a sudden gust of wind. The musical notes, with all the secrets they carry, tumble from their staffs, and they float and spin and fall in with the song of a bird on a branch. The notes roll out with the bird's full-throated warble.

Day, dead or alive, will bring music to Paris.

I'm in my pajamas, sitting on the corner of the bed, looking at the door, when Blue walks through it. Two of the girls walk in behind him. I fear I'm inventing them. I'm hallucinating. I thought we'd sent all the girls away.

He bends over slightly, to look in my face. He says something to me, but I quickly forget what it is. His voice is an echo down a tunnel.

"I'm going to bed," I tell him.

"No," he says. "You're getting up." He puts his hand on my elbow, but I pull my elbow away.

"It's time I got to bed," I say. I'm trying to scramble away from whatever I'm dreaming, to fall back into the black of sleep. I begin to turn toward the quilts. I tug at them, but I'm tugged away. I'm dizzy, as if I were drunk, and it feels like the whole house is tipping. I feel like I'm on Day's old houseboat. I square up my feet, to keep from falling over, but it's no good. I'm falling off the bed. But I don't fall on the floor. I'm steady after all, on my feet, in Blue's arms. He leads me to the door.

I don't want to go out there. "That's where the nightmares go," I say, but even I don't know what I mean. It's real, my terror of the doorway, and the corridor. Maybe I'm in a nightmare now. Maybe everything is only a nightmare. It might as well be a cliff's edge Blue's pushing me off. I dig my heels into the rug, but the rug slips away, out from under me. The girls surround me too, these fairies of destruction, chirping goodwill in my ear. They coo-coo and tut-tut.

Leave me be, I think I say, or maybe I'm not speaking at all. I let my legs go limp so I'm every ounce of deadweight I can muster. I claw at their clothes to drag them down with me. But they're determined, this little troop of do-gooders. They insist that I'm sick.

"I know," I say.

"A hot bath will do you good," someone says.

"There's no water," I say, "no heat," as if this will free me from them.

Now I'm crying, and all my sobbing weakens me. I lean into Blue, and he holds me up. The girls help me with my balance.

Before I even realize we've crossed the threshold of the bedroom, I'm at sea, in the water, pajamas and all. They hold me, to keep me from slipping in the tub, and I fight them when I first feel the water soaking me. It feels cold, but then I'm shivering the chills away, and I feel the warmth of it settling in, finding my bones. And I can't deny the ease I feel. I give in.

Blue says, as he leaves, "I'm letting the girls see to your bath. I'm respecting your dignity." The girls unbutton my wet pajamas and peel them off me. I help them.

I fall under the spell of the ritual. They use a pitcher to pour warm water over me. Over my head. Down my back. I sit up. Lean forward. I realize I've been gripping the edge of the tub, and I let my fingers relax. I cross my arms beneath my breasts. Cup my bony elbows in my hands.

And Annick is here now. Or maybe she's always been here. She dismisses the girls. Her necktie, this time, is all pink elephants. There's a low wooden stool with four legs, a teak stool from Japan, and she brings it to the side of the tub to sit with me. She presses a sponge to my back, the back of my neck.

She uncorks a bottle and tips some liquid into my bath, a honey-water she fixed in my kitchen herself, from a recipe in one of my books. I know in an instant that it's expert, a perfect rendering. I haven't made it in some time. It's sour and spice: bruised lemon rind, crushed clove.

Bees. I remember a Lalique comb I stole right off a woman's head. The bees across the comb were made of gold, and they had made the woman look like her hair was crawling with insects.

I think I'm thinking this only to myself, but I must be thinking out loud. Annick says, "The queen bee leaves pheromones in her path, in her footprints. To send messages. By scent, actually. It's like a perfume, I suppose. It fades as she gets old."

Drip drip drip, more tipping of the honey-water.

Annick tilts her head with sympathy. Or pity. Sympathy, pity; one's much the same as the other, I suppose. She puts a hand to my cheek, then leans in to place a kiss on my forehead, on my temple. Her kiss is so gentle, so kind, it'd break my heart if my heart weren't already shattered.

"I feel like I've been awake every night for days," I say, "but I also feel like I've been sleeping for days. It's like when you try to remember a dream, and it keeps skittering away from you." I begin to worry that I'm describing senility. I'm talking like old people do when they snap, when they slip away.

I feel compelled to ask Annick if she knows much about love, but I don't ask. I'm thinking of M. Can someone truly pine away for years and years? Have I done that?

I haven't, I don't think. My love for M did fade, so it's the memory of the love that so moves me now. I miss knowing it, being distracted by it. You think you're hypnotized when you're in the thick of it. Asphyxiated, a suffocation of flowers. Now it's all out of reach, but only just, and it sometimes seems close enough that you can fall back into the trance of it. You can be haunted again by it all; you can fall in love with your memories.

···· 71 ····

Blue's decided we'll celebrate Day. After my bath, I find him in my bedroom; he's laid out my entire costume for me, draped it over the quilts, all of it situated just so, as if a gentleman had lain back for a moment and then turned to mist, slipping away from his clothes, lifted by the rapture. But none of it is anything I've seen before. "Very dapper," I say. The suit is rushing summer, a thin linen of powder blue, with very light, very thin stripes of pale rose. The stripes are barely a stitch, barely a thread. At the ghost's throat is a partially knotted necktie of lime green. And at the tie's center, a pin, a grasshopper of emerald, with golden wings, flown in from my past on the farm, a tribute to my childhood plague of locusts.

"Not gold," he says, as if he's read my mind. He taps his finger on a wing. "Gold-painted tin."

I reach out to lift a sleeve. "Did you at least seduce the dandy before you stripped him of his clothes?" I say.

"None of this is secondhand," he says. "All the haberdasheries are open to bargaining these days."

"I hope you at least flirted with someone," I say.

"I flirt even when I don't mean to," he says, and it's true. It's his cross to bear, that he can't keep people from falling in love with him.

"The bath made me very tired," I say. "It's getting dark already. The nights keep getting longer."

"They're actually getting shorter."

I sit on the edge of the bed. "But then they'll just get long again."

"Day died a hero," he says. "So you can't pay your respects by pulling your sheets up over your head."

I've taken too many risks. I can't help but think that the whole house will collapse, that we all *will* be arrested, and my failure will be an infection that works its way up the entire vein of the Resistance, and all the way down to the nuns in the south, and I'll have poisoned everyone.

As Blue and Annick help me dress, I say, "All of this is my punishment for breaking the rules."

Blue slips my arm through a sleeve. "We don't make the rules," he says, "so we shouldn't be blamed for breaking them." He slips my other arm through the other sleeve.

"That, my darling, is a criminal logic."

"We *are* criminals," he says. He buttons me up.

···· 72 ····

We can't help but cry a little as we walk in the cold rain, after dark, all of us tucked in under the few umbrellas we could find. But we sing past our tears, Blue leading everyone in Day's song "Where Were You When" as he walks backward before us, shouting the words above the wind like a drill sergeant, his voice rising far over his usual soft-spokenness. We shout them back at him with the same military bleat. *Where were you when I loved you the most? Did you think of me much, did you keep my heart close?*

Arrest us. Charge us for breaking curfew. How could we care?

From the outside, Café Roche looks shuttered and dark, and I fear it's closed for the night. But Blue, still directing us, bumps his hip against the door, and it swings wide open for him. It's not empty at all. The place is packed with the people of Paris, and they're sitting in only the glow of candlelight. I suspect everyone's gone out in the rain just so the rain could chase them into cafés and bars.

They look up from their mostly empty cups and cocktail glasses, and we keep singing Day's song. We sing even louder, even the girls who sing the wrong words. There's only one empty table, and it's too small, but we all gather around it. A few girls sit on other girls' laps. Blue pulls the bench down from the top of the piano, lifts the lid, and begins to play.

Here, with the racket of the rain muffled, we slow the song down, and we soften it up, and we sing it the way Day did. Blue waves his arms at the others in the café, and some of them join in too. When we finish and start over, more join in. We keep singing the song, over and over, and everyone in the joint's singing along.

Madame Roche tugs on the sleeve of one of our girls, and they go to the cellar, and they come up with their arms overloaded with bottles, most of them half full at best. Some of them have only a few sips, or even just a drop. I'd even guess that a few just had a sticky lip for the licking. But it's all her very very finest, the cognacs and liqueurs that you had to ask for, that you had to know about, that you had to pronounce correctly or she wouldn't bring them to you. She'd pretend she had no idea what you meant.

She'd hidden what was left in her cabinets when the Nazis came. And now she was offering it all up to everyone in the house. We pass the bottles around, take what we want. Madame Roche returns to the cellar and comes up with even more. The bottles keep moving, from table to table, and we keep singing.

The beauty of the song is that it's simple. It's sentimental. There are no complicated notes to be reached, no clever bridges to cross. Day was such a young woman when she sang it—a girl, really—and we all heard in her sweet, innocent voice every brokenhearted sweetheart who sent her boy to fight. The tune wasn't catchy by any means, but it was so singable, you couldn't keep quiet once it was struck up; the singing reached inside of you and drew the song out.

And the record came out just after the War Before, only months after it ended. It was a promise, and a blown kiss, to the soldiers who fought.

Where were you when I thought of you always?
Do you sing along when our song plays?
What'd you do with the love that I sent?
Did you always know the words that I meant?

She recorded it in the only language she knew then, English, but they listened to it everywhere there were war wounded and war dead.

For some folks, "Where Were You When" was the only English they ever learned. There was no way to distort the power of that song, even if it was sung by the enemy. It was about every hero who'd ever fought, whether he'd won or not. And when it played, wherever it played, men and women stood, put their arms around each other, and sang it with more heart than they'd ever sung any national anthem. They even recited the song's first words, along with Day, a dedication that was spoken not sung: *This song is for you, whoever you are.*

···· 73 ····

After I settled in Paris a little over a decade ago, I got a few letters from M, then nothing for two years. And I'd not moved an inch. I wrote to him, and I wrote again. Certainly there'd been long stretches of silence before, a silence I might as well have begged for, foolishly, in my letters, in my efforts to be poetic, or erotic. *When I don't hear from you, I think of you constantly,* I'd write. Or: *You'd be easier to forget if I heard from you often. You would become a habit. An idle conversation. An easy waltz. As it is, it's a dark emptiness I'm always calling into, always listening close for more than an echo.*

Finally, I received a package—a large, fat envelope—with M's address on the return label. Eight years ago, now.

Inside the envelope were more envelopes, a bundle of letters, tied together with a silk ribbon. Not only had M finally written me again, I thought, but he'd written letter after letter. Or, even more enticing: these were letters that had sat unsent in a desk drawer for years. I loved the idea of hearing all the things he hadn't dared tell me.

But as I loosened the ribbon, I saw that these letters weren't unsent. They'd been marked up by post-office stamps and cancellations. They were addressed, but not to me. They were all addressed to him, *by* me. He'd returned to me the many letters I'd sent him.

I searched the package for an explanation, and found a separate envelope, with no writing across it. I opened it and was relieved to read the first line: *I've waited too long to write.* But then it occurred to me that this wasn't M's penmanship. I turned the sheet over, to see the signature. *Mrs. Oliver Somerset.*

What I learned from Mrs. Oliver Somerset, in this one page of stationery, front and back, was that M had a daughter I never knew about. M had this daughter, with his mister, shortly after I left Manhattan. This daughter, this Mrs. Oliver Somerset, was married herself now, with children of her own. She had a name of her own too—Clementine. And this Clementine, wife of Oliver Somerset, mother of Wilbur Somerset (thirteen years old), and Evelyn Somerset (eleven), and Annabel Somerset (eight), was writing me on this day because I was her mother's friend, and she was sure I'd want to know the sad news that M had passed away.

She gave no details of her mother's death, whether it was sudden or expected, peaceful or fraught. And I sensed from the letter that her *not* telling me was a kind of refusal, a way to insist on the intimacy of family, to remind me that I was not part of M's life. I was to be grateful, the letter didn't say, that she'd bothered to write me at all. Every sentence, though polite and kind and charitable, carried with it that clipped hint of finality—I could just hear her voice, like those of the church ladies of my childhood, that gaggle of do-gooders who had only just time enough to bless you with an update on their piety, on their family's health, on their baking, their quilting, their housewifely diligence, leaning forward, nodding fast, smiling tightly, before a *So good to see you in church* and a quick gathering of skirts, off to attend to the people who mattered.

Every empty sentence was only carrying the letter closer to its end. I knew, before I even finished, that Mrs. Somerset would not ask me to respond, would ask no questions about me, about my life, about my days with M, and would indicate nothing about the bundle of letters she was returning to me. She didn't even mention them, as if they'd somehow found their way into the envelope unnoticed while she busied herself with her letter about her husband and children.

Clementine, you and I share a name! she wrote, her only acknowledgment of having given the letters half a glance.

I was sad, yes, to hear of M's death, sad beyond belief, but in the moment, I was most distracted, and baffled, by how M, my M, could have raised someone like this. I hated Mrs. Oliver Somerset. I wanted M to have had a daughter who would long to come to Paris to meet me. I could picture *that* Clementine as any number of amazing women—maybe an actress, a poet, a sculptor. Maybe she'd be an aviatrix who'd pilot her own plane from her city to mine. The loss of *that* woman, this fictional daughter, was what tore at my heart.

In the months that followed, after reading and rereading that letter from Mrs. Somerset, I came to understand it differently. I even came to have some affection for Mrs. Somerset, and sympathy for the predicament she was in when faced with her mother's proof of another life lived. Suddenly, out of nowhere, her mother was someone she'd never met before. But Mrs. Oliver Somerset gathered her wits and did me this kindness. And that rushing of the sentences I'd imagined before began to slow down; the sentences even seemed painstaking, the words deliberate. Oh, that sweet and sad exclamation point at the end of *you and I share a name!* You and I share a name. You and I share a name. I never tired of reading it, and I could sense Clementine trying to say so much more than she could.

But those first days after receiving the letter, those eight years ago, I only felt insulted. And the only crying I could do was a kind of exasperated sputtering. Only hunger drove me out of the house. I went to Café Roche for a cup of coffee and a pale gray, wrinkled steak that I could barely saw through with Madame Roche's toothless table knife. Usually I brought my own silverware, because not only was Madame Roche's very feeble, but she charged a fee for its use. The food at Café Roche was never very good, even before the war.

And, wouldn't you know, that's the moment my grief chose to consume me. First you suspect you'll let yourself shed a tear or two; you can always dab your damp cheeks with the cuff of your sleeve. But then your efforts to keep from crying tremble your hands, and start your knife and fork clattering against the plate. Your embarrassment provokes more tears. And when you realize there's no stopping what you started, you give in, and once you give in, you're done for. And you sit there shaking, and weeping, and snorting, asserting yourself into everyone's evening, wordlessly insisting that everyone consider your condition and weigh their responsibilities to you, a stranger. And just like that, the night becomes that night when no one knew what to do for the old woman in trousers bawling her eyes out.

It broke my heart to not know what they'd buried M in. A dress, most likely. I wished I knew, at least, what the dress looked like. And then I began to cry for someone else too, someone I didn't even know, someone named Abraham who had belonged to the club in Manhattan, our gentlemen's club, the Brothers of the Sisterhood, whose death made the newspaper as a bit of comedy—the weird tale of how a man died, and the undertaker declared that the man had not been a man at all, never, not once, no matter what he wore and how he signed his name. This undertaker took Abraham's whole life away from him as he lay dead on a slab, indefensible forever and ever, amen.

I'd noticed a woman sitting at the next table with three men, a beautiful woman with a complexion that was both dark and light, with orange freckles across her nose and cheeks. She wore a summery hat so big it went on for ages, the front brim popped up. She wore a dress that looked like there should be something to wear under it; it was like an apron, her naked breasts barely hidden by its lacy ruffles. And like an apron, or a dish towel, might be, it was patterned with pears and apples and walnuts.

Across her shoulders she wore a long pale blue chiffon scarf patterned with see-through stars. Her legs were crossed, most likely to show off a shoe that was a checkerboard of lime-green silk and yellow rhinestones.

Ladies and gentlemen, Day Shabillée.

When Madame Roche brought to her table a bottle of champagne on a tray, with glasses, Day rose from her chair, plucked up the bottle and two champagne coupes, and left the three men. The men groaned and objected, they begged for her return, but she ignored them and plopped down across from me. She handed me a handkerchief, then began to pull at the cork of the bottle.

"I don't drink," I said, in English. I knew she was American right off.

"You'll drink *this*," she said. "I made those brats order me the best bottle in the house, because they've insulted me." She nearly missed the glasses as she poured from the heavy bottle with her thin wrists, splashing the wine all around. "I'm living here at the café, upstairs. My demi-pension rate only includes breakfast, so I have to dress scantily . . ." She paused. Looked up in thought. "Scantily and scandalously, I guess." She shrugged. "I have to flirt for my supper. But some of the less reputable cafés around here rent their rooms by the hour, and that just confuses some of these boys." She picked up my glass and handed it to me, so she could clink hers against mine. "I'm actually a very popular singer," she said. "I had a song, some years ago, that everyone was singing everywhere. You couldn't get away from it if you tried." She picked up my fork and speared a slice of potato from my plate. Ate it, then ate another. "Why *are* you crying? But you don't have to tell me if you don't want to."

I knew that *this* was the daughter I would have preferred for M. Not Mrs. Somerset, but Day Shabillée. The daughter I wanted for M *and myself*. I'd longed for her, and now here she was.

Does the jeweler discover the facets of a diamond with the *tip-tap* of his chisel, or does he tip-tap the facets in? It's like how the ancient Romans suggested the atom, and then centuries later, Einstein found it. You theorize, then invent your proof.

A perfumer creates a fragrance from thin air, then breathes it in.

I cleared my throat. "A man I loved has died," I said.

Day tilted her head. "That's the most tragic thing I've ever heard in my life," she said. It was melodrama, but it didn't offend me. She asked for the handkerchief back. "Now *I* need that," she said, and she did. Though the tears were real, she did perform a bit. She fluttered the hankie at her face, making sure the men at the next table saw her so overcome.

74

I've been giving up my life of crime for decades, my every theft my last. I got rich enough at a young-enough age that I could easily picture myself becoming someone else. But that someone else was always doing something that didn't seem quite doable.

I'd get so frustrated by the notion of learning a new way of living that I'd fall back on what I knew all too well.

At least three or four times a year, I would commit my final crime and trumpet my retirement to the underground of snakes-in-the-grass. If you were a villain like I was, you fell in with the others, like in any other industry of corruption. We'd bump into each other in all the places we didn't belong.

And I always wanted them to know that I wasn't one of them. I wanted to believe in a network of misfits so everyone could take note of my disappearance from their ranks. I wanted all the most-wanted, the crooks with the biggest bounties on their heads, to envy me my new leaf. I longed to be respected for finally disrespecting my disreputable life.

But what would I do instead?

"Before I opened my shop, I never imagined I would be a perfumer," I tell the girls. "Or that I could be." A few of the courtesans who've escaped Boulette's, and a few others from other houses, have lingered here. They just can't bear to leave Paris. I'm teaching them the art, philosophy, and manufacture of scent. I lead them on tours of the boilers and stills in my house. Blue has set up a laboratory in what was once the dining hall of the boys' academy, and I instruct the girls on the use of the paper cones, the heating coils, the glass plates, the flasks, the cylinders, the pots, the ladles. "Sunlight steals the scent away," I tell them as I lead them through the academy's shadows. "We keep our bottles away from the windows."

But mostly I teach what can't be taught. Inspiration can come from anywhere, I tell them, from all the senses. I once created a perfume inspired only by the very particular ticking of M's pocket watch; not just the sound of it, but the feel of it, its tiny, tinny *tip-tap* against my chest as he held me close. I've created a perfume based on Blue's gentle voice onstage, the first time he got a speaking part in a play, as a jilted lover who had only one line, a line delivered too soft to hear, even as we all leaned forward to listen. I heard in that pretty boy's voice the spun-sugar scent of candy floss, and the faint ruin of an orchid corsage wilting at the end of a long night.

And though I want more than anything for Blue to let Félix go, so his heart would be up for grabs again and he could love someone else, he's still holding on. I've made Blue a perfume that speaks of all the mythmaking of our everyday—so many gone, so much stolen, so many lies, so much heroism and villainy. It's a perfume made of whispers, of secrets written in the cream of your coffee with the tip of your spoon. Codes tapped with your tongue on the roof of your mouth.

But some in my house aren't so interested in romance. One of the girls wants to nuzzle her nose again in the balls of a barley farmer. I help her make an elixir of bamboo extract, apple peel, burnt tobacco. Some want sweat, skin, blood. Opium, absinthe. One girl will only write on a piece of paper her request: *Son sperme sentait comme le gingembre épluché.* His semen smelled like peeled ginger.

Annick has invited in strays of her own. One recent afternoon, she stumbled across a teenage girl begging, and that girl had a brother, a boy of ten. Their house had been stolen, their parents dragged off. Then, only a few days after, Annick brought home another homeless child, an eleven-year-old, and the day after that, a six-year-old, all from Jewish families. I didn't want to believe Paris was now a city of urchins, so I half suspected Annick of kidnapping. I preferred to picture her as a witch luring babies away with lollipops.

It sent a shiver up my back to think that at any given moment, you could stumble across a lost waif. In spite of all the horrors of this war, I simply couldn't quite all-the-way believe in all these orphans.

I left America when I did because I had to, but I wanted to leave too. We left America, so many of us, to be free of its oppressions. And we were, for a while. Paris had been invented for us, inspired by our imaginations. But this city we're now in . . . I never wanted to live like this.

Still, here we are. The house gets so full, our ration cards can't keep up, and the black market's getting skimpy too. I install locks on the cupboards so no one'll sneak more than their share, but the children, our little Hansels and Gretels, sometimes unscrew the hinges to steal the chocolate. We've even resorted to reading cookbooks aloud to each other. *English pheasant pie. Saddles of Kentucky mutton. Tongue au gratin. Walnut mocha cake.*

Much of the time, we're in our laboratory. Blue has carried up all my apothecary jars of spices and herbs, and my cabinets with drawers full of dried petals and powders. All the materials I've collected and stockpiled over the years. We have jugs and bottles and ginger pots of oils and essences.

Though I created many scents for Day over the years, this one, the newest one, will take me years to get right. I'm thinking I smell sweetbriar in it, and forget-me-nots, which are always most fragrant in the evening.

Do people recover from guilt like this? From regret? I did everything wrong. I should have spent all my time, my every minute, with Day. I should have begged her to stay out of trouble. I should have nagged. I should've wept and threatened. And I should have kept out of trouble myself, locked up in my own rooms, rattling my bottles and soaking my roses.

Blue tries to comfort me, to tell me that Day knew what she was doing. She wasn't innocent. We should be proud of the risks she took, he says. We should be pleased she was so hated by our enemy. Our little Day, so dangerous.

"They'll write songs about her someday," he says.

We find salvation in our work. We find each other.

Voss, so far, has kept his promise, and we've not been bothered, we've not been watched. Someday he'll discover that the blueprint is fake, if he hasn't already. Maybe he knew all along. He seemed skeptical of it. He perhaps knew better than to pass it along, to risk the ridicule of it all. The *real* blueprint, I've sent on along a line of Resistance fighters. They'll know where to take it.

I've seen nothing of Lutz either. I like to think they refuse to punish me because they refuse to admit any kind of defeat I've delivered. I'm a little old lady who peddles perfume. And I'd been doing my damage for weeks, as they watched. How humiliating.

So now we've been sneaky, Blue and my ladies and me.

We've been using our perfumes to serve the Resistance. It's a quiet way of asserting our presence. Of providing our identities. Of sending messages. We'll stroll into a café, or along a street corner, and whichever perfume wafts in our path answers questions without a word, without a gesture. We don't even have to be in the room to whisper our clues—we just linger beforehand, reeking of our secret message.

Our perfumes are codes, like Day's musical notes. The messages we interpret come from the networks Blue has established, or from backstage at his theater. Or they come from the nuns who traffic in refugees. Or we serve the queer lot who haunt the cocktail clubs. We're interwoven with the city's malcontents.

We might put an electrical fan in a window and spray our perfumes at the blades, sending the scent out. We might flutter paper fans at our perfumed throats.

We drip our messages into snuff bottles, and little glass vials, and we drop these signals into coat pockets, into purses gaping open, or tuck them into a trouser cuff as a gentleman crosses his legs while sitting at a café table preoccupied with his meager splash of wine. We've slipped them into hatbands, into bouquets of flowers, into the backs of collars, up sleeves like an extra ace in a poker game. We leave them on doorsteps and drop them through mail slots. We put them in the baskets of parked bicycles.

We know how to step lightly, to silence our footfalls. We anticipate corners to slip around and doorways to hide us, while our scent sends its message. We're simply the spirit of the city, as light as ether.

We leave our bottles under the loose floorboards of our own house, and in the backs of our cabinets. We make holes in the walls to slip the bottles through. Someday someone will find them, and they'll lift the stoppers, and they'll know our story just by breathing it in.

A Note from the Author

While entirely a work of fiction, my portrait of Paris of 1941, and Manhattan of the late 1890s and 1920s, is drawn largely from the historical record; even some of the more fantastical elements, such as the lepidopterist's hunt for butterfly scent, and Fanny's mention of the subcutaneous perfume craze of Paris, and even Fanny herself (a ballerina/Civil War veteran) arose from the many margins of the research.

To flesh out Clementine's professional, criminal, and romantic pursuits, I had to learn my way around the art and business of perfume, how her sexuality would have influenced her life, and the living conditions (and daily risks) of the occupation.

For the hinges of all Clem's plots I relied heavily on science—specifically chemists' reports in journals and newsletters on perfume-making, poison, invisible ink (and other tools of the amateur and professional spy), and chemical warfare. Reading about one topic often led me to another that was parallel, until all the various threads seemed to stitch themselves together. It was research into perfume and poison that led me to the unfounded but widely recorded rumors of Gabrielle d'Estrées's murder by poisoned gloves, which led me to explore the queer interpretations of the painting of her and her sister, which led to my invention of a lesbian perfume to puzzle and thwart Oscar Voss.

While Clem's engagement with a queer resistance does have some foundation in fact, much of that history has been lost; a secret within a secret can be tough to trace. And what history there is has been corrupted by the homophobic interpretation of queers as giddy, oversexed collaborators, happy to canoodle with the manly men in uniform or, at the very least, sing and dance for them—many of the LGBTQ Parisians living openly were in the arts, determined to maintain their careers and avoid arrest. Though there are certainly convincing instances of gay collaboration with the Nazis, there are among these cases ambiguity and possibility; historians of lesbian cabaret singer and nightclub owner Suzy Solidor, for example, have made the case that her entertaining of the German troops might have allowed for work as a double agent, to gather information for delivery to the French Resistance. And *any* gay expression, such as Solidor's explicitly lesbian lyrics, has been interpreted as resistance in an era of anti-gay laws and discrimination.

One queer performer who did directly influence *The Perfume Thief* was Josephine Baker. To develop the character of Day, I followed Baker's well-documented stage career. Day is far less famous than Baker was, and Day's particular methods of musical cryptography and fact-gathering are distinctly her own, but Baker did famously smuggle secrets to the French Resistance shuffled in among sheets of music or written directly on the sheets in invisible ink. Baker's methods, style, and legacy certainly inform the sensibility of all the characters in *The Perfume Thief*. Her life, including her espionage, is vibrantly portrayed in *Josephine: The Hungry Heart* by Jean-Claude Baker and Chris Chase.

In the many months since I started writing the novel, some excellent LGBTQ histories of the Resistance have emerged; the Council of Europe released *Queer in Europe During the Second World War* (edited by Régis Schlagdenhauffen), which includes mention of Pascal Copeau's work for the French Resistance and of resistance networks in Czechoslovakia composed entirely of LGBTQ members. *Resistance: The LGBT Fight Against Fascism in WWII* (Avery Cassell and Diane Kanzler) is a comprehensive collection of brief and enlightening biographies. I'm about to delve into the brand-new *Paper Bullets: Two Artists Who Risked Their Lives to Defy the Nazis* (by Jeffrey H. Jackson) about the anti-Nazi propaganda schemes of the lesbian avant-garde artists Claude Cahun and Marcel Moore. Other notable queer members of the French Resistance were Rose Valland (who saved thousands of works of art while documenting the German pillaging of museums and Jewish-owned collections), Édith Thomas (the subject of *Édith Thomas: A Passion for Resistance* by Dorothy Kaufmann), poet Jean Desbordes, and critic Roger Stéphane. Last year, author Charles Dantzig accomplished his years-long commitment to having a street in Paris named for gay novelist and Resistance fighter Pierre Herbart.

And at the very moment I'm writing these words, I've learned of the death of art dealer Daniel Cordier, who, at the age of one hundred, was one of the last living Companions of the Liberation as decorated by Charles de Gaulle. Cordier wrote of his sexuality, and his work for the French Resistance, in his memoir, *Alias Caracalla* (2009).

The *New York Times* archive reveals even more than one might expect when seeking stories of queer turn-of-the-century Manhattan—reading between the lines, and intuiting codes, one can learn a little something about the stories its writers didn't dare tell. And the paper's reporting on Paris during the war offered many intimate and fascinating glimpses of the modes of survival in the city.

It was in the *Times* archive that I found a few hints about French perfumers' engagement with war chemicals, including a brief and provocative article from 1933: "Deadlier Gas Discovered in Research on Perfume." And I gained insights into the politics of perfume from an article in the *Business History Review:* "Marketing for Socialism: Soviet Cosmetics in the 1930s" by Olga Kravets and Özlem Sandıkçı (2013).

I reached even further back to gather notes on perfume, chemicals, and tea-tasting from a number of newsletters and trade/professional journals, from as early as the 1830s (*A Treatise on Poisons: In Rela-*

tion to Medical Jurisprudence, Physiology, and the Practice of Physic by Robert Christison and *The Dispensatory of the United States of America*). Other publications from the late 1800s and early 1900s that I consulted were: *Journal of the Society of Chemical Industry, Practical Druggist, Popular Engineer, Annual Report on Essential Oils, Synthetic Perfumes, Etc., American Soap Journal and Perfume Gazette*, and *American Perfumer and Essential Oil Review*, as well as the popular cultural magazines *Putnam's, Harper's, Scribner's*, and *Cosmopolitan*. I relied also on the Library of Congress's Chronicling America digital newspaper project, and the New York Public Library archives. The gateway for much of my research was via Google Books and Love Library of the University of Nebraska–Lincoln.

The *Vogue* archive provided tantalizing insights into the influences of the war on the fashion industry and the effect of its deprivations. I also looked past the feature articles in magazines and newspapers to the art, design, and fanciful descriptions in advertising, where so much of America's proclivity for style, fashion, and beauty is given an oblique yet revealing language, most often intended for women.

In many ways, *The Perfume Thief* is also a story of paper and ink, of love letters and their sentiments, so I learned about the sophisticated and highly efficient postal service of turn-of-the-century New York from the *New York Times* archive, and also from *The Postal Record*, the newsletter of the National Association of Letter Carriers. I learned about perfumed stationery, disappearing ink, and other romantic trends in correspondence from *Paper Trade Journal* and *Bookseller, Newsdealer and Stationer*.

While I looked to well-known books on perfume, such as G. W. Septimus Piesse's *The Art of Perfumery* and Eugène Rimmel's *The Book of Perfumes*, I was most enamored of an oddball obscurity from 1892, by J. C. Sawer: *Odorographia: A Natural History of Raw Materials and Drugs Used in the Perfume Industry, Including the Aromatics Used in Flavouring*. In fact, I was so enamored of it, the book itself becomes a prop in the novel, a gift from M to Clem, which inspires Clem's escape into the scents of the world.

Butterfly-Hunting in Many Lands: Notes of a Field Naturalist (1912) by George Blundell Longstaff introduced me to the scent research, and its baroque olfactory schemata, gathered by Fritz Müller and Frederick A. Dixey.

I've relied also on twenty-first-century historians and their scholarship, especially those books and articles on war and entertainment. Among them: *And the Show Went On: Cultural Life in Nazi-Occupied Paris* by Alan Riding, *The Shameful Peace: How French Artists and Intellectuals Survived the Nazi Occupation* by Frederic Spotts, *When Paris Went Dark: The City of Light Under German Occupation, 1940–1944* by Ronald C. Rosbottom, and *Wine and War* by Donald Kladstrup and Petie Kladstrup.

All these recent works were preceded by such excellent sources as *Resistance: France, 1940–1945* by Blake Ehrlich (1965), *Surrender on Demand* by Varian Fry (1945), and *Memory of Justice* (1976), the documentary film by Marcel Ophüls. For a firsthand account of a Nazi-occupied Paris bordello, I read *Palace of Sweet Sin*, by Fabienne Jamet (1977).

Some of my favorite portraits of Paris were *My Blue Notebooks* by the infamous courtesan Liane de Pougy and *Shakespeare and Company* by bookseller and publisher Sylvia Beach. I was able to get a sense of war-era Illiers (the setting for Marcel Proust's fiction) from a 1948 article in *Vogue* and one in a 1952 edition of *Western Humanities Review*, as well as a recent portrait of the town by William Friedkin in *The New York Times Style Magazine*.

Perhaps the most sublime component of building Clementine's world was exploring the Paris she fell in love with. To stroll the avenues of Paris before the war, I sought out tour guides from the 1920s and '30s that told the city's story by way of its shops, cafés, jazz clubs, confectioners, galleries, flea markets, and vendors. Among these books: *The Spirit of Paris* by Paul Cohen-Portheim (1937); *The Paris*

That's Not in the Guide Books by Basil Woon (1931); *From a Paris Garret* by Richard Le Gallienne (1936); *Paris on Parade* by Robert Forrest Wilson (1925); *The Lantern Show of Paris* by F. G. Hurrell (1930); and *Paris with the Lid Lifted* by Bruce Reynolds (1927), which dips us into the underbelly to acquaint us with the male vamp, the habitués of brothels, and the hostesses of cafés.

Acknowledgments

A number of people have contributed significantly to the development and publication of *The Perfume Thief*. Margo Shickmanter, my editor, had an extraordinary vision for this book and a profound commitment to its story and characters, and I'm so grateful to have had the opportunity to work with her. Alice Tasman, my agent, is always an inspiration, a marvel, and a blessing. I'd like to thank the fine people of Doubleday for all they do for their books. Cara Reilly offered keen editorial insights. And many thanks to Jennifer Weltz and all at the Jean Naggar Literary Agency.

In the English Department at the University of Nebraska–Lincoln, I've received a great deal of support from Marco Abel, as well as from Jonis Agee, Joy Castro, and Kwame Dawes. I've benefited also from discussions of process and research with my graduate student advisees: Scott Guild, Rachel Cochran, David Henson, Ilana Masad, Kathrine Schwartman, Avee Chaudhuri, Jonathan Wlodarski, and Adrienne Christian.

In 1970, the English Department offered the first interdisciplinary LGBTQ course in the nation, so I'm grateful to such pioneers as Louis Crompton, who created the course and devoted his career to LGBTQ scholarship. And I was personally inspired by Barbara DiBernard, our own local resistance fighter, who introduced me to new writers and new ways of reading.

I'm fortunate to have creative friendships that inform my writing and research; many thanks to: Janet Lura, Byron Chavez, Maud Casey, Jim Baker, Orenda Fink, and Jami Attenberg, and my god-daughter Miranda Andersen. I've explored some of the research for this novel in columns for *Enchanted Living* magazine, edited by my great enabler, Carolyn Turgeon. I'm grateful for Amy Mather's insights into perfume, and for all the conversations about art with Matthew Clouse, José Villarrubia, and Wendy Bantam, and conversations about language with Frank Bramlett, and any number of conversations about books and movies with emily danforth. Thanks also to Shellee Dill for sharing a trove of letters written by her grandfather, who served in France during World War II.

Always much love to Mary Mignon, and to Judy Slater, who helped me find my voice as a writer. I cherish my New York City cocktails with Rhonda Sherman and Laura Mitchell, and my various escapades with Lauren Cerand. David Ebershoff helped me to discover the title for this book. And I thank Greg Michalson for the care and attention he gave the publication of my earliest novels.

And I'd like to salute our booksellers, so hard hit by the pandemic. I'm forever in their debt. Many thanks to the Bookworm, and to Beth Black, Andrea Gunther, and Janet Grojean, and to Stephanie Budell.

Much love to my parents, Larry and Donita, who set me on the right path. And love to my husband, Rodney Rahl, my coconspirator in all my plots.

ABOUT THE AUTHOR

Timothy Schaffert is the author of five previous novels: *The Swan Gondola*, *The Coffins of Little Hope*, *Devils in the Sugar Shop*, *The Singing and Dancing Daughters of God*, and *The Phantom Limbs of the Rollow Sisters*. He is a professor of English and director of Creative Writing at the University of Nebraska–Lincoln, and he writes the column The Eccentricities of Gentlemen for the popular lifestyle magazine *Enchanted Living*.